IF I SEEM QUIET...

A novel
by Dave Hughes

Prickly Pair Publishing
Chandler, Arizona, USA

Also by Dave Hughes:
Maybe Next Year
Instant Adult
Open Books, Closed Sets

Watch for two more books in this series.

Visit AuthorDaveHughes.com to learn more about Dave, gain background information and insights into Dave's books and the writing process, and receive advance notice of upcoming book releases (and subscriber pre-release discounts). You will receive Dave's short story, *Cruise Virgins*, free when you subscribe to his bi-weekly newsletter. If you would like to contact the author, please send an email to Dave@AuthorDaveHughes.com.

Cover photo: Daria Lixovetckay (licensed from Shutterstock)
Cover design: Dave Hughes

Library of Congress Control Number: 2023921016

ISBN: 978-0-9970018-0-8

A Fridge Full of Nothing to Eat

Wednesday, March 23, 2016

Aaron Bradbury opened the freezer door of his refrigerator to contemplate his dinner options. The realization hit him, like the blast of cold air from his freezer, that the state of his refrigerator said a lot about the state of his life.

There were ten frozen entrees, two personal-size pizzas, a bag of salmon fillets, and several vegetable bags. *Meh*, Aaron thought.

His refrigerator held an assortment of condiments and salad dressings with nothing to pour them on, a 2-liter bottle of Dr Pepper, and an egg carton with three eggs remaining. He spotted the clamshell container that held the leftovers from his dinner three nights ago when he celebrated his 28th birthday at a chain steakhouse by himself. He popped open the lid and peeked inside. The juice from the steak had congealed into white goo and the remainder of the onion bloom appetizer was soggy and limp. He tossed it in the trash.

In the back of the fridge, he saw a bottle of Chardonnay. He bought it at a winery in Scottsdale he visited on an outing organized by a Meetup group for young singles. He had been saving it for a special occasion. He sighed when he realized he had purchased it over a year ago.

Aaron's mood sank as he realized that his food options, like his life, had fallen into a boring, predictable rut. Nothing in his refrigerator inspired him. This would be another evening of dining at one of the nearby restaurants. Besides, it was a beautiful spring day and he felt like getting out of the apartment and seeing other human beings.

By all reasonable standards, Aaron lived a comfortable, even enviable, life. He lived in a modern, upscale apartment complex with three pools and two in-ground jacuzzis. He lived a three-minute walk from two shopping centers, so he had easy access to a supermarket, an independent bookstore, a discount department store, and more. The HealthPro drugstore where he worked as a pharmacist sat on the corner. There were nine fast-food restaurants he had patronized many times during the past year and nine months. On the other side of his apartment complex, a canal stretched for miles in either direction. Its wide dirt trails on either side were ideal for joggers and bikers. Aaron ran along the canal several times a week.

Aaron had everything he needed within walking distance – except a life.

He wasn't sure what he felt like eating as he began the familiar walk to the L-shaped shopping centers at the nearby intersection. He chose Wok Around the Clok, his default choice on days like today when he craved nothing in particular.

Wok Around the Clok's menu offered a variety of rice or noodle bowls topped with various meats, vegetables, and sauces, as well as an assortment of sushi rolls. It wasn't authentic Asian food by any stretch of the imagination. In fact, Aaron couldn't recall ever seeing an Asian person dining there. But it was decent enough, it was reasonably priced, and it was relatively healthy for fast food.

The biggest thing Wok Around the Clok had going for it was that it differed from anything in Troy, Ohio, where he grew up.

Aaron pushed the door open and walked inside. He was greeted by Maribel, a perpetually cheerful, motherly woman who seemed to be on duty every time he dined there.

"Hi, Hon. How are you today?"

Normally, Aaron detested being called 'hon' or 'dear,' but coming from Maribel it was somehow endearing and comforting. Aaron felt as if she genuinely wanted to know how his day was going.

"Oh, pretty good. How are you, Maribel?"

"Can't complain! What can I get for you today - your usual?"

Aaron scanned the menu board mounted above Maribel's head for about two seconds. He had tried everything at least once, but his favorite was chicken over brown rice with extra Teriyaki sauce, and a medley of peas, mushrooms, and shredded carrots. It came as a combo with a vegetable spring roll, a tiny side salad with an unidentifiable brown dressing, and a medium soda. Once in a while, he ordered something different to change things up, but not today. Aaron was not in the mood to make choices.

"Yeah, the usual."

Geez... I'm so familiar and predictable the server knows what I always order and asks if I want 'the usual.' I guess it could be worse – the question could be coming from a bartender at some dive bar.

Aaron paid for his dinner, picked up his tray, and turned toward the dining area.

Aaron's favorite seat was at a table against the wall near the back. It was quieter, close to the self-serve soda dispenser, and good for people-watching. Today, someone was sitting in his favorite seat.

Since I'm such a regular customer here, they should mount a little plaque on the wall above this table that says, 'Reserved for Aaron Bradbury. Please relinquish this table upon request.' Then he realized how pathetic that was.

The guy who was sitting in Aaron's usual seat looked like he was settled in for the long haul. The remains of his dinner were shoved off to the far side of the table. He was focused on his laptop, with his cell phone close at hand and a drink he had probably refilled at least four times. He obviously wouldn't be leaving anytime soon.

The table next to him was empty, but sitting there would violate the Relative Personal Space Rule of restaurant dining. This was the same Relative Personal Space Rule that applied to standing in an elevator or choosing a urinal. There were plenty of other empty tables in the restaurant, so it would be creepy to sit next to him.

Aaron picked the table with the most Relative Personal Space. He set his tray down and carried his drink cup to the soda dispenser.

As he passed his usual seat, he noticed Laptop Guy was wearing a purple T-shirt with white block letters that said something about "If I seem quiet…". The laptop obscured the rest of the T-shirt's message. Oddly, there was also what appeared to be a white silhouette drawing of a person playing a trombone. Aaron didn't want to approach the guy and stare at his shirt, so he filled his cup with Dr Pepper and returned to his seat.

Aaron's chair didn't face Laptop Guy directly – he was off to his right side. Aaron kept his attention focused forward. But somehow, he got the feeling that Laptop Guy was frequently looking at him. He tried to shake it off. He was probably just imagining things. Besides, he liked to watch other people in restaurants, so he had no reason to complain if Laptop Guy looked at him.

The drawing of the trombone player on Laptop Guy's shirt prompted Aaron to think back to when he played trombone in his high school band. He wasn't popular in high school, but he fit in well with the band geeks. He and his friends had so much fun at band camp, on bus rides to away games, and even during rehearsals. *Those were probably the happiest days of my life. Too bad I didn't realize it or appreciate it then. I miss those days. I'm friends with some of my band buddies on Facebook, but that's not the same.*

When Aaron went to Ohio State, he played in their famous marching band as an undergrad. But after he started pharmacy school, he figured he wouldn't have time for music and stopped playing his trombone. He wondered if it was still somewhere at his parents' home in Troy. For all he knew, they sold it at a garage sale or gave it away or made a planter out of it. Maybe it's now nailed to the wall in a trendy restaurant somewhere.

Maybe I shouldn't have moved away from Ohio. At least I would still have some of my friends left. But I guess most of them have moved away too, and they've gotten on with their lives. Face it, those days are gone.

Aaron had little success making friends in Tempe. He tried Meetup groups for young professionals, talking with people at the pool, and even online dating, but nothing had come of it. Back when he was in the band, he didn't have to work at making friends. They were readily available.

His work schedule didn't help, either. At HealthPro, he worked with only one other pharmacist. One of them had to be there whenever the pharmacy was open, which was 8:00 a.m. to 10:00 p.m. Monday through Friday, 9:00 a.m. to 6:00 p.m. on Saturday, and 10:00 a.m. to 6:00 p.m. on Sunday. That's 87 hours a week to split between two people. Aaron and his counterpart, Charlie, divided the week so Aaron worked Monday and Tuesday, Charlie worked Wednesday and Thursday, and they alternated working Friday, Saturday, and Sunday. That schedule made it challenging to find times when he could get together with people.

As Aaron poked at his food and contemplated the current state of his life, he realized he was now only two years away from 30. He dreaded turning 30. After 30, it would be all downhill.

It's funny how we spend all our childhood looking forward to being older. First, we look forward to turning 16 so we can drive. Then we look forward to turning 18 so we can vote and be an adult. Then we look forward to graduating from high school and going to college. Then we look forward to turning 21 so we can buy alcohol. Then we look forward to graduating from college so we can get a job and make money and finally be done with school.

Now I'm out of school, I have a decent job, and I make good money. I live in a warm, sunny climate in a nice apartment with everything I need close at hand - and my life sucks.

Something had to change, but Aaron had no idea what it would be or how to go about it.

Aaron looked down and saw there were two bites left in his bowl. He had eaten his entire dinner on auto-pilot, not tasting or enjoying any of it. He glanced at Maribel, who was cheerfully greeting customers and assembling rice bowls. *She always seems happy. How does she do it?*

Aaron carried his tray to the trash can, then headed back to the soda dispenser for one last refill to go. Laptop Guy was shutting down his computer. He grabbed his cup and started toward the soda dispenser. He looked up, saw Aaron approaching, and motioned for him to go first.

Aaron could now see his entire T-shirt. It said, 'If I seem quiet it's because you haven't seen me with my trombone.' The white silhouette depicted a guy wailing on his trombone, slide pointed to the sky.

Aaron smiled. "Nice shirt!"

Laptop Guy looked down as if he had to remind himself of what he was wearing today. He smiled back. "Oh… Thanks!"

As Aaron refilled his drink, he asked, "Are you a trombone player?"

"Yes, I am."

"I used to play trombone in high school and college, but I haven't touched it for almost six years. Are you a professional musician?"

"Nah, I just play for fun. I'm in a community concert band."

"No kidding! I didn't know there was such a thing."

"Oh, yeah, there are a lot of them around. We're having a concert on Sunday afternoon. You should come!"

Spending a Sunday afternoon at a band concert wasn't on Aaron's radar, but he decided to at least humor the guy. "Where is it?"

"At the Maricopa Cultural Center just north of downtown Phoenix. It starts at 3:00." Laptop Guy reached into his wallet and pulled out a business card. "Here. Send me an email or a text and I'll send you all the info."

"Thanks!" Aaron accepted the card and glanced at it. Laptop Guy's name was actually Rob Chilcott. There was a picture of him holding his trombone, his phone number, and his email address: bonehead60@gmail.com. Clever.

"I'm Rob." Rob extended his hand and Aaron shook it.

"Aaron."

"Nice to meet you, Aaron."

"You too. Thanks for the info."

Aaron's mood improved as he walked back to his apartment. *So there are actually bands for adults! Who knew? I wonder if some of them have people I could make friends with, like in high school. I wonder if they're any good. I wonder what the age range is, and if there are very many young single women.*

When he arrived back at his apartment, he placed the card next to his computer. He would decide later what to do with it, if anything.

Band Memories

Sunday, March 27, 2016

At 2:45, Aaron parked his car in the garage next to the Maricopa Cultural Center and walked toward the entrance. He purchased a ticket at the box office and walked inside.

The auditorium was beautiful and, as he would soon learn, acoustically brilliant. He chose a seat in the back row, which was still reasonably close to the stage in the comfortable, medium-sized venue. *I'm amazed that a community concert band could perform in a venue this nice. I was expecting something like a high school auditorium.*

Aaron glanced at the program. The name of this band was Desert Pride Wind Symphony. The program stated that this was an 'LGBTQ and allies' band.

The musicians filed on stage and tuned. *Are all these people really gay? It says 'and allies,' so maybe some of them are straight. But why would straight people want to play in a gay band?*

The lights dimmed and the conductor entered to a round of polite applause. He stepped onto the podium, lifted his baton, and launched the band into a brisk opening number.

Soon, Aaron was swept into the world of symphonic band music. *Wow… this is just like my high school symphonic band, only the people are older. I remember all the fun we had during band rehearsals. We probably drove the director crazy with all our clowning around, but by the time the concert came, we always sounded pretty good.*

Aaron thought about his band friends and wondered which ones still played their instruments. He was friends with some of them on Facebook. Others, he had lost track of.

I wonder if these people are having as much fun as I had. I wonder if they have the same kind of camaraderie and friendships I had in high school.

The third song on the program was one Aaron played when he was in the wind symphony at Ohio State. He closed his eyes and tried to remember playing the trombone part. He recalled sitting in band rehearsals in Hughes Hall and performing concerts outdoors near Mirror Lake at the end of the spring quarter.

Aaron looked around the audience. The majority were older folks, but there were people of all ages. There were pairs of men and women whom he assumed were couples. Some people sat in small groups of either all men, all women, or both, and some people sat by themselves. Perhaps they were the partners of people in the band. He couldn't tell whether most of the people were gay or straight. It dawned on him that maybe he had bought into stereotypes that weren't accurate.

I wonder if anyone else is looking around the audience and assuming I'm gay. What if someone comes up to me after the show and wants to ask me out or something? I'll leave as quickly as possible when it's over.

Aaron enjoyed the second half of the concert as much as the first. He felt nostalgic for the good times, good friends, and musical fulfillment he had experienced in his various high school and college bands. He missed having music in his life.

After the concert, Aaron noticed a small art gallery at the other end of the lobby. He decided to check it out. Ten minutes later, he had seen all there was to see, so he headed back across the lobby to the door. During the time he was in the gallery, band members had emerged from backstage and were mingling among the attendees.

Before he made it to the door, Rob spotted him. He excused himself from his friends and hurried up to Aaron. "Aaron! I'm glad you came. How did you like it?"

"The band sounded great! I really enjoyed it. It brought back a lot of memories from my bands in high school and college."

"Thanks. A lot of people in our band stopped playing when they left school, and they really enjoy playing again."

"I quit playing when I started pharmacy school. It took up so much time, you know? I didn't have time for anything besides classes and studying."

"Yeah, I'll bet. Anyway, now that you're working, you probably have some spare time. You should start playing again!"

"I don't know… it's been five years…" *and I don't think I'd join a gay band anyway. I wonder if there are any other bands out there.*

Rob laughed. "We have people who hadn't played in twenty or thirty years. I think the longest is 38 years. You'd be surprised at how quickly it comes back. I didn't play for 13 years, and I got back to my previous level in about two months."

"That's good to know. Anyway, my trombone is still at my parents' house in Ohio. That's assuming they haven't gotten rid of it by now."

"If you're interested, you can borrow my old trombone. It plays okay. I use it for parades and stuff like that, so I don't have to be too concerned about it getting dinged or something."

Aaron thought, *Really? You'd loan one of your instruments to somebody you barely know?*

Rob could tell Aaron was thinking about it. "Just come to a rehearsal or two and check it out. No commitment. We rehearse on Thursday evenings. We're taking this Thursday off, but we'll be back the following week. The first rehearsal is always a sight-reading rehearsal, and we welcome new people who want to come and try it out. If it doesn't work for you, you can give my trombone back. No harm, no foul."

"So, would I have to audition or anything?"

"Nope. It's a non-audition band. We try to be as welcoming and inclusive as we can, for people at every skill level." Rob paused, then added, "gay or straight."

Aaron said, "Really? You guys sounded too good to be a non-audition band."

The conversation had gone on this long, so it was obvious Aaron was interested.

Rob said, "So, would you like to borrow my trombone and give it a try?"

Aaron tried to think of a polite excuse, but he couldn't come up with one. The lame objections he had put up so far had been addressed. There was no way he could say, 'I really don't want to play with a bunch of gay people,' without sounding like a terrible human being, so he said, "Yeah, okay."

"So let's talk about how we can get my trombone to you. In what part of town do you live?"

"Tempe. You know Wok Around the Clok where we met? I live near that."

"Hmmm… I don't get to Tempe all that often. Do you ever come to uptown Phoenix?"

"No, but I don't mind driving. Besides, you're the one doing me a favor. I should come to you."

"Okay. Have you ever been to Kahuna's Tiki Paradise?"

"Never heard of it."

"It's on Central, a few blocks south of Camelback. It's one of my favorite places. They have Hawaiian and Polynesian-inspired food, and the cocktails are fabulous! I'll buy you a Mai Tai."

"Well, okay…"

"How about this Thursday at 5:30? It will still be happy hour."

"Yeah, that should work."

"You have my phone number – text me if something comes up."

Aaron nodded.

"Well, I should let you go. There are a few more people I want to say hi to, then I have to help load the instrument truck. See you on Thursday!" Rob gave Aaron a friendly pat on the side of his shoulder, then turned and walked over to another cluster of people.

Aaron left the building and walked through the parking garage to his car. As he drove home, he replayed his conversation with Rob. *What the hell just happened? Some gay guy I met less than a week ago just invited me to join a gay band – and I said yes. He's going to loan me his trombone, even though he doesn't know me from Adam. And he invited me out for a drink! I wonder if Kahuna's Tiki Paradise is some kind of gay place. And… is this like a date or something? This is crazy! I should just text him and say no.*

When he got home, he searched for Kahuna's Tiki Paradise on his computer. It looked festive and appealing. There were both women and men in the pictures, so it probably wasn't a gay restaurant. He checked out the menu and the pictures of the food and drinks. They looked delicious.

All week, Aaron waffled back and forth. The idea of playing trombone again appealed to him. It would be a great way to get out of his routine and meet some new people. But they were gay – most of them, anyway.

Tiki Time

Thursday, March 31, 2016

By 5:00 on Thursday afternoon, Aaron had not worked up the nerve to tell Rob he had changed his mind and would not be borrowing his trombone or joining the gay band. He knew he wanted to start playing again. He planned to ask his parents to bring his trombone when they came to visit at the end of April, regardless of whether he joined this band or some other one.

It was the gay thing that bothered him, and he felt guilty about it. A few guys in his college bands were gay, and they were decent guys. He didn't have any issues with them being gay or with being around them. There were probably others he didn't know about – maybe even one or two of his friends. He considered himself reasonably progressive, so he supported gay people having equal rights. He voted for Barack Obama in 2012 and planned to vote for Hillary Clinton in 2016. Intellectually, he knew gay people were pretty much like everyone else and there was no good reason to be uncomfortable around them.

Still, he felt uneasy.

He knew he needed to start driving into Phoenix now or he would be late for meeting Rob. He couldn't back out now.

Traffic was worse than Aaron expected. Since he walked to work, he completely forgot that most of the working population had to deal with rush hour. At 5:34, he pulled into the parking lot behind Kahuna's Tiki Paradise and shut off his car.

He placed his hand on the door handle but he couldn't pull it. Something in his subconscious mind was preventing the muscles and tendons in his hand from performing this simple task. He sat paralyzed in his car as a wave of panic swept over him. His pulse rate and breathing accelerated. Since the engine was off and the air conditioner was not running, the temperature inside the car rose quickly. He could feel perspiration forming on his warm face.

After three minutes had passed, Aaron took a few slow, deep breaths of hot, stuffy air. He chided himself for being such a coward and for making himself even later for his meeting with Rob. He pulled on the door handle and emerged from his car. As he walked toward the restaurant, he grew more apprehensive. His rational mind tried to convince his irrational mind that he was being paranoid for no reason and nothing bad was about to happen.

The front door was propped open to take advantage of the beautiful spring day. Aaron walked in and spotted Rob sitting at the near end of a long, raised table. His trombone case was standing upright on the floor. Rob's expression conveyed a combination of annoyance and concern, but he smiled when he saw Aaron approach. He hopped off his stool and extended his hand. "Glad you made it. I was starting to get concerned."

Aaron shook his hand and said, "Yeah, sorry. Traffic was worse than I thought it would be." He knew that didn't sound convincing.

"Well, anyway, you're here. Have a seat!"

Aaron sat down across from Rob. Two water glasses sat on the table. Rob's was already half empty. He scanned the room. A wooden bar spanned the entire length of the opposite wall, with a thatched roof extending over the bar and the bar stools. Several tall wooden tikis were positioned around the room. An assortment of glassware, from pineapple-shaped mugs to Charlie Chan ceramic glasses, was displayed on a long, narrow shelf near the ceiling. Polynesian-themed artwork adorned the walls. "This is quite a place," Aaron said.

"Yeah, they put a lot of effort into creating the right ambiance."

A perky waitress arrived at the table. "Can I get you guys started off with something to drink? One of our signature Mai Tais, perhaps?"

Rob smiled at Aaron. "Their Mai Tais are the best. Their other drinks are good too. And it's on me."

"Yeah, sure, I'll try the Mai Tai."

"Make that two." He turned back to Aaron. "Want to split an order of ceviche?"

"What's that?"

"Seafood cooked in citrus juice. You'll love it."

"Okay." Rob seemed intent on ordering something, so Aaron figured he should go along. If he didn't like it, Rob could eat the rest of it.

Rob turned back to the waitress and nodded. She said, "Two Mai Tais and an order of ceviche. I'll get that started for you." She turned and hurried away.

Rob said, "So, Aaron… you said you haven't played since you started pharmacy school. Where did you go?"

"Ohio State. I was in their marching band for three years."

"Ahh… the Pride of the Buckeyes! The Best Damn Band in the Land!"

Aaron perked up. "That's the one!"

"I'll bet that was quite an experience."

"Yeah, it was. It was probably the greatest experience of my life. What about you? Where did you go?"

"Arizona State. I'm a Phoenix native. You won't find too many of us around here. Most everyone has moved here from someplace else."

"Were you in the marching band?"

"Yeah. It was a lot of fun. I was in it for four years, but I only got to go to one bowl game. That was the Rose Bowl in 1996, my senior year."

Aaron did some quick math in his head. If Rob was a senior in 1996, that would make him about 42 now.

Rob continued, "The football team kinda sucked from the late 80s through the early 90s. But that year, we had a great quarterback and a star defensive linebacker. We went undefeated and won the Pac-10 conference, so we got to go to the Rose Bowl. Ironically, we lost to Ohio State. Their coach had previously been the coach at ASU, and their star quarterback came from Mesa. If we had won, we would have won the national championship that year, but… oh well. So yeah, a lot of ASU fans hated Ohio State after that. But I gotta say, you have a truly remarkable marching band. And it's all brass and percussion, right?"

"Yeah, that's right. I didn't make the band my freshman year, but I made it in my sophomore year. So I was only in it for three years. We played for the national championship game at the Sugar Bowl after the 2007 season. Then we went to the Fiesta Bowl in 2008 and the Rose Bowl in 2009. When we came out here for the Fiesta Bowl, I really liked the area. I loved that it was warm and there was no snow. That's one of the main reasons I took a job out here after I graduated."

The waitress arrived carrying two brown, frothy drinks in short, fat glasses. Another employee tagged along, carrying the plate of ceviche and two smaller plates. The waitress asked, "Have you decided what you want to order, or do you need a few more minutes?"

Rob replied, "We're just here for drinks and appetizers today."

"Sure, no problem. I'll check in with you later to see if you need anything else."

Aaron lifted his glass and took a small sip through the bright orange straw. "Oh my God, this is awesome!"

Rob smiled. He placed one of the small plates in front of Aaron. "Now try the ceviche. Put a few chunks on top of one of the chips."

Aaron tried a bite. "Very good. I don't think they have this back in Ohio. At least I've never heard of it."

"Oh, there's probably a tiki restaurant somewhere in a city the size of Columbus. But yeah, this is kind of a niche. Anyway, help yourself. There's no way I'll eat all this."

They took a few more sips of their Mai Tais and bites of ceviche.

Rob said, "Getting back to something you said a moment ago… What do you mean, you didn't make the band?"

"I got cut during tryouts. At least I made it to the last round of cuts, so I almost got in."

Rob looked puzzled. "You mean they have tryouts for the marching band at Ohio State? I've never heard of that. At ASU, anyone who wants to be in the band is in. I thought it was that way everywhere else." Rob wondered if Aaron was a crappy trombone player and if inviting him to join Desert Pride was a mistake. He remembered Aaron asked whether he would have to audition.

"That's right. The OSU Marching Band has fixed instrumentation – only so many people on each instrument. So there are always 224 people in the band, plus the drum major and assistant drum major. Each year, between 350 and 375 people try out. So yeah… a lot of people get cut."

Rob looked astonished. "I guess that explains why your band is so good. You only take the better people."

"Yeah. And it means everyone has to worker harder to get in."

"But enough about college. How do you like living in Arizona?"

"It's been okay. I enjoy the warm, sunny weather and I sure don't miss the snow. But I'm finding it hard to make friends out here."

"Well, joining Desert Pride is a great way to meet people. We have a lot of nice folks in the band."

"Yeah, but…" Aaron stopped himself before he said, 'They're all gay.'

"But what?"

"I don't know. Nothing, I guess."

Rob smiled. "But we're a gay band."

"Well, yeah, but it's not like there's anything wrong with that."

Rob didn't say anything while he waited to see what Aaron would say next.

"It's just that I don't know whether I'd fit in. What do you guys do?"

"We meet once a week, get out our instruments, and rehearse concert band music – like you would do in any other band." He paused and smiled. "They're rehearsals, not orgies."

"Then what's the point of having a gay band if it's the same as any other band?"

"It's so gay people can have a place where they feel like they belong. Someplace where they know it's okay to mention their partner and other people won't be telling fag jokes."

Aaron looked perplexed. "Is that really a problem for you?"

"It can be. It was a problem back when I was in high school and college. You're younger, so hopefully it wasn't as bad at your schools."

The waitress reappeared. "Can I get you guys anything else? A couple more Mai Tais?"

Rob said, "No, I think we're fine. Would you bring the check, please? I'm paying."

The waitress nodded. "I'll be right back."

Aaron thought back to his time in the marching band and some of the crude songs they sang on bus trips. To him, it was all in fun. It never occurred to him until now that those songs could have been hurtful to some people.

Rob said, "Plus, we're kind of like cultural ambassadors of the LGBTQ community to the community at large. Any straight people who come to our concerts see we're just people playing music like anyone else. Music helps build bridges and break down barriers."

"Yeah. When I was at the concert, I remember thinking that if I walked in off the street and didn't know, I wouldn't have figured out it was a gay band."

"Exactly."

"Well, okay, I get all that. But still, I don't understand why straight people would want to be in a gay band."

"Maybe… because we're good? Maybe because we're nice people and we're fun to be around? I know a couple of the straight women in the band have daughters who are lesbians. Another one has a gay brother."

Okay, but none of that applies to me. "So how will the other people know I'm not gay?"

"Does it really matter? Like I said, they're rehearsals, not orgies. You don't have to suck a cock to get in."

Aaron felt embarrassed. "I didn't mean it that way. Sorry if that came across wrong."

"I don't think you'll have any problems. I doubt that anyone will say or do anything inappropriate. Just be nice to people and let them be nice to you. If anyone shows any interest, just say, 'Thanks, but I'm straight.' But if you're that uncomfortable, it would be better if you didn't come. There are plenty of other community bands you could join."

The waitress returned with the check. "No hurry. Whenever you're ready." Rob motioned for her to stay. He pulled his credit card from his wallet and handed it to her along with the check.

Aaron thought, *What is wrong with me? He probably thinks I'm homophobic. I don't think I'm homophobic, but am I? If I'm not, I shouldn't have any issue with this. He's being nice to me. He's offering to loan me his trombone! He's giving me an opportunity to play in a band, and I know they're good. What is my problem?*

Aaron said, "No, I want to give it a try. I'll start practicing this evening. But a week from now, I'll probably still sound pretty bad."

"Don't worry about it. Most people in the band hadn't played their instrument for years when they joined. Everyone remembers what it was like. We won't judge you too harshly."

"Well, if you say so…"

"I'm sure of it. So… see you next Thursday at 7:00. I'll text you the address. Anyway, I need to be on my way. I'm having dinner with a few friends." The waitress returned with the check and Rob's credit card. He added a tip and signed it.

Aaron said, "Thanks for the Mai Tai and the ceviche – and for loaning me your trombone."

"My pleasure. See you next week." He hurried out the door.

Aaron flagged down the waitress. "May I see the menu again? I'd like to order dinner."

Aaron's First Rehearsal

Thursday, April 7, 2016

At 6:45, Aaron turned his car into the parking lot of the church where Desert Pride Symphonic Band rehearsed. He selected a parking space at the far corner of the lot and backed into it. He sat in his car and watched other people arrive and walk inside. Everyone looked pretty normal. What did he expect them to look like? He glanced at his watch. 6:53. He knew he was stalling, and he wasn't sure why. Maybe to avoid small talk with people he didn't know yet.

He got out of his car, retrieved Rob's trombone from the trunk, and headed into the church. He followed a few other people so he would know where to go once he was inside. He walked into the rehearsal room and spotted Rob sitting in the first chair of the last row on the left, the same place he sat at the concert. Rob saw him, smiled, and waved him over.

"Welcome! Glad you made it!"

"Thanks. I've been practicing all week. I don't think I'll sound too bad. I don't know if I'll be able to play for two hours, though."

"Don't worry… it's not like we play constantly. Just do what you can. What part did you play when you were in school."

"First. But since I'm starting again, it's fine if they put me on second or third. Whatever."

"No, play first. Why don't you sit there, on the other side of Stephen?" He pointed to the third chair in the row, which was empty. "We'll decide who sits where later."

Aaron scooted past the 30-ish guy seated next to Rob and sat down. He opened his trombone case and began assembling Rob's trombone. The guy seated next to him said, "Hi! I'm Stephen." He extended his hand for Aaron to shake.

"Hi, I'm Aaron."

"Welcome!"

"Thanks. I haven't played for, like, five years, so I'll probably suck."

He immediately regretted that choice of words. Stephen seemed not to notice.

"No problem. I hadn't played for six years when I joined. You'll be surprised at how quickly it comes back."

Stephen seemed nice enough. Aaron turned toward the guy on his left. "Hi. I'm Aaron."

The other guy said, "Jeremy," and they shook hands. Jeremy smiled at Aaron, and Aaron felt slightly less nervous. The director stepped onto his podium and the cacophony of chatter and random horn-blowing subsided.

"Hello and welcome back! Nice to see a few new faces. I'd like to ask each of the new people to stand up and tell us your name, how long it's been since you last played your instrument, and something interesting about yourself. It doesn't have to be anything too personal." He scanned the flutists in the front row. "Why don't we start with you?"

A middle-aged guy stood up and said, "My name is Paul. I'm just getting back into playing flute after 15 years. As for something interesting about myself, hmmm... well... besides working as a technical trainer, I'm a medium."

Jeremy turned toward Aaron, Stephen, and Rob and whispered, "He's a medium? I saw him in the men's room before rehearsal. He's definitely a large!" Stephen and Rob snickered. Aaron smiled and made a mental note to avoid using the restroom here.

Several more people stood and introduced themselves. In the sax section, a new guy introduced himself as Stephen. The Stephen to Aaron's right muttered, "Great. Another Stephen."

Finally, it was Aaron's turn. He stood up and said, "Hi. I'm Aaron. I'm from Ohio. In fact, I was in the Ohio State marching band. I've been out here – er, I mean *living* here for almost two years. I hadn't played trombone for five years until about a week ago. Something interesting about me... Hmmm, I don't know... I'm straight." He immediately wished he hadn't said that. He added, "And I'm a Pharmacist."

He quickly sat down. The room felt awkward – or maybe it was only him. The director moved on by asking a new person in the percussion section to go next.

In the French horn section, yet another Stephen turned to the guy next to him, Kent, and whispered, "He's straight all right – straight to bed!"

Kent whispered back, "If that's the guy Rob told me about, he *is* straight. At least that's what he says."

Stephen smirked dismissively. "Hmmph. Twenty bucks says he wants his weenie washed."

Kent shook his hand. "You're on."

The first half of the rehearsal passed quickly. Once they started playing, Aaron felt more comfortable and allowed himself to enjoy the experience. He played better than he expected. He was a good sight-reader so he made only a few mistakes. At least he wasn't embarrassing himself.

After an hour, the director released the band for a ten-minute break. Rob motioned for Aaron to follow him up to the podium to meet the director. Rob said, "Aaron, this is our Artistic Director, Lee Parker. Lee, this is Aaron Bradbury." They shook hands.

Lee said, "Welcome to Desert Pride. I heard you say you were in the Ohio State University Marching Band. So was I!"

"Really! When?"

"Oh, it was back in the early 80s."

"I was in from 2007 to 2009."

"Cool. What brought you out here?"

"My job. And I wanted to live someplace warmer."

"I know what you mean. We came out here for the Fiesta Bowl twice – in 1980 and 1983. I liked the area and decided I wanted to live here. I've been here since 1985."

"Nice. So Rob said you want me to play for you so you can decide which part I should play."

Rob interjected, "He told me he played first in high school and college. And he's sounding pretty good so far today."

Lee said, "If you were good enough to make the Ohio State University Marching Band, you're good enough to play first in Desert Pride. So as far as I'm concerned, you can stay right where you are."

Aaron smiled and said, "Thanks! And nice to meet you."

"I'm sure we have some band stories we can share at some point."

"Yeah, that would be fun."

Lee turned to deal with someone else, and Rob said, "Well, I need to go hit the little boys' room before we start back up." Aaron wandered into the courtyard, where band members were standing in clusters chatting.

Kent and Stephen, the French horn players, walked up to Aaron.

Kent extended his hand and said, "Welcome. I'm Kent."

Aaron shook his hand. "Aaron."

Stephen glided forward and offered his hand, palm down and limp at the wrist. "And I'm Stephen." Aaron gently shook his hand. "So what brings a nice straight boy like you to the *faaabulous* Desert Pride Symphonic Band?"

Aaron wasn't sure how to respond. Kent rolled his eyes and said, "Don't mind Miss Thing here. Welcome! But seriously, how did you find out about us?"

"Well… I happened to run into Rob at a restaurant a couple of weeks ago, and he was wearing this shirt that said, 'If I seem quiet, it's because you haven't seen me with my trombone–'"

Stephen cut in. "Oh, that tacky old thing? I can't be-*lieve* he wears that out in public!"

"Anyway, I said, 'Nice shirt,' and he asked if I was a trombone player, and it went from there. He told me about your concert. So I went, and you guys sounded great. Anyway, it kind of made me want to start playing my trombone again, so Rob invited me to come here tonight to check it out."

Kent said, "How do you like it so far?"

"Oh, I love it. And Lee's a very good director."

The break ended and people started filing back into the rehearsal room. Stephen leaned closer to Aaron and whispered, "But one thing, honey. Be careful! I hear there are *homosexuals* in this band!"

"Uh… yeah, I kinda knew that."

Kent said, "And he's the only one you have to watch out for." He grabbed Stephen's arm and pulled him away.

When rehearsal concluded, Lee announced, "Welcome to all the new people who came tonight. Just so you know, some of the people in the band meet at a local restaurant each week before rehearsal. We announce which restaurant we're going to in our Facebook group. Once we have your new member form, we'll invite you to join that group. Also, a bunch of people usually go to Raise! for a drink after rehearsal. It's a couple of miles up 7th Street. So feel free to join us for either or both of those things."

As Aaron crossed the parking lot on the way to his car, Jeremy called out, "Hey! Are you going to join us at the bar?"

Aaron hadn't planned on it, but he didn't want to seem unfriendly to one of his new section mates, so he said, "I don't know. I guess rehearsal was the only thing on my radar for tonight."

"Come on. I'll buy you a drink. You can follow me there."

"Well… okay."

As Aaron drove to the bar, he thought, *I can't believe I'm doing this. First, I went to a gay band rehearsal, and now I'm going to a gay bar. If my parents ever found out, they'd freak. I'll just stay for one drink.*

Raise! The Bar

Thursday, April 7, 2016

Aaron followed Jeremy's Acura north on 7th Street until he spotted a sign with a pink neon outline that said RAISE! in all capital letters, with smaller letters underneath that said, THE BAR. He smiled; it was a clever name. He turned into the parking lot and pulled into one of the few remaining spaces. He met up with Jeremy and they walked into the bar together.

Aaron said, "The place looks packed, especially for a Thursday night."

Jeremy replied, "It's 2-for-1. Plus, friends of people in the band know we'll be here tonight, so they come out too."

Aaron had no idea what he was about to encounter, but Jeremy seemed like a nice guy, as did Stephen the trombonist, Rob, Kent, and Lee. He didn't know what to make of Stephen the French horn player. He could leave if it got too weird.

Jeremy led him up to the bar. A couple of people were lined up to buy drinks. Jeremy got in line behind them. "What'll you have?"

Aaron had no idea what to order in a gay bar. Up to this point, he drank simple drinks like Rum and Coke or Jack and Coke, or beer. He recalled how much he liked the Mai Tai from Kahuna's Tiki Paradise, so he said, "I'll have a Mai Tai."

The bartender handed drinks to the people ahead of them, and they turned and left. Jeremy stepped up to the bar. "I'll have a Long Island Iced Tea and my friend will have a Mai Tai." The bartender nodded and went to work. A moment later, he handed Jeremy a drink that looked like iced tea in a tall, slender glass with a lemon wedge and a cherry on top. He handed Aaron a yellowish drink in a shorter glass with a pineapple wedge, a cherry, and a pink paper umbrella. Aaron was horrified. This was not the same drink he was served at Kahuna's. He pulled the umbrella out of his drink and left it on the edge of the bar.

Jeremy paid for their drinks and the waiter handed him two white register receipts. Jeremy handed one to Aaron.

"What's this?"

"That's your 2-for-1 ticket. Give it to them when you want your second drink."

"Does it have to be the same drink?"

"Yeah, I think so."

Jeremy and Aaron weaved their way through the crowd to a long table near the back of the bar, where a dozen other band members had already gathered. As Aaron walked through the bar, he looked around. It was dimly lit but comfortable. There was a pool table and a dartboard. The bar ran the full length of the left side. There were stools all along the bar, three high-top tables including the one the band members had claimed, and a sitting area with a couple of couches and comfortable chairs. Television monitors mounted around the room were showing fast-paced, trippy music videos. It was noisy, but not too loud for conversation.

Aaron glanced at the other people as he passed. They seemed like average, everyday people. The crowd was mostly men, but there were some women too. Aaron wondered if other people could tell he was a straight man invading their gay space, but then he realized he couldn't tell whether most of the other people were gay or straight. If he encountered them someplace other than in a gay bar, it wouldn't even occur to him. By the time he reached the band crowd, he decided that everyone else in the bar probably couldn't tell whether he was gay or straight, and nobody seemed to care anyway. That was a relief.

Several others introduced themselves to Aaron and engaged in small talk. Thankfully, nobody grilled Aaron with questions about why he, a self-proclaimed straight guy, had joined a gay band and come out to a gay bar.

Kent and Stephen from the French horn section were sitting at one end of the table, along with a man Aaron didn't recognize from the rehearsal. Kent introduced him as his husband, Justin. One of the percussionists was standing nearby and introduced himself as Stephen. Aaron said, "Another Stephen! How many Stephens are in this band? There's you two, and the guy I was sitting next to, and the new guy in the sax section."

Stephen, the flamboyant French horn player, let out an exaggerated sigh, raised the back of his hand to his forehead, and gasped, "Oh, I *know*! It's just so *overwhelming*! How will you ever keep it … straight? Well, here. Let's make it a little easier. You can call me Petunia!"

Everyone within earshot had paused their conversations to listen to this exchange. When they heard that, everyone busted out laughing. Aaron had no idea how to react, but he forced a chuckle.

From that moment forward, Petunia was never called Stephen again.

Aaron soon realized he was having a good time. The other guys and a couple of the women from the band all seemed nice and treated him like one of them. He finished his Mai Tai. Although it was fruitier and sweeter than he expected and not as good as the Mai Tai at Kahuna's, it was all right. Jeremy finished his drink and noticed Aaron's glass was empty, so he said, "Ready for another one?" Aaron nodded. "Give me your drink ticket."

Aaron fished the ticket out of his pocket and handed it to Jeremy. "Thanks. Oh, and… where's the restroom?"

"C'mon, I'll show you."

Jeremy led Aaron through the crowd, past the pool table, and into the men's room in the corner. The small restroom contained three urinals with no dividers, one stall, and one sink. The restroom was dimly lit and there were mirrors everywhere. Thankfully, there was nobody else in the restroom at the moment. Aaron stepped up to the urinal farthest from the sink. Jeremy left the customary one-urinal gap and stepped up to the urinal at the other end. Aaron hoped a stranger would not walk in and stand right next to him. He tried to stay focused on the mirror in front of him, but he surreptitiously shifted his eyes to see if he could triangulate a glance through one or two mirrors to get a glimpse of Jeremy. He could. He tried his best not to stare. Jeremy didn't seem to notice.

Throughout the evening, people circulated from one conversational group to another. Aaron was enjoying getting to know the people in the band. He had no concept of how much time was passing. His glass was empty, so he decided to get something else. That Long Island Iced Tea Jeremy ordered looked good. He remembered having one at a party when he was in college. He walked up to Jeremy and said, "I'm going up for a Long Island. Do you want one?"

Jeremy looked concerned and said, "Nah… I'll switch to Diet Coke."

A few minutes later, Aaron returned with a Long Island and a Diet Coke.

After a half-hour, Aaron redeemed his drink ticket for his second Long Island. As he returned to the band table, he noticed the crowd in the bar had dwindled to about a quarter of its original size. One or two at a time, band members circulated around their group and said goodbye, usually with a hug.

Some people, without thinking about it, hugged Aaron. The hugs were friendly and not sexual, so he didn't mind.

When there were only six band members left, Jeremy said, "Well, it's time for me to go." He gave each of the others a quick hug and a goodbye. When he ended up in front of Aaron, Aaron hopped off his tall chair and, for an instant, lost his balance. Jeremy grabbed him by the shoulders to keep him from falling. Aaron rocked slightly as he said, "Thanks for inviting me to come out tonight. And thanks for the drinks." He took the initiative to hug Jeremy and held him for almost five seconds. It felt good. Afterward, Jeremy looked at Aaron with concern. "Are you okay?"

"Yeah, I'm fine."

"Well, you be careful." He turned and left, along with Petunia and Stephen the percussionist. Aaron looked around. Only Kent and Justin remained. Kent approached Aaron and said, "You're pretty drunk. I don't think you should be driving home tonight."

Aaron was about to insist that he would be okay to drive, but he knew he wasn't.

Justin said, "I think maybe you had one too many. Those Long Islands can be pretty strong."

Aaron started to think about how much a taxi or an Uber would cost to get from here to Tempe.

Kent said, "We live right around the corner. You can sleep on the couch."

Aaron nodded.

"Give me your keys. I'll drive your car."

Aaron knew Kent and Justin were right, so he handed his keys to Kent.

As they walked toward the front of the bar, Aaron realized he was staggering. He wasn't feeling good. "Will you guys excuse me for a moment?"

Without waiting for a reply, he bolted for the restroom. Thankfully, the stall was vacant and he made it in time to heave.

The Morning After

Friday, April 8, 2016

When Aaron woke up, he had no idea where he was, what time it was, or why he was sleeping on a hide-a-bed. He pulled the sheet and comforter off to one side, pivoted, and sat up. He was wearing underwear, which was not his custom at home. As he looked around Kent and Justin's living room, he started to remember bits and pieces from last night. His head throbbed and he was hungry.

He saw the shorts and T-shirt he wore last night on a nearby chair. His shoes and socks were on the floor in front of the chair. Aaron stood up, yawned, and put his clothes on. Then he went in search of a bathroom.

As he walked past the kitchen, Kent called out, "It lives! How do you feel this morning?"

"Like shit. May I use your bathroom?"

"Sure, it's the first door on the left."

When Aaron returned, he asked, "What time is it?"

"9:15. Would you like coffee?"

Aaron wasn't in the habit of drinking coffee, but he needed a caffeine jolt. "Yes, please." He sat down on one of the stools at the kitchen island. "Where's Jeremy?"

Kent scowled. He knew Aaron made a simple mistake, but he wasn't amused by this situation. "You mean Justin."

"Yeah, Justin. Sorry."

"He already left for work."

"What about you?"

"I called and told them I'd be working from home this morning. I have a flexible schedule, so I can do that."

Aaron felt like crap physically, and now he felt like crap for inconveniencing Kent and Justin.

Kent poured his coffee and said, "You had quite a night last night."

"Yeah, I guess I overdid it."

"When we saw you going for your third drink and you came back with a Long Island, we figured we should keep an eye on you."

"Thanks. I really appreciate it. And I appreciate you letting me stay here."

"You're welcome. But be more careful from now on. Their drinks aren't watered down. Most of us limit ourselves to two."

Aaron nodded and took a sip of the coffee.

Kent said, "But all that aside, did you have fun last night?"

"At the rehearsal or the bar?"

"Both."

"Yeah, it was great. It felt so good to play in a band again. And everybody was really nice."

"Many of our best friends are band people."

Aaron nodded. "I remember when I was in band in high school and college, most of my best friends were in the band too. That's why I wanted to try this out."

"So what else do you do when you're not working?"

"I go running a lot. There's a canal right next to my apartment, so I run along that. And sometimes I run through the neighborhoods around my apartment. But other than that, nothing. And that's the problem. I've lived out here for over a year and a half, and I don't know very many people."

"What did you think about your first visit to a gay bar? At least, I assume it was your first."

"I didn't know what to expect, but actually, it was fun."

"You seemed like you were having a good time."

"Yeah. I'll probably go out with you guys on the weeks I don't have to work the next day."

Kent glanced at his watch. "I have to dial into a meeting in a few minutes."

"Then I'll get out of your way. But thanks! I really appreciate it."

Kent walked Aaron to the door and opened it.

Aaron said, "Thanks again."

Kent gave him a quick hug, then closed the door.

Across the parking lot, Petunia was leaving his apartment to go run some errands. He saw Kent and Aaron hugging in Kent's doorway. He quickly stepped back inside and closed the door. He pulled out his phone and stepped over to his front window.

Once outside, Aaron stood in front of the door and scanned the parking lot looking for his car. He didn't see it anywhere to his right, but then he spotted it to his left in front of the next building.

Petunia took several pictures of Aaron standing in front of Kent and Justin's door. He picked the best one and texted it to Kent with the caption, 'You owe me $20, bitch!'

Petunia waited a few minutes for Aaron to leave before he opened his door again. When he sat down in his car, a text came in from Kent.

> Sorry to wilt your petals, Petunia, but nothing happened.

> Yeah, right. Everyone knows you're shameless whores. You probably double-banged him.

> We may play around, but we don't take advantage of drunk people – let alone drunk straight people.

> Bitch, please! He was all over Jeremy when they said goodbye. So will you be using Venmo, Zelle, or PayPal?

> None of the above. Later, bitch.

***

When Aaron arrived at his apartment, he decided to go for a run before he took his shower. He was tired, but he knew he could run at least three or four miles.

It was almost eleven by the time he reached the canal and started running down the path on the north bank. The canal was deserted. It was hot, so he pulled his tank top over his head and tucked it into the waistband of his shorts in the back. Soon, he spotted another man running toward him. He was shirtless too. As he approached, Aaron could see he was tall and slender. His hairless chest glistened and perspiration dripped from his wavy dark blond hair. Aaron had never seen this guy before. Perhaps he usually ran at this time of day. The man was running at a brisk pace. As they passed, Aaron smiled and said 'hi,' as he often did when he passed other runners. This guy nodded and waved as he sped past.

A couple of steps later, Aaron turned to look back. The runner's well-toned legs moved efficiently, propelling him forward gracefully. His minimal arm swings were perfectly coordinated with his stride. Sweat rolled down his back and dampened the back of his silky running shorts. Aaron wondered whether the other runner would turn and look back at him. He didn't.

At the next street crossing, Aaron turned back. He was getting tired. Maybe the other guy would turn around at some point and they would cross paths again.

As Aaron approached his apartment complex, he decided to continue running. After running for two more miles, there was still no sign of the tall, slender, blond runner. Aaron stopped and walked for a little while, sipping from his water bottle. Finally, he headed home.

***

After Aaron took a shower and ate a microwaved entrée for lunch, he sat down at his computer. He checked his email, then pulled up Facebook. He was pleasantly surprised to find eleven friend requests and an invitation to join the Desert Pride Members Only group. He was already friends with Rob, but now he had requests from Stephen the trombone player, Justin, Kent, Lee, the Stephen now known as Petunia, and a few others he had talked with at the bar. He accepted each request and looked briefly at their pages. Before he finished, another friend request popped in – from Jeremy.

He accepted Jeremy's request and started reading the posts on his timeline. He learned that Jeremy was originally from Yuma, Arizona, was five years older, and liked to hike. There were numerous pictures of Jeremy hiking with a bunch of other guys – probably some sort of gay hiking group. Kent and Justin were in some of the pictures. Aaron also discovered that Jeremy was newly single after ending a 14-year relationship a couple of months ago.

While he was scrolling through Jeremy's timeline, a private message from Jeremy arrived.

Hey, how's it going?

Pretty good. Just went for a run and took a shower.

So you got home okay?

I stayed with Kent & Justin. They live near the bar.

Good - glad you didn't drive home.

Yeah, I kinda overdid it. Sorry!

No prob... we've all been there.

Did I say or do anything embarrassing?

You were pretty chatty, but no worries.

Thx for inviting me. And thx for the drinks.

So you're glad you went?

Totally. Had a great time except for getting too drunk.

Are you coming back to band next week?

Definitely. Didn't realize how much I missed music.

Cool. CU then.

C'ya. Bye!

A moment later, Jeremy was offline.

Aaron returned to his email and composed a message to his mom.

Dear Mom,

    I'm looking forward to having you and Dad visit in a couple of weeks.

    Do you still have my trombone? If so, would you please bring it with you? I've found a local community band I'm going to start playing in.

    Tell Dad I said hi.

    Love,

    Aaron

Aaron's Second Rehearsal

Thursday, April 14, 2016

Now that Aaron was a member of the Desert Pride Members Only Facebook group, he learned that this week's pre-rehearsal dinner would at Angeloberto's, a local Mexican fast-food chain. He decided to try it out. He sent messages to Rob, Jeremy, and Kent asking if they were planning to go. He'd feel a little more comfortable if at least one person he already knew was there. Kent replied with a maybe, depending on whether he could finish work in time. Rob said he would be there.

At 4:45, as Aaron was about to shut off his computer and head out the door, a message came in from Jeremy. He'd be there. Aaron smiled.

When Aaron arrived at Angeloberto's, Rob and a few other band members were standing in line at the counter to order. By the time he finished ordering, the others had shoved some tables together to create seating for 20. Aaron chose a seat next to a woman he recognized from the clarinet section. A few minutes later, Jeremy arrived. Thankfully, by the time he made it to the table, the seat across from Aaron was still available.

The conversation flowed easily. Some people talked about the Pride parade which had taken place two weeks earlier. People expressed opinions about the music Lee had selected for their June concert. At one point, the clarinetist seated to his left asked Aaron where he was from and what he did for work. Several others asked more questions. At first, Aaron felt like he was being interviewed or interrogated. But then he realized they were just trying to get to know him and make him feel included. At one point, the clarinetist mentioned her husband, so Aaron knew there was at least one other straight person there.

Dinner ended and the band members migrated to the rehearsal hall.

After rehearsal, Jeremy asked, "Are you coming out to the bar tonight?"

"Nah, I can't. This is my weekend to work and my days are pretty long. I'll be there next week, though! ... Oh, wait, no I can't. My parents are coming to visit. So I won't be at rehearsal next week either. Shit! Oh well."

"Okay, then, see you in a couple of weeks." Jeremy nodded and left.

Aaron's Parents Visit

Thursday, April 21, 2016

Aaron woke up at 6:45. He usually slept in on his days off, but he had too much on his mind today. His parents would be arriving sometime in the afternoon.

They had rented a Class C motorhome and were driving it all the way from Ohio. After visiting Aaron for a few days, they would head up to the Grand Canyon. Following that, they planned to continue north to a couple of the national parks in Utah, then up to Yellowstone, and then back to Ohio. It was a chance for them to experience the RV lifestyle in anticipation of their retirement. If they enjoyed the trip in their rental, they would buy an RV and spend months at a time on the road, exploring the country.

Aaron went for a run along the canal. As he ran, he tried to make sense of the mixed emotions he was feeling about his parents' visit. Of course, he loved his parents and it would be great to see them. And they were bringing his trombone, which he was eager to play again. He had places around town he wanted to take them. He wanted to show them his trendy, upscale apartment. Most of all, he wanted them to see that he had created a nice life for himself in Tempe.

He wasn't about to let on that only a month ago, he was depressed and lonely. Playing in Desert Pride and the new friends he was making changed all that.

On the other hand, he dreaded the questions they might ask. Was he going to church? Was he meeting any nice girls? And why does he have to live so far away? What's wrong with Ohio?

At 3:30, Aaron's phone chirped. He glanced at the caller ID and accepted the call.

"Hi, Mom!"

"Hello, dear. Just callin' to let you know we've arrived."

"How was the trip?"

"Exhausting! Oh, my lord! The first part of the trip wasn't bad, but each day seemed to get longer and longer! And the further west we went, the more we drove and drove without seeing anything! Everything's so far apart out here!"

"Yeah, it sure is. Well anyway, I'm glad you made it. Do you want me to head over there now?"

"Not yet. We want to relax for a while and get settled in. Your dad might take a little nap. Why don't you come by for dinner? Let's go out somewhere. I don't feel like cookin'."

"Okay, how about 6:00? I've got this great place I want to take you."

"It's not too fancy, is it? I don't feel like dressin' up."

"Oh, no. It's totally casual."

"Well, okay, then. Why don't you call before you leave to make sure we're ready?"

"Okay. See you in a couple of hours. Bye!"

"Goodbye, dear. I love you."

"Love you too, Mom."

***

At 6:00, Aaron pulled into the Desert Breeze RV Resort in Mesa. It was located in a rather unappealing part of town. It wasn't unsafe, just plain, run-down, and lower-class. Everything looked like a throwback to the fifties. Many of the buildings looked like they had barely been maintained. Aaron shuddered to think that this part of town was their first impression of Phoenix.

He drove around the perimeter road of the RV park. Some of the units looked like larger mobile homes which rested there permanently. Other spaces held a variety of travel trailers and motor homes. Some spaces were vacant since many of the snowbirds had already headed back to their northern homes.

He found space #26 and parked his car in one of the nearby guest parking spaces. He walked up to the unit parked there – an extra-long and tall van with a canopy that provided a covered area outside the door. He knocked on the door, and his mom opened it.

"Aaron! Honey!" She stepped down out of the RV and gave Aaron a huge kiss and an enthusiastic hug. "My baby! Awww… it's so good to see you!" She was practically crying with joy. She leaned into the RV and called out, "Ralph, Aaron's here!"

Aaron heard Ralph's muffled voice say, "I'm comin'."

Martha turned to Aaron and said, "He just got up from his nap. He was exhausted from that drive. Anyway, come on in and let me show you this thing."

Aaron followed his mother inside the RV. He had to lower his head to get in the door, but inside he could stand up straight with about an inch to spare. "Wow. This is pretty nice!"

Martha replied, "Yeah. That tiny little kitchen takes some gettin' used to, and everything's a little smaller than I'd like."

Ralph said, "Especially the bathroom! You can hardly turn around! It has a shower, but I can barely fit in it. Whenever we stay at a place that has bathroom facilities, we take our showers there. Stick your head in there and take a look." Aaron stuck his head in the door. It was, indeed, compact.

Aaron said, "So, how does it drive?"

Ralph replied, "Oh, it drives fine. The seats are real comfortable. They're the most comfortable part of this whole thing!"

"Cool. Well anyway, let's go eat! I have this really cool place I want to take you to. It's my favorite restaurant."

Martha asked, "Is it close by?"

Aaron grimaced. There was nothing but fast food chains and questionable-looking mom-and-pop restaurants in this part of town. "No, it's in Phoenix. It'll only take us 15 or 20 minutes to get there."

His parents didn't argue since it was clear Aaron had his heart set on taking them to this place. But they were exhausted from traveling for five of the last six days, and they didn't want him to spend a lot of money on them.

They stepped out of the RV and climbed into Aaron's Toyota Corolla, which previously belonged to his maternal grandmother. Martha asked, "How's the car holding up?"

"Great! I don't drive it that much. I live close to the drugstore where I work and there's a grocery store and a bunch of restaurants and everything else I need close by. So I walk everywhere."

Aaron navigated through the streets of Mesa to Loop 202. He drove west on the freeway toward downtown Phoenix. He hoped they would enjoy the beautiful mountains on the horizon. As they drove through Tempe, Aaron pointed to the left and said, "There's Arizona State's football stadium. And that's Tempe Town Lake. I think those office buildings and condos on the far side are really cool. You should see them lit up at night!"

Ralph said, "Good lord! This freeway's six lanes wide! I-75's just three lanes, and that's plenty. All this traffic would drive me nuts!"

Martha said, "And everyone's drivin' so fast. How fast are you going, dear?" She leaned over. "Eighty! God Almighty, honey, slow down! You're gonna get us all killed!"

Aaron rolled his eyes. He maneuvered to the right lane and slowed down to 65. All the other cars whizzed past.

Although it was 6:25 and the rush hour traffic was abating, they hit a backup a mile before the I-10 interchange. Aaron slowed to a crawl. Ralph sighed and said, "I don't understand why you had to haul us all over Hell's half-acre just to go to a restaurant. We passed a bunch of restaurants within a mile of the trailer park."

"We'll be there in ten minutes. I promise you'll love it. It'll be totally worth the drive."

Aaron turned into the parking lot at around 6:40. Ralph looked at the sign and said, "Kahuna's Tiki Paradise? What the hell kind of place is this?"

Aaron said, "It's Polynesian and Hawaiian-inspired food. It's delicious!"

"God, I remember that time in the Navy when we were docked in Bangkok. I tried some of that food and I had the shits for three days!"

Martha thought, *That's not all you had.* She said, "Honestly, Ralph! Do you have to talk like that right before we eat?"

Aaron led them to the greeter's stand and said, "Hi, Ashley. I'd like a table for three, please. If you have a booth near the windows, that would be great."

Ashley smiled and said, "Wait just a moment, please. I'll see what's available."

While they were standing inside the entrance waiting to be seated, a group of four diners came in from the outdoor patio. Aaron panicked. It was Kent, Justin, Stephen the sax player ... and Petunia. Aaron turned to face his parents, hoping the guys hadn't seen his face yet.

They had.

Petunia sashayed up to Aaron and exclaimed, using his most flamboyant campiness, "Wellll...! Look who's here! Fancy meeting you here, darling."

Aaron continued to face his parents and tried to ignore Petunia.

Petunia wasn't having it. He glanced at his watch. "Oh dear... you're going to be late for rehearsal!"

Aaron turned to Petunia and glared at him. "I won't be there tonight."

Petunia feigned shock and raised one hand to his chest. "Oh."

Before he could say anything else, Kent muttered, "Come on!" He grabbed Petunia's wrist and yanked him toward the door.

Petunia turned back toward Aaron, waved, and blew him a kiss. "Ta-ta!"

As soon as they were out the door, Ralph said, "Who the hell was *that*?"

Aaron had no idea how he was going to explain what just happened. Thankfully, Ashley returned and said, "Right this way, please."

It was a lovely evening, so the large glass-paned garage doors were open to allow the evening breeze in. Ashley led them to a booth near the open doors. They sat down and she handed them menus. "Enjoy your dinner!"

Aaron said, "The Mai Tais here are amazing. So's everything else."

Ralph said, "Is that one of those fruity drinks with a little pink umbrella stuck in it?"

"No, Dad. It's got a dark rum and lime taste. It's pretty bold."

"Can't I just have a beer?"

"Yes, they have beer here."

The waiter arrived and said, "My name's Jason. I'll be taking care of you guys. Can I start you off with something to drink? Maybe a Mai Tai or a Tropical Itch?"

Ralph said, "What kind of beer you got on tap?"

"Kona Longboard Lager and Big Wave Golden Ale."

"Never heard of 'em. Ain'tcha got Budweiser or Miller?"

"We have Bud Light and Miller Light in bottles."

Ralph frowned. "Whatcha got that ain't light?"

"Heineken."

"That'll do."

Martha said, "I'll have a Coke."

Aaron said, "Definitely a Mai Tai."

Jason asked, "Would you like to start off with any appetizers?"

Aaron lit up. He said to his parents, "They have this dish called ceviche. It's fish marinated in citrus juice. It's really good."

Martha looked shocked. "Raw fish? No thanks! Your Aunt Carolyn tried to get me to eat sushi one time. I said, 'No way!'"

"It's not raw. The acid in the citrus juice cooks it."

Ralph scanned the appetizer list. "They have wings. How 'bout that?"

Aaron sighed and turned to Jason. "We'll have an order of wings."

Jason said, "Excellent. I'll get that started for you guys." He turned and left.

Martha said, "These kids today. They call everybody 'guys.' I'm not a guy, I'm a woman."

Aaron said, "It's become sort of a gender-neutral term. The girls where I work say 'you guys' to each other all the time."

"Whatever happened to 'sir' and 'ma'am?' Or 'ladies' and 'gentlemen?' Or even 'folks.' That's much more polite."

Ralph scowled as he looked up and down the menu. "Ahi? Mahi? Hapu? What the hell is all that?"

"It's fish, Dad."

"Well, I ain't eatin' nothin' that lives in its own toilet. God, I've never heard of half of this stuff. What the hell is sun-dried tomato pesto aioli? Everything's got some kind of foofy sauce on it. Nobody eats this kind of stuff in Troy."

"That's kinda the point, Dad. I thought you might like to try something different."

"Nah, I know what I like – a thick, juicy steak."

"They have steak. There at the bottom."

Ralph grimaced. "Yeah, but it's got Teriyaki sauce smeared all over it. Why do they have to ruin a perfectly good steak? And what the hell are shit-take mushrooms?"

"It's pronounced shuh-tah-kee. They're large mushrooms from Japan. And you can ask them not to put Teriyaki sauce on your steak. Or get the ribs or the pulled pork. The pulled pork's really good."

Martha said, "Good heavens! I don't understand most of this stuff either. What's jerk chicken? Or fried sweet plantains? Or jungle curry sauce? Maybe I oughta just have a salad."

"There are several salads on the other side of the menu."

Martha turned the menu over. "Oh, my word! They want fifteen dollars for a salad!"

"Don't worry about it. I'm paying for it. And they're large and they have a lot of stuff on them."

"I don't want anything too large. For the life of me, I can't figure out why restaurants think they have to give you such large portions. No wonder there are so many fat people in America."

"You can take what you don't eat home with you and have it for lunch tomorrow."

Martha scowled as she looked at her choices. "This is all too fancy for me. Don't they have a regular salad?"

"I don't know. We can ask."

"This spicy shrimp Caesar salad might be all right. How spicy is it? I don't wanna burn my mouth out."

"I tried it once. It's not too spicy. But we can ask them to hold back on the spices."

Jason returned with their wings and beverages and then took their order.

They devoured the wings and Ralph downed half of his beer. Aaron knew he should have only one Mai Tai in front of his parents, especially since he was driving, so he sipped it slowly.

After Ralph licked off his fingers and wiped the corners of his mouth with his napkin, he asked, "So who was that pansy that came up to you while we were waiting?"

He's not a pansy, he's a petunia, Aaron thought. "He's in the band I play in. I don't really know him."

"You mean they let fairies in your band?"

Martha said to Ralph, "Honey, they probably have to. There's probably some law that says they can't discriminate."

Aaron said, "Everyone is welcome in this band."

Ralph said, "Maybe so, but can't you find some other band where they don't have any?"

"What am I supposed to do, walk into a rehearsal and ask, 'Are there any gay people in here?' Besides, any time you have a group of 50 or more people, a few of them are bound to be gay. There were gay kids in my bands in high school and college."

Martha said, "Well, you stay away from them. If you're not careful, they'll try 'n' recruit you."

Ralph added, "Steer clear of the queers." He smiled like he was proud of himself for coming up with that one. "Those other guys he was with looked a little light in the loafers, too. I can spot a homo a mile away."

Aaron said, "Oh, really. How do you do that?"

"It's easy. You've gotta know what to look for. Like their hair. If it's a little shorter and more stylish and combed perfectly, like they're using hair spray or some kind of gel on it, they're probably queer. Of if a guy has long hair, he probably wants to receive, if you know what I mean. Like he's trying to look like a woman."

Aaron said, "So if they have short hair or long hair, they're gay."

Ralph continued. "And their clothes. They tend to wear stylish, designer-name clothes, and they wear them a little too tight, you know? Like they're tryin' to show off their crotch or their ass. And if it looks like they spend all their time at the gym? You know, like their chests are all built up and stretching their shirts – that's a dead giveaway."

"So let me see if I've got this right. If a guy is well-groomed and dresses well and keeps himself in good shape, that means he's gay."

"Yeah. And you can always tell by the way they walk. Like they're more delicate. They kinda prance."

"And wait, let me guess. If they swish, and their wrists are limp, and they lisp when they talk."

"Oh, those are dead giveaways. Like that pansy who came up to you at the door."

Jason and a helper arrived at the table loaded down with food, and they distributed it to Ralph, Martha, and Aaron. "Can I get you anything else? Another beer, perhaps?"

Ralph said, "Yeah, I'll have another beer." He took a large swig and finished off the bottle. He plunked it down on the table in front of Jason.

Jason said to Martha, "I'll bring you a refill of your Coke." He turned to Aaron. "Another Mai Tai?"

"Yes, please." *Screw it. I need it.*

Jason nodded and left.

Martha said, "Honey, are you sure? I don't want you drivin' home if you've had too many."

Ralph said, "Oh, for Christ's sake, Martha. He's not a little boy anymore, he's a grown man. And Bradbury men can handle their liquor."

Martha rolled her eyes.

Ralph said, "And you know what? I'll bet our waiter's queer. A lot of 'em are. I mean, what kind of man wants a job waiting tables? Used to be, only women did that."

Aaron said, "Oh, yes. And flight attendants. And hairdressers. And interior decorators. And let me think… what else? Oh, yeah… priests.”

Ralph frowned, unaware that he was being mocked. “Now, you keep men of the cloth out of this.”

Martha said, “Speaking of church, some churches have bands now. You should check around with local churches to see if any of them need a trombonist.”

Aaron desperately wanted to change the subject to anything else. He asked, “How's your food?”

Martha said, “This salad is pretty good!”

“So the shrimp aren't too spicy?”

“No, it's fine. I don't think I'll be able to eat all this though.”

“Dad, how's your steak?”

Ralph nodded and said, with his mouth half full, “All right! Better than I thought it would be.”

Martha said, “Do they have a band at your church?”

Uh-oh. “Uh… I'm not going to church at this time.”

Martha frowned.

“I haven't found one I like. Plus, I work every other Sunday.”

“Well, keep lookin'. Like I said, maybe you can find one with a band you can play in.”

Aaron asked, “So what do you want to do while you're out here?”

Martha replied, “Rest, for one thing. Drivin' for five days really takes it out of you. I know you're just sittin', but it's still tiring.”

Aaron said, “I'd like to take you to the Musical Instrument Museum. It's amazing! Or Taliesin West – you know, where Frank Lloyd Wright lived and taught architecture.”

Neither of them seemed interested.

After a moment, Martha said, “Well, I don't want to be standin' on my feet for too long. And it's so hot out… I don't know. Why don't we take it one day at a time?”

Aaron was starting to dread the rest of this visit.

They ate in silence for a few minutes. Then Martha asked, “So, have you met any nice girls? Have you been on any dates?”

Oh no, not this. “No. I guess I've been more focused on my job. I work really long days. And I'm still learning the area. I haven't met that many people yet besides the people I work with. That's one reason I wanted to join a band. In high school and college, all my friends were in the band.”

Ralph said, "Well, you ain't gonna meet any women if you're playin' in a band full of queers."

"There are straight people in the band too. And women." *Of course, most of them are lesbians, and most of the straight women are married.* "And I'm just looking to make friends. I'm not really focused on dating right now."

Martha said, "Well, I don't wanna die before I get to see my grandchildren."

"Relax, Mom. You're not going to die anytime soon. Now can we move on to something else? Tell me about your trip."

Jeremy

Thursday, April 28, 2016

Aaron was happy to be back at band rehearsal. He regretted missing the rehearsal last week, especially since the dinner with his parents went so badly. He felt guilty when he realized he would have preferred to be here with his new friends than with his parents. But that's how he felt.

He really wanted to go out to the bar with his bandmates after rehearsal, even though he had to work tomorrow from 8:00 a.m. to 10:00 p.m.

When Aaron arrived at Raise! the Bar, the band table was already full and several people were standing around the chairs. He saw Kent, Justin, Stephen, and Petunia at one end. He definitely wanted to say hi to Kent and Justin. He would have preferred not to deal with Petunia after what he did last week, but he was there and Aaron didn't have much choice.

As he approached the table, Kent and Justin got up and gave him a quick hug. Petunia seemed uncomfortable. After the initial round of hellos, Petunia approached Aaron and said, "May I talk with you for a moment?"

They walked to a quieter area off to the side.

Petunia said, "I want to apologize for what I did last week at Kahuna's. I guess I had one too many to drink, and I was in a catty mood, and… well, Kent and Justin called me out on it, and, uh, they were right. It was wrong of me to act like that in front of your parents. I'm sorry." Petunia offered Aaron a masculine handshake, as opposed to the swishy, effeminate handshake he had offered when they met three weeks ago.

Aaron shook his hand. "Okay, thanks."

"I hope I didn't cause any problems."

"Well, actually, you did. They grilled me about why I was in a band with gay people, and how I should try to find a church band instead. Let's just say my parents aren't the most progressive, enlightened people."

"Oh, dear. Well, like I said, I'm really sorry."

"I forgive you."

"Thanks. I appreciate it."

And with that, they headed back to the table and rejoined the others. There was an empty chair next to Jeremy, so Aaron sat down on it. After saying hi to each other, Aaron said, "You have a lot of pictures on Facebook of you hiking."

"Yeah. That's one of the great things about living here. There's all kinds of good hiking within an hour or so."

"Those guys you were with... is that some sort of hiking club?"

"I guess you could say that. It's not an official organization. It's just a bunch of friends. The guy who organizes it set up a Facebook group and we communicate about upcoming hikes and post pictures. There are like 50 or 60 guys who belong to the group now. Usually, about ten or fifteen will show up for any given hike."

"Oh, cool. Are they all gay?"

"I think so. People invite their friends. Everyone assumes everyone else is gay, but nobody actually asks."

"Sounds like fun. I need to find something like that. I'd enjoy hiking, but I have no idea where to go. And it would be more fun to have other people to hike with."

"You live in Tempe, right?" Aaron nodded. Jeremy continued, "Well, there's South Mountain, to the west of you. There are lots of trails, from easy to moderate. Just Google 'South Mountain hiking trails' and you can find a map. The ones at the east end are pretty easy, but they're also the most crowded."

"Okay, thanks." Aaron didn't want to press Jeremy to invite him to their next hike, because… well, it was a gay group. Not that Aaron would mind. He was enjoying being part of Desert Pride, after all.

With no more to say about hiking, Jeremy turned his attention to the conversation that was going on to his right. Aaron went to the bar to redeem his 2-for-1 receipt for his second drink.

He returned to the band table and chatted with a few others. He glanced at his watch and saw that it was already 10:45. He knew he shouldn't have stayed out this late, but the socialization did him good. He started circulating around the table to say goodbye.

When he reached Jeremy to tell him goodbye, Jeremy said, "Hey, we've got a hike coming up on Saturday morning. You wanna come along?"

Aaron grinned for a second, but then he realized he couldn't. "Oh, man… I'd love to, but I can't. I work every other weekend, and this weekend

I work. But maybe next time."

Jeremy thought for a moment. "Well, why don't you and I go for a hike next weekend? I live near the main entrance to South Mountain, and I know some good trails."

Aaron smiled. "Sure, that would be great!"

"How about 7:00 a.m. next Sunday? Is that too early? It's getting pretty hot out."

"No, that's fine. I don't mind getting up early." *Especially for this.*

"Okay, I'll send you a Facebook message with my address. You can meet me at my house, and I'll drive us in."

"Great! Thanks! Okay, well, I'm gonna be on my way. See you at rehearsal next week!"

Jeremy hopped off his chair and gave Aaron a hug. Then he caught himself. "Oh, sorry. I forgot."

"No problem. I'm fine with hugs." *No problem at all.*

Name That Band

Saturday, May 7, 2016

On Saturday afternoon, Aaron was sitting at his computer surfing Facebook. He was chatting with Jeremy and Rob, and scrolling through the timelines of his new friends in Desert Pride.

His phone rang. It was his mom, so he picked up. "Hi, Mom!"

Martha said, "Hi, Honey! How are you? What are you up to?"

"I'm fine. I went for a swim in the pool earlier. Now I'm catching up on the computer. I'm gonna start fixing dinner pretty soon."

"Okay, well, I just wanted to let you know we made it home safely."

"Good. How was the rest of your trip?"

"Long. Really long. But it was nice. We really enjoyed the Grand Canyon and Yellowstone, and the other parks were nice too. The wonders of God's creation never cease to amaze me. I wish He had done more with South Dakota, though."

"Did you see Mount Rushmore?"

"Yeah, but we didn't have time for much else. Your father has to be back at work on Monday."

"So how did you like traveling in an RV?"

"It took some gettin' used to, but it's cheaper than stayin' in motels and eatin' all your meals in restaurants."

"Just think, after you retire, you won't have to worry about when you get back home. You can take your time and go wherever you want."

"Unless our backs give out first. All that driving wore us out!"

"Well anyway, I'm glad you had a good trip and you got home safely."

"Thank you, dear. Oh, and I wanted to ask you a question. What's the name of that band you joined?"

Uh-oh. I have to tell her. I'm not going to lie and make something up. "Desert Pride Symphonic Band."

"That's a funny name. Why would a band be proud of the desert?"

"I don't know, Mom. I didn't make it up."

"Well, anyway. You take care, sweetheart. And remember what I said about finding a church. You might find one that's looking for a trombone player. And maybe you'll meet some nice girls."

"Okay, Mom. Tell Dad I said hi. I love you."

"I love you too. Bye!"

"Bye."

Aaron pushed the button to end the call. He set the phone down and let out a long sigh.

***

Forty-five minutes later, Aaron's phone rang again. It was his mother. "Hi, Mom."

"Aaron, I just did some searching – you know, on the internet – and it says the Desert Pride Symphonic Band is an LGBT band. You know, for homosexuals."

"It's LGBT *and allies*, Mom. Straight people are welcome in the band, too."

"Well, of course they want straight people to join the band – so they can recruit 'em!"

"Mom, that's ridiculous. Nobody's trying to recruit me."

"Well, why on earth would you want to be in a band like that anyway? What will people think?"

"What people? I hardly know anybody here. And besides, I don't care what anyone else thinks."

"You should care about what God thinks. And God makes it perfectly clear in the Bible that homosexuality is a sin."

"I never said I was a homosexual."

"But why would you want to hang around with them? You should be careful about the people you choose to associate with."

"They're nice people. I'm enjoying playing my trombone again and I'm making friends."

"Phoenix is a big city. There must be other bands that aren't full of homosexuals. Try searchin' on the internet! They have all kinds of information on there now."

"I know how to search for things on the internet."

"Well then, search for a good church to join. You need to start goin' to church again and hangin' around with good Christian people. And who knows, you might meet a nice girl. You're 28, you know."

"Yes. And being 28 means I'm an adult and I can make decisions for myself. Now if you'll excuse me, my dinner's getting cold."

"Well, okay. But you think about what I said."

"Right. Bye, Mom. Love you."

"I love you too, sweetheart. But you be careful."

Hiking with Jeremy

Sunday, May 8, 2016

At 6:00 a.m., Aaron sprang out of bed. He put on his new hiking boots, shorts, and the T-shirt he bought made of material that was supposed to wick moisture away from his skin. He stepped out onto his balcony and sprayed his exposed skin with sunblock. He ate a quick breakfast and filled his new water pack with ice cubes and water. At 6:30, he climbed into his car and headed for Jeremy's house.

He arrived early, so he parked down the street and sat in his car until 6:59. Then he drove up to Jeremy's house and parked in front.

Jeremy invited Aaron in and greeted him with a quick hug. "Welcome to my humble abode – at least for now."

Aaron scanned the living room. It was sparsely furnished, but what was there was nice. Jeremy led him into the combination kitchen and family room. Aaron glanced out the sliding glass door and saw a sparkling pool.

"Wow… this is nice."

"Thanks."

"So… it's none of my business, but… why did you say, 'at least for now?'"

Jeremy sighed. "My ex-partner and I broke up a couple of months ago. He moved out and I'm staying here for the time being. But either I have to buy him out and keep paying the mortgage myself or sell it and we split the equity. I'll probably sell it, but I'm still thinking about what my next steps are going to be."

"You could get a roommate."

"Yeah. But I'd still have to come up with the money to buy out his half and then refinance the mortgage by myself."

"That's a shame. This place is beautiful."

"Thanks. When we bought it, it was kinda like a dream come true for me. I've wanted a house with a swimming pool ever since I was a little kid. And we dropped a ton of money on that barbecue island."

Aaron thought, *I'd be your roommate. It would be a step up from my apartment, and it would allow you to stay here.*

Jeremy said, "But enough of that. Let's get going." He opened the door to his garage and pressed the button to open the garage door. His sporty Acura coupe looked lonely by itself in the two-car garage. Jeremy pressed his remote and the trunk popped open. "You can drop your water pack in there. Did you bring sunblock?"

"I put some on before we left."

They got in the car. Jeremy zigzagged through some residential streets, then turned south onto Central Avenue and drove to the main entrance of South Mountain Park. As they entered, Jeremy said, "South Mountain is the largest city park in the world. Have you been here yet?"

"No, I haven't. I'm coming up on two years of living here, and there's still a lot I haven't done yet. I'm trying to change that."

They drove a bit further into the park. At one intersection, Jeremy said, "If you turn left here, this road will take you to a scenic overlook at the top. You can see all over Phoenix. It's beautiful, as long as the pollution's not too bad."

"Yeah, I'll bet."

"The best time to go up there is at sunset."

They kept driving down the main road. There were fewer cars and fewer side roads the further they went.

Aaron wondered, *Where is he taking me? We've passed plenty of trails already.* He said, "Wow. This park really is big."

"Yeah. In case you're wondering, I'm taking you to the western end of the National Trail. I like to come out here because it's never crowded. It's more peaceful. Sometimes I don't see anyone else at all."

Wait a minute. I'm being taken out to some deserted place by a gay man I hardly know. I mean, he seems nice, but... what if he has something in mind? He tried to shake that thought from his head. "How long is it?"

Jeremy glanced over at Aaron and smirked. "Oh, you mean the *trail.* It's 16 miles end to end. It runs the whole length of the park, mostly across the mountain tops."

Aaron looked confused. *Yes, the trail. What else would I be talking about? ... Oh. I get it.* "Are you thinking we'll go all the way?" *Oh, shit. Did I just say that?* "I mean, are we going to hike all 16 miles?"

"No, no, of course not. That would take, like, seven hours each way."

Jeremy paused. "I was thinking we'd just go a couple of miles. We can turn back whenever you think you've gone far enough. Does that sound okay?"

I wonder if I've gone too far already. "Yeah, that sounds good."

Jeremy sensed that Aaron felt awkward, but he couldn't figure out why. He pulled the car into a small, semi-circular parking lot with a lone picnic table under a roof. There were no other cars. They got out, Jeremy popped the trunk, and they put their water packs on their backs.

Jeremy led them across the road and they started down the trail. Aaron asked, "Have you ever hiked the whole trail?"

"Not all at one time. I've done different sections. I've probably done almost all of it at various times."

"Have you ever thought about doing the whole thing?"

"I've thought about it. Maybe during winter when it's cooler. And I'd want to arrange it so someone parks their car at the other end. I don't think I'd be up for going there and back."

After a few minutes of silence, Jeremy asked, "So, how do you like being in Desert Pride?"

"Oh, I love it. It feels so good to be playing my trombone again. And everyone's so nice."

"Yeah, it's a great bunch of people. They were a big help when Juan and I broke up."

"How long were you guys together?" He knew, but he didn't want to let on that he had scoured Jeremy's entire Facebook feed. Plus, he wanted to encourage conversation.

"Over 14 years. We met when we were freshmen at ASU. I'm 33 now, so yeah – it would have been 15 years this fall."

Aaron had no idea what to say to someone who had just broken up after 14-plus years. Still, he felt like he needed to say something. "How are you doing?"

"Okay. When we first broke up, I thought I was handling it well. Everybody was checking in on me and asking if I was okay and all that. It felt good to have so much support. A lot of people said I made the right choice and I'd be better off without him. And I probably will be. But it's been kinda rough lately. It's like everyone else has gone back to their lives, and it's starting to sink in that I'm alone now. I've never been alone. And now I have to think about selling the house and what's going to happen next and all that stuff."

"Yeah, I can see how that would be rough."

"Have you ever been in a relationship?"

"Not really. In college, I asked a few girls out but nothing happened. I guess I was more focused on band and studying and hanging out with my friends. When I went home for the summer after my freshman year, I hung out with this girl I knew from high school. We messed around a little bit, but then summer was over and we went back to our separate colleges. Once I got out here, I tried joining a couple of Meetup groups, but nothing ever came of that. So, long answer to a short question, but no."

They hiked in silence for a few minutes. Then Jeremy said, "Here's a shady spot. Wanna stop for a minute?"

"Sure."

They sat down on rocks and took a few swigs of water from their water packs.

Then Jeremy asked, "So, I hope you don't mind me asking, but if you're straight, why did you join Desert Pride?"

Aaron realized he didn't have a clear answer to that question. "I don't know."

"I mean, it's fine… We're glad you're here, and straight people are welcome, but… I was just wondering."

"I guess it was the first opportunity that came up. I happened to meet Rob at a restaurant near my apartment. He was wearing this T-shirt that looked like it had a trombone on it. That started a conversation and Rob ended up inviting me to your concert in March. Next thing I knew, I was in the band."

They stood up and started hiking again.

Jeremy asked, "So your parents were recently out here, right? How did that go?"

"Not so well. Terrible, actually. I took them to Kahuna's for dinner, which was a huge mistake. I mean, they're just plain folks from Ohio. They had no idea what a lot of the stuff on the menu was, and they had no interest in trying it. My dad, especially. All he wants is steak and potatoes. I took them out to Western Corral the next night, and they were in heaven."

"Ewww…"

"I know, right? But that wasn't the worst. When we first got to Kahuna's, Petunia and several of the others were leaving. And Petunia walked up to me and said, in his own special way, 'Fancy meeting you here, darling!' And then he blew me a kiss as he was leaving."

"Yeah, I heard about that. That was totally uncalled for."

"He apologized later, but the damage was done. For the rest of the dinner, it was homophobia on parade. Like, 'Why do they let fairies in your band?' and 'Watch out, they'll try to recruit you.' Then Dad went on about how he can spot a homo a mile away. Mom was all about how I needed to start going to church again and play in a church band instead of Desert Pride."

"Sounds awful."

"Yeah. And then for the rest of the visit, I couldn't get them to do anything interesting or fun. Like I wanted to take them to the Musical Instrument Museum or Taliesin West, but it was either too much standing up or too much time outside because it's too damn hot or they're too tired and they just want to relax. And I get it. They drove for five days and that's tiring. But I think the truth is they didn't want to do anything where they might learn something new or get exposed to any kind of culture. Hell, if there was a monster truck rally in town, they probably would have gone to that."

"Or a WWE match."

"Yeah, exactly. But wait, it gets worse. So yesterday, Mom called me to let me know they made it home safely. But then she asked me what the name of the band is. When I told her she said, 'That's a funny name. Why would a band be proud of the desert?'"

Jeremy laughed. "That's funny. Like it didn't even occur to her what that means."

"Yeah, but then 45 minutes later she called back. She found the band's website and she started going on about how 'it's a band for homosexuals! Why would you want to be in it? They'll recruit you!' and all that bullshit. And then more shit about going to church and meeting a nice girl and what it says in the bible and all that."

"Oh, wow. I'm sorry."

"Thanks. Geez, can you imagine how much worse it would have been if I actually told them I'm gay?" After a few seconds, Aaron added, "I mean, if I was."

"Actually, that's probably the same response you'd get either way. Sounds like they're already treating it like you are. Or like it's just a matter of time before we win you over."

They hiked in silence for a few minutes. Then Aaron asked, "Do your parents know you're gay?"

"Yeah. I told them not too long after I got out of college. While I was in college, I could say Juan was my roommate. But then when we graduated and got an apartment together, it became pretty obvious."

"How did they react?"

"Not very well at first. I got a lot of the same stuff about 'the bible says it's a sin' and all that crap, but they warmed up to it after a while. At least they were polite to Juan. Finally, they realized this is the way it is and they needed to accept it and deal with it."

"When did you know?"

"That I'm gay? Oh, pretty much my entire life. I mean, I always kinda knew I was different, but I wasn't sure why. Then around third grade, I started to realize I liked some of the other boys in my class, and not in a 'just friends' kind of way. When I went to bed at night, I imagined one of my friends was spending the night with me – you know, like a sleepover – and we'd be in bed together kissing and stuff like that."

"And stuff like what?"

Jeremy paused, then said, "You know, sucking each other's little third-grade weenies. And I actually fantasized that we'd spoon up against each other, and it would go in."

"Wow. All that in third grade?"

"Yeah. And see, here's the thing. Nobody ever told me about any of that stuff. I totally imagined it on my own. Years later, I realized those thoughts came to me as naturally as thoughts about what to do with a woman came to straight boys. I knew what I wanted, even way back then."

Aaron tried to remember what he was thinking about in third grade.

They reached a clearing at the top of one of the higher mountains. They took swigs of water while they admired the view.

Aaron said, "Wow – this is amazing! You can see in every direction." He pulled his phone out of his pocket and adjusted the camera settings. "I'm gonna take one of those 360° panoramic photos." He selected a spot with the best vantage point, pushed the button, and slowly rotated until he completed a circle. Jeremy moved behind Aaron so he would stay out of the picture.

Aaron said, "You could have stayed in the picture."

"I didn't want to foul up the beautiful view. But here… let's take a selfie."

Jeremy pulled out his phone and set the camera to use the self-facing lens. He stepped closer to Aaron and said, "Here, turn this way so we see the Phoenix skyline in the background." He extended his right arm and moved it up and down until he had the picture framed to his satisfaction. He casually draped his left arm over Aaron's shoulder in pulled him closer, so their faces were only a few inches apart and filled the lower half of the frame. He snapped the picture. "Let's take another one with our sunglasses off." He snapped another picture. He lowered his left arm but stayed close to Aaron. "Let's see how they turned out."

He opened the picture roll and showed both pictures to Aaron. Aaron said, "They both turned out well, but I like the first one slightly better."

"Yeah, me too."

"Send those to me, will ya?"

"Sure. So, you wanna continue on, or are you ready to head back?"

Aaron was loving this adventure, but he realized it was getting hotter and he already drank more than half of his water. "Maybe a little farther."

They started hiking again. Aaron said, "It's incredible that all this wide-open space exists in the middle of a major city."

"Yeah. I'm glad someone had the foresight to protect it as parkland. There are places on the south side of the mountain that aren't part of the park, and they've already built luxury houses there."

"That's too bad."

"Yeah, but I'm thankful for what we have. And there's lots of other great hiking in the area too, like Camelback Mountain, Piestewa Peak, the Superstitions, and a bunch of others. My hiking group has gone to a lot of different places."

I'd love to come along, Aaron thought. But he didn't want to push things too much.

Twenty minutes later, they turned around and headed back. It was after 11:00 when they made it back to Jeremy's car. Aaron said, "That was great, but I was starting to get overheated."

"Yeah, we probably should've turned back sooner."

They got into the car. Despite the reflective shade they had put in the windshield, the car was an oven. Jeremy blasted the air conditioner at full force, but it still felt uncomfortable for a few minutes. Aaron felt bad that his profuse perspiration was soaking into the seat and it would stink up Jeremy's car for a while. But then, Jeremy was hot and sweaty too.

When they arrived back at Jeremy's house, they walked into the kitchen. Jeremy asked, "Would you like a glass of water?"

"Yes, please. And lots of ice."

As they drank their water, Aaron said, "Man, I am still burning up. I'll bet your pool would feel great right now."

Jeremy paused. *That was pretty forward of him. I wasn't planning on getting in the pool with him. But we're both still overheated.* "It's probably around 80 degrees. I know that sounds warm, but it's really cold when you get in. I don't normally get in until it hits 84, which is usually closer to Memorial Day."

"Oh, that wouldn't bother me. The pool we used to go to back in Ohio was colder than that sometimes. It was cold when you first got in, but after a minute it was fine."

Jeremy walked outside and fished the floating thermometer out of the pool "Eighty-two. I guess that's not too bad. So yeah, we can get in if you want." He added, "We might have a shrinkage issue."

Aaron chuckled and said, "I don't care."

For an awkward moment, neither of them said or did anything. Then Jeremy asked, "So, are you going to swim in your shorts or your underwear? Or I guess I could let you use one of my swimsuits."

"What do you usually do?"

"I usually swim naked, but that was when it was Juan and me, or only me."

Aaron considered his options. He didn't want to drive home in wet underwear or wet shorts. It seemed kind of weird to wear someone else's swimsuit – kind of like wearing someone else's underwear. What the heck? He'd been in locker room showers with other naked guys many times. "Naked is fine. Let's go – I'm burning up."

Jeremy seemed surprised that this straight guy would have no problem getting in a pool naked with a gay guy. Jeremy had no issue with nudity, but this seemed a little weird. But it was happening. He said, "I'll get a couple of towels. Do you want more water?"

"Yes, please."

Jeremy handed Aaron the towels, then carried their glasses over to the water dispenser, refilled them, and added some more ice. They walked out onto the back patio. Jeremy set the glasses down at the edge of the pool, and Aaron set the towels down on one of the lounge chairs near the steps.

They looked at each other as if to say, 'Well, now's the time.' They peeled their clothes off. Aaron knew it wouldn't be cool to turn and look at Jeremy's cock, so he headed for the pool steps. He placed his foot on the first step, then hurried down the remaining steps into the pool until the water was covering his shoulders. He turned and looked at Jeremy, who was still standing on the deck. *That's the thickest dick I've ever seen. Even if it shrinks some... wow!*

Jeremy hesitantly took the first step, then the second. He shivered. "Oh my God... this is freezing."

"It's better to get it over with quickly. I'm already used to it. It's refreshing."

Jeremy knew he was right, so he stepped quickly the rest of the way in and hoped he wouldn't pass out.

They didn't say much as they cooled off and drank their water.

Finally, Aaron said, "This is great. It must be nice to have a pool. Back in Ohio, very few people had in-ground pools. Sometimes people put up above-ground pools, but Mom and Dad never let me have one. They said it would leave a big dead spot in the grass."

"Yeah, it probably would."

"They're kind of lame anyway."

"Yeah. Like I said, it was always a dream of mine to have a house with a pool."

"I can see why. Especially out here."

"It's a lot of maintenance, but it's worth it. To me, anyway."

After a moment, Aaron said, "I don't think I've ever skinny-dipped before."

Jeremy couldn't remember the last time he heard someone say 'skinny dip.' "When we were looking at houses, I told Juan I wanted a private backyard with no two-story houses around, so we could swim naked. It actually feels odd to wear a swimsuit now. We would wear them whenever we had other people over." He paused while he debated whether to say the next thing on his mind. "There were a few of our friends we'd swim naked with. But mostly not."

Aaron wondered what the boundaries for appropriate questions should be at this point. But Jeremy seemed willing to answer whatever he was asked, so he took a chance. "So, did you like..."

"Have sex? Not with others. But Juan and I had sex out here a lot."

"Really? You can have sex in a pool? How does that even work?" Aaron tried to imagine what that would be like.

"Oh, it's great. You have to be quiet, so no moaning or screaming 'Harder, harder!' or 'Oh God, I'm cumming!' or anything like that. You use silicone lube because the regular water-based stuff will wash away. But the feel of the cool water against your skin while you're doing it feels fantastic. It's a whole different sensation!"

Aaron had seen pictures of Juan on Jeremy's Facebook feed. He imagined Juan being in the pool with Jeremy and what they might have done together.

After a moment, Jeremy said, "Uh… Aaron?"

Aaron snapped out of his daydream. "Oh. Yeah?"

Jeremy said, "It's after twelve, and I've got some stuff I need to do this afternoon."

"Oh… okay. I guess I'd better get going then."

Jeremy passed Aaron as he walked toward the steps at the shallow end. Aaron glanced down. After fantasizing about Jeremy and Juan, he was three-quarters hard. *Oh, shit. I wonder if he saw it. I can't get out of the pool now.*

Aaron turned away from Jeremy and submerged himself one last time to cool off his face. He stayed under for around ten seconds. He tried to think about anything other than Jeremy and Juan having sex in the pool. It wasn't working. Trying to think about not having an erection only kept his erection from going down.

He stood up and opened his eyes. Jeremy was standing on the deck facing away, holding his towel by the ends and drying off his back. Aaron bolted for the steps, hoping he could reach his towel and unfurl it in front of him before Jeremy turned around. He barely made it. Jeremy finished drying himself off and started putting his clothes on. Aaron turned away and dried off his legs and back. He was able to put his underwear and shorts on while still facing away. With his dick now constrained, it went soft quickly. *Whew! Crisis averted.*

Aaron said, "Thanks a lot! I really enjoyed the hike and the dip in the pool."

Jeremy smiled and replied, "Me too. It's a lot more fun to hike with someone else than by yourself. And it was nice to have you here. I'm still getting used to being alone in this house."

"Maybe you can take me to a few of the other places you talked about."

"Yeah, sure."

After a few seconds of awkward silence, Aaron said, "Well, I'll be on my way. I hope you get all your stuff done."

"Thanks. And good luck with your parents."

Aaron hadn't thought about his parents since the subject came up during the hike. It was nice to have a break from it.

Jeremy led Aaron to the front door. Before he opened it, he turned around and gave Aaron a hug. It was more than a friendly goodbye hug but less than a romantic or sexual hug. It was more of an 'I need to be hugged' kind of hug.

They stepped apart and smiled. Jeremy turned and opened the door. Aaron said, "Bye!" and stepped outside.

"Bye!" Jeremy watched Aaron walk to his car. When Aaron turned and looked back, Jeremy waved. Aaron waved back. Jeremy slowly closed the door.

***

When Aaron returned home, he remembered he had left his phone in his water pack while he swam with Jeremy. He retrieved it from the side pocket and unlocked it. There was a voicemail from his mother and a text message from Jeremy awaiting his attention.

He opened the message from Jeremy first. It contained the two selfies he had taken on the mountaintop. Aaron gazed at the first photo, then the second. He swiped back to the first photo to look at it some more, then back to the second. In the first one, they looked cool with their sunglasses on. Aaron decided he liked the second one better because he could see their eyes, even though he was squinting a little bit.

He hardly noticed the scenic view that filled the background behind their heads. The thing that struck him the most about both pictures was their smiles. Both of them wore unforced, natural, happy-in-the-moment smiles. Aaron realized he hadn't smiled much over the past couple of years. Those were definitely pics he would transfer to his computer and save.

He looked at the panoramic picture he had taken. It looked nice too, but the picture did not convey the true grandeur of the vista they had enjoyed, nor did it stir any memories of the elation he felt at that moment.

He replied to Jeremy and texted

He attached the photo and sent it. As an afterthought, he sent a second text.

> I had a great time today. Thanks!

Then he decided he might as well deal with his mom's call. He pulled up her voicemail and held the phone to his ear.

Hi, Honey. Since you're not home, I hope that means you went to church this morning. I sent you an email too. Give me a call when you get home. We're going to visit your grandmother from two to four, then we'll be eating dinner at around five. So call anytime before or after that. Oh – that's Ohio time, not Arizona time. Anyway... call me soon, okay? We need to talk. Love you. Oh, and your father says hi. Bye!

Aaron sighed. He didn't feel like calling her back yet. He wanted to see what was in her email first.

He powered up his computer and attached the charging cable to his phone so he could transfer the pictures. He felt some trepidation as he opened his email.

Sure enough, there was an email from his mom.

Dear Aaron,

I was talking with Pastor Fleming after church today, and he suggested a website you should take a look at. It's called Family-Focused Ministries. They have a whole section on there about homosexuals, and how people who think they might be homosexual can escape from that lifestyle. They have some articles you can read and videos you can watch. I took a look at a few of them, and they're really good. You need to take a look at them. And whatever you do, you need to get out of that band. I don't want you hanging around with those people anymore. Or maybe you can forward some of this information to them – it might help save their souls if it's not too late. Especially that real sissy one we saw.

Call me soon!

Love,

Mom

Aaron closed the email and sighed. He had no idea what he'd say to his mom, but he had to come up with something.

The Dream

Sunday, May 8, 2016

Aaron felt a strong hand grab him by the arm just below his shoulder, tugging firmly to get him out of bed. Aaron realized he had no choice but to get up, so he pulled the sheet aside with his free hand, sat up, and pivoted his legs over the side of the bed.

It was definitely his bed, but he couldn't see anything else in the room. Everything was enveloped in a mysterious fog. His bed seemed to be floating in nothingness.

As he tried to figure out what was happening, the only thing he could see was the man who was holding onto his arm. He was muscular and hairy. He was wearing nothing but leather – a leather police officer's hat, a leather harness that emphasized his chiseled chest and well-defined abs, leather bands around his biceps, a leather pouch covering his ample manhood, and leather chaps. A thick mustache and goatee accented his well-defined jawline. His eyes were hidden behind large mirrored sunglasses reminiscent of the 70s. Hyper-masculinity oozed from every pore on his body.

As Aaron stood up, another similarly clad figure emerged from the fog and grabbed his other arm. Without saying a word, they led him into the fog. Their grip was firm but not painful. Aaron knew he had no choice but to go wherever they were leading him. He was not given an opportunity to put on clothing.

As Aaron walked with his two escorts, he couldn't see or feel the floor beneath his feet. He couldn't see anything but the sides of the two men. He glanced at his captors with his peripheral vision, but they said nothing and remained focused straight ahead.

They stopped in front of a solid metal double door with no door handle, like the exterior of a fire escape door. One of the men knocked on the door, and two more leather-clad guards opened the doors from the inside. The doors swing outward, and Aaron's escorts lead him into a large room. They released their grip on his arms and stepped back, leaving Aaron standing naked and alone in the center of the room.

The fog cleared, revealing a luxurious, ornate room that resembled a large parlor in a mansion. The room was adorned with oversized floral arrangements, flickering vanilla-scented candles, and tasteful artwork. Aaron could hear the faint thumping beat of dance music coming from somewhere else.

Three figures rose from luxurious chairs and approached Aaron. They wore fabulous glittery gowns, flamboyant jewelry, garish yet elegant make-up, and huge, outlandish hair-dos. One was Black, one was White, and the third appeared to be Latina. They were overblown caricatures of women, yet stunningly beautiful. They could easily have been contestants on Ru Paul's Drag Race.

Behind their chairs, at least a dozen gorgeous young men of various races were sitting or reclining on a variety of couches and huge, overstuffed floor pillows. They looked to be about 20, with perfectly coiffed short hair and slender, hairless bodies. They wore nothing but white thongs, tailored with ample pouches which they filled impressively. They looked like a harem of some sort. The beautiful young men gazed at Aaron with interest. He had no idea what to make of any of this.

The Black drag queen spoke first. "Wellll… look who's here."

The White one added, "He's a little late to the party, but whatever. He's here now."

They slowly glided around him, examining him head to toe from every angle, as if they were inspecting merchandise. Aaron never felt so objectified and vulnerable in his life.

The Latina said, "Oh, look. The poor dear is terrified." She was right – he was scared shitless. She spoke to Aaron, with an almost condescending tone. "Awww… Don't worry, honey, we won't hurt you."

With that, the Black one, the sassiest of the three, reached down and playfully smacked one of Aaron's butt cheeks. "Well, it might hurt a little at first!"

The other two let out an affected, high-pitched, "Ooooo!" as if to say, "Oh no, gurrrl, you *didn't*!"

Aaron felt like a piece of meat. He wanted to say something, but he had no idea what. He remained silent. Lacking any other options, he decided he might as well let them do whatever they were going to do.

The White one said, "So… what do you think, girls?"

The Black one responded, "Oh, he's fiiine… just look at that cute little bubble butt!"

Aaron glanced at the harem of twinks. They were all smiling and nodding in agreement. He wondered if he was about to be thrown into the middle of them. He felt his dick start to get hard. *Oh God, no. Please, no.*

Finally, Aaron spoke. "Who are you? Where am I? Why am I here?"

The Latina answered, "Honey, you are right where you belong."

With that, the two leather men stepped forward again and grabbed him by each arm – more gently this time. The three drag queens took a couple of steps back toward their chairs. The men turned Aaron to the left and led him to another set of double doors. Two more leather men stood on either side of the doors. As Aaron approached, they opened them to reveal a huge ballroom. Some kind of dance party was taking place. The music, which he heard only faintly before, was now louder. They were playing "Get the Party Started," by P!nk.

Once Aaron had taken a few steps into the room, the leather men let go of his arms and receded into the background. He didn't turn around to look, but he could tell the doors had closed behind him.

Aaron couldn't see the far wall of the room. Either there was a wall of mirrors or the opposite wall was too far away to see. The massive ballroom seemed to hold hundreds if not thousands of people. In the foreground, people were standing in clusters around small high-top cocktail tables, sipping drinks and talking. Beyond that, he could see a large bar and, in the distance, a dance floor.

Aaron recognized a few people in one of the groups closest to him. There was Travis Tucker, a gay guy he knew when he was in the Ohio State University Marching Band. There was his high school history teacher, Mr. Blaine. There were a couple of gay people from his pharmacy class at college. When they saw him, they waved him over to their table. Travis spoke first. "Aaron! Welcome to the club!"

Aaron concluded he was in a humongous nightclub of some sort. Still, something about this place seemed surreal. *Are these people real? Why does it seem like everyone has been expecting me to show up?*

Then a possibility hit him like a brick. "Have I died?"

Mr. Blaine replied, "Oh, no! Quite the opposite. You're just beginning to live!"

Aaron had no idea what he meant. At that moment, a server wearing a pink bow tie and mini vest arrived with a tray of champagne glasses. Everybody at the table took one, so Aaron did too. Someone said, "Cheers!" and everyone clinked their glasses and took a sip.

As Aaron continued to look around, it became clear that everyone in this room was LGBT.

At a nearby table, he spotted Sammy. He was a nerdy kid in junior high everyone teased and picked on because they thought he was a sissy. Aaron was ashamed to admit that sometimes he had teased him too. Sammy looked at Aaron with recognition but didn't smile.

Aaron glanced down and noticed he was still completely naked. Everyone else in the room was clothed, but they acted like his being naked was not unusual or inappropriate. It was as if they didn't even notice. Suddenly, Aaron felt self-conscious. He wanted to run from the room and put some clothes on, but he didn't see any doors. He turned around and couldn't see the doors through which he had entered. There was no way to escape.

Aaron thought, Maybe I can at least find something to wrap around me, like this sheet – this sheet on the bed I'm sitting on. Why am I sitting naked on a bed when everyone else is standing around me? He looked around and started noticing the features of his bedroom. The people, the ballroom, the drinks, and the party faded away.

Aaron laid back down on his bed and stared at the ceiling.

What the hell was that about? That room I ended up in – where was that? And the people I knew –why were they there? Were they there because of me? How did they all know each other already?

He thought back to the beginning of the dream.

Why was I dragged away by tough guys in leather? And those drag queens – why were they examining me like that? And all the cute young guys in their little thongs – what were they all about?

Aaron thought back to their cute faces and lean, toned bodies. He reimagined their skimpy white thongs, and how full they seemed. As he drifted into a light slumber, he imagined them standing up, dropping their thongs, and playing with each other's growing erections. He wondered if he would be forced to join in.

Still half asleep, Aaron reached down. His cock was hard as a rock. He began stroking it, but within a few seconds, he realized what he was doing and it jolted him awake.

The fact that Aaron had become aroused by this dream troubled him.

The more Aaron thought about the dream and replayed it in his head, the more shaken up he became. To his knowledge, he had never had a panic attack. He didn't even know what having a panic attack would feel like, but he wondered if he might be having one now.

He got out of bed and walked to the kitchen. He glanced at the time on the microwave clock – 2:15. *Shit. I need to get back to sleep or I'm going to be worthless at work tomorrow.*

He pulled his bottle of Jack Daniels down from its place in the cupboard. He reached into the refrigerator for a bottle of Coke, but then thought, *The last thing I need now is caffeine.* He retrieved a juice glass from the cupboard and filled it with ice cubes. He poured a shot of whiskey over the ice cubes. He took a sip. He had never sipped liquor straight, so the strength of the alcohol jolted him. As the ice melted, each sip became a little easier. He finished the drink in about a minute.

He wandered into the bathroom and laid a couple of tissues on the counter in front of him. He thought about Megan, the girl from high school he had messed around with the summer after his freshman year. He tried to remember the special sensations he felt with her. He wondered what it would be like to do it with her in a pool. He tried to imagine the sensation of cool water on his skin as their bodies rocked against each other. He imagined Megan with her legs wrapped around his waist and her arms wrapped around the back of his neck. He wondered if this was the same way Jeremy and Juan did it. He wondered who would be standing and who would have his legs and arms wrapped around the other. Before long it was Jeremy, not Megan, who had his arms and legs wrapped around him, rocking against him.

He exploded all over the bathroom sink.

He grabbed several more tissues and wiped up everything, then flushed them down the toilet. The whiskey was starting to take over, and he felt drained following his orgasm. He climbed back into bed and fell asleep.

What Do You Think About...?

Wednesday, May 11, 2016

This week was one of Aaron's two-days-on, five-days-off weeks. Monday and Tuesday were busy days at work, which forced Aaron to stay focused on his job instead of everything that had happened over the past couple of weeks.

His mom wasn't letting up. She tried calling him twice on Monday, but he let her calls go to voicemail since he was at work. He sent her a text telling her not to call him at work unless it was an emergency.

Apparently, she viewed her crusade to stop him from associating with homosexuals as an emergency, because she called again on Tuesday. Aaron hadn't listened to her voicemails yet. She also emailed him a list of 18 right-wing churches within a ten-mile radius of Tempe. "Some of them say they have praise bands on their websites. You should check them out first."

On Wednesday morning, Aaron lay in bed for a while before getting up. He usually enjoyed his days off, but today was going to be difficult. He knew he needed to deal with his mother, but he wasn't ready for it yet. No doubt, she would call at some point today.

Aaron turned his computer on and opened his email. Not surprisingly, there was an email from his mother. This one contained a list of other community concert bands in the Phoenix area. She implored him to check them out and switch to one of those.

He launched Facebook for the first time since Sunday. As he scrolled through his feed, he saw that Jeremy had posted one of the selfies from their hike on South Mountain. The photo had received 26 likes or loves and a few complimentary comments, mostly from people in the band. Petunia commented, 'You two look so cute together!'

Aaron couldn't argue. They did look cute together. But until this moment, he hadn't thought about that photo appearing on Facebook. He wondered what everyone would assume.

He scanned up and down the right column. He noticed Rob was online, so he clicked on his name to open a chat window.

Good morning

Hey, good morning. What's up?

I am, finally. Slept in today.

Must be your day off.

Yeah. Hey, are you available for lunch or dinner, today or sometime soon?

Sure. How about lunch today?

Cool. Pick a place near you.

Have you been to Salad Daze? It's a healthy eating place on 7th St north of Bethany Home Rd.

No, but it sounds good. 11:45?

Cool. C U soon.

Aaron closed Facebook. He found the address of Salad Daze and jotted it down. Then he shut off his computer and went for a run along the canal. He figured a run might help him process things and clear his head a little.

***

When Aaron arrived at Salad Daze, Rob was waiting for him at the entrance.

Aaron scanned the menu board above the counter. In addition to salads, there were quinoa bowls and cauliflower-rice bowls with a variety of vegetable, legume, and tofu toppings. He was relieved to spot a few items that included chicken, so he ordered a blackened chicken Caesar salad. They didn't offer Coke or Pepsi products, so he settled for a large mango-infused iced green tea.

Rob said, "It's a nice day. Want to eat out on the patio?"

"Sure." Aaron felt it might be a little less noisy and offer them more privacy.

After they had settled in their chairs and exchanged a few pleasantries, Rob asked, "So, what's on your mind?"

Aaron chuckled. "Is it that obvious?"

"Yes."

"Well, a couple of things. First, my parents. You know they visited here about three weeks ago."

"Uh-huh…"

Aaron told Rob about their encounter with Petunia at Kahuna's and the ensuing homophobic conversation.

"Yeah, I heard about that."

"Okay, so first of all, does everybody in the band talk to everyone else about everything? It seems like any time something happens, everyone else knows about it within, like, half a day."

"Yeah, we're a pretty close-knit bunch. It's more about being interested in each other and sharing information. I don't think it's ever malicious."

"Well, except maybe for Petunia."

"True. He can be a bit much sometimes."

"A bit? None of that stuff with my parents would have happened if it wasn't for him being 'a bit much.' Anyway, so my parents got all bent out of shape about there being homosexuals in the band, and how I need to stay away from them or else they'll recruit me."

"Oh, no…"

"Yeah. And then my mom started going on about how I should find a church that has a praise band instead. But then this past Saturday, after they got back to Ohio, Mom called and asked what the name of the band is. Of course, I couldn't lie to her, so I told her. And then, like, 45 minutes later she called back and she's all outraged that this is 'a band for homosexuals' as she called it. And she hasn't let up since. She's calling me every day, and she's emailing me all this stuff about local churches I should join and other bands in the area. And – get this, this is the worst part – she sent links to articles on Family-Focused Ministries' website about how terrible gays are and how people can be rescued from 'the homosexual lifestyle,' as they put it."

"Sounds like you have your hands full."

"Yeah. I haven't returned her calls from the past couple of days. I know she's going to call again today, and I'm trying to figure out what I'm going to say to get her to back off."

Aaron's phone vibrated. He glanced down at the screen. "Guess who?" He let the call go to voicemail.

Rob said, "Well, I suppose you can thank her for her concern and assure her that you're in no danger. Then politely ask her to stop calling you about it and sending you stuff."

"Yeah, I guess, but I don't think she's going to let up until I tell her I've quit the band and started going to church again."

"There are gay-welcoming churches."

"I'm not interested in going to church. But if I did, she'd ask what church I was going to, then she'd check it out. And if it's not a Baptist church or some other right-wing denomination, I'd get the same thing all over again."

"Well, I'd hate to see you go, but you could quit this band and join a straight band."

"Yeah, but I don't want to. One, I'm enjoying this, and two, I don't want to give in to their homophobia. Besides, I'm 28 now. I'm not a kid anymore. They shouldn't think they can tell me what to do."

"Maybe you should tell her exactly that."

"Yeah, but it's hard. And she'll say something like, 'But we'll never stop caring about you.'"

"Sometimes doing the right thing is the most difficult. Taking the easy way out may alleviate the situation now, but it will only make it worse later on."

"Yeah, I guess."

They took a few bites of their salads in silence. Then Rob asked, "So, what else is there?"

Aaron took a deep breath, stared out toward the parking lot, and sighed. "I'm not even sure how to bring this up." He paused while Rob waited expectantly. "Okay, so you know Jeremy?"

Rob smiled. "Of course. That was a nice picture of you two up on South Mountain, by the way."

"Yeah. Anyway, he's been really nice to me. After the first rehearsal I came to, he invited me out to the bar and bought me a drink. I didn't think much about it at the time, but now I wonder why he did that. I mean, maybe it was just to be nice, but I don't know. Anyway, so we chat with each other on Facebook almost every day and he's always friendly."

"Okay, so he's nice and you're becoming friends. What's the problem?"

"Well, after we got back from the hike, we were hot and sweaty, so we went for a swim in his pool. And…" Rob was listening intently. Aaron saw his expression and said, "No, no, nothing happened. But we were naked in the pool together. See, I didn't even know he had a pool so I didn't expect that we'd go swimming. Anyway, he offered to let me wear one of his swimsuits. But that seemed kind of weird, you know, like wearing someone else's underwear. So I figured, I've seen guys naked before, so why not?"

Rob shrugged and said, "Again… so?"

Aaron hesitated, then said, "I don't know. I wonder if I enjoyed it a little more than I should have. I mean, I was kinda nervous at first, but then once we saw each other's dicks it was kind of like 'so what' after that, you know? And whenever I'm on Facebook and I see a message from him, I always perk up a little bit. And when he posted that picture of the two of us? I looked at it for, like, five minutes."

Rob said, "Well, okay. But didn't you tell me that since you moved here from Ohio, you haven't made very many friends until now?"

"I wouldn't even call them friends. More like acquaintances."

"Okay, so you've been lonely. Now you're making friends. Of course, it feels good. And you're playing your trombone again. No wonder you're happier now."

Aaron considered this. Is that really all it is? Just being happy to have friends and play music again? That could explain it with most of the other guys, but… with Jeremy, it's different.

Rob knew Aaron had more to say, but he decided not to try to pull it out of him.

Finally, Aaron said, "May I ask you something kind of personal?"

Rob smiled and said, "You can ask. I reserve the right to not answer."

Aaron chuckled nervously. "Fair enough. Okay… So, how did you know you were gay?"

Rob said, "I think I've always kind of known. I remember back in elementary school, I was always more interested in the other boys. I mean, not even sexually – not back then. When I was a teenager, I tried dating girls, because that's what everyone else did and I knew that was expected of me. And of course, I wanted to fit in, 'cause I always felt like I was different. As far as I could tell, none of the other boys felt the same way I did. I was certain I was the only one. Of course, now I know there were other boys in my junior high and high school who were interested in boys, too. I'm sure they felt like they were the only ones, too.

"Anyway, in high school, I definitely knew I was interested in boys – a few of them in particular. But I had no idea what to say to them. And with my luck, the ones I liked were probably straight anyway. But I kept dating girls, one, because I wanted to fit in, and two, I thought if I just found the right one, those other feelings would go away. Of course, they never did. During my sophomore year of college, I gave up the façade of trying to date girls, but I still had no idea how to tell which guys might be gay or how to approach them. In hindsight, I missed some pretty obvious clues, but oh well…"

Aaron was listening intently.

"Then, one day I was in this bookstore near campus. I was looking to see if they had any books about gay people. They had a small section, like part of one shelf. There was a book called *The Frontrunner*, by Patricia Nell Warren. I worked up the nerve to buy it. I kept it hidden in a drawer in my dorm room, and I only took it out to read when I knew my roommate would be gone for a while. But as I read it, I realized I could relate to the gay characters in the book. I knew I was like them."

"Very interesting. So… again, I know this is personal, so you don't have to answer, but… What did you do after that? How did you start meeting guys? And when did you start… you know…" Aaron was too nervous to finish.

"Having sex?"

Aaron nodded.

"It's funny how that happened. One day, I left the book on my desk. I was reading it, but then I had to go to the bathroom, which was down the hall. While I was gone, my roommate came back to the room. When I got back and saw him there, I almost had a heart attack. He didn't say anything about it then, but a few days later, he asked about the book I was reading. I guess he looked for it on my desk while I was gone and didn't see it anywhere. So I told him it was a novel about some track runners. He asked if he could see it again, so I got it out and handed it to him. I was sure when he figured out it was a gay book, he'd tell everyone else on the floor and try to move to another room or something. But he said, 'Can I read it after you're through?' And I said, 'Okay.'

"So after he finished reading it and gave it back to me, I asked him what he thought of it. He said, 'It was interesting.' That evening, I could tell there was some sort of nervousness or tension in the air. Sort of like an awkward feeling of anticipation. So anyway, we started playing around with each other, and I ended up going down on him. He was pretty freaked out about it the next day, but then a few nights later he wanted to do it again. I told him if he wanted me to go down on him, he needed to go down on me too. So he did. But the next day, he got all freaked out again, so nothing else ever happened."

"Are you guys still in touch with each other?"

"No. I'm surprised we made it through the rest of the year living in the same room. He was never comfortable with me after that. Out of curiosity, I looked for him on Facebook a few years ago. He's married and has two kids, so I never reached out."

"Do you think he was really gay or just curious? Or just horny?"

"I think deep down, he's probably gay. But he was pretty religious and he just couldn't deal with it. He started going to a bible study group after those two nights we played around with each other. But it confirmed for me that this was who I am and what I want."

They ate a few bites in silence while Aaron thought about everything Rob had just said. Then Aaron asked, "But if he's married to a woman and presumably having sex with her, doesn't that make him straight?"

"I guess it depends on how you define gay and straight. If it's who you're having sex with, then I guess that makes him straight. But if it's who you're attracted to, then he might be gay. But I'll never know and I don't care. I can't crawl inside his head and see what he thinks about while he has sex with his wife, or what he thinks about when he masturbates."

What he thinks about when he masturbates. Those words hit Aaron hard.

Aaron knew he thought about Jeremy frequently. He often replayed moments from their hike, their time in the pool, and times they hung out together at Raise! the Bar. He realized he was checking his email and Facebook more often these days – and the main reason was to see if Jeremy sent him anything. He created a folder for Jeremy and kept all his emails in it.

What he thinks about when he masturbates.

Last Sunday night, he knew it was the thought of him and Jeremy in the pool that pushed him over the edge.

Rob spoke and jolted Aaron back into the present moment. "Well, I should probably be on my way in a few minutes."

"Oh… yeah. Sorry. I guess I got lost in thought for a while."

"That's okay. I hope our conversation was helpful. Is there anything else you want to talk about?"

Aaron blurted out, "I think I might be gay."

Rob smiled and resisted the urge to say, "Well, duh!!!" Instead, he said, "Well, you seem to be comfortable around all the gay people in the band. But that doesn't necessarily make you gay."

"I know, but… I don't know… it seems like I've found a home. It feels like where I belong."

"Did you ever wonder if you were gay before you started coming to Desert Pride?"

Aaron thought about that for a moment. "I guess I didn't want to get close enough to that topic to even ask the question. Like, don't even think about it. But now that I look back, I realize I've always been more interested in looking at guys than girls. We had plenty of both in my marching band at college, but it was always the guys I wanted to look at and be friends with."

Rob nodded. He had plenty he wanted to say, but he knew it was best to let Aaron talk.

"And I guess another reason I avoided even thinking about it is my parents. I knew I could never come out to them. They're not very open-minded or tolerant. Their visit really drove that home. Plus, I'm an only child. They're counting on me to bring them grandchildren and all that. And based on how they're reacting to me simply being in the same band with a bunch of gay people, yeah… they'd totally lose their shit if I came out to them."

"Well, you don't have to come out to them right away."

"Yeah, but the topic's kind of on the table already."

"Still, you said, 'I *think* I *might* be gay.' Think. Might. Are you not sure?"

"I'm pretty sure. But I guess I won't know for sure until I do it and I see whether I like it. And like, I kinda want to find out, but I kinda don't want to know for sure, either."

Rob said, "Well, as I said earlier, it's not so much about who you're having sex with, it's more about who you're more attracted to."

"It's about who you think about when you masturbate."

"Yeah. But you don't have to tell me, just answer honestly to yourself."

"Jeremy."

"Huh?"

"Jeremy. I think about Jeremy when I masturbate. I think about doing all kinds of other things with him. I think about him all day long. I keep looking at that picture of us together. I keep looking forward to the next time I get an email or a Facebook message from him."

"Jeremy is a sweetheart – and he's definitely attractive."

"Yeah. He reaches me on so many levels, you know? Anyway, I have no idea what to say or do. I'm totally new to this."

"Well, keep in mind that he's recently out of a long-term relationship. Generally, people need a while to process all the hurt and anger they've experienced."

"How long?"

"At least a few months. Maybe a year. Rebound relationships usually don't work out very well."

Aaron sighed. He didn't want to wait a few months. He wanted something to happen now.

"Well, okay, but how will I know when it's the right time?"

"I don't know. But you will, and so will he. When it's the right time to move forward, it will be clear to both of you."

"I guess. Well, anyway, thanks a lot for having lunch with me, especially on short notice."

"You're welcome. I hope I could be of some help."

"Oh, you definitely helped. More than you know."

"And hang in there with your parents. Give them time to adjust. Once they calm down about you being in a gay band, then you can tell them – if you want to."

"Okay, thanks."

They got up from the table and carried their trays to the busing station. Once they were out in the parking lot, Rob gave Aaron a nice hug. "You'll be fine. And welcome to the fraternity."

"Thanks."

No Son of Mine

Wednesday, May 11, 2016

Aaron hardly noticed the scenery as he drove from Salad Daze in north-central Phoenix back to his apartment in Tempe. He was so consumed by replaying the lunch and thinking about his mom's calls and emails he could barely remember anything about the drive. It was a wonder he didn't cause an accident.

He had just come out of the closet. He had just told another person he was gay. And he had just told that person about his attraction to Jeremy.

Instead of feeling relieved, he felt apprehensive. *What do I say to the rest of the band? I've told them I'm straight up to this point, now I'm gay? What do I say to Jeremy, and when? Should I say nothing and see where things go? How do I tell him I want I want to do with him? Is it too soon? What will it be like to have sex with a guy?*

He glanced at his phone and remembered that his mother had called during lunch. He needed to return her call soon. *What can I possibly say to my parents? There's no way I'm going to come out to them – at least not in the foreseeable future. How can I get her to stop with all the calls and emails?*

When he got home, he turned on his computer. He could stall for a little while by checking his email and Facebook. He sighed when he saw his mother had sent him two more emails with links to articles about the evils of homosexuality.

He opened Facebook and caught up on his newsfeed.

What was he going to say to his mother? He thought back to lunch when he said to Rob, 'I'm 28 now. I'm not a kid anymore. They shouldn't think they can tell me what to do.' Rob had replied, 'Maybe you should tell her exactly that.'

Aaron picked up his phone, took a deep breath, and called his mom.

She picked up the phone after one ring. "Hi, Honey. It's about time you called back. I was startin' to worry that you'd been hit by a truck or something."

"Hi, Mom. Sorry. The past two days were my long work days – 8 a.m. to 10 p.m. with only a half-hour for lunch and dinner. And today, I had lunch with a friend. Anyway, here I am. I know it's 5:00 your time so it's getting close to dinner. I can call back later if you want."

"No, no, dinner can wait. Your father isn't home yet anyway. He should be walkin' in the door any minute. So listen… did you get my emails?"

Aaron rolled his eyes. "Yes, Mom. I haven't had time to read them all."

"Well, make sure you do that today. There's a lot of important information. You really need to read them. So who were you having lunch with?"

"A friend of mine from the band."

"Honey, for heaven's sake, you have to stop hangin' around with those people. You need to be careful who you associate with."

"Mom, I'm entitled to pick my own friends."

"Well, you're not doin' a very good job. Wait, your father's walking in the door now." Aaron could hear his mother say, "Welcome home, dear. Aaron's on the phone. Here, let me see if I can remember how to put him on the speaker." A few seconds later, she said, "There. Can you hear me now?"

"Yes, Mom. Hi, Dad."

Ralph said, "Hello, Son."

"How was your day at work?"

"Long and tiring. I tell ya… I need to retire soon. I'm gettin' too old for this. I come home at night and I'm so tired I can hardly do anything 'cept watch Sean Hannity."

Aaron was glad they weren't on Facetime and they couldn't see him rolling his eyes.

Martha said, "Well, enough of that. He hasn't had a chance to read through my emails yet, but he just told me he had lunch with one of the people from that band."

Ralph said, "Son, you need to get out of that band. You don't need to be hangin' around no faggots or sissies."

Martha said, "In one of those emails I sent you a list of other bands in the area. You should check them out."

Ralph said, "And make sure you keep your eyes open. Take a good look at the other men and remember our talk about how you can spot homosexuals."

Aaron said, "I'm not going to find another band. I'm staying in Desert Pride."

Martha said, "Honey, at least start going to church again. I sent you a list of good churches in the area."

Aaron said, "Mom? Dad? Just cool it, okay? I mean seriously, just stop! I'm 28 years old. I'm an adult. I'm out on my own. I can choose my own friends. I can choose what band I want to play in. I can choose whether or not I go to church and if I do, where I'll go. I really don't need your input and I sure as hell don't need your approval."

Aaron couldn't remember if he had ever cursed at his parents before, or even pushed back this hard.

After a few seconds of stunned silence, Martha said, "Well, yes, you are an adult now. But we'll always be your parents and we'll always care about you. And right now, we're concerned."

"You have nothing to be concerned about. I'm perfectly fine. In fact, I'm the happiest I've been since I got out here. I'm making friends and playing music again, and I like it."

Martha said, "Yes, but why do you have to make friends with homosexuals? Why can't you find some good Christian people to make friends with?"

"Mom, I'm tired of hearing about it. Just stop, okay?"

Ralph said, "Watch how you talk to your mother. She's right. I don't want you hangin' around with no homosexuals. Next thing you know, one of them's going to try something on you."

"Oh, don't be stupid. It's a band, not a sex club. And I can take care of myself."

Ralph hollered, "Now don't you be callin' me stupid. You think you're so damn smart now that you've got your college degree, but let me tell you something. You hang around them long enough, and sooner or later they're gonna turn you into one of them. And no son of mine is gonna be a goddamn faggot. You hear me?"

Aaron yelled back, "Yeah, I hear you. And now you listen to me, 'cause I've got news for you. Your son already is a goddamn faggot. And they didn't recruit me. I've been gay my entire life, only now I'm brave enough to admit it. I love this band and I love the people in it because for once in my life, I feel like I belong somewhere. I'm happy, because now I can finally be myself, and they'll love me for exactly who I am." He paused and took a breath. "Now let's see if you can do the same."

Ralph said, "Oh, Jesus Christ, now look what you've done. Your mother's over here cryin' her eyes out and I'm so mad I can barely see straight. You need to get yourself to some kind of therapist right now before this goes any further. Jesus Fucking Christ. I never thought I'd say this, but I'm ashamed of you. You're a disgrace to–"

Aaron hung up. He threw his phone against the wall. It left a sizable dent but fell onto the couch undamaged.

Two minutes later, the phone rang. He picked it up, saw his mother's name on the caller ID, and pressed Decline. Then he pulled up their names and numbers in his Contacts and blocked them.

He went back to his computer, sorted his emails by sender, and deleted all the emails his mom had sent over the past several days. He set up a rule to send all emails from his mother to the Deleted Items folder.

He paced around his apartment, processing everything that happened. His fucking homophobic parents could eat shit and go to hell.

***

As the afternoon progressed, the enormity of everything that had transpired weighed more and more heavily on Aaron. Gradually, his thoughts turned from cutting off his parents to how he was going to proceed with Jeremy.

First, he needed to tell Jeremy he had come out. Now that he was gay, not presumably straight, would that change anything about their dynamic? Up to this point, would Jeremy have treated him any differently if he knew he was gay?

Telling Jeremy he was gay would be the easy part. Telling him he was totally smitten with him would be much trickier. Aaron had no idea what to say or do. Maybe Jeremy had already figured it out.

Aaron sat down at his computer and pulled up Facebook. He debated whether he should post about coming out. And he debated what, if anything, he should say about the blow-up with his parents and their subsequent dissociation.

He decided the part about his parents should remain unsaid. It might come across as too much drama. Besides, he was friends with a few of his high school classmates.

He decided not to come out to Facebook World yet. He wanted to tell Jeremy first, then maybe he'd post something on the band's group page. That would be enough for the time being.

He wondered if Rob had already started telling people. Probably not. Rob seemed too thoughtful and responsible to do that.

Aaron opened the message window for his chats with Jeremy. He typed

Hey. Hope you're having a good day. Lots of stuff has happened. Can we talk? Maybe over dinner? You can pick the place. HUGS!

Before he pressed Send, he thought twice about the 'HUGS!' at the end. He changed it to 'Thanks!'

Aaron decided to take a brief walk outside. He walked around his apartment complex, then debated going to the bookstore in the shopping center nearby. Maybe they had some books that dealt with coming out or gay relationships. He decided to push that off until tomorrow. He walked to the mailboxes, picked up his mail, and returned to his apartment.

Jeremy had replied.

Sure. Dinner tonight would be great. How about my place at 6:00?

Can I bring anything?

Maybe a bottle of white wine?

Great! C U soon!

Sunset Over Phoenix

Wednesday, May 11, 2016

At 5:30, Aaron grabbed the bottle of Chardonnay he had been saving for a special occasion. He didn't know where their conversation might lead, but if there was any chance that thinking of this as a special occasion would help make it so, he wanted to take that chance. He left his apartment and began driving toward Jeremy's house.

As he maneuvered through the stop-and-go traffic on Baseline Road, he rehearsed what he wanted to say and how he wanted to say it. He tried to anticipate how Jeremy might react and how he would respond in return. Then he realized he was only making himself more nervous and he should just relax and let the evening flow naturally. But it was all he could think about. This new world of gay romance, dating, and sex was perplexing.

He turned onto Jeremy's street a few minutes early, so he parked at the beginning of the street for a few minutes. He closed his eyes and took a few deep breaths. *It will be fine. Just relax and be yourself. He may want to start dating or he may not. It may be too soon for that. Don't push too hard. Things will happen when – and if – they're meant to happen.*

He continued to repeat affirmations and encouragement to himself. Finally, he opened his eyes and glanced at his watch. 6:08. *Shit! Now I'm late. Gah!!!*

He drove up to Jeremy's house, got out, and approached the door. Before he made it to the doorbell, Jeremy opened the door and smiled.

Once they were inside, Jeremy gave Aaron a big hug. Aaron wanted to go in for a kiss but he knew it was too soon for that. He handed Jeremy the wine, and Jeremy said, "Chardonnay. Excellent choice! I've never heard of this brand."

"I bought it at a winery in Scottsdale. Maybe we can go there sometime."

"Cool. Should be delicious, then."

Jeremy led Aaron into the kitchen and gestured for him to sit down on one of the stools at the kitchen island. Aaron spotted two large chicken breasts marinating in a plastic container and two ears of corn wrapped in foil. "Wow – you're really going all out here."

Jeremy replied, "Yeah, I guess. I haven't cooked for two for at least two months. I guess I'm less inclined to fix a nice meal only for myself. I'm glad you suggested getting together for dinner tonight. I could use the company. And you said you had stuff you wanted to talk about."

"Yeah, kinda."

Jeremy carried the chicken and corn out to the grill, which was already hot, and put the food on it. He came back inside. "You want something to drink? Maybe a martini?"

"Sure. Just make me whatever you're going to make for yourself."

Aaron watched as Jeremy expertly prepared their cocktails. He peeled two perfect spirals of lemon rind, dropped them into the glasses, and gave one to Aaron. "Cheers!"

They clinked glasses and sipped. Jeremy's culinary and bartending skills made Aaron all the more enamored of him.

Aaron remained seated on the stool. They exchanged small talk and sipped the martinis in between Jeremy's trips to the patio to check on the chicken. When the chicken and corn were almost ready, he retrieved two small salads from the refrigerator and carried them to the table. A timer dinged, and he pulled a foil-wrapped loaf of garlic bread from the oven and transferred it to a basket lined with a cloth to wrap around the bread. He opened the wine bottle and poured five ounces into elegant-looking wine glasses. Then he took one final trip to the patio and returned with the chicken and corn.

After they sat down and clinked wine glasses, Jeremy took a sip and said, "Delicious!"

"Thanks. I've been saving it for a special occasion." Aaron immediately thought, *Shit. Was that too much?*

Jeremy seemed surprised that Aaron would call this a special occasion, but he didn't say anything. Instead, he asked, "So what's on your mind?"

Aaron took a generous sip of wine. *Here goes.* "Okay, so you remember on Sunday I was talking about how my folks were giving me shit because I was in a gay band?"

Jeremy nodded.

"Well, Mom hasn't let up. She called Monday and Tuesday while I was at work and she's been sending more emails. She made lists of all the

Baptist churches in the area and all the other concert bands in town. Anyway, earlier today I had lunch with Rob and asked him for advice. He said I need to be firm and tell them I'm 28, I'm not a kid anymore, and I'll make my own decisions. I mean, he's right, of course, but that's easier said than done. Especially with my parents."

"Wow. Sounds like they're pretty pushy."

"Yeah. Because, of course, that's what the Bible says."

"The Bible says you shouldn't play in a gay band?"

"To them, it does. It might as well. By the way, this chicken is delicious! So is everything else."

"Thanks."

"It's done just right. Whenever I try to grill chicken, it's either still raw in the middle or I overdo it and it gets all dried out."

"I think marinating it gives it more moisture. Hey, do you want more wine?"

"Sure." *I'll need it.*

Jeremy topped off their glasses and sat back down.

Aaron said, "So while I was having lunch with Rob, we talked about something else, too. And… basically… I came out to him."

For a moment, Jeremy just looked at Aaron. Aaron couldn't figure out what his expression conveyed. Jeremy was debating what he should say next. Finally, he said, "So, you're now officially gay."

"Yeah."

"Have you been wondering whether you're gay for a long time, or did this suddenly come up?"

Well, my dick suddenly came up while we were in the pool together. That was a clue. "I guess I've been trying to avoid it for years. You know, like don't even go there. For one thing, I knew my parents would freak out. I guess I kept hoping that one day I'd meet the right girl and, you know, those feelings would go away. Anyway, talking with Rob really helped me sort things out. One thing he said was, being gay isn't so much about whether you're actually having sex with men, it's more about who you feel attracted to."

"Yeah, I would agree with that."

"Anyway, after I got back from my lunch, I called my parents and we got into this big argument. I don't think we've ever yelled at each other like that before. They were going on about how, if I keep hanging around with homos, I'll turn into one. And then my dad was like, 'No son of mine is going to be a goddamn faggot!' And then I said, 'Well, your son is already a goddamn faggot!' And it went downhill from there. I ended up hanging up on them and blocking their numbers."

Jeremy was stunned by what he was hearing.

Aaron started to sob. "So yeah, now I'm gay. Well, I always have been, but now I'm finally admitting it. And you know how other people say, 'When I came out it was such a relief and such a load off my mind?' Well, it's not. Now I feel worse than ever. It's like I can't help feeling this way, but my parents will never accept it, and it's either I cut them off or they'll never stop giving me shit about it."

The tears started flowing more heavily. *Shit. He cooked this nice meal for me and everything was going so well, and now I'm ruining it.*

Jeremy stood up and walked around to Aaron's side. "Come here."

Aaron stood up, and Jeremy wrapped his arms around him. He placed his head on Aaron's shoulder and held him while Aaron cried some more.

When Aaron's sobbing began to subside, Jeremy took a step back so he could look at Aaron's face. "It's gonna be okay. It will get better."

"Really? Will it?"

"Probably. But I'm proud of you for coming out. You need to live your life honestly or you'll never truly be happy. Yeah, it will be rough at times. You'll lose some people along the way. But you'll gain so much more."

Aaron's tears stopped flowing and he tried to pull himself back together. "Yeah, I guess. It occurred to me that since I joined Desert Pride, I've been happier than I've been for several years. And it wasn't just playing my trombone again, it was making new friends. I really like all the people in the band. And… well, I feel like I belong there."

"You *do.*"

Aaron picked up his napkin and wiped his eyes and cheeks. "Thanks."

They sat down and finished their dinners in silence. Jeremy could see Aaron was still wrestling with the situation with his parents and whatever else was going through his mind. What he wanted to talk about could wait until later.

After they had cleared the table, Jeremy asked, "How are you doing right now?"

"Better. I still have a lot on my mind."

"What do you feel up to doing this evening?" Then he added, "If anything."

Aaron thought for a second. He knew what he wanted to do, but he had no idea how to ask for it, or even how to bring up the topic. Then he had an idea. "Do you think we could get in the pool?" *What the heck, there's no harm in asking.*

"I dunno, it's still pretty cold. Let me go check the temperature." Jeremy walked outside and fished the thermometer out of the pool. He walked back in and said, "Eighty-one. I know we got in on Sunday, but the sun was beating down and we were overheated. Now that the sun's going down and it's getting cooler, it's too cold for me."

Crap, Aaron thought. *I mean, he's right, it's probably too cold. But now what? Maybe go for a walk?*

Jeremy said, "Tell ya what, though. We could get in the hot tub."

"Yeah, we could do that." Aaron hoped that sounded sufficiently nonchalant. He didn't want to seem too eager.

"Okay, let me go turn it on."

"How long will it take to heat up?"

"An hour to an hour and a half."

Aaron followed Jeremy outside. Jeremy unlatched the cover and raised it long enough to set the temperature control. The pump sprang to life, and he lowered the cover.

Jeremy looked west and said, "It's going to be a beautiful sunset tonight."

"Would you be willing to take me up to that place you were talking about on top of the mountain? We could watch the sunset from there."

Jeremy said, "Yeah, sure. We probably have about half an hour until the sun goes down. We can make it if we get going now."

Aaron said, "If you want, I'll drive."

"Okay. Wait... let me put the rest of the wine in the fridge."

Fifteen minutes later, Aaron's old Toyota was straining to climb Summit Road. When they arrived at Dobbins Lookout, the sun was about five minutes away from touching the horizon. There were only a few cars in the parking lot. Most of the other people were clustered on or around an open-air stone building that might have been home to a few Native Americans a century or two ago. They walked down the footpath until they reached a spot that afforded them a nice view with enough privacy that they could talk without others hearing.

Aaron said, "Wow! You weren't kidding. This is beautiful!"

Aaron and Jeremy looked north across downtown Phoenix. The setting sun painted Camelback Mountain and Piestewa Peak with swatches of deep brownish-red, accented with black shadows. The sky to the west sported hues of brilliant yellow, orange, and red. Aaron looked east toward Tempe and tried to trace the roads to his apartment complex.

When he turned back, the sun had just touched the horizon. They stood in silence as the sun slowly disappeared. The sky would remain light for another twenty or thirty minutes. Aaron scanned the sky from west to east, marveling at the gradual transition from light to dark blue. He wanted to hold Jeremy's hand, but he didn't know how the people at the stone structure would react. For that matter, he had no idea how Jeremy would react. But in an hour, they would be sitting in a hot tub together. He could probably hold his hand there. Then he thought, *Are we going to get in naked? We were naked in the pool on Sunday, but we were several feet apart in broad daylight, not sitting right next to each other in the dark. Will he insist that we wear something? And if we're naked...*

Jeremy interrupted Aaron's fanciful daydream. "So, what are you thinking about?"

What Aaron was thinking about was the last thing he should say. "Oh… I was just admiring the beauty. Like how the color of the sky changes from west to east. Phoenix looks so much different from up here."

"Yeah. It really shows how spread out it is."

"A few minutes ago, I was trying to find my apartment in Tempe."

"Did you find it?"

"I think so."

"You can't see my house from here, it's obscured by the mountain."

Aaron asked, "Have you lived here all your life?"

"No, I came here when I went to ASU. I'm from Yuma, which is in the southwest corner of Arizona, near the Colorado River. So I've lived in Arizona all my life, but here for almost 15 years."

"Do you like it here?"

"Yeah. But after my breakup, I've been thinking it might be time for a change."

That statement horrified Aaron.

Jeremy continued. "As I've been standing here looking at all the buildings and roads and stuff, I've been thinking about all the places I've been and things I've done and people I've known. Good times. Lots of memories."

"Then why would you want to leave?"

"All those things are in the past. But this has gotten kind of old, you know? I'd like to try something new – a new place, with new people to meet and new things to discover."

"Where would you go?"

"I don't know. I'm still thinking about it. Someplace warm, with a good gay community, that has culture and some character. That's one thing about Phoenix. It's kind of bland."

"Really? I don't think so."

"Yeah, but you're still relatively new here. And you came here from Ohio."

For an instant, Aaron felt defensive. *How dare he insult Ohio! But then, I moved out here to get away from Ohio. I needed new scenery but for different reasons. Reasons I didn't fully understand at the time.*

Jeremy said, "Sorry, I shouldn't have said that."

"That's okay. You're probably right."

"Where are you from in Ohio?"

"Troy. It's a little town about 20 miles north of Dayton."

"How many people?"

"Around 25,000."

"Wow, that *is* small. Yuma has almost 100,000."

"That's still kind of small, compared to here anyway. But we both came from small towns and went to big cities to go to huge universities."

"Yeah. So what brought you out here?"

"I don't know. I liked Columbus. I mean, if I had to stay in the Midwest, I'd want to live in Columbus. But I wanted to get away and try something else – preferably someplace warmer."

"I get it. And now I've reached a point where I want to get away and try something else."

Even with no relationship experience to speak of, Aaron knew it would be foolish to try to rush things. But something about Jeremy made his heart sing, and he knew he'd have to work quickly to give Jeremy a reason to stay.

Aaron glanced up at the stone structure. The other people were heading back to their cars. There was still some color on the western horizon, but the sunset was almost over.

Aaron said, "Shoot. I wish I had taken a few pictures."

Jeremy said, "Yeah. But a lot of times, they don't fully capture the beauty. I'd rather just enjoy it. Sometimes, I think people get so wrapped up in taking pictures of everything, they never really enjoy the moment."

They stood next to each other and watched the last few moments of the sunset. Aaron moved in close to Jeremy's right side and put his left arm around his shoulder. To his relief, Jeremy put his arm around Aaron's waist. Aaron savored the dwindling light, the warm breeze, and the touch of another man. He glanced at Jeremy out of the corner of his eye. His eyes were gazing into the distance and his face was expressionless. Aaron couldn't tell if he was watching the tail end of the sunset or staring at nothing, lost in thought. Aaron glanced up the hill. Everyone else had departed. He turned toward Jeremy, and Jeremy turned to look at him. Aaron kissed Jeremy on his right cheek. Without saying a word, Jeremy turned to face Aaron and kissed him on the lips. They wrapped their arms around each other and kissed for the next two minutes.

When they separated, a sweet, almost embarrassed smile appeared on Jeremy's face, as if to say, 'Well, I certainly didn't expect *that*.'

They started walking back to the car. Aaron realized this was the first time he had ever held and kissed a man on the lips. That he was able to do it in such a romantic setting was indescribable.

As they drove downhill on Summit Road, neither of them said much. Aaron was replaying the scene that had just occurred and anticipating what might happen in the hot tub. *I can't believe I waited until today to come out. This is what I've been missing? Geez... How many years have I wasted?*

Aaron glanced over at Jeremy. He seemed to be lost in thought too, but with a pensive look on his face. Aaron said, "So, what are you thinking about?"

Jeremy snapped back into the present moment. "Oh... I don't know. I guess I was thinking back to me and Juan." He paused while he debated whether he should share more. He knew he needed to. "I don't think we ever did anything like that."

"I thought you said you've gone up there to watch the sunset before."

"Yeah, we did, a couple of times. But we never had a moment like that when we kissed. It was always like, 'Hey, wasn't that beautiful?' 'Yeah.' And then we'd leave." Jeremy sighed. "Juan wasn't exactly what you'd call romantic."

Aaron thought, *See what you've been missing?*

Jeremy continued, "And we'd go hiking sometimes like you and I did on Sunday. There would be times when nobody else was around, and I wanted to stop and kiss him for a few minutes. But he never seemed comfortable with it. Like, someone could come along at any moment. Hell, I wish we could have fucked out there, right out in the open, right in the middle of all that beautiful nature. But there was no way that was ever going to happen."

Aaron made a mental note to add outdoor sex to his bucket list. Of course, he had to *have* sex first.

Aaron wasn't sure what, if anything, he should say at this moment. So he reached over and placed his right hand on Jeremy's thigh. Jeremy put his hand on top of Aaron's and held it for a moment.

At the next sharp curve, Aaron had to take his hand away to steer. But it had been a moment.

Jeremy said, "Oh well. I don't want to think about that stuff anymore." But Aaron knew he still was.

Firsts

Wednesday, May 11, 2016

When they arrived back at Jeremy's house, he checked the hot tub. "It's about ready. I usually set it for 98 and it's 97 now. You wanna finish off that Chardonnay?"

"Sure."

Jeremy reached into his cupboard and found a couple of clear plastic wine glasses. He retrieved the Chardonnay from the refrigerator and divided the remaining wine between them.

"Would you grab a couple of towels from that basket by the door?"

Jeremy carried the two wine glasses toward the sliding glass door. Aaron said, "Here, let me get that for you," and opened the door. Jeremy set the glasses down on the drink shelf on the side of the hot tub, then raised the cover.

They walked back inside, then turned and looked at each other. After a few awkward seconds, Aaron said, "I'm okay with getting in naked if you are. But if you'd rather not…"

"No, that's okay." They disrobed quickly and headed out to the tub.

They eased their way into the hot, bubbling water. Neither of them said anything and there seemed to be a bit of tension. Aaron's mind was racing. He took a few sips of wine, gazed up at the clear night sky, and tried to let the water jets pound some relaxation into him. He closed his eyes and focused on the humming pump and the feel of the water jets against his back, lower legs, and feet. It was a sort of meditation to calm his mind.

A few moments later, he opened his eyes and glanced over at Jeremy. He was staring into the sky. Aaron said, "I love hot tubs. We have a couple at my apartment complex. Of course, I can't go naked in those, even though I'm usually the only one there."

"Yeah. They're great for when it's too cold to get in the pool. But in a couple of weeks, it will be too hot to do this."

"It's funny… Lots of people have hot tubs out here where it's already hot, but not that many people have them in Ohio, where they'd get more use out of them."

"I see what you mean. But would you really want to get in or out of the hot tub when it's 20 degrees out?"

"Good point. Plus, out here we have walls for privacy. In Ohio, they either have chain-link fences or nothing at all."

"Yeah, there's that too."

After a few minutes of silence, Aaron asked, "So what have you been thinking about?"

Jeremy paused, then said, "How much I'm going to miss this place. I was thinking back to when Juan and I bought this house five years ago. It was just being built, so we were able to choose all the options for carpeting and tile and countertops and all that stuff. I wanted to have a backyard where we could entertain friends and enjoy nights like this. We went all-out on the pool, the hot tub, the barbecue island, and the landscaping."

"Well, you don't have to go. You could get a roommate to help you cover expenses. Heck, I'd live here!"

"No, I need to sell it and move on. I tried working the numbers, and I can't swing buying him out for his half of the house. But it's more than that. This was supposed to be *our* home. *Our* life together. *Our* dream. If I stay here, it will keep reminding me of that."

"You could buy a smaller house and still have a pool and stuff."

"Yeah, I know. There will be another house, another pool, and another hot tub. But it's still painful to let go of this. It's not just the physical things, it's what they represent. They're the physical trappings of the relationship that's now over."

"I know you'll find another man you can share it all with." *Like, maybe me.*

"Yeah, I guess. But enough of that happy talk. What's on your mind?"

"Well, while we're on the topic of ruined relationships, I've been thinking about my parents. I don't know what I'm going to do about them. I don't want to spend the rest of my life never talking to them again. But I don't want to talk to them if they're going to shove religious garbage in my face. And I'm not willing to live my life the way they want me to – going to church every Sunday, marrying a woman, and bringing them grandkids."

"Give them some time. All that stuff they said was just a knee-jerk reaction. And you have to admit, coming out in the middle of an argument when you were both angry wasn't the nicest way to break the news to them."

"Well, how was I supposed to do it?"

"I don't know, but it doesn't matter now. It's done."

"Okay, so now what?"

"Now it's time for the repair work. And that's going to take time – and willingness on the part of both you and them."

"Yeah, but I'm gay no matter what. That's not going to change. They're going to have to accept that. I don't see how we can have a good relationship if they can't accept who I am."

"Well, perhaps you both need some time to cool off. But then, reach out to them. Try to be patient with them. Just talk. Be willing to answer questions, even if they seem stupid. They're probably holding onto a lot of stereotypes and mistaken beliefs about what being gay is like, especially if they're as religious as you say."

"I guess."

Jeremy said, "Think about this. You're what, 28? Look how many years it took you to accept that you're gay. It's not fair to expect them to accept it overnight. They're going to need time, too."

"With them, that could take years."

"Well, it took you many years, too. But the sooner you start on that journey, the sooner you'll reach the end of it. A lot depends on whether you're willing to be patient with them and help them along or just shut them off."

"Okay. Well, like you said earlier, enough happy talk. What else would you like to talk about?"

"Oh, I don't know. I'm sorry. I guess I kind of killed the mood. I'm not too cheerful these days. You pick something."

Aaron thought, *What can I change the subject to that might make him happier? I hoped this evening might go somewhere. It was heading in that direction when we kissed on the mountaintop and then got in the hot tub naked. But now, it seems like that's off the table. Oh well. I think he needs someone to talk to; someone to be with. Maybe that's the best thing I can do for him tonight. So… maybe another time. Heck, I don't even know what he likes to do. But how do I ask that?*

Aaron thought for a moment, then said, "Okay, so now that I know I'm gay, there are a couple of things I've been wondering. And if this gets too awkward or anything, just say so. Anyway… When two guys, you know… get together, how do they decide what they're going to do? You know, like who's going to do what?"

Jeremy said, "You mean, like, who's going to be the top and who's going to be the bottom?"

"Yeah. Or even if they're going to fuck or just suck or, I don't know, jerk each other off or whatever."

"Well, I guess that depends on the guys involved. From what other people have told me, some guys are more into sucking. For others, sucking is more like foreplay before fucking. I knew this one guy who wasn't into either sucking or fucking. He just wanted to rub their bodies together and get off that way."

"Hmmm… okay. But like, how do you know what the other guy wants to do?"

"Well, on apps like Grindr, guys pretty much tell you what they want."

"What's Grindr?"

Jeremy chuckled. "I forgot you just came out today. It's a hook-up app for gay guys."

"You mean you can just open an app and find guys to have sex with?"

"Yep. It tells you when there are other gay guys near you – assuming they're on Grindr too. But hooking up is the main idea."

"I don't think I want to get into that stuff. I don't want to just hook up with someone. I'd like to at least get to know them a little bit."

"I'm the same way. I've never had to think about that kind of stuff until now. Juan and I met when we were freshmen, so I've never had to deal with putting myself out there and trying to find a guy."

"Is Juan the only guy you've ever slept with?"

"Yep. He was the one and only. We were a monogamous couple – up until I discovered we weren't. But let's not go there now."

"So how did you guys decide who did what?"

"Well, he kind of decided for me. He only wanted to be the top, so that meant I had to be the bottom."

"How come?"

"Well, he's Latino, and in many Latino cultures, there's this concept of machismo. From what he told me, his culture isn't very accepting of gays. It might be acceptable to have sex with a man if you're the one putting your dick in the other guy's hole. It's not acceptable to be the one getting fucked – that's what a woman does. But you don't call yourself gay even if you have sex with men, and it isn't talked about."

"And you were okay with that?"

"I loved him and I wanted the relationship to work, so I had to accept that that was the way it was going to be. At the time, I was fresh out of the closet and I didn't know many other gay guys. So I figured I needed to do whatever it took to hang onto him if I wanted a partner."

"Was he out to his family?"

"Not officially. I think they all knew, especially the women, but I doubt that he ever actually said 'I'm gay' to anybody. I mean, come on, he was living with the same guy for fourteen years – from sharing a dorm room to renting an apartment to buying a house together. They had to know. He'd take me with him to family gatherings sometimes, but I was just Jeremy, not his partner Jeremy. And they were nice to me and made me feel welcome. But there were plenty of occasions when I got the message that I wasn't quite part of the family. Like when we went to visit his family for Christmas, they'd have a stocking for me and give me some presents. But when they'd all gather around for a picture, someone would hand me the camera to take the picture. Like I wasn't family enough to be *in* the picture."

"So when same-sex marriage became legal here, did you guys get married?"

Jeremy sighed. "No. I asked him to marry me, but he wouldn't. To him, everything was fine the way it was. And not being willing to be out to his family was a big part of it. Like, either he'd have to tell them and invite them all to the wedding or do it without telling them. Then he'd have to worry about remembering to take his ring off every time he saw them and all that stuff. In hindsight, that was the beginning of the end. I was really hurt by that."

"So is that why you broke up?"

"No, I broke up with him after Petunia showed me his profile on Grindr."

"Ouch."

"Tell me about it. And he was looking for young guys – 18 to 25. I think after I turned 30, I was too old for him."

"How old is he?"

"Oh, he's 33, like me. But I guess he still wants to fuck twinks. And apparently, he was."

"Wow. That sucks. I'm so sorry."

"Thanks."

"And that was a shitty thing for Petunia to do. I mean, what's his problem? He's the one who practically outed me to my parents. Why does he think he needs to stick his nose into other people's business?"

"Actually, I'm glad he told me. I needed to know. That's one thing about Petunia. As much as I don't get into his queeny, swishy act, he's honest. He doesn't tolerate other people's bullshit. If there's a truth he thinks needs to be told, he'll tell it. Most people won't say anything. But as unpleasant as it was, I'd rather know the truth than naïvely think everything was okay when it wasn't. I mean, I don't know if Juan was using condoms or not. He could have caught some STD and brought it home to me – not that we were doing it very often anyway. Obviously, he was gettin' it someplace else." He paused. "Oh, and for the record, I got tested for HIV after we broke up. Thankfully, it came back negative."

Aaron could see that Jeremy was getting sadder by the minute, and he looked like he was on the verge of tears. He scooted closer to Jeremy and put his arm around his shoulder. In doing so, his right leg brushed up against Jeremy's left leg. Jeremy placed his left hand on Aaron's right knee.

Aaron said, "I am so sorry. You're such a nice guy. You didn't deserve this."

Jeremy sniffled, then replied, "Thanks. And I'm sorry about tonight. I didn't mean to drag the whole evening down with all this talk about my breakup. I guess I'm not much fun to be around, am I?"

"I enjoy being around you. And I dragged it down with all that talk about my parents." Aaron squeezed his hand on Jeremy's shoulder. "I think we both had some stuff we needed to get off our chests. Maybe talking about this was good for both of us. Anyway, I'm happy to listen."

"Thanks. In the long run, I know I'll be better off. Now I can see that I did all the compromising. I put most of the effort into trying to make the relationship work. I know someday, I'll find a guy who's more my equal. Someone who wants a relationship as much as I do. Someone who wants to get married and be open about it. Someone who's monogamous." He paused. "And versatile. Is that too much to ask for?"

How about me? Aaron thought. *I'd be a great husband. I'd do all that for you.*

"So, you mean you've never been able to fuck another guy?"

"No. Well, kinda. We tried a couple of times, but as soon as I got a little bit in, he'd go, 'Ow! It hurts, it hurts! I can't do it!' The fact is, he didn't really want to. So I gave up."

Aaron blurted out, "I'd do it for you." *Oh, God, did I just say that out loud?*

"What?"

"I'd let you fuck me. I'd bottom for you."

"But… you've never done it, have you?"

"No. But want to! I've got to start sometime. And I'd rather have it be you than anyone else."

Jeremy's mind was swirling. *Oh my God, should I do this? He just came out earlier today. We've just been friends up to this point – it's not like we're dating. And after dumping all this garbage about my breakup? I'm hardly in the mood for sex. But… now's my chance to finally be a top. I know, there will probably be other chances, but who knows when? And it's his first time. He's offering me his virginity.*

Jeremy turned toward Aaron. He lifted his right arm out of the water and placed it behind Aaron's head. He pulled Aaron's head toward his and pressed his lips against Aaron's. Within seconds, they were kissing passionately. With their free hands, they stroked up and down each other's backs. Soon, their hands were exploring each other's chests, then sliding downward.

When Aaron's hand reached Jeremy's chub, he was taken aback – so much so that he stopped everything else he was doing. When he tried to reach his hand around it, he couldn't touch his fingertips to his thumb.

Jeremy whispered, with a hint of bravado in his voice, "I'm a grower, not a shower."

Aaron resumed kissing Jeremy, caressing his chest with one hand and stroking his cock and balls with the other. *Maybe this is why Juan wouldn't let Jeremy fuck him,* he wondered. *But I've pushed us this far. I can't back out now. And… I want so much to do this for him. I want to do for him what Juan couldn't – or wouldn't. I want to be his first. Somehow, I'll make it work – even if it hurts.*

Jeremy said, "Stand up."

Aaron looked at him quizzically.

"Stand up."

Aaron stood up, and Jeremy sat upright on the edge of the seat. Aaron's rock-hard stiffy was pointing right at Jeremy's face.

Not surprisingly, Jeremy possessed far more expertise than Megan. Thirty seconds later, Aaron whispered, "Better slow down!"

Jeremy said, "Let's go inside."

They climbed out of the hot tub and towel-dried themselves quickly. Then Jeremy led Aaron into the master bedroom.

Aaron said, "Just go slow and try to be gentle, okay?"

***

An hour later, they lay in each other's arms, blissfully exhausted.

"May 11, 2016," Jeremy said softly.

"Huh?"

"May 11, 2016. I'll never forget this day as long as I live."

Aaron smiled. "Me neither. That was incredible. I've never felt anything like that before."

"I didn't hurt you, did I?"

It hurt like hell at first. "A little. But then once I got more relaxed… oh my God! I had no idea it would feel so good."

"You did great. Especially for your first time. And second time."

"Thanks. It was definitely a challenge. But I wanted to do it for you."

"You have no idea how much this means to me."

Aaron kissed Jeremy on the cheek. "And thanks for letting me do it to you too. It was fantastic." *So much better than Megan.*

They gazed affectionately into each other's eyes and smiled.

Jeremy said, "I could easily fall asleep any second now. Will you stay?"

"Sure. I don't have to work tomorrow."

"Well, I do, so we'll have to get up at around 6:30."

"That's fine. Do you have a toothbrush I could use?"

"Yeah."

They got up. Jeremy returned to the back patio. He reset the hot tub to its normal temperature and closed and latched the lid. He brought their empty wine glasses in and put them in the sink. They brushed their teeth, got back into bed, and fell asleep in each other's arms.

On Top of the World

Thursday, May 17, 2016

The next morning, Aaron felt euphoric as he drove home from Jeremy's. The long waits at traffic lights and the frantic drivers with their erratic lane changes could not bring Aaron down from his cloud. He turned the radio to a station that played pop and light R&B and cranked the volume. Every song seemed to be about 'giving me your love,' 'you and I together,' 'the man of my dreams,' 'you're my one and only,' and so on.

When he arrived at his apartment, he changed into his running clothes and hit the canal trail. As he ran, he replayed last night's moments over and over in his head – the lovely dinner, the kiss during the sunset, their make-out session in the hot tub, and, of course, his initiation into the wondrous world of gay sex. He recalled the shower they took together this morning, playfully soaping each other all over and ending with an encore performance. Jeremy reveled in his newfound opportunity to be a top and seemed eager to make up for lost time. Aaron was thrilled to be the one to do that for him.

When he wasn't thinking about Jeremy, he was thinking about his conversation with Rob and the wisdom he had imparted. He couldn't wait to tell Rob all about his experience last night.

All this had happened in less than 24 hours. Yesterday at this time, he was still in the closet and fretting over his parents. But now, everything was right with the world. Everything was just as it was supposed to be.

He wondered how he should tell his bandmates. Should he make an announcement at rehearsal tonight? Post about it in the band's Facebook group? Maybe he'd ask Rob if he saw him online.

Aaron thought ahead to rehearsal this evening. *Should I join the others for pre-rehearsal dinner or ask Jeremy if he wants to eat someplace else, just the two of us? Dammit, I have to work this weekend, so I shouldn't go out to the bar after rehearsal. But I really want to. Or maybe Jeremy and I could go home together instead of going to the bar.*

And what about this weekend? I have to work, so we can't go hiking.

But since I get off at six, maybe I could invite him over for dinner on Saturday and he can stay over. We can go hiking the following weekend, or maybe go up to Sedona or something.

Aaron returned to his apartment and turned on his computer. He had fourteen new emails, but they could wait. He opened Facebook. Neither Jeremy nor Rob was online. He opened a private message window for Jeremy and typed,

> Hey, how are you? Just got in from running. Can't stop thinking about last night. It was amazing! Have a great day!

He got up to take a shower. When he returned, Rob was online. Aaron opened a window and typed,

> Good morning!

> Good morning! How RU?

> FANTASTIC!

> That's good. How come?

> Had dinner with Jeremy last night. It was wonderful! We went up to the top of South Mountain and watched the sunset. And we kissed! For like five minutes.

> Nice!

Then we came back and got in the hot tub. Had some serious talk, but then we kissed some more.

Oh my...

He said Juan never let him top. Seriously! He's 33 and he's never fucked a guy before! Can you believe that?

Aaron... TMI

And I SO wanted to do that for him. So while we were kissing our hands started going down there and OMIGOD!

I don't need to know this.

You wouldn't believe how thick it is! I wasn't sure I'd be able to handle it. Cuz it was my first time.

STOP TYPING!!!

But then we went back to his bedroom and we did it! OMIGOD it was so amazing!

STOP!!! NOW!!!

???

Aaron, this is none of my business. What happened is between you and him. Don't go telling other people about it.

I figured I could tell you.

NO. Don't tell anybody. Completely inappropriate. If it gets back to him, he'll be really angry. And rightfully so.

Oh.

Don't worry, I won't tell anyone. But don't go telling other people about your sex life. It's his sex life too, and he has the right to his privacy.

Yeah, I guess.

Anyway, so you had sex. First time with a guy, right?

Yes. And second. And third.

TMI

Sorry

Congratulations! I'm happy for you.

Thanks! Now I'm kicking myself for waiting so long to come out.

Better late than never.

Anyway... Jeremy is so nice!

Yes, he's a real sweet guy.

I can't stop thinking about him.

Any updates on your parents?

Well... I came out to them yesterday afternoon.

How did it go?

Terrible. Worse than I expected.

I'm sorry. But give them some time. They'll probably come around.

Yeah, that's what Jeremy said too. Anyway, I'm over them. Being gay is great. I'm so much happier now. If they don't like it, too f'n bad.

Well, gotta run. CU tonight.

OK. Bye!

And with that, Rob dropped offline.

Aaron thought some more about the chat they just had. *Rob was probably right – I shouldn't tell other people who I have sex with. But I want to shout it from the mountain top!*

He thought some more about how and when to come out to his bandmates. *Maybe I should just tell Petunia, then sit back and see how fast everyone else finds out.*

Aaron opened his Facebook profile and clicked on the About section. Then he clicked on Contact and Basic Info and scrolled down to the field labeled 'Interested In.' He changed it to Men, then saved it. It was a start.

He clicked on Family and Relationships. In the Family section, there was Martha Bradbury, his mother. He had unfollowed her page a long time ago, because she constantly posted smarmy feel-good memes, cat pictures, and, more recently, pro-Trump propaganda. He avoided posting anything about the band up to this point since he didn't want his parents to know about it. But now that he had a big, fabulous gay life ahead of him, he didn't want them to see what he posted. Besides, he was tired of her leaving an obligatory comment on every single thing he posted. So he unfriended her.

Then he looked up at the Relationship section. He couldn't wait to add 'In a relationship with Jeremy Stanton.' Soon!

As if on cue, a notification popped up that Jeremy had replied to his message. Aaron eagerly opened the window.

Hi! Yeah, last night was nice. Thanks!

How's your day going?

Great! I just got some good news.

About?

A position I posted for at work. Just found out I got it.

Congratulations! We should celebrate!

Definitely.

Maybe after band tonight? (wink, wink)

Sorry, can't. Not going to band. I have an early flight to Austin tomorrow morning for some meetings.

Maybe dinner?

Thanks, but no. Gotta pack and get to bed early.

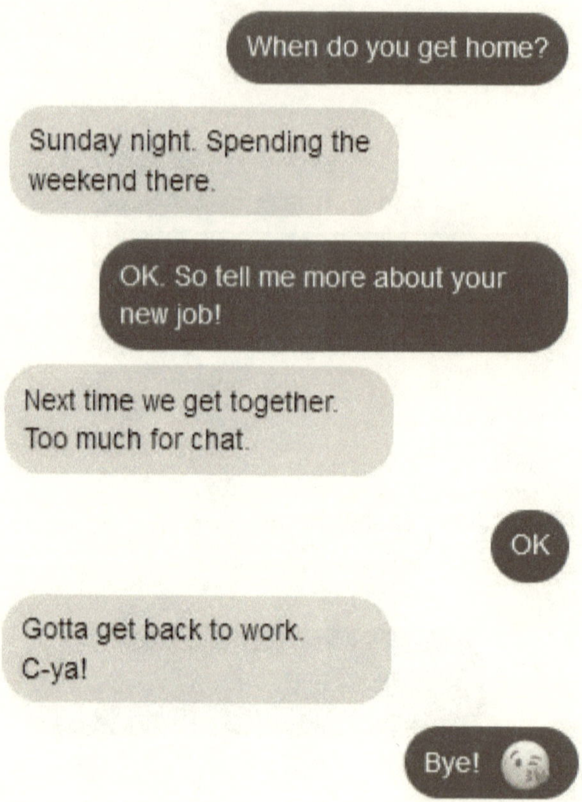

Then Jeremy dropped off.

That's odd, Aaron thought. *He never said anything about going to Austin last night.*

* * *

Aaron arrived at band rehearsal about ten minutes early. He sat down in his seat next to Rob and began putting his trombone together. He leaned over and whispered, "Sorry about those texts earlier. I guess I was too excited to think straight. Errr... gay. Or whatever."

"That's okay. You were thinking with your other head."

Aaron chuckled. "Yeah, I guess so. Anyway, so I was wondering... How should I go about letting everyone else know I'm gay? I mean, I don't feel like standing up and making an announcement. And it seems kind of awkward to start going up to people and saying, 'Hi! Oh, by the way, I'm gay now.'"

"You could take out an ad in the next concert program."

Aaron was stunned. "Are you serious?"

"No, of course not. Just tell a few of the people you know better. Other people will find out sooner or later – sooner, depending on who you tell."

"Yeah, I was thinking all I need to do is tell Petunia, and he'll do the rest."

"You read my mind. Besides, if things work out with you and Jeremy and people see you two hanging around each other all the time, they'll get the idea."

"Yeah, there's that."

During the break, Aaron spotted Petunia and Kent chatting in the courtyard. He wandered up and said hi.

Petunia said, "Well, hello, pumpkin. Where's your boyfriend this evening?"

Aaron looked surprised. "Huh? How did you know?" *Has Jeremy been telling everyone about last night?*

Petunia exclaimed, "Ah-HA! I knew it! Straight, my ass!"

"No, seriously, how did you know?"

"Oh, honey, that picture he posted of you two said it all. Helen Keller could see the sparks flying between you two. Yep… there was love in the air on that mountaintop!"

Kent said to Petunia, "Then maybe *you* should go up there sometime."

"Oh, no, dear. All that perspiration would ruin my hair! I don't want my men hot and sweaty until after I'm done with them."

Petunia sure is a piece of work, Aaron thought.

Kent asked, "Will you be joining us at the bar?"

"Not tonight."

Petunia said, "Oh, I see how it is. Lover Boy won't be there, so you have no use for the rest of us. Hmmph."

"I have to get up early. This is my weekend to work. Anyway, if you'll excuse me, I'm going to go refill my water bottle before break's over."

Aaron turned and walked away. *Yep. By the time everyone leaves the bar tonight, they'll all know.*

Petunia put his hand out in front of Kent, palm turned upward. Kent sighed, pulled out his wallet, and gave Petunia a twenty-dollar bill.

Jeremy's New Job

Friday, May 20, 2016

During the week following Jeremy's trip to Austin, he was friendly with Aaron online but he seemed resistant to getting together. He said things were busy at work and he had a lot of stuff to do at home. He didn't have time for band rehearsal on Thursday, but he agreed to go out to dinner with Aaron on Friday evening to celebrate his new job and tell him all about it.

Aaron could hardly contain his excitement as he drove to Jeremy's house. The rush hour traffic was a little worse than usual, and he hoped he wouldn't be late. They had reservations for 6:30 at Taste of Oaxaca, a small Mexican restaurant that specialized in cuisine from that state. Jeremy described it as a small mom-and-pop place run by people who had actually lived in Oaxaca. They prepared their food using the authentic recipes they brought from their homeland.

Aaron packed an overnight bag with toiletries and hiking gear, in case they decided to go hiking in the morning. He was filled with anticipation for the evening – and the night and morning to come, hopefully. And whatever else. Aaron had nothing on his schedule and he would be happy to hang out with Jeremy for the rest of the weekend if he was up for it.

Aaron turned the corner onto Jeremy's street at 6:05. As Jeremy's house came into view, he saw a For Sale sign in his front yard.

Aaron's heart sank. Jeremy had talked about selling his house but still, the prospect of Jeremy losing his dream house made Aaron sad. Besides, he was looking forward to frolicking in the pool and the hot tub in the weeks and months to come, and someday moving in with Jeremy. Maybe Jeremy's next house would have those amenities, too.

Aaron decided to leave his overnight bag in the trunk. He could bring it in with him when they returned from dinner. He grabbed the cold bottle of champagne he had purchased on the way, hurried to the front door, and rang the doorbell.

In a few seconds, Jeremy opened the door and let Aaron in. He was smiling, but not as overjoyed as Aaron expected him to be. Aaron hugged Jeremy and planted a light kiss on his lips.

Aaron held the bottle up and said, "I brought you something."

Jeremy took the bottle and looked at the label. "Oh, wow! Thanks! You didn't have to do that."

"I wanted to celebrate you getting your new job. And dinner's on me."

Jeremy smiled, then glanced at his watch. "We should leave for the restaurant in a few minutes. Let me put this in the refrigerator and we'll have some when we get back. Taste of Oaxaca has excellent margaritas, so I don't want to do more drinking before we get there."

"Oh, that's how you pronounce it? Wa-ha-ka? I thought it would be O-a-za-ka."

"Yeah, it doesn't sound the way it looks. Anyway, let me put this in the fridge, then we can go." Jeremy hurried into the kitchen.

Aaron glanced around the living room and noticed there were already a dozen cardboard boxes stacked along one wall. The home was already sparsely furnished since Juan had taken his things when he moved out. Aaron noticed some of the nick-nacks and clutter on the end tables and coffee table were no longer there.

Jeremy returned. "Your car or mine?"

Aaron said, "I'll drive. So, I couldn't help but notice the For Sale sign. And you're packing already?"

"Yeah." Jeremy held the front door open for Aaron to exit. He followed him out and locked the door behind them. They got in Aaron's car and began their journey to the restaurant. "Make your way to Central Avenue, then head north. So anyway, Daniella Whitehurst came over on Monday night and I signed the contract to list the house with her. She's one of the flutists in the band. She's also a very good realtor. She found this house for us. She said the house should have enough furniture that it looks lived-in but not crowded. She said to get rid of all the clutter – both so it looks tidier and so people don't steal anything."

"Really? People steal stuff when they look at houses?"

"I guess it happens. I'll need to pack it all up anyway – or get rid of it. I'm going to try to get rid of a lot of stuff rather than move it."

"So, you're really going to sell the house."

"Yeah. It has to be done. But someday I'll have another nice house with a swimming pool, barbecue island, and hot tub."

"And someone to share it with."

"Yeah, hopefully. When I'm ready for that again. Okay, we're almost there. Turn right at the next light." Aaron turned. "Now, see that little street on the left? Turn there."

Aaron turned onto a narrow street that was more like an alley than a city street.

"Okay, it will be a little brick building on your right, in about half a block. You'll see a neon Modelo sign in the window … Slow down … There it is. Turn right. There are a few parking spaces in the back."

Aaron parked and they got out of the car. "How did you find out about this place?"

"There used to be a guy in the band named Carlos. He played trumpet. Not too long after we bought the house, we had a pool party for people in the band. When he saw how close we lived, he told me about it." Jeremy held the door open for Aaron. "You'll love it. It's really authentic."

The interior of the restaurant was cozy and inviting. Colorful Mexican tiles adorned the trim and archways. The décor consisted of blankets, pottery, and sombreros mounted here and there along the walls and shelves. A motherly, brown-skinned lady approached the door and immediately recognized Jeremy.

"¡Buenas noches, señores! ¡Bienvenido!" She grabbed a couple of menus from the welcome stand. "Por aquí, por favor." She led them to a booth in the corner.

They scooted into their seats and she placed the menus in front of them. Jeremy said, "¡Gracias, Maria!"

Maria smiled, but she had a curious look on her face. "¿Dónde está Juan?"

Jeremy shook his head. "No mas."

Maria nodded like she understood what Jeremy meant.

Jeremy said, "Este es mi amigo Aaron."

Maria smiled. "Hola, Aaron. ¡Bienvenido!"

Aaron said, "Thank you! Er… ¡Gracias!"

Maria departed. Aaron scanned the menu. Most of the dishes were pictured and described in both Spanish and English. They all looked delicious.

Moments later, a handsome young man delivered a generous bowl of chips, two small bowls of salsa, and a bowl of bean dip. Jeremy said, "Gracias, Pedro."

Pedro nodded and smiled. "Would you like anything to drink from the bar?"

Jeremy looked at Aaron and asked, "Wanna split a pitcher of margaritas? They're the best in town."

Aaron asked, "How big is a pitcher?"

Pedro said, "About two glasses each."

Aaron said, "Sure. Why not?"

Pedro smiled and said, "I'll be right back."

Aaron said, "You must come here often if you're on a first-name basis with everyone."

"Yeah. Not so much in the past couple of months. It's not as much fun to eat out alone."

"I hear that. It's all I've done for the past two years. I went out to a steak house for my birthday alone. But I figured it was either that or stay home."

"Yeah. I had a nice conversation with Rob not long after Juan and I broke up. He's been through a couple of break-ups himself. He gave me some good advice on what to expect. He said you have to take yourself out on dates every so often, even if you don't have someone else to go with. It's kind of like you need to be your own boyfriend. Treat yourself every now and then."

"So what's good here?"

"Everything. I'm going to have the tamales with the mole negro. It's incredible."

"What's mole negro?"

"Mole is a sauce. There are seven moles in Oaxacan cuisine. Mole negro, or black sauce, has a bunch of different chilis and chocolate."

"Really? I didn't know there was such a thing as chocolate sauce on Mexican food."

"Well, it's not like the chocolate sauce you'd pour on ice cream. But there's chocolate in it. Anyway, there's also mole verde – green sauce – and a bunch of others."

"I'll take your recommendation and try the tamales with mole negro."

Pedro arrived with the pitcher and two glasses. He filled the glasses and set the pitcher down near the edge of the table. As soon as he left, Maria returned and took their order.

Aaron took a sip of his margarita. "Mmmm… you're right. This is excellent."

"The best in town."

"This bean dip is to die for, too."

"These little hole-in-the-wall places are the best. They put a lot of care into every dish they make, unlike larger places where they hire whomever they can get and crank the meals out as fast as they can."

Aaron said, "So… tell me about your new position!"

"It's in Fraud Detection and Prevention. Basically, they try to keep one step ahead of whatever the next scam is. They're constantly testing ways to adjust the algorithms that detect unusual spending patterns or other signs of stolen credit card numbers."

"Sounds interesting – and challenging."

"Yeah, that's what appealed to me. They tell me it's constantly changing, so it shouldn't get boring. I've been working in Mortgage Servicing for about four years now. It's pretty routine and predictable, so I'm ready for something new."

"So, will you be working in the same building you're in now?"

Jeremy paused, then said, "No, I'm moving to Austin."

Aaron froze.

"That's why I went to Austin last weekend. I had an in-person meeting with my new boss and met my new team. Then I spent the weekend looking at apartments. I found a really nice one only half a mile from work."

"You're moving away?" It was part question and part statement of disbelief.

"Yep. Next Friday is my last day here. I'll finish packing everything up next week, then drive a U-Haul there over Memorial Day weekend. Kent and Justin are coming along too. They'll drive my car, help me unload the truck, and then fly back to Phoenix. I'll start my new job on the day after Memorial Day."

"You told me you were getting a new position. You didn't say it was going to be somewhere else." *That's a pretty important piece of information to leave out.*

"I wanted to tell you in person. That day last week when we were messaging each other back and forth, I had to be in a meeting in, like, thirty seconds. Between wrapping things up at my current job, training my replacement, and packing everything up at home, I've been incredibly busy. It's a relief to take tonight off and chill. I need it."

Aaron sat in stunned silence.

Jeremy continued. "Banktopia has offices all over the country. I also applied for jobs in Portland, Denver, San Diego, Houston, and Dallas. I was really hoping for San Diego. Have you ever been there?"

Aaron shook his head.

"It's amazing! You'd love it. It's beautiful, the weather's nice, it's right there on the ocean, and there's a big gay community. There's a neighborhood called Hillcrest that's one of the best gayborhoods in the country. And they have an amazing gay pride weekend every year in July. You should check it out!"

Aaron was only half paying attention. Jeremy was moving away. And he seemed happy about it.

Jeremy continued. "Anyway, Austin came through first. It's pretty cool, too. I think I'm going to like it. They've got a great live music scene and lots of cool restaurants and bars. It's a lot more progressive than the rest of Texas. But yeah. A change of scenery will do me good. I need to start a new chapter. The other night when we were standing up on South Mountain and looking out over Phoenix, remember how I said I was thinking back on all the places I had been and things I had done?"

Aaron nodded. *How could I ever forget that evening we watched the sunset together and kissed? It was so romantic.*

"I knew then I was ready to move on. You know, like been there, done that, what's next? I mean, Phoenix is nice and I've enjoyed living here. I've met lots of nice people – including you – but if I stayed here it would be same ol' same ol'."

You aren't even thinking about me, are you? Was I just a one-nighter? Is it just 'been there, done that, what's next' with me, too?

The food hadn't come yet, but Aaron was already finished with his first margarita.

Jeremy said, "And to be honest, it'll be nice not to worry about running into Juan. I mean, I don't hate him. If we saw each other at a party or something, we would be civil. But I'd rather not, you know? It would bring back a lot of pain and sadness. Especially if I see him with someone new."

"So you're willing to give up all your friends, and band, and *me*, just so you won't run into Juan somewhere?"

"That's a small part of it. But regardless, I'm ready to move on. They have a good gay community in Austin. And you can find nice people to be friends with wherever you go."

Pedro arrived and delivered their food. "Careful, amigos, the plates are very hot."

Jeremy smiled at Pedro and said, "¿Muy caliente?"

Pedro winked and smiled back. "Si, señor. ¡Muy caliente!"

Is Jeremy actually flirting with Pedro? And is he flirting back?

By now, Aaron's heart had been ripped out of his rib cage and lay dying on the floor. He was torn between crying and erupting in a fit of anger. He knew doing either would be pointless and would only make matters worse. He tried his best to show no emotion.

They dug into their food, resulting in a lull in the conversation. Aaron had no idea what to say. *It's hopeless. There is nothing I can do. Unless…*

Aaron took another bite. As he chewed, a possibility dawned on him and he started to perk up. *HealthPro has locations in Austin! I could get a transfer there!*

Jeremy said, "More margarita?"

Aaron nodded and Jeremy divided the remaining margarita between their two glasses. Jeremy noticed the change in Aaron's demeanor and asked, "Whatcha thinkin'?"

"Oh, just trying to process all this new information."

"How do you like the food?"

"It's great. I've never had Mexican food this good."

"Yeah. A lot of the Mexican restaurants in this country are okay, but they're Americanized. This is the real deal."

Jeremy took another bite. Then he said, "That's one thing I'll miss about Juan – his family gatherings. His mom and his aunts cooked wonderful food! And there was always plenty of it. They'd send us home with homemade tamales and tortillas and stuff all the time. In the south part of Tucson, where they live, there are little hole-in-the-wall places. Nothing fancy like this. A lot of times they're just little block buildings with a patio and a few picnic tables. And there would be a window where you order and you can see right into the kitchen. Real basic and simple, but boy was it good!"

"Was Juan from Oaxaca?"

"No, he was born in the US. His parents and their relatives came here from Hermosillo. It's about three hours south of Tucson." Jeremy paused to take another bite. "Mexico is different in different parts of the country, like the US. Each region has its own cuisine. Oaxaca is especially well-known for its food. Mexico City has some of the best food in the world. There are Michelin five-star restaurants there."

"So did you go to Mexico very often?"

"Just a few times. Mostly to PV. That's where the gay people usually go."

"PV?"

"Puerto Vallarta. It's on the west coast, about halfway down. It's only a two-hour flight from here."

They ate in silence for a few minutes. The small talk about Mexico was only moderately interesting, but it diffused the tension and kept the focus away from the elephant in the room. Aaron didn't have anything to contribute to the conversation, but that was okay. He wasn't sure what he wanted to say, if anything, or how to say it. Letting Jeremy prattle on about Mexican food was just as well.

They finished their food. Pedro came and cleared the table, and Maria came by with the check. Since she knew Jeremy, she placed the check on his side of the table. He was probably the one who paid when he and Juan came here.

Jeremy started to reach for his wallet. Aaron reached across the table and took the check. "I said this meal would be on me." Even though the experience had turned out nothing like Aaron had hoped, he wasn't going to go back on his word.

He paid the check and they headed out the door. Jeremy made a few attempts at small talk as they drove home, but Aaron didn't engage.

When they arrived at Jeremy's house, Aaron pulled his car into the driveway but left the engine running.

Jeremy said, "Come on in, and let's enjoy that champagne!"

"No thanks, I'd rather not."

Jeremy turned toward Aaron and put his hand on his shoulder. "It would mean a lot to me if you would. I think we need to talk some more. Please?"

Aaron turned the car off. Silently, they got out and Jeremy led Aaron in through the front door. "Have a seat," Jeremy said as he gestured toward the couch.

Aaron sat down facing straight ahead. Jeremy sat a few inches away and angled himself toward Aaron. "So what's on your mind? Come on, talk to me."

Aaron sighed. *Oh well, there was nothing to lose. Everything was lost already.* "Okay, I'll be honest with you. I'm crushed. I've spent so many years in the closet, and now that I've finally come out, I meet a wonderful guy and I'm happy and I think, great! Now I have someone to love and spend my life with and everything's going to be wonderful. And then this. I feel like the rug has been pulled out from under me. It's like, 'Look what you could have!' and then whoosh! It all gets taken away."

Jeremy listened intently and tried to show empathy. "Okay, I hear what you're saying. And yeah, I felt you were falling for me too quickly, and a little more than you should be."

"Yeah, but… it was so perfect! I thought we really connected. Didn't you think so? Didn't you feel it too?"

"Yes, we did share a wonderful connection that evening. The experience we had together was sweet. And it was just what we both needed at that moment in time. You've recently come out and you were eager to have your first gay experience. I was in the dumps for two months after Juan and I broke up. And to be honest, that relationship effectively ended years before we finally called it quits. We were just going through the motions. There was no spark. He had checked out a long time ago. He wasn't interested in me anymore. Do you know how that feels?"

Aaron shook his head.

Jeremy said, "I had forgotten what it's like to have someone be interested in me. When we kissed on the mountaintop, it was magical. When we were talking in the hot tub, even though some of it was unpleasant, I felt like you really wanted to listen and you cared about what I was feeling. And then when we had sex, it was fireworks – like it was the first few times Juan and I did it. You gave me that. You lifted me out of my doldrums. You let me know I'm still desirable, that it's still possible to feel those things with someone. And I finally got to be the top. I'll never forget you for that."

"Well, okay, but still. I feel like you took advantage of me. You knew you were going to move away. You knew there was no possibility for a relationship, but you did it with me anyway."

"I wasn't thinking it would turn into a relationship. And I didn't think having sex with you would lead you to think we were starting a relationship."

"So for you, it was just a one-nighter. Just casual sex that didn't mean anything."

"I think that's a bit too far to the other extreme. It's not like we hooked up online and you showed up, we fucked, and you left. We shared a wonderful evening. It meant something. We talked, we got to know each other, we built a connection, and finally, well, our desires took over. I know you're new to this, Aaron, but people have sex for all kinds of reasons and in all kinds of scenarios. It's not always about being in a relationship. Sometimes people do it because, at that point in time, they want to."

Aaron realized Jeremy was right. "I guess you wanted one thing and I wanted another."

"I guess so. But I want to go back to something you said a couple of minutes ago. You said you felt like I took advantage of you. If I recall correctly, you're the one who initiated it. I said I've never topped a guy, and you said, 'I'd do that for you. I'd let you fuck me. I'd bottom for you.' I don't think that's taking advantage of you. You said you wanted to do it. You pushed us over the edge."

"Yeah, but you knew you were about to move and I didn't. I thought maybe we'd have a future."

"And at that point, I didn't know either. I got the job offer the next day. Up until that point, nothing I applied for had come through. I didn't know whether I'd be moving somewhere else or not."

"Fair enough. But can't you back out of your new assignment? Can't you take your house off the market? Can't you stay so we can see if we can make this work?"

"No. I've gone too far to turn back now. And there's another thing. Aaron, you're fresh out of the closet. I'm the first guy you've ever had sex with, and maybe the first guy you've ever felt attracted to. You're in the same position I was in when I was a freshman in college and I met Juan. He was one of the first gay people I met after I came out of the closet. He's the first guy I felt attracted to and the first guy I had sex with. And I did what you're trying to do now. I grabbed onto him, thinking he was the only chance I'd have for someone to spend my life with. I was so naïve. I didn't know if I'd ever meet another guy I could fall in love with. In hindsight, that was foolish. I didn't see him for who he really was. Not that he was bad or anything, but he had faults like everyone else, and I was blind to them at first. We didn't have that much in common, other than being gay. In hindsight, I shouldn't have rushed into it. I should have met other guys and dated around. I should have learned more about myself and what I wanted from another man and what to look for in a partner. I don't want to see you make the same mistake I made."

Aaron said, "Yeah, but now we'll never know. We'll never even get to try. We won't know whether it might have lasted forever or it wouldn't."

Jeremy placed his hand on Aaron's knee and said, "Look, Aaron. You're really nice. You're decent and honest and good-looking and fun to be around. You have a lot to offer. There's a man out there for you somewhere. There are plenty of guys who will be interested in you. Just keep putting yourself out there and meeting new people. The right one will come along. But don't rush into it. Don't grab onto the next guy who comes along. The next time you meet a guy you really like, take your time and get to know him. And remember, nobody's perfect, and no relationship is perfect. If someone seems perfect to you, you're only seeing the shininess on the surface. You're seeing him through rose-colored glasses. That doesn't last. It wears off sooner or later – usually sooner. And when it does, you'll know if you still love each other and you still want to spend the rest of your lives together. *Then* you have a relationship."

"Yeah, I guess you're right."

"Trust me on this. And another thing. Even if I wasn't moving, I'm not ready for another relationship. I need time to heal from my last one. I need time to work through the pain and find myself again. So don't go after a guy who's recently broken up with someone. Rebound relationships rarely work out."

"Okay."

Jeremy smiled and stood up. "So… are we okay?"

Aaron stood up and said, "Yeah, I guess so."

Jeremy hugged Aaron. Aaron felt stiff and reluctant at first, but after a few seconds, he relaxed and hugged Jeremy back.

"Now, how about that champagne?"

Aaron smiled. "Sure. Why not?"

Jeremy led Aaron into the kitchen. He pulled the bottle of champagne from the refrigerator, then reached into the freezer and retrieved the two champagne flutes he had placed there before they left for the restaurant. He opened the bottle and poured some bubbly into the glasses, then gave one to Aaron.

Aaron said, "This evening was supposed to be about celebrating your new job. So… Here's to a new job, a new city, and a fresh start!"

They clinked their glasses and took a sip.

Jeremy said, "Mmmm… that's delicious."

They stood facing each other for a moment. Then Jeremy said, "It's a lovely evening. Wanna sit out on the back patio?"

"Sure."

They walked out onto the patio. Jeremy turned off the motion-activated back porch light so they could better see the sky. They sat at the round outdoor dining table, angling their chairs so they were sitting almost side-by-side facing the expansive night sky with their backs to the house. For a few minutes, neither of them said anything while they sipped their champagne and stared at the stars.

Jeremy broke the silence. "So… whatcha thinking about?"

Aaron smiled. He figured he might as well tell him. It would be something nicer to talk about than the confrontation they just had. "Oh, I was thinking back over the last few weeks. Joining the band, going out to the bar afterward, and the whole thing with my parents. I wouldn't have gone to the bar if you hadn't invited me. You even bought me a couple of drinks."

Jeremy smiled. "Yeah, I remember that."

"That was so nice of you. I had no idea what to order in a gay bar. I was at Kahuna's the week before and had one of their Mai Tais. So I ordered a Mai Tai at Raise! and it came with a pink umbrella. I mean, seriously? I took it off and left it on the counter."

"Yeah, I saw you do that. That was funny. When I went back and got your second drink, I told the bartender not to give you one."

"Thanks!" Aaron paused. *Should I ask the question that's on my mind? Oh, why not? He's about to move away.* "Okay, true confession time. I'd like you to tell me something, and then I'll tell you something."

"Okaaaay…"

"So, when you bought me those drinks, were you just being friendly or did you have anything else in mind?"

Jeremy chuckled. "I was just being friendly. But I have to admit, I was sort of attracted to you and I was curious about whether you were really straight. Anyway, I could tell you were nervous about the whole thing, so I thought a drink or two would relax you – and it did."

"Yeah. I got a little too relaxed. God, that was so embarrassing."

"Don't worry, it happens to all of us at one point or another. Anyway, I wasn't going to try to take you home or anything."

Aaron said, "Besides, with me being that drunk it would have been a disaster anyway."

"So yeah… I did it to be nice and to hopefully make a friend, which I did. Okay, now what was it you were going to tell me?"

"Well, do you remember how, when you went to leave, I hugged you? And I kind of held on a little longer?"

"Yeah. I thought you were just trying to stay upright."

"Well, maybe that too, but I really wanted to hug you. It felt so good. And that's part of what made me realize I'm gay."

"That, and you were checking me out in the restroom."

"OMIGOD! You saw me checking you out?"

"Come on! There were mirrors all over the place. I gave it a couple of extra shakes just for you."

"God… I'm so embarrassed."

"Don't be. It didn't bother me at all. In fact, it helped answer the question. Besides, it's not an uncommon occurrence in a gay bar restroom – or any restroom, for that matter. More champagne?"

Aaron nodded, and Jeremy refilled their glasses.

Aaron said, "And then there was the time we got in the pool together after we went hiking. Hard to believe that was less than two weeks ago."

Jeremy chuckled. "Yeah, that was another thing. First, you asked if we could get in the pool, then you were okay with getting in naked."

"Guilty as charged. And then later we got to talking about you and Juan having sex in the pool."

"Annnnnd…?"

Aaron decided to go ahead and say it. "Well… I got a hard-on while we were talking about it."

"Yeah, I noticed."

"WHAT???"

Jeremy reached over and placed his hand on top of Aaron's. "It's okay."

"So you had me figured out all along."

"Mostly. But it's not like I could say anything. I knew I needed to wait until you were ready to tell me."

Aaron said, "The thing that settled it for me was when I had lunch with Rob last week. He said something that really made me stop and think. He said, 'What do you think about when you masturbate?'"

"Yeah, that's a pretty good indication."

"And I realized that…" Aaron stopped. *Should I really say this? Oh well, I've started the sentence. I can't stop now.* "Okay, so since we're doing true confessions…" He took a swig of champagne. "Well… I realized I had masturbated while I thought about you and Juan having sex in the pool." *And you and me having sex in the pool. But I am absolutely not going to say that.*

Aaron paused, and Jeremy didn't say anything.

Aaron said, "So yeah, that's when I knew." He took the last swallow of champagne. "Well, I kinda knew all along, but that's when I finally stopped playing games and admitted it to myself."

Jeremy said, "It's when you ended the denial."

"Yeah."

For a few moments, they gazed up at the stars in silence. Then Jeremy said, "I guess I played a pretty big role in you coming out."

"Yes, you did. Now, do you see why I fell so hard for you?"

"Yeah. But that aside, I'm honored. And flattered. Thanks for telling me all that stuff. That took courage."

Aaron said, "You know, even though I got too wrapped up in you and after all the stuff that happened earlier tonight, I'm still glad this happened."

Jeremy reached over and held Aaron's hand again. "Me too."

Aaron leaned over and kissed Jeremy. He didn't intend for it to be a make-out kiss, but more of an 'I appreciate you' kiss." Still, it was a sweet moment for both of them.

Jeremy got up and walked over to the edge of the pool. He fished out the thermometer and looked at it. "Thanks to the hundred-degree days we've had this week, it's 85." He turned to Aaron and smiled. "Wanna get in?"

"I could be tempted. Especially if you get your silicone lube."

The Tall Guy

Saturday, May 21, 2016

Aaron and Jeremy's playful romp in the pool under the moonlit sky was wonderful. It certainly salvaged an evening that had been a disaster earlier. Since they had reached an understanding of what their friendship was and was not, they could simply enjoy each other without the baggage of relationship expectations that would go unfulfilled. Aaron discovered that pool sex was every bit as fantastic as Jeremy said it was, and he resolved that any house he owned would have a pool and a private backyard.

Aaron didn't spend the night. Jeremy needed to resume packing first thing in the morning. Given the boundaries of their friendship, it seemed less appropriate.

After he ran, showered, and ate breakfast, Aaron sat down at his computer. He saw Kent online.

Yeah, pretty much.

Who needs CNN when you have Petunia?

LOL! Ain't that the truth? What are you up to this weekend?

Not much. How about you?

Doing chores today. Running club tomorrow morning.

Running club?

Yeah. We're in a gay running club.

I love running! I run on the canal next to my apartment all the time.

Come join us. We start at 7.

Aaron thought, *Seven o'clock in the morning? Seriously? But then, it is hot out. Why not? It's not like I have anything better to do.*

Where do you meet? How far do you go?

***

The next morning, Aaron got up at 6:00 and ate breakfast. By 6:30, he was driving north on Loop 101. He arrived in the parking lot at 6:55 and spotted a group of about a dozen guys in a grassy area next to the parking lot. Some were stretching their legs while others were standing around chatting.

Aaron said hi to Kent and Justin. A couple of the other guys approached Aaron and introduced themselves.

A couple of stragglers arrived a few minutes after 7:00. Then Justin counted the people and said, "Okay, I think we have everyone we're expecting. Let's get going!"

They started running north on a multi-use trail that ran alongside Hayden Road. After the first mile, the trail veered away from the road. Soon, the trail passed along the edge of a golf course. The runners were spreading out, as some naturally ran faster than others.

The lead runner was a tall, slender man with dark blond hair who looked to be in his mid-20s. Aaron guessed he was somewhere around six and a half feet tall. He was setting a brisk 8-minute-mile pace and seemed to be doing it effortlessly. With legs that long, he was able to cover more ground with each stride. Every few minutes he turned and looked back to check on his followers. Aaron and a few others were keeping up but with a bit more effort.

He looked familiar. Aaron stared at his tall, lanky body and the smooth motion of his legs and arms as he ran, and tried to figure out where he had seen this guy before.

Finally, he remembered. It was the day after his first band rehearsal and first visit to Raise! the Bar. When he went running along the canal, he passed a tall, slender, dark blond guy who caught his attention. He remembered looking back after the guy passed and watching him as he ran. *That should have been another clue I'm gay,* he thought. *Anyway, this guy looks just like him.*

Two miles later, the trail weaved through an upscale residential neighborhood with a beautiful lake on one side and the backyards of luxurious houses on the other. It was spectacular scenery, but Aaron barely noticed. The most beautiful scenery in Aaron's eyes was the lead runner.

After half an hour, the trail passed through a tunnel under a road and emerged at the edge of another beautiful lake. By this time, only Aaron and three other guys had kept up. The lead runner slowed to a walk, then stopped in a grassy area under a large shade tree. "Let's take a break here and wait for the others to catch up."

Aaron was already fascinated with this guy, but his deep, rich voice made Aaron swoon. Within minutes, most of the others arrived. Nobody said much as they drank from their water packs and mopped sweat off their faces with their shirts. Tall Guy was standing off to one side, so Aaron approached him and said, "You really set a good pace. That's a little faster than I usually run."

"Thanks. Good job keeping up."

Aaron paused for a moment. *What the heck? Go for it. Nothing ventured, nothing gained.*

"So, I hope you don't mind me asking, but do you ever run along the canal that runs east-west through Tempe, between Elliot and Guadalupe?"

Tall Guy thought for a second, then said, "No, I've never been there."

"Oh, okay. You look like a guy I saw on the trail a month or so ago. I was just wondering if you might be him."

God, that sounded creepy. Like I keep a mental image of every guy I see when I run.

"Nope, it wasn't me. Must have been a handsome guy, though." Tall Guy smiled to let Aaron know he intended that to be humorous.

"Yeah, he was." *Oof. Move on – quickly.* "That canal runs right next to my apartment complex, so that's where I usually run. I run by myself, and I think I keep up a pretty good pace, but not like this! You really pushed me."

"Thanks. I was on my track team in high school. I can't run as fast as I did back then, but I still run to keep in shape."

Aaron ran out of things to say. Since their brief conversation had come to an end, Tall Guy called out, "Okay, are we ready to get going again?"

Some of the guys nodded, and those who had laid down in the grass got back up.

"How much farther do you want to go?" Tall Guy asked no one in particular. Most of the guys looked at each other, deferring to someone else to answer.

Justin said, "Maybe up to Shea?"

Another guy said, "Hmmm… That's like three more miles. It's already getting hot out. I wouldn't mind heading back now."

Tall Guy said, "We could go as far as Via Linda. That's like a mile, maybe a little more."

Aaron looked around the group and saw the uncertainty on many of the guys' faces.

Justin said, "Okay, well how about if those of us who want to go a little further go, and the rest of you can get a head start going back?"

Everyone seemed to agree with this plan, so Tall Guy took one more swig of his water and started running. Aaron, Justin, and four others took off behind him.

Aaron didn't know where any of those streets were, but he was bound and determined to keep up with Tall Guy no matter how far or how fast he went.

Tall Guy slowed his pace so the others, some of whom were visibly tired already, could keep up. When they reached Via Linda a mile later, they turned around. When they returned to the spot where they took their last break, they stopped again.

Aaron wandered over to Tall Guy and asked, "Where do you usually run?"

"Mostly on this trail. I live nearby. If you head west on that road right next to us, you'd get to my neighborhood in about a quarter of a mile."

Aaron glanced down the road where Tall Guy had pointed. He couldn't see very far, but the houses on the other side of the lake were luxurious. Aaron wondered how Tall Guy could afford to live in this upper-class part of town. Maybe he still lived with his parents.

Aaron said, "Wow. This is beautiful. The canal where I run is straight and flat for miles and miles. The houses are okay, but nothing like this."

"Well, my house isn't as big as those over there, but yeah… I'm very fortunate to be able to live in this area."

"Where do you work?"

"I work for a company called Technovations. Their office is next to the 101 up by Raintree. I did an internship there after my junior year, and I stayed with a guy who lives not too far from here. I liked it, so when they offered me a job, I took it."

Aaron thought, *So, he's in high-tech. Maybe that's how he can afford to live here. Still, he looks like he's about my age.*

Tall Guy called out to the others, "Ready to get going again?"

Nobody objected, so Tall Guy started running again, with Aaron close behind.

***

By the time the runners reached their cars, Aaron was exhausted. This had been a longer and faster run than any he had ever taken along the canal.

Everyone said goodbye to each other and got in their cars. As Aaron walked toward his car, he noticed Tall Guy walking toward the BMW parked next to him.

Tall Guy asked, "Is that your Toyota?"

Aaron immediately felt self-conscious about his old Toyota Corolla. "Yeah. It gets me around."

"I used to have one of those, except mine was blue. That's what – a '95?"

"Yeah."

"So was mine. I got it when I was a senior in high school. It already had 120,000 miles on it. I figured it must have only been driven by a little old lady to church every Sunday."

Aaron chuckled and said, "I got mine from my grandmother. She moved into a retirement community while I was in college. So mine was literally driven by an old lady to church every Sunday."

"Nothing beats a Toyota for longevity. How many miles has it got on it?"

"About 80,000. I don't drive it much either. My apartment is a three-minute walk to where I work, and everything else I need is in the shopping centers at that corner, so I walk everywhere."

Tall Guy nodded.

Aaron asked, "How long have you had your BMW?"

"Let's see… four years, now. I got it when I graduated from college and came out here. It belonged to my best friend. He was moving to London and didn't need it anymore, so he sold it to me." He turned toward his car and clicked his remote to unlock the door.

Sensing that his time with Tall Guy was ending, Aaron said, "Hey, nice running with you. Will you be here in a couple of weeks?"

Tall Guy turned back toward Aaron and gave him a confused look.

"I have to work every other weekend, so I won't be able to come next week."

Tall Guy smiled and said, "Oh, I guess Justin didn't tell you. We take off between Memorial Day and Labor Day. It's too hot, and not enough guys are willing to start earlier than 7:00. So we won't be running again until September."

Damn.

Tall Guy asked, "So, what do you do, that you have to work every other weekend?"

"I'm a pharmacist. I work at a HealthPro store in Tempe. There's only one other pharmacist there and the store is open seven days a week, so I work five days one week and two days the next."

"So you get a five-day weekend every other week? Must be nice!"

"Yeah, but on the weekdays, we work from eight in the morning until ten at night."

"Fourteen hours a day? Damn… That sounds brutal."

"I'm used to it. And I get time off for lunch and dinner. On Saturday and Sunday, we close at six, so that's a little better. Oh, by the way, I'm Aaron."

"Ryan."

Aaron extended his hand and Ryan shook it. "So, uh, you wanna get together and run sometime? I don't mind getting up early."

Ryan said, "Yeah, sure."

"Are you on Facebook?"

"No, I don't do social media."

"Okay, well… could I text you?"

"Sure."

"Hang on a sec."

Aaron opened the passenger door of his car and retrieved his phone from the glove compartment. He unlocked it and opened his contacts while he walked back toward Ryan. "Okay, what's your number?"

Ryan gave it to him.

Aaron said, "I'll send you a text so you'll have my number."

Ryan started walking around to the driver's side of his car. He turned and waved goodbye to Aaron. "See ya."

Aaron waved back. "See ya soon!"

Ryan

Sunday, May 22, 2016

Aaron was tired, sore, and sweaty as he drove home, but he was alive with excitement. He alternated between replaying the snippets of conversation he had with Ryan and thinking, *Whoa. Not so fast. Don't start falling for a guy you've only met once. Take it slow. Give it time to develop. Remember what happened with Jeremy.*

Regardless of what might or might not happen with Ryan, moving on after Jeremy just got a little easier.

After Aaron had showered, eaten, and gotten dressed, he picked up his phone and sat down at his computer.

He pulled up Ryan's phone number. He didn't get Ryan's last name, so he did a reverse phone number lookup and discovered that his last name is Robertson. "Ryan Robertson," he said out loud to no one. "Ryan Robertson." He smiled. He liked the sound of it with the two alliterated Rs. The name rolled easily off his tongue.

After more searching, he found Ryan's address. He opened Google Maps and found that it was, indeed, only a few blocks from the place they had rested this morning. He switched into Satellite mode and zoomed into Ryan's property. He could see a pool in his backyard, along with some trees and shrubs, some lounge chairs and tables, and something that looked like a thatched roof. He switched to Street View and gazed at the exterior of Ryan's house, then moved up and down the street. It seemed a bit smaller and less opulent than the houses that backed up to the lake, but it was still enviably nice. It was a far cry from his parents' modest home in Troy, Ohio.

Must be nice, he thought.

He launched Zillow and typed in the address. The house's estimated value was $739,000. *This guy must make a fortune if he can afford to live in a house like this and drive a BMW. Am I even in his league?*

I wonder how old he is. Wait… he said he got his BMW four years ago when he got out of college. So, if he has a Bachelor's degree, that would make him 26. But if he's working for a tech firm and he's making that kind of money, maybe he has a Masters or a PhD. No wait... he said he interned there after his junior year and started working there a year after that.

Aaron's mood sank. *Ryan's already seen my 21-year-old Toyota. He didn't act like he looked down on me for having it, but he has certainly traded up from his. I told him I live in an apartment in Tempe, and look where he lives! Do I even want him to visit my place?*

Besides, I don't even know if he's single. I don't know anything about him other than he runs fast, he works for a tech company, and he seems to be well off. Oh, and he's hot! There's definitely that.

Aaron opened a search window and typed 'Ryan Robertson Scottsdale Arizona.' Various people finder websites popped up in the search results, so he started going through them. He learned that Ryan's middle initial is B and he's 26 years old. He had two previous addresses – an apartment in Scottsdale and a house in Los Angeles, near UCLA.

Aaron looked at the time on his computer. He had devoted nearly an hour to investigating Ryan Robertson and had learned little more than his age, the value of his house, and that he, at one point, lived in Los Angeles. He probably went to UCLA.

Aaron thought, *Oh, well. Enough investigative work for one day. All for someone who's probably out of my league anyway.*

Aaron opened Facebook. He received an invitation to join the Rainbow Runners Facebook group and a private message from Justin.

> Did you have fun today?

> Yes! I'm tired, though. I don't usually run that far or that fast.

> You did great! You kept up with Ryan.

> Yeah, I don't push myself that hard when it's only me.

Saw you chatting with Ryan there at the end. 😊

Is he single?

As far as I know.

Thx

Interested? 😊

Maybe...

Aaron waited a moment. Justin didn't type anything.

I asked if he wanted to go running sometime. He seemed interested. I got his digits.

Good luck! Hope it works out.

We'll see. Nothing ventured, nothing gained.

True. Gotta go grab lunch. Kent says hi.

Tell him I said hi. TTYL

Aaron accepted the invitation to join the Rainbow Runners group. He scanned up and down the member list. There were at least 60 members. He recognized some of the others from this morning's run. He didn't see Ryan, but then he remembered Ryan didn't use social media.

Aaron looked at his calendar. He had Wednesday and Thursday off, as usual. He assumed Ryan had a Monday through Friday job. But he didn't know. He could ask.

Next weekend was his work weekend. And it was Memorial Day weekend. He had to work Monday, too. Shit. He wouldn't be able to run with Ryan until two weeks from now.

Aaron decided to call Ryan on Wednesday. He wanted to call him right now, but he knew he shouldn't seem too eager.

Nothing Ventured, Nothing Gained

Wednesday, May 25, 2016

For three days after meeting Ryan, Aaron could think of little else.

On Wednesday morning during his run along the canal, Aaron contemplated what his next step with Ryan should be. He couldn't go running with him until the weekend after next, but he wanted to make some kind of contact sooner than that. But what should that be?

Aaron visualized them running together along the canal. He pushed himself to match the pace Ryan had set on Sunday morning.

He imagined running with Ryan near his home in Scottsdale. Since they would be hot and sweaty afterward, they could take a dip in Ryan's pool to cool off – hopefully naked. Aaron thought back to his tryst with Jeremy in his pool and fantasized about doing that with Ryan. He pictured himself clinging to Ryan, his legs wrapped around Ryan's waist and his arms wrapped around his neck. They'd kiss passionately while he bounced up and down on Ryan's cock.

Between fantasy scenes, Aaron chastised himself for getting so obsessed with this guy he had only met once and knew so little about.

He returned home, showered, and checked his email and Facebook. *I wonder why Ryan isn't on Facebook.* He shut off his computer and fixed lunch for himself. As he ate, he thought, *I want to call him tonight, but I need something to say other than setting up a time to go running a week and a half from now. Maybe we can just talk for a while. I don't want to sound pushy. How do gay guys get started with each other?*

Come on, man, you're 28 years old. You're acting like a junior high girl with a teenage crush. For God's sake, just man up and call him.

I don't want to wait until this evening, but I don't want to bother him at work. Maybe I should start by texting him. Then we can set up a time to talk if he's interested.

Aaron picked up his phone. He opened a new text message and thought about what to type. He spent five minutes choosing his words, typing, then erasing what he had just typed. Finally, he settled on a message.

> Hey Ryan, it's Aaron Bradbury. We met last Sunday at Rainbow Runners. I was wondering if I could call you this evening. We could set up a time to go running and maybe chat for a bit. Let me know a good time for you. Thanks, Aaron

Aaron re-read it three times to make sure it sounded okay and there were no typos. He took a deep breath and pressed Send.

Aaron put his phone down next to his computer. Nothing to do now but wait. He decided to walk over to Food World, the grocery store in the nearby shopping center. They had sushi on sale every Wednesday, so that had become his weekly routine.

Half an hour later, he arrived back at his apartment carrying a container of sushi, a bottle of sake, and several other grocery items. He glanced at his phone. He had received a text message from Ryan! Aaron lit up as he opened the message.

> Hey there! Would love to chat. I'm not much of a phone person, so would you like to meet for a drink tomorrow after work? How about 6:00 at Kahuna's in downtown Scottsdale? I'm open to other options. Let me know. Ryan

Aaron was bursting with excitement. *Ryan likes Kahuna's too! Oh my God, could this be any better? Oh, wait. I have band tomorrow night. I'd have to leave Kahuna's by 6:30 at the latest to get to rehearsal on time. Still, I can't say no.*

Aaron hit Reply and started typing.

Aaron pressed Send. A few minutes later, Ryan replied.

Aaron thought, *Wait a minute. Is that coming on too strong?* He backspaced to erase the last sentence. Then he thought, *No. Now it looks too terse. I am looking forward to it, so why not say so?* He retyped the last sentence but used a period instead of an exclamation mark. He pressed Send.

***

At 5:00, Aaron walked into his closet and tried on several shirts. A T-shirt seemed too casual. He tried on a light blue dress shirt. *No, too stiff and dressy. Since it was Kahuna's, maybe a Hawaiian shirt? No, too loud.* He settled on a short-sleeved shirt with a more subdued floral pattern. It was kind of island-inspired, kind of festive, but not too overboard.

At 5:15, he got in his car. The map app said it would take 25 minutes, but he didn't want to take any chances and be late. Plus, he'd have to find a parking space.

At 5:50, he arrived. He stood outside the entrance and waited. Less than a minute later, Ryan's black BMW pulled into an empty space across the street. He crossed the street with a spring in his step and a friendly smile. As he approached, he extended his hand and said, "Hey!"

Aaron replied, "Hey!" As they shook hands, Ryan reached forward with his left hand and briefly put it on Aaron's right shoulder, one step shy of giving him a hug. They turned and walked into the restaurant.

The hostess asked, "Would you like a table or are you going to sit at the bar?"

Ryan turned to Aaron. Aaron shrugged. Ryan replied, "How about that table in the front by the sidewalk?"

"Right this way, please." The hostess gave them two dinner menus and two happy hour menus.

Ryan said, "You've been here before, right?"

"I've been to the one on Seventh Street, but not this one. The menu's the same, though." Aaron didn't need to look at the drink menu. "They have the best Mai Tais here. I usually start with that. Their other drinks are good too, but I only order a second if I'm eating dinner."

"Yeah, I love their Mai Tais too." Ryan glanced up and down the appetizer side of the happy hour menu. "You want to split an order of ceviche?"

"Sure!" Aaron was delighted that Ryan seemed to like all the same things he did.

The waiter arrived with two glasses of water and took their order. With that business taken care of, Ryan asked, "So you mentioned you have a band rehearsal tomorrow. What kind of band?"

"I'm in Desert Pride. It's Phoenix's LGBT wind symphony. Kent's in it too."

"What do you play?"

"Trombone."

"Oh, cool. I used to play trumpet back in high school and college."

"You should totally join the band! It's really good. And there's lots of nice people."

"Yeah, Kent tried to get me to join. But I don't know. It's been, like, four years since I've played."

"It was six years for me. You'd be surprised at how quickly it comes back. I'm pretty much back to where I was in college."

"I'll think about it."

"We've got a concert coming up on Sunday, June 19. If you're free that day, come check it out."

"Sure. Remind me closer to the time. So, how long have you been in the band?"

"I just joined a couple of months ago. I went to hear their concert in

March. It brought back all kinds of memories from when I was in band in high school and college. And I realized how much I missed playing music. But honestly, what I really missed was the friendships. Since I moved out here two years ago, I hadn't made very many friends. Now that I'm in Desert Pride, that problem's solved."

"Cool."

Aaron wondered what to say next. Ryan beat him to it. "So are you originally from here?"

"No, I'm from Ohio. I grew up in a little town called Troy, north of Dayton. I went to Ohio State."

"What brought you out here from Ohio?"

"I wanted to live someplace warmer, where it doesn't snow. I mean, snow's fun when you're a kid and you build snowmen and go sledding and all that. But when you're a grown-up and it means shoveling snow and scraping ice off your windshield and trying to drive in it, it's not nearly so much fun. When I was in the marching band at Ohio State, we came out here to the Fiesta Bowl one year. I loved how it was warm and sunny in December instead of cold and snowy. When I graduated from pharmacy school, I got a job offer from HealthPro. They have locations all over the country, so I chose here."

"Smart choice."

"Yeah, especially now that I'm making friends and stuff. How about you? Where are you from, and what brought you here?"

Ryan had been smiling up to this point, but now he looked uncomfortable. But then the waiter delivered their Mai Tais and ceviche. He asked, "Are you ready to order dinner or do you need a few more minutes?"

Ryan said, "We'll stick with drinks and appetizers, at least for now."

"Okay, well I'll check back in a little while and see how you're doing."

Ryan took a sip of his drink, loaded some ceviche onto a chip, and took a bite. Then he took another swallow of his drink. Finally, he answered the question.

"I'm originally from Kansas – one of the suburbs of Kansas City. I moved out to Los Angeles to go to school at UCLA. After I graduated, I took a job here in Scottsdale."

"How do you like it? And how did you like LA?"

"I like it here. Some people say Phoenix is Little LA, but I don't think so. I guess there are some similarities, but I like this better. LA was okay. I lived in Westwood, which is right next to UCLA. It's really nice. And there were mountains not too far away that I went hiking in several times, and of course, the beach. That's one thing Phoenix doesn't have. But aside from that, LA is too big. The freeways are insane, and the suburbs go on forever. Once I graduated, there was no real reason to stay. And I was ready for something else. Scottsdale is beautiful and much more laid-back. The whole area is a lot more manageable."

"Yeah. I haven't seen much of Scottsdale, but when we were running on Sunday, I couldn't get over how nice everything looks."

They each scooped more ceviche onto a chip and ate it. With that topic exhausted, it was time for something else.

Aaron asked, "So when you were at UCLA, were you in the marching band?"

"No, unfortunately. I wish I could have, but I had to work and I couldn't do both."

"Yeah, being in a marching band takes up a lot of time."

"I was in one of their jazz ensembles, though. So that gave me a place to play my trumpet during college."

"Cool. I was in my high school jazz ensemble."

"So you like jazz?"

"Yeah, although I don't listen to it that much. I like big band, but there's a lot of other jazz I don't know that much about. Desert Pride has a jazz ensemble too, but I can't be in it since they rehearse on Monday nights and I always have to work."

Ryan's face lit up. "Will they be playing at the concert in June?"

"Yeah, I think they're going to play three or four songs."

"Cool. Well, I'll definitely be there."

The waiter returned. "Would you like another round of Mai Tais? Maybe another appetizer?"

Ryan smiled at Aaron. "You wanna stay for dinner?"

"Sure!" Aaron hoped that didn't come across as *too* excited.

The waiter asked, "Do you need a couple more minutes?"

Aaron and Ryan exchanged glances. Aaron said, "I know what I want." *In more ways than one.*

Ryan nodded. The waiter took their orders and scurried away.

Ryan asked, "So how long have you known Kent and Justin?"

"I met them when I joined the band back in April."

"Oh, I thought maybe you already knew them and they invited you to the concert. So how did you find out about it?"

"That's kind of a funny story." Aaron told Ryan how he met Rob at Wok Around the Clok, and he said something to Rob because his T-shirt had a trombone on it. He talked about how Rob had invited him to the concert and even offered to loan him his trombone.

Ryan said, "Wait a minute. This guy, who you just met at a fast-food place, was willing to loan you a trombone?"

"Yeah. Rob's really nice. He's become kind of like a big brother to me, especially while I was coming out and dealing with my parents."

"So, you recently came out to your parents?"

"Yeah. Actually, I just recently came out to myself. I almost didn't go to the concert when I found out it was an LGBT band. But Rob kept saying straight people are welcome too. And it's true – there are some straight people in the band. But after I was in the band for a few weeks, I felt comfortable around everyone, and I realized this is who I am and where I belong. Well, that... and I kinda fell for a guy."

Ryan laughed, "Yeah, that would be a tip-off. So what happened with that? I mean, if you're willing to share. It's none of my business."

"No, that's okay. His name is Jeremy. He also plays trombone. He sat next to me. Anyway, after band rehearsals, some of the people go out to this bar called Raise! the Bar. I wasn't planning on going, 'cause, you know, it's a gay bar and I still thought I was straight. But Jeremy invited me and said he'd buy me a drink, and I thought, 'Sure, why not?' I mean, I didn't want to seem unfriendly and stand-offish. Anyway, I went and had a great time, and I met Kent and Justin there. Kent's the one in the band, but they live close to the bar so Justin usually comes out and joins us." Aaron decided to leave out the part about him getting drunk.

Their food and second drinks arrived, so they took a few moments to dig in. Then Aaron continued. "So, a couple of weeks went by, and I realized I was thinking about Jeremy a lot. So one day I had lunch with Rob and told him everything that was going on. By the end of the lunch, I was ready to admit to myself that I'm gay."

Ryan asked, "And that was – how long ago?"

Aaron thought for a second. "Two weeks ago today. Kinda seems like it's been longer than that."

"So you've already had a boyfriend and broken up in less than two weeks?"

"Well, it's not quite like that. We weren't actually boyfriends. We already knew each other for a month, and we went hiking together the weekend before I came out. Here, let me show you this picture we took." Aaron got out his phone and found one of the selfies they had taken on the mountain peak. He showed it to Ryan.

"Awww… that's sweet. You guys look good together. Where was that taken?"

"South Mountain. Have you ever been there?"

"No, I've been meaning to go someday. But, I dunno… It's kind of hard for me to get motivated when it's only me. It's easier to just go for a run."

"I know what you mean. So yeah… We could go hiking together sometime."

"Maybe once it cools off. So anyway, back to Jeremy."

"Right. It's funny, we got together for dinner that night… yeah, it was Wednesday, the same day I had lunch with Rob. So I came out to him. And after dinner, we went up to the top of South Mountain to watch the sunset. He lives pretty close to the park entrance. So we were up there, and it was really beautiful! We stayed after everyone else left and it was starting to get dark and … well, we kissed. And it was perfect. It was so romantic! So anyway, when we got back to his house, we got in the hot tub, and… well… one thing led to another, and…"

"I get the idea. So that was two weeks ago. What happened since?"

"Well, one thing I didn't tell you was he broke up with his partner a couple of months before that. He posted for some jobs at his company in other cities, 'cause he felt like he needed a fresh start somewhere else. And the next day, he found out he got a job he applied for in Austin. So, he's moving there this weekend. He's probably packing right now. In fact, Kent and Justin are going to drive there with him and help him unload the rental truck."

"That must have been disappointing."

"Yeah, tell me about it. He was really nice. But besides the new job in Austin, he said getting into a new relationship so soon after breaking up with his ex probably wasn't a good idea. So, it wasn't meant to be. But I'm still glad it happened."

Ryan said, "Thank you for telling me all that."

Aaron asked, "So how long have you been out?"

Ryan's mood suddenly turned somber again. "Since the summer after my junior year in high school. My best friend and I realized we were in love with each other."

"Oh, cool! So what happened?"

"I'd rather not talk about it. It's kind of painful."

"Oh. Okay. Sorry."

For an awkward moment, nobody said anything. Desperate to get dinner back on the right track, Aaron searched for another topic. "So… I know you like to run, and you'd like to go hiking if you had someone to go with. What else do you do for fun?"

"I like to travel. One of my housemates when I lived in LA now has a job where he works in different major cities around the world. Like, he'll live in one place for a couple of years, then move on to the next place. So I go visit him wherever he happens to be. So far, I've visited him in London and Berlin. Actually, that's how I met Kent and Justin. I went to visit Ted – that's my friend – in London, but then we went on a gay cruise from Amsterdam to Barcelona. I met Kent and Justin on the ship."

Aaron's eyes popped wide open. "They have gay cruises?"

"Yep. It was a lot of fun. I wasn't sure whether I'd like it, but I did. Anyway, on the first day of the cruise, I saw these two guys on deck trying to take a selfie. So I asked if they'd like me to take the picture for them. We introduced ourselves and found out we lived in the same city. They're the ones who invited me to join the running club." Ryan decided not to mention that he had hooked up with them on the ship.

"That's funny – you went on a cruise in Europe and met people who live here. Where is Ted now?"

"He's in Buenos Aires, but I haven't been to see him yet. I usually wait until he's been there several months so he knows his way around."

"Wow! That sounds exciting!"

"Yeah. He really enjoys living somewhere else and experiencing the lifestyle and culture there. It's totally different from just going there on vacation for a few days. Anyway, so besides traveling, I listen to a lot of music. As I said, I'm really into jazz. I like to watch live concerts on YouTube and I've collected a lot of CDs and videos. Back in Kansas, my best friend and I used to go to Kansas City and spend a couple of hours in their used record stores. I'd come home with all kinds of stuff. And there were some fantastic used record stores in LA! I'd hit them all pretty regularly."

Aaron asked, "How about here?"

"There are a few. But used record stores are kind of fading away.

Everyone buys and sells stuff on Amazon now. I get a lot of stuff from there, but I miss going to used record stores and browsing through all their stuff. I could get lost in there for hours."

"Do you ever go to concerts?"

"Yeah. There are some great concert venues around town – Scottsdale, Tempe, and Chandler all have Centers for the Arts, there's the MIM… and there's a jazz club downtown."

"I love the MIM! I went there not long after I moved here. I need to go back. I tried to take my parents there when they visited a couple of months ago, but they weren't interested."

"Let's do it! I love going back there. They always have some new stuff I haven't seen."

"Great. And next time there's a concert you want to see at any of those places, let me know and I'll go with you if I can. I mean, if I'm not working."

"What's this weekend look like?"

Aaron sighed. "I have to work. But I get off at 6:00 on Saturday and Sunday, so I could go to something after that."

Ryan pulled out his phone and started typing. "I'm looking to see who's playing at Bird's Nest. That's the jazz club downtown." Neither of them said anything while Ryan tapped and scrolled on his phone. "Oh, cool. This band called the Loose Lions is playing on Saturday night. I like them. They're sort of, shall we say, progressive. They can get kind of out there."

"Sounds good! I'd love to get out and hear some live music." *And spend more time with you.* "Except for the Desert Pride concert, I haven't been to a concert since I moved here."

"Well, okay then. I'll still check to see what's happening at the other places, but if there's nobody good, we'll go to the jazz club. They start at 7:30."

Aaron was all smiles. The check arrived, and Aaron reached for his wallet. Ryan said, "Nope. Let me get it."

"Are you sure?"

"I'm sure." Ryan handed his credit card to the waiter and he left to process the charge.

"Thanks! That was really nice of you. I'll get it next time."

"Whatever. I'm not worried. It'll all even out."

"Ryan, I'm glad you suggested this. I really enjoyed dinner – both the food and getting to know you."

"Me too. I'll send you a text to firm up the details about Saturday night."

"Cool. I'm looking forward to it!"

The waiter returned with the receipt for Ryan to sign. He scrawled his name with a quick flourish, grabbed his credit card and the duplicate copy, and stood up.

Aaron stood up reluctantly. I could stay here another three hours. Oh, well, better to leave some for next time.

Once outside the door, they stood still, like neither of them wanted to head back to their car just yet.

Ryan said, "Have fun at band rehearsal tomorrow."

"Thanks! If you want, you could join us at Raise! after rehearsal. We usually get there around 9:45. Kent and Justin will be there, and I can introduce you to some of my other friends."

"Thanks, but I'll pass. I'm not much of a bar person."

For a brief moment, neither of them said anything else. Then Ryan stepped forward and opened his arms. They hugged and said goodbye. Aaron strolled toward his car. Ryan scampered across the street. When he reached his car, he turned and waved. Aaron smiled and waved back.

Moving On Quickly

Thursday, May 26, 2016

Jeremy didn't attend the rehearsal. He needed time to pack, and since he would be gone before the concert took place, the director preferred to rehearse the band with the musicians who would be performing.

At Raise!, Aaron was standing in line to order his drink when Jeremy walked in the door. Jeremy said hi and gave Aaron a quick kiss.

Aaron said, "So what would you like? I'm buying tonight."

"You don't have to do that."

"I want to."

"Okay, then, I'll have a Long Island."

"Cool. I'll see you back there in a few minutes."

Jeremy walked to the band table in the back of the bar and began his round of hello hugs.

At one point midway through the evening, Aaron found himself at one end of the table with Kent, Justin, and Rob. Jeremy was talking with another group of people at the other end.

Aaron said, "So, last night I had dinner with Ryan."

Justin and Kent each put their hand in the air and high-fived Aaron.

Justin said, "Well! You're moving quickly."

"Actually, he's the one who suggested getting together. I just wanted to chat on the phone. We met at the Kahuna's in Scottsdale for a drink, and that turned into dinner."

Kent said, "So I guess it went pretty well."

"Yeah! We're getting together on Saturday night to hear some live jazz."

Rob asked, "So who is this Ryan guy? And so soon after Jeremy?"

"Hey, I'm making up for lost time. Anyway, he's this tall, handsome guy I met last Sunday when I went running with their running group."

Kent said, "I can vouch for that. He's *very* tall. And *very* handsome."

Justin grinned and added, "And *verrry–*" Kent kicked Justin's leg under the table. Justin pivoted quickly. "...well educated."

Aaron wondered what that was about, but whatever. "Yeah. He works at a technology research company called Technovations."

Rob said, "So if he's into jazz, does he plan an instrument?"

Aaron said, "He plays trumpet. At least he used to. He said he hasn't played it since he left college several years ago."

Rob said, "Well, we all know that's no excuse."

"Yeah, I invited him to our concert and I think he's going to come. And I told him we have a jazz ensemble too. He was pretty excited about that."

Rob said, "And as you well know, to hear us is to join us."

Aaron turned to Kent and Justin and asked, "How well do you guys know him?"

Kent replied, "Hmmm... I dunno... Not that well. He's invited us to his house for dinner a couple of times. And sometimes he goes to parties when someone in the running club has one. But we've never had any deep conversations with him."

Justin said, "He's a rather private person. We can talk about surface-level things like world events or things to do around town, but anytime we ask about where he came from, or his family, or anything about his past, he shuts down pretty quickly."

Kent said, "Yeah. So we've learned to steer clear of that stuff."

Aaron said, "Yeah, that happened last night. We were talking about me coming out, and that was going fine, but then I asked him when he came out. He kinda got quiet, but then he said after his junior year of high school, he and his best friend realized they were in love with each other."

Kent said, "That's more than we ever got."

"But then I asked him what happened and he said he didn't want to talk about it. So I moved on to something else."

Rob said, "Sounds like you need to go slow with this guy."

Aaron asked, "You guys said you've been to his house. What's it like?"

Justin said, "It's pretty nice, and it's certainly in a nice part of town."

Aaron paused for a moment. "So, if he's about my age, how do you think he can afford such a nice house in a rich part of Scottsdale?"

Kent and Justin looked at each other and waited to see which one of them would say something first. Then Kent said, "Well, I wouldn't be surprised if his job pays well, considering what he does."

"Yeah probably. And he drives a BMW and I drive my grandmother's old Toyota. So I guess what I'm wondering is… I don't know…"

Rob said, "You're wondering if you're good enough for him."

"Yeah."

"Well, why don't you let him decide that? You're nice, you're good-looking, you're well-educated, and you have a good job. And you have things in common, like running and music. So why wouldn't you be good enough for him?"

Kent said, "Rob's right. It's up to you to decide whether he's good enough for you. It's up to him to decide whether you're good enough for him. Why should you make that decision for him? You don't know what his criteria are. You might be exactly what he's looking for."

Rob said, "Good relationships aren't built on comparing bank accounts and investment portfolios."

Justin added, "Besides, you don't know. He might be mortgaged to the hilt and in debt up to his eyeballs."

Kent said, "During the time we've known him, we've never seen him in a relationship. At least he's never mentioned anyone. And we're like, why doesn't he have guys hanging all over him? But you know, maybe everyone else writes him off because they think he's too good for them. As a result, he has no one."

Justin said, "I kinda got the impression he and that guy he was with on the cruise were an item. But he says they're just good friends."

Aaron said, "He mentioned him yesterday at dinner. He said they lived in the same house at UCLA. He has a job where he can live in cities all over the world for a year or two. He's lived in London and Berlin, and now he's in Buenos Aires. Ryan goes to visit him in each place."

Rob said, "Must be nice. It's possible they're in a long-distance relationship. Maybe his heart belongs to this guy."

Justin smiled as he recalled the evening he, Kent, and Ryan hooked up on the cruise. "No, I'm pretty sure they're not in a relationship."

Kent shot Justin a glance that said, 'Shut up.' Then he said, "Well, in any case, he seems to be interested in you, so I hope it goes well. Just go slow. And good luck with getting him to open up to you."

Aaron said, "Thanks, guys. I appreciate the advice."

They realized this topic had run its course. Aaron wandered over to Jeremy. Fifteen minutes later, Jeremy said, "Well, I'm tired. I guess I should get going." He worked his way around the table, saying goodbye and hugging everyone. Since this was the last time he would see everyone before moving to Austin, he spent a little more time with each person. Aaron positioned himself so he would be the last person Jeremy reached before he left.

When Jeremy finally reached Aaron, Aaron kissed him and gave him a long hug. They leaned back and looked into each other's eyes.

Jeremy thought, *It would be nice to have one more time with him, but I'm tired and I really need to get to bed.*

Aaron thought, *It would be nice to have one more time with him, but I don't know… I'm more interested in Ryan now. Maybe I should hold out for him.*

After a few seconds of silence, they both realized they were on the same page. They smiled and the tension evaporated.

Jeremy said, "Come visit me in Austin after I get settled in. You're always welcome."

Aaron said, "I'd love to." *…unless things get serious with Ryan.* "Let's stay in touch."

"For sure!"

They kissed and hugged again. As they hugged, Aaron whispered into Jeremy's ear, "I'll never forget you."

"I'll never forget you either."

They kissed one more time. Then Jeremy said goodbye and turned toward the door.

Loose Lions in the Bird's Nest

Saturday, May 28, 2016

At 6:00 on Saturday, Aaron hurried out of the HealthPro pharmacy and practically ran home. He pulled a frozen entrée from this freezer, placed it in the microwave, and pushed the 3-minute button. He rushed into his bedroom, pulled off his work clothes, and left them strewn across his bed. He donned a nice pair of shorts, a casual short-sleeved shirt, and shoes.

The microwave dinged. He rushed into the kitchen, stirred the mishmash of chicken, broccoli, and pasta, and placed the meal back in the microwave for another two minutes.

He stepped into the bathroom, shaved quickly, and examined his nose up close to make sure there were no stray nose hairs or boogers. His hair looked fine, but he ran his comb through it to put any loose hair back into place.

The microwave dinged again, and he rushed into the kitchen. He ate his food as fast as he could without choking on it. Then he hurried back to the bathroom to brush his teeth.

He glanced at his watch as he headed for the door. 6:32. Hopefully there would be no traffic along I-10 and he would be able to find a close parking space.

He entered Bird's Nest at 7:10. When he reached the ticket counter, he said, "I'm Aaron Bradbury. There should be a ticket waiting for me."

One of the volunteers smiled and reached for a piece of paper off to the side. She scanned the ticket and said, "Your friend is seated at table B-3." She gestured toward a partially open black curtain behind Aaron. Through the opening, Aaron could see a cozy room crammed full of small tables and chairs. An electric tea-light candle adorned each table.

Aaron stepped into the room, and immediately Ryan stood up and waved. Aaron scooted past a few other patrons and arrived at the table. He wasn't sure whether a hug would be an appropriate greeting, but that question was answered when Ryan offered his hand for a quick shake. "Glad you made it!"

"I got here as fast as I could."

"Plenty of time. Hey, you wanna split a bottle of wine?"

"Yeah, sure." After operating on overdrive for the last hour and 15 minutes, some wine might help him chill a bit.

"White or red?"

"Either's fine. You pick."

Ryan got up, scooted his way back to the lobby, and got in line at the snack bar. He returned a few minutes later with a bottle of Chardonnay, two clear plastic glasses, and a bag of something that resembled Chex mix. He sat down and poured them both a glass.

After he had taken a few sips, Aaron started to relax. He looked around the room. Portraits of famous jazz musicians adorned the walls. He recognized Duke Ellington and Miles Davis, but he wasn't sure about the others. A small stage held a grand piano and an electric keyboard, a drum set, a string bass laying on its side in front of an amp, several microphones, and a few music stands. The energy in the room was positive. The other patrons seemed to be in a good mood as they anticipated the start of the show.

Aaron said, "Tell me more about the band we're seeing tonight."

"They're local guys, but they're really good. I've heard them once before and I bought their two CDs. They play almost all original music. If they cover a song, they take it in a totally different direction."

"So what you're saying is I may not recognize anything I hear tonight."

"Probably not. But that's kinda the point. See, with jazz, and especially with this band, it isn't so much about the melody. I mean, that's the starting point, but it's more about improvisation. It's about what they create on the spot, right before your eyes – and ears. And it's amazing to watch how the musicians interact. Like, if whoever's taking a solo goes off in one direction, the rhythm section responds to it and follows him. These guys have been playing together for several years and it shows in how they interact. Oh, and of course, they're all monster players."

Aaron had no idea whether he would like what he was about to hear or even understand it. But it was clearly something Ryan was passionate about.

Aaron asked, "So how did you get so into jazz?"

"Well, my high school had a good jazz ensemble. Our director taught us a lot about jazz. I remember one time during my freshman year in high school. It was October 21, 2004. I'll never forget that date. The director took a bunch of us to see Maynard Ferguson. He was playing at some small college in this tiny little town called Baldwin City, Kansas. But oh man! He blew me away! And everyone else in the room. Not just him and how high he could play on his trumpet, but his whole band. It was full of energy! They had so many great soloists. The band was on fire and the audience was stoked... it was amazing. I'll never forget that night. From that point on, I knew I loved jazz. I wanted to be able to play high notes like Maynard Ferguson, and for a high school kid, I did pretty well. I spent hours learning how to improvise with play-along records." *With Chris, but I won't mention that.* "And I've got, like, 500 CDs – almost all jazz. I like to analyze how the musicians structure their solos and how the music's arranged."

Up to this point, Ryan had talked non-stop. When he stopped for a few seconds to take a sip of wine, Aaron said, "I'm surprised you didn't major in music."

"I thought about it. But I looked at my band director's situation. They don't pay teachers very well. He had to spend all his spare time playing in churches and teaching lessons – just to make enough to get by. And if I wanted to be a performer – well, that's even tougher. I thought about Maynard Ferguson and the guys in his band. They spend all their time riding on a bus from one little town to the next. They barely make enough to get by and they don't have any kind of home life. The guys in this band probably have it the best. I think they all teach at the local community colleges, so they make regular salaries and they can still play in places like this. Anyway, I was also interested in website design and computer technology, so I figured I would depend on that to earn a living but keep music as something I can do on the side for fun."

Aaron thought, *But are you?*

As if Ryan heard his thought, he added, "But I guess I haven't really done that."

"See? You need to join Desert Pride. And see if you can join their jazz ensemble!"

"Yeah, I guess."

"At least it will get you playing your trumpet again."

Six musicians emerged from a side room and made their way to the stage. Some of them said hi to people they knew as they passed. Two sax players juggled several instruments, while another guy carried both a trumpet and a trombone.

Ryan turned to Aaron and said, "Oh, and I didn't tell you. The horn players are versatile. You never know what they're going to pick up and play next. And sometimes they use electronic effects. That's really wild!" Aaron nodded.

Someone from Bird's Nest stepped up to a microphone and introduced the Loose Lions. The band launched into an energetic opening number in an unusual time signature Aaron couldn't quite figure out. The band members navigated the complex piece as easily as if it were in basic 4/4 time.

Each song seemed to last at least ten minutes, with several musicians taking lengthy solos. Sometimes Aaron lost track of where they were in the chord progression, or even if they were in one at all. But their virtuosity and cohesion were amazing, as Ryan had described.

Two hours later, the band finished to enthusiastic applause. Ryan and Aaron left the club. Once they were outside, they stepped off to one side of the sidewalk.

Ryan was exuberant. "Wow! Wasn't that amazing?"

"Yeah. Those guys were really good like you said."

"Where are you parked?"

Aaron pointed down a side street. "A couple of blocks that way."

Ryan said, "I'm over there across the street." He paused. "Did you like it?"

Truthfully, the performance didn't do nearly as much for Aaron as it did for Ryan. He took care to phrase his answer favorably. "Well, I didn't understand it as much as you did. Sometimes I thought they were just playing lots and lots of notes. But it was interesting. So yeah, I liked it pretty well."

"I get that. They get pretty avant-garde and cerebral at times."

"But I could tell they were excellent musicians with a lot of talent."

"Cool. So, uh… what are you doing tomorrow?"

Aaron sighed. "I have to work, remember?"

"Oh, yeah, that's right. Sorry, I forgot."

"That's okay. I have a weird schedule."

"But you get off at six, right?"

"Yeah…"

"Would you like to come up to my place for dinner?"

Aaron smiled. This was a pleasant surprise. "Yeah, sure. I should be able to get there at like 6:45. Seven at the latest. I know that's kind of late for dinner on a Sunday."

"No, that's fine. I'll text you my address."

Aaron didn't let on that he already had it as a result of his internet stalking. "Okay, cool. Should I bring anything?"

"Nah… I haven't decided what I'm going to make yet. Besides, if you have to work all day, you won't have time to make or pick up anything."

"True."

"Any food allergies or dislikes?"

"No allergies… hmmm… I don't like liver and onions, but other than that, I'll eat just about anything."

"Cool. Well, then, I'll see you tomorrow at around 6:45 or 7:00. Text me if you're going to be later than that."

Aaron nodded. They both glanced around. Most people had left the jazz club, so there was practically no one on the sidewalk.

Aaron said, "I had fun tonight. Thanks for suggesting this."

Ryan smiled, opened his arms, and took a step toward Aaron. They hugged for about three seconds, then stepped apart. Aaron smiled and gazed up at Ryan. Ryan smiled, gave Aaron a quick goodbye wave, and turned to cross the street.

A Sunday Evening Tradition

Sunday, May 29, 2016

When 6:00 rolled around, Aaron closed the pharmacy quickly. For the second straight night, he needed to hurry. He had someplace to be! And someone to be there with!

As he walked through the store, he passed the wine aisle. He stopped and looked at the selection. He didn't know what Ryan was planning to serve, not that he knew much about wine pairing anyway. He knew Ryan liked Chardonnay since that's what he bought last night. He picked a bottle of one of the major brands and paid for it at the checkout. He didn't know whether it was a good brand or not, but he figured Ryan would appreciate the gesture.

Thankfully, traffic was light and Aaron made it to Ryan's home by 6:45. As he walked up Ryan's driveway, he looked up and down the street. The Zillow photos hadn't done the house or the neighborhood justice. This was a beautiful place to live.

Ryan answered the doorbell promptly. He swung the door open and welcomed Aaron inside. After he closed the door, he gave Aaron a nice hug. It was more of a friendly hello hug than a romantic hug, but it still felt nice. Aaron heard big band jazz playing on speakers mounted high on the wall. The volume was just loud enough to hear the music but not so loud as to impede conversation.

Aaron handed Ryan the wine and said, "I don't know whether this will go with what you're serving for dinner, but I wanted to bring it anyway. You can have it now or later, whichever you prefer."

Ryan said, "Thanks! I made a pizza. I was thinking a Long Island Iced Tea or a Jack and Coke would go well with it, or I have beer if you'd prefer that."

Homemade pizza, Aaron thought. *All this, and he can cook too.* "A Long Island would be delicious if it's not too much trouble. They have those at Raise! the Bar, where the band goes after rehearsals."

"No problem at all. That's what I was going to have. C'mon, let me put the pizza in the oven. I wanted to wait until you got here to start it." Ryan led Aaron into the kitchen.

As Aaron followed Ryan through the living room, he looked right and left to take it all in. Ryan had surprisingly nice furniture – very tasteful and modern. The kitchen was part of a great room, with a large island separating the kitchen from the family room area. The music was playing in there, too.

On the island was a wooden pizza peel holding a large, generously topped pizza. Ryan said, "I guess I should have texted you earlier. Is there anything you don't like on pizza?"

"No, I like pretty much everything."

Ryan grabbed the handle of the pizza peel and slid the pizza into the oven. He set the timer for 12 minutes. While he was doing that, Aaron looked around. He could see a separate dining room to the left of the kitchen. On the opposite wall in the family room area, there was a large TV inside an entertainment center with a nice home theater system and audio equipment. The couch and recliners looked substantial and comfortable, the type you could relax on for hours. Then Aaron looked out the sliding glass doors and saw a small but beautiful pool. A waterfall cascaded into the pool on the opposite side, flanked by raised platforms holding large pots with blooming flowers. Oleanders, roses, and cacti adorned the perimeter of the yard.

Aaron said, "This is quite a place you have here." *How the hell can you afford this?*

"Yeah, thanks. It's my little refuge from the world."

"How long have you lived here?"

"Hmmm… let's see. I bought it in March of 2013 and moved in in May, so yeah… it's been three years this month! I hadn't thought about it until you asked."

With the pizza in the oven and the timer set, Ryan walked over to a wet bar on the side of the family room and proceeded to make two Long Island Iced Teas. Aaron followed him, and after admiring Ryan's mixology expertise, his eyes wandered to the wall near the bar. There was a nicely arranged collection of framed photos, some of which showed college-aged guys dressed up and holding cocktails. They looked like they were at some sort of fancy party. Aaron saw a much younger Ryan in a couple of the pictures. He looked young enough to still be in high school or maybe a freshman in college – yet he was holding a cocktail. Next to that, there was a framed professional headshot of a beautiful black lady, elegantly dressed and perfectly made up.

The picture was autographed with the inscription:

To Ryan, my favorite "Friend of Dorothy."
All my love, Whitney Austin

Aaron asked, "Who's this?"

Ryan looked up from mixing their drinks to see where Aaron was pointing. "Oh, that's Darnell. He's one of the guys I lived with while I was going to UCLA."

Aaron looked confused. "But this is a woman named Whitney."

"Yes, Whitney Austin is Darnell's drag name."

"You mean that's a man???"

"Yep. Pretty convincing, huh? And you should hear him sing! Darnell doesn't just lip-sync, he sings in his real voice. He's amazing. He has power and range like you wouldn't believe."

"Well, okay, but why?"

"Why what?"

"Why does he dress up like a woman? Why doesn't he just sing as a man?"

Ryan finished mixing their drinks and offered one to Aaron.

Aaron took one sip and said, "Oh, man, this is delicious! This is even better than the ones at Raise!"

"Well, I'm not a professional bartender, but I have more time to measure the ingredients. They have to throw them together quickly. And I probably use better quality liquors. Anyway… You *are* newly out, aren't you? I remember when I was fresh out of the closet, I didn't understand drag queens, either. But I learned they're a significant part of our culture. The short story is that back in the bad old days when gay people had to be secretive, the only place they could go was to bars. Even then, they had to be careful. The police would raid the bars every now and then. Anyway, I guess some guys dressed up like the divas of the day and lip-synced to their songs. It was probably the only entertainment they had. Anyway, on June 28, 1969, the police raided the Stonewall Inn in Greenwich Village in New York City. This time, the patrons fought back. The drag queens led the way. The riot went on all night. And that event is considered the beginning of the "modern gay rights movement. Since then, drag queens often perform for charity events and fundraisers. So they give a lot to the community."

Aaron gestured toward the other photos. "And who are these guys?"

"They're some of the other guys I lived with. That's Ted, that's Ricky, and that's Hal. He's the guy that owned the place. And the Vietnamese guy I'm with? His name is Mike. He and I went to the senior prom at our high school together."

"Oh, wow! You went to your prom with a guy? How did that go?"

"We were nervous at first. And there was one tense moment when they played a slow dance. Mike and I and my best friend LaTanya and her girlfriend danced together. For a minute everyone stopped and stared at us. But then a few of our straight friends paired up as two girls or two guys and started dancing together. A few minutes later, it was no big deal. Everybody got over it and moved on. In hindsight, I'm sorry we waited until so late in the dance."

"So were these pictures taken that night?"

"No, they were taken the following weekend. Every year, there's a big banquet for the Los Angeles LGBT Youth Project. Hal was a big supporter of that organization. Every year, he bought a table of ten and invited us and a few of his friends. Those pictures are of us having cocktails at the house before we left to go to the banquet. Hal rented a limo and everything!"

"So you were still in high school then?"

"Yeah, I was a senior. All the other guys were in college."

Aaron thought back to his senior year of high school. He couldn't imagine going to a fancy banquet in a limousine. And certainly not drinking. "Sounds like you had a pretty fancy life."

"I've had my share of ups and downs. But the ups were pretty incredible."

The timer on the oven went off. Ryan walked back into the kitchen and pulled the pizza from the oven. It looked amazing. The edge of the crust was golden brown, and the cheese on top had melted into stringy, gooey goodness. He transferred the pizza to a metal restaurant-style pizza pan and cut the pizza into eight slices with a roller. "It's a nice night. Wanna eat on the patio?"

"Sure, why not?"

Ryan set the pizza down on the counter. He hurried out of the kitchen and down a hallway towards the bedrooms. A few seconds later, he was back. He stepped into the pantry and returned with a serving tray, which he loaded with two plates, napkins, a jar of grated cheese, and a jar of crushed red peppers. He added his drink to the tray and said, "Would you mind carrying this out?" He handed Aaron the tray and opened the sliding glass door. Ryan followed with the pizza. When Aaron stepped outside, he heard the same big band music coming from a pair of speakers mounted under the eaves of the patio roof.

After they had taken a few bites of pizza, Aaron said, "This is incredible! How did you learn to make pizza like this?"

"Hal taught me. You know, the guy who owned the house I lived in. You should have seen that house. It was kinda like this, only bigger and nicer. He lived in the master suite, which was big enough for his home office, too. There were four bedrooms he rented out to college guys – me, Ted, Darnell, and Ricky. After Ted graduated and moved out, a guy named Mykel moved in. Hal was the greatest guy. He was really generous and he loved to help people. During the week, we were all responsible for our own food. But every Sunday night, we'd have Family Night. Hal would fix dinner for everyone, and we'd all talk about our week and what was going on in our lives. Then we'd do something together like play games or watch a movie. Hal was a great cook. Most of the time, he'd make something like pizza or chili, or he'd grill hamburgers or chicken. The day I turned 18 happened to be a Sunday, so he cooked steak for everyone."

"Oh, man, that sounds wonderful."

"Yeah, those were good times. Those guys were like brothers to me. And Hal was like a father. I said that to him once, and he got all bent out of shape because he didn't want us to think of him as being that much older than us. So maybe mentor or role model would be a better way to put it. Anyway, they gave me so much love and support while I was coming out and adjusting to living on my own. I don't know where I'd be without them, especially Hal."

"Are you still in touch with those guys?"

Ryan's demeanor shifted from upbeat to neutral. He took a drink of his Long Island, then said, "Some of them, yes. I have the most contact with Ted. Of course, he's now moving from place to place around the world, so I don't get to see him very often. We talk by Skype every month or two. Sometimes they fly him back to Los Angeles for meetings or training, so I'll drive over and see him there. And I try to visit him at least once in each city he lives in. In fact, I'm flying down to Buenos Aires to see him next month."

This revelation caught Aaron off-guard. "So, uh... When will you be in Buenos Aires?"

Ryan thought for a moment, then replied, "I fly out this Saturday afternoon and get back on Sunday morning, June 19. So I'll be back in time for your concert. I may be a bit jet-lagged, but I'll be there. Anyway, Darnell is in Atlanta now. He's a nurse practitioner, so he's building up his practice while he takes care of his mom."

"Does he still do Whitney Austin?"

"Not as much as he used to. While he was in school, he had entire summers off, so he could perform for eight weeks in P-town and entertain on gay cruises. He still takes a week off here and there for a cruise, but now he mostly does local events."

"What's P-town?"

"Provincetown, Massachusetts. It's a town on the tip of Cape Cod that's a popular vacation spot for gays. According to Darnell, it's overflowing with gay men all summer long."

Aaron made a mental note to visit P-town sometime. "Cool. How about the others?"

"I'm not in touch with them anymore. Ricky developed a drug problem. He really needed to go into rehab but he wouldn't, so Hal kicked him out. He kinda disappeared after that. And Mykel moved out of the house suddenly, and it was pretty clear he didn't want to have any further communication."

For a moment, Ryan and Aaron looked at each other silently. Ryan could tell Aaron was thinking, 'What about Hal?' Ryan's heart sank. He didn't want to start crying in front of Aaron, but he needed to tell him something. "And as for Hal, well… He passed away suddenly at the end of my senior year of college, right before I graduated. It was really tragic, and I'd prefer not to go into it now. Let's keep the evening light, okay?"

Aaron nodded.

"Anyway, I cook a nice meal every Sunday night, like Hal used to. Sometimes I invite one or two people over but usually, I cook for myself. I make enough so I can have leftovers later in the week. I think it's good to do something special for yourself every now and then. When you live alone, it's easy to eat out a lot or fix microwave meals. But I want to have at least one home-cooked meal a week. So, Sunday night dinner is a tradition for me. I do it to honor Hal's memory."

"Yeah, I totally get that. I eat out a lot and go through a lot of microwave meals. Sometimes I buy stuff at the grocery store to cook, but most of the time I can't get motivated to cook for just myself."

Aaron decided to switch to another topic. "So, tell me about your family."

"I just did."

Aaron looked puzzled. "No, I mean your mom and dad. And your siblings, if you have any."

Ryan thought about how he wanted to respond to this. He wanted to keep things with Aaron positive and focus on the future, not the past.

"Okay. So, I believe we have two families – our biological family and our logical family. Or I guess you could say our chosen family. My chosen family was Hal, Ted, Darnell, and Ricky. It's still Ted and Darnell and a couple of guys here. One is the guy named Eddie I roomed with when I came here for my summer internship back in 2011. He works at Technovations, too. He's sort of taken Hal's place as my older, wiser mentor."

Ryan paused. "Now as for my biological family, I don't have any contact with them. I haven't since 2007. I really don't want to get into what happened, 'cause it was ugly and kind of painful. Let's just say my parents couldn't deal with me being gay. But that's in the past. I want to stay focused on the present and the future."

Aaron said, "Yeah, I know what you mean. When my parents found out Desert Pride is a gay band, they gave me all kinds of shit. Like, I hadn't even come out yet, but they didn't want me hanging around with … homosexuals, as they would call them, although sometimes my dad used worse words than that. Anyway, Mom started calling me every day and sending me emails with, like, lists of all the fundamentalist churches in the area, lists of other bands I could play in, bullshit from Family-Focused Ministries… stuff like that. Anyway, once I finally accepted that I'm gay, I told them and they totally lost their shit. So I hung up on them, blocked their calls, and set up an email rule that sends their emails to the Trash. So yeah, I'm not talking to my parents anymore either."

Ryan thought, *Whoa. That was kind of extreme. He flies off the handle pretty quickly. His parents weren't trying to force him to see a therapist or send him off to a gay conversion therapy camp like mine did.*

Aaron asked, "Do you have any siblings?"

Ryan looked away, an expression of heartbreak on his face. "One little brother, Brandon. He's eight years younger than me. I haven't seen him since I left home."

Ryan again looked like he could cry at any moment. Aaron thought, *I so wish I hadn't asked that. What was I thinking? God, I'm such an idiot.*

They ate some more of their dinner in awkward silence. Aaron thought, *How can I salvage this evening?* "Have you seen any good movies lately?"

Ryan replied, "I don't see movies in theaters very often. I've got a whole bunch of movies here. A lot of gay classics. After Hal died, the executor of his estate said I could take any of them I wanted. I took them all. Otherwise, they probably would have been thrown away."

Aaron said, "Or donated."

Ryan smiled, "Um… some of those movies aren't very … donatable." He smiled, hoping Aaron would get the drift. He didn't.

"How come?"

"They're porn." Ryan saw the surprised look on Aaron's face. "Not all of them, just maybe a third of them. But there are a lot of gay classics like *Priscilla, Queen of the Desert, Brokeback Mountain, the Bird Cage, Sordid Lives…* stuff like that." Ryan thought for a moment. He and his housemates often watched a movie together after dinner on Family Night. "Wanna watch a movie after dinner?"

Aaron wondered, *Does he mean porn or not porn? If he wants to watch porn, things could get interesting. It's 7:35 now. I was hoping to be home by 9:00 so I could get a good night's sleep, but I want to spend time with him.* "Yeah, I guess so, as long as I don't stay out too late." *Dammit. I just told him that I'm not open to anything else happening this evening.* "I guess we can kinda play it by ear."

They carried their plates, glasses, and the empty pizza pan back into the kitchen. Then Ryan led Aaron down the hallway and into the first room on the right. "This is my media room. My videos are on those shelves over there. Why don't you take a look through them and see if anything pops out at you?"

Aaron glanced around the room. There were several shelf units with CDs, one with books, and two that were full of DVDs, Blu-rays, and a few old VHS tapes. There was an entertainment center with a receiver, a turntable, a CD player, and a couple other pieces of equipment Aaron couldn't identify. In the center of the room was a comfortable recliner with a small table next to it and a floor lamp behind it. Large speakers faced the chair, positioned to achieve good stereo separation. There were a few fake plants here and there. In the corner was an empty music stand and Ryan's trumpet case.

Aaron scanned some of the videos and recognized only a few titles. "Umm… How can I tell which ones are porn and which ones aren't?"

Ryan laughed. "Don't worry, none of them are. I keep the porn in my bedroom for obvious reasons. The bottom three shelves are jazz videos."

Aaron scanned the shelves. "I don't recognize most of these. Why don't you suggest something?"

"What kind of movies do you like?"

"Comedy, drama, rom-com – anything, really, as long as it's not too violent."

"Oh, I hate violent movies. So, let me think… How about *Priscilla, Queen of the Desert*?" Ryan pulled the case off the shelf and looked at the back. "It's an hour and 43 minutes long. Is that okay or should I pick something shorter?"

Aaron thought about asking for something shorter but decided he could stay a little later in the interest of spending more time with Ryan. "That sounds fine." He took another look around. "This is quite a set-up you have here."

"Yeah, thanks. I decided to put all my music and audio stuff in this room since it's closest to the center of the house. I ran speaker cables from the closet up into the attic, then to various places around the house. I have speakers in here, the living room, the dining room, the family room, my office, my bedroom, and outdoors on the patio and next to the pool. I can choose which ones are on and off. That way I can hear the music wherever I go in the house." He pressed a few buttons and turned the system off, then led Aaron back into the family room. He powered up the TV and entertainment center. "Would you like another Long Island?"

"I probably shouldn't, since I have to drive home and get up early tomorrow. It was great, though! If you have Dr Pepper or something like that, that would be good. If not, water would be fine."

"I have Dr Pepper! It's my favorite, too."

Aaron sat down on the sofa in the middle of the room. Ryan returned with two large glasses of Dr Pepper on ice and started the movie. He sat down on the sofa, leaving a couple of feet between him and Aaron.

They didn't say much as they watched the movie. When it finished, Ryan asked, "How did you like it?"

Aaron had a hard time understanding some of the dialog due to the Australian accents and what he assumed were references to gay culture he didn't get. "It was a lot of fun." He would have liked to stay longer and discuss the movie, but he knew he shouldn't. "I should probably get going. But I really had a great time this evening."

"Thanks. So did I. I'm glad you came over."

"That pizza was amazing. So was the Long Island." *So are you.*

"Thanks. It was nice to have someone to cook for."

"Well... Have a great week."

"You too."

Ryan ushered Aaron to the door and they hugged.

Aaron said, "Maybe we can get together later in the week, before you head off to Buenos Aires."

"Yeah, that would be great."

"I'll text you."

Ryan smiled. "Sounds good."

Aaron had no idea what to do next. Kiss him? Hug him? Just turn and leave?

For an awkward moment, they just looked at each other. Then Ryan hugged Aaron again. They smiled at each other. Ryan opened the door for Aaron and said, "Have a safe trip home."

"I will."

As Aaron walked to his car, he thought, *I'm such a klutz.*

A Wednesday Evening Tradition

Wednesday, June 1, 2016

On Wednesday morning, after Aaron ran, showered, and ate, he sat down at his computer. Since he had little time to be online on Monday and Tuesday, Wednesday was always a catch-up day. Before he got into his email and Facebook, he sent Ryan a text.

Hey! How's your week going?

Fine. &U?

Good. Two long days, but now I have five days off. 😊

Cool. Must be nice.

Yeah, in some ways.

Want to go running Saturday morning?

How early? I ran at 8 today and it was already hot.

How about 7?

> Sounds good. Meet at your place?

Several minutes passed before Ryan responded. Aaron thought, *Maybe he got a phone call or someone stopped by his office.* He waited anxiously for Ryan's reply.

> Okay. But I don't mind going to your place some of the time. It's not fair to make you do all the driving.

Aaron thought, *Yeah, but I don't want him to see where I live. Compared to his house, this is a slum. Oh well, he's going to see it sooner or later. And it would be nice to see him before Saturday.* Then he had an idea.

> Would you like to come to my place for dinner this evening? I usually have sushi on Wednesday.

> That would be fun. I love sushi.

> And sake too? ☺

> Definitely. What time?

> Whatever's good for you. I'm here all day.

> How about 6:15?

> Cool

Aaron typed his address into a text message and sent it.

Aaron set his phone down and began pacing around his apartment. He felt an odd mixture of elation and apprehension. He walked to his front door and turned around to face his living room. He tried to imagine what first impressions someone would form upon seeing his abode for the first time.

Aaron spent the next five hours decluttering his entire apartment. He had cleaned his apartment thoroughly when his parents came to visit in April, but that was six weeks ago. He vacuumed, dusted, cleaned the entire kitchen, and scrubbed the toilet. He had no idea whether they might end up in the bedroom, but he washed the sheets and pillowcases anyway. Finally, at around 2:30, he realized he hadn't eaten lunch yet. He cobbled together an assortment of leftovers from the refrigerator. It would be good to have those gone anyway, in case Ryan looked in there for some reason.

After lunch, Aaron visited a nearby department store and bought a few artificial plants, nice chopsticks, and a sake set. Since it was the beginning of Pride Month, they had a display of rainbow-colored merchandise and T-shirts. Aaron was amazed that stores would even sell such things. Wouldn't they attract protesters and boycotts? Aaron marveled at the array of products that were available in rainbow colors. He bought a rainbow-striped candle, a few rainbow drinking glasses, a set of rainbow-themed potholders and an oven mitt, and a set of six drink coasters, one in each color.

Next, he stopped at Food World, where he bought sushi every Wednesday. He debated whether to buy a more expensive assortment instead of the usual rolls that were on sale for $5. But if he was going to introduce Ryan to his Wednesday sushi tradition, he needed to go with the usual fare. He did spring for a more expensive bottle of sake.

Aaron returned home at 5:00. He had just over an hour until Ryan was due to arrive. He positioned his new plants around the living room, placed the rainbow coasters and candle on the coffee table, and took one more look around. *I wish I had bought some artwork for the walls. Oh well, this is as good as it's going to get for today.*

He took a shower and put on fresh clothes. He debated what sort of music he should play, if any. He didn't have much in the way of jazz or other music that would settle comfortably in the background. He chose a solo guitar

CD that was kind of new-agey and improvisational. He could set it to repeat and hopefully, Ryan wouldn't notice.

***

Ryan knocked on the door of Aaron's apartment at 6:15 on the dot. Aaron hurried to the door, paused long enough to take a deep breath, then swung the door open wide. "Hey! Come in, come in!"

Ryan smiled. Once Aaron had closed the door, they hugged. Ryan held Aaron slightly longer than a typical hello hug among friends.

Aaron asked, "Did you have any trouble finding the place?" *Duh! Of course not. He arrived right on time. That was dumb.*

"No, your directions were perfect."

"Great."

"Here, I brought you something." Ryan handed Aaron a brown paper bag. Aaron pulled out a bottle of amaretto.

"Oh, wow, thanks! So, uh… I've never had this before. Do you mix it with something or do you sip it?"

"Either. It goes well with Dr Pepper or you can just sip it on the rocks."

"Cool. So, anyway, welcome to my humble abode. There's not much to it… just what you see here and two bedrooms – one for my bed and one I use for my office. Oh, and a bathroom, of course."

Ryan scanned the room. "This is a lot like the apartment I had when I first moved to Scottsdale. It's nice."

"So, how was your day?"

"It was okay. I spent most of it in meetings. Sometimes when I leave work at the end of the day, I wonder whether I got anything important done."

"I guess that's one good thing about my job. I never have to go to meetings. Speaking of which, did you notice the HealthPro store on the corner where you turned left to get here?"

Ryan nodded.

"That's where I work. I can walk to work, which is nice. And there are all kinds of stores and restaurants at that corner, so I pretty much have everything I need within walking distance."

"Nice. That's one thing about my place. If I want anything, I have to get in the car and drive a couple of miles."

With the small talk out of the way, there was a brief, awkward silence.

Aaron said, "So, are you hungry? Wanna get started?"

"I'm starving. I've been looking forward to this all day."

So have I. You have no idea. Aaron smiled and led Ryan over to his kitchen table. "Have a seat." He opened the oven, where two small plates with spring rolls were staying warm. He grabbed two of his new rainbow potholders, pulled them out, and carried them over to the table. Then he retrieved two small ramekins with dipping sauce from the refrigerator and set them next to the plates.

Ryan smiled and said, "When you first reached into the oven I thought, he didn't bake the sushi, did he?"

Aaron chuckled self-consciously. "No, I at least know enough not to do that.*" Oh, God. Now I made it sound like he insulted me. C'mon, Aaron, get your act together. Stop saying stupid shit.*

Ryan said, "Of course. I didn't mean to imply that–"

"Oh, I know. I don't know why I said that. So, uh, would you like some sake?"

"Of course!"

Aaron opened the refrigerator and pulled out the sake bottle. He filled each of their small sake cups, then poured more in the little pitcher that came with the sake set. He put the bottle back in the fridge and sat down.

Ryan lifted his cup and held it toward Aaron. "Cheers! To good food and good friends!"

Aaron clinked his cup against Ryan's and took a sip.

Ryan said, "That's delicious." He dipped the end of one of his spring rolls into the sauce and took a bite. "MMMmmm… These are good."

"Yeah. I don't usually have that with my sushi. But for tonight, I thought, what the heck? Why not?"

"So what did you do today?"

"To be honest, I cleaned all day."

"Well, you did a great job. The place looks immaculate. But you didn't need to go to all the effort for me."

"That's okay, it needed it. I haven't given the place a good thorough cleaning since my parents were here six weeks ago." *Oh, great. I just told him I'm usually a slob.*

They finished their spring rolls. Aaron jumped up, removed their plates, and brought out two plates of sushi from the fridge. At least he thought to transfer the sushi out of the rectangular plastic containers they came in.

"Would you like some more sake?"

"Sure."

Aaron picked up the small pitcher and started to pour sake into Ryan's glass. He underestimated how fast it would come out, and sake spilled over the edge of the glass and onto the table. "Shit!"

Aaron rushed over to the paper towel dispenser and disengaged the roll from the holder. He began frantically wiping the spill from the table while Ryan lifted his plate. "Oh, geez, I'm sorry. I'm such a klutz."

Ryan smiled. "Don't worry. I've been known to spill things too."

After Aaron had mopped up the spill, he threw the wet wad of paper towel in the trash can and returned the paper towel roll to its holder. *Jesus Christ, could this be going any worse?*

As Aaron returned to the table with a flustered look on his face, Ryan stood up. "C'mere." Ryan wrapped his arms around Aaron and held him until he could feel the tension in Aaron's body start to relax. He ran one hand gently up and down Aaron's back. He whispered, "Relax… it's okay." Finally, he took a step back so he could look into Aaron's eyes. He moved his hands to Aaron's sides, just above his waist. "You seem awfully nervous. Is everything okay?"

Aaron sighed. "Kinda. Well, not really. I guess I wanted everything to be just right."

"And it's not?"

"No. Well, it's not just that. It's… I guess I feel kind of self-conscious about my apartment. And where I live. And, well, everything. I mean, you have this nice house in Scottsdale with a pool and everything. Then you made that incredible homemade pizza, and here I am serving you store-bought sushi that was on sale. And, well, I… I… I guess I wonder what you must think, and–"

"Aaron?"

"I just wanted to make a good first impression, but now–"

"Aaron?" Ryan gently placed his finger against Aaron's lips to get him to stop talking.

"Aaron, you made a good first impression on me a week and a half ago. And as for what I think of you, well, obviously I must think you're pretty nice or I wouldn't be getting together with you so often. Look… I didn't come here to inspect your apartment or compare it to my house. This is a nice place. There's nothing wrong with it. And the sushi's fine. I love sushi. No… I came here to see *you*."

Ryan gave Aaron a quick kiss on the cheek. "Relax. Everything's fine. I like you. Let's just enjoy hanging out together, okay?"

Aaron forced a smile. "Okay."

"Now let's dig into that sushi!"

They sat down and each took a bite. Aaron didn't say anything, and Ryan could tell he was still nervous. "Tell me more about Desert Pride."

"What do you want to know?"

"Whatever. Do you like the people? Do you like the music? How good are they?"

"The people are really nice. It's great to be a part of a group again and have friends. Up until a couple of months ago, I was pretty lonely and unhappy. I mean, I like living out here and everything, but I hadn't made any real friends yet. And I didn't realize how much I missed playing music. I stopped playing when I started pharmacy school, and I guess I never thought about when, or if, I'd ever play again. The music is typical concert band stuff. The director's good; he has good rehearsal technique and he's nice. So between playing my trombone again, having a bunch of new friends, and finally coming out of the closet, I've been really happy lately."

"That's great. I'm surrounded by people at work every day. It's not like they're close friends, but they're nice. So I have people to say hi to and eat lunch with if I want to. But yeah, I miss music."

"Are you out at work?"

"Kinda. Like I don't tell people in so many words, but I know most of my co-workers have figured it out. I'm pretty sure my manager is a lesbian, but we've never talked about it. They have an LGBT employee group at work. Eddie, the guy I stayed with during my internship, belongs to it and he said I should check it out. He's introduced me to some of his friends who work there. But I guess I'm not that interested in having everyone at work know I'm gay. I'd rather keep my work and my social life separate."

Aaron asked, "Aside from the running group, do you have many gay friends?"

"Not really. I'm not that close to most of the other guys in the running group. I mean, they're nice and I chat with them when we're there. Once in a while, someone will have a party and I'll go to that. But mostly it's just Eddie and a couple of other guys at work. And now you."

Ryan paused while he ate a bite of sushi, and to give Aaron a chance to talk if he wanted to say something. He didn't, so Ryan said, "And that's okay. I'm an introvert, so I don't have to be around people a lot. I prefer to deal with people one-on-one or in small groups. I don't like crowds, which is why I don't go out to bars and I'm not so inclined to join the gay group at work."

Aaron thought, *And that means you might not join the band.*

They finished their sushi, so Aaron got up and cleared the plates from the table. He loaded them into the dishwasher, then asked, "Would you like some more sake or do you want to switch to Dr Pepper?"

"Dr Pepper would be nice. Thanks."

Aaron retrieved two of his new rainbow-striped glasses from the cupboard, added ice, and filled them with Dr Pepper. He handed one glass to Ryan. Ryan looked at the glass with a hint of disapproval, but he took the glass and said, "Thanks."

"Wanna go sit in the living room?"

"Sure." When they sat down on the couch, Ryan noticed the rainbow-colored candle and coasters. "For someone who's only been out of the closet for two months, you're really into the rainbow thing, aren't you?"

"Yeah, I guess. Now that I'm not hiding from myself anymore, it's like … I dunno … a whole new world has opened up for me. I finally feel like I have somewhere I belong. But anyway, I was out earlier today picking up a few things, and they had this display of all kinds of rainbow stuff. I guess it's Pride Month. I was actually surprised that a regular store would sell that kind of stuff. Like, wouldn't other people complain? Anyway, I guess I made a few impulse purchases. Just to support a gay-friendly business, you know?"

"Yeah, I guess. It's hard to know whether they really support gay people year-round or if they see an opportunity to make money off of us. And perpetuate stereotypes."

"What do you mean?"

"Well, just because we're gay, does that mean we all want to fly rainbow flags and wear rainbow clothes and buy rainbow things? I mean, I'm not ashamed of being gay but I don't see a need to go around labeling myself."

Aaron had no idea what to say. Thinking back on it, he wasn't sure why he purchased those things. It seemed like a good idea at the time.

Ryan said, "Anyway, if you like this stuff, that's fine. It's funny… this reminds me of this time right after my junior year of high school. That was what, 2007? Yeah. Nine years ago. Seems like forever. Anyway, my best friend Chris and I went to Kansas City one Saturday morning to go to some used record stores. Then we ate lunch at a barbecue place that's popular in KC. After that, we drove past a park where they were having a gay pride festival. Chris wanted to go, so I said okay. He was like a kid in a candy store. It was like gay, gay, gay all over the place and he was totally into it. There was a booth where they were selling all kinds of gay T-shirts, and he bought several. Like there was this one that said, 'I'm not gay, but my boyfriend is,' and it had an arrow pointing one way. And there were others that had the arrow pointing the other way. So he wanted to buy one of each and I'm like 'There's no way in hell I can wear that shirt anywhere.' Anyway, he was all enthusiastic about the whole gay community thing, and I was like, 'Why do I have to label myself and be part of some community?' It's nobody else's business. Anyway, you kind of remind me of him."

"Uhhh… Is that a good thing or a bad thing?"

"Neither. It just is. I mean, he was so excited about being gay and finding out there's a gay community and lots of other gay people. And you're kind of in the same place now. It's cute, really. But I was so terrified about my parents finding out I couldn't get into it with that level of enthusiasm. I was like yeah, I'm gay, so let's just get on with life, you know?"

Aaron nodded, but he wasn't sure he knew. "So, what do you feel like doing? Wanna watch a movie or something? I don't have a video collection like yours, but we can watch something on Netflix."

Ryan thought for a moment. "Nah, we watched a movie on Sunday. It's nice out. You wanna go for a walk?"

Aaron thought quickly. They could walk through the nice residential neighborhood east of the apartment complex. "Sure."

They spent an hour and a half walking up and down tree-lined streets with upper-middle-class houses. It was still hot out, but with the sun down and a breeze blowing, it was quite pleasant. They talked about their jobs, and Ryan asked Aaron to tell him about his experiences in the Ohio State University Marching Band and pharmacy school. Aaron was aware that he was doing most of the talking, but Ryan seemed interested and kept asking questions to keep the conversation flowing.

When they arrived back at Aaron's apartment at around 8:30, Ryan said, "This has been fun. Thanks for inviting me over."

"Thanks for being willing to join me for my weekly Wednesday night sushi routine. I know it was kind of simple, but…"

"Sometimes the simple things in life are the best. I'd be happy to join you for Wednesday night sushi anytime you want."

For a moment, neither of them said anything. Aaron was trying to figure out a way to ask Ryan if he'd like to stay a while longer, but he couldn't think of what to say that wouldn't seem too pushy. At least he knew that 'Wanna fuck?' wouldn't be the best thing to say right now. 'Let me show you my bedroom' would be almost as bad.

Ryan said, "Well, I should probably be on my way…"

"Sorry I was such a dork earlier. I'm usually not that uptight and klutzy."

Ryan chuckled. "No worries. I could tell you were a little nervous at first, but after we got settled in, I had a great time."

"I don't know what happened. I just–"

"I do."

Aaron stopped.

Ryan smiled. "Having me come over tonight was a big deal to you. You were worried about what I'd think. You wanted everything to be perfect. So you ended up putting a lot of pressure on yourself, which made everything harder than it needed to be."

Aaron averted his eyes downward. "Yeah, that pretty much sums it up."

Ryan placed two fingers under Aaron's chin and lifted it gently so Aaron could look him in the eyes. When he did, Ryan placed his hands on Aaron's sides. "Everything *was* perfect. And I'm flattered that you placed so much importance on this. It makes me feel special."

Aaron smiled sheepishly.

Ryan said, "And for the record, I spent all day Sunday cleaning my house for you." He wrapped his arms around Aaron and kissed him. After about ten seconds of romantic bliss, but before the kisses would reach the next level of passionate energy, Ryan pulled away. "Well, I guess I'll see you Saturday morning at seven."

"Wait a minute. Isn't that the day you fly to Buenos Aires?"

"Yeah. But I don't need to leave for the airport until 11:30 that morning."

"Are you sure you don't mind having me come over on the morning you leave for your trip?"

"It'll be okay. Once the flight leaves Dallas, it's 11 hours to Buenos

Aires. I'll sleep on the plane. And I'd like to see you again before I go."

"Well, okay, then. Oh, and uh… We'll probably be pretty hot and sweaty when we're done. Do you think maybe we could get in your pool? Just for a little bit?"

Ryan thought for a moment. *If we start running at 7:00, we'll probably be done by 8:30. That's kind of early to get in the pool, but he's right… we'll be overheated. I guess as long as we're done by 9:00, it'll be okay. But I know what he has in mind.* "Yeah, okay, we can get in the pool for a little while. So bring your swimsuit. I have plenty of towels."

That wasn't quite what Aaron was hoping to hear, but he said, "Okay, then. See you Saturday morning at seven."

"Okay. Bye!" Ryan leaned in and gave Aaron a quick kiss on the lips. He smiled, turned, and walked out the door.

Running

Saturday, June 4, 2016

Aaron arrived at Ryan's house at 7:00 a.m., dressed in his running attire. He brought a gym bag with his swimsuit and regular clothes to change into afterward. Ryan greeted him at the door. As soon as Aaron stepped in, Ryan gave him a quick kiss and said, "Ready?"

Aaron placed his gym bag on the nearest chair and said, "Sure. Let's do this."

They ran along the streets in Ryan's neighborhood until they reached the same multi-use trail they ran on two weeks ago. They turned north and ran five miles, well past the point where the running club had turned around. They didn't say much as they ran since heavy breathing made conversation difficult. When they reached their turning point and rested, Aaron was too tired to say much of anything. The heat and Ryan's fast pace were taking a toll. As they got up to begin their return journey, Aaron said, "Could we slow down a little?"

Ryan smiled. "Sure. It's pretty hot out."

"That pool is going to feel sooo good."

When they returned to Ryan's home at 8:30, Aaron was exhausted. He wondered if he would have the energy to drive home. Hopefully, the pool would refresh him.

Ryan said, "Why don't you change in the hall bathroom? I'll meet you in the kitchen in a few minutes."

Aaron changed into the Speedo he wore as a swimmer on his high school swim team and as a lifeguard during the summers while he was in college. Thanks to his regular running, his swimsuit still fit well. When he entered the kitchen, he saw Ryan wearing oversized board shorts. For a moment, he was nervous about the obvious mismatch, but Ryan didn't seem to care.

Ryan asked, "What do you want to drink? Dr Pepper? Water?"

"Water, please. And lots of ice."

Ryan filled two large plastic glasses with ice and water, then they headed out to the pool.

Once they were in the pool, Aaron said, "So, you said you were on the track team at your high school. What was that like?"

"It was fun – more fun than I thought it would be. Chris was on the team too, so that helped. We ran together a lot during the off-season. Anyway, my junior year, the team did really well, so we went to the state championship track meet in Wichita."

"Oh, wow! You went to the state championships?"

"Yeah. Well, keep in mind, this was Kansas. Not one of your more populous states."

"But still! How did you do?"

"It was kind of mixed. I finished first in the 300-meter hurdles, but only fourth in the 100-meter. And our 4x440 relay team with me and Chris and two other guys finished third. I know that sounds good, but on a better day I probably could have finished first in all of them."

"What happened?"

Ryan paused as he debated how much he wanted to say. "Well, that's kind of an interesting story. See, the state championship meet is a two-day event. Since Wichita was three hours away, we stayed in this cheap hotel Friday night. Of course, Chris and I shared a room. Anyway, to make a long story short, that was the night when we both discovered the other one was gay."

"Ahhh! I'll bet that was a fun night!"

"Well, not as fun as it might have been. We both kinda suspected the other one was gay, but we had no idea how to bring it up. And like, what if you say, 'I'm gay,' and the other guy isn't? That could have ruined our friendship. Besides, I was so scared to come out, I wasn't even ready to admit to myself that I was gay yet."

"So what happened? If you don't mind, of course."

"Well... first, we were looking to see what was on TV, and *Brokeback Mountain* was on HBO. Have you ever seen it?"

"I've heard of it, but I've never seen it."

"We'll have to watch it sometime. It's about two gay cowboys back in the sixties. Anyway, that at least brought up the topic of homosexuality. So we were lying in bed that night, and I couldn't fall asleep to save my life. Part of it was being in a strange bed, but mostly it was wondering if anything was going to happen with Chris. I had no idea what to say or do, and I guess he didn't either. So finally, he said, 'Are you still awake?' And I said, 'Yeah, I can't fall asleep.' And I gave him all these excuses about being in a strange bed, the noisy air conditioner, thinking about the meet tomorrow, and all that. Then he said, 'Maybe we can't sleep because we're both wondering if something is going to happen.' And of course, that was it. So we did a bunch of hugging and kissing. We were actually making out pretty hot and heavy. But I wasn't ready to go any further. I mean, I knew I wanted to, but I still wondered if it was wrong, you know? I had a lot of religious baggage back then. So nothing happened beyond kissing. At least, not that night."

Aaron's cock was straining at his swimsuit. Thank God the material was substantial enough to keep it from showing too much. He hoped Ryan wouldn't see it. He seemed too focused on telling the story to notice.

Ryan continued. "Anyway, we didn't get to sleep until 3:00 a.m. So we were really tired the next day. When I ran my first hurdles event, the 100-meter, I knocked down four of the ten hurdles. I mean, I've never done that badly. And then during the relay, Chris ran third and I ran fourth, and when we handed off the baton, I dropped it."

"Oh, shit."

"Yeah, really. So I picked it up and somehow I found the energy to overtake a couple of the guys that had passed, and I almost caught up with one more. Anyway, we ended up finishing third, but if I hadn't dropped the baton, we would have won."

"Wow, that really sucks."

"Tell me about it. I felt terrible about it at the time, but in the long run – no pun intended – it was just a high school track meet. Life goes on."

"So, are you in touch with Chris?"

Ryan became uncomfortable. "Once in a while. He has a partner he's been with for like eight years now and they live in DC. Anyway, I should probably let you go. I need to finish packing for my trip."

They got out of the pool and dried off. Aaron returned to the hall bathroom to change into his street clothes. When he emerged, Ryan was in the family room.

Ryan said, "I'm sorry I ended our pool time abruptly. I just... well, I guess sometimes it's a little difficult for me to talk about Chris."

"That's okay. And I know you need to get things done. But I'm glad you made time for me this morning."

"So am I. Anyway, I'm looking forward to your concert. Since it's Sunday, you wanna come here for dinner afterward?"

"Sure. I have to do some stuff like help load the instrument truck and unload it at the church where we rehearse. That'll take about an hour and a half, but I can come up after that."

"That'll be fine. It will give me some time to get stuff ready."

"Okay, well... I guess I'll see you then. Have a great trip."

"I will."

They paused.

Aaron had several things I wanted to say, but this probably wasn't the time to say them. It was time for him to leave. He simply said, "I'll miss you."

Ryan smiled. "I'll be thinking about you. I'll send you a couple of emails when I get the chance."

They kissed. Then Aaron picked up his gym bag and turned toward the door. "Bye!"

"Bye!"

***

Later that day, when Aaron was on Facebook, he received a message from Kent.

> Hey, how's it going?

> Okay. U?

> Pretty good. Trying to stay cool.

> Yeah, it's pretty hot out.

> RU seeing Ryan this weekend?

We went running this morning. But now he's on his way to Buenos Aires for two weeks to see his friend Ted.

So how's it going with you two?

Pretty good, but kinda weird.

How so?

Mixed signals. Like he seems interested but he doesn't want to get physical.

That *is* weird.

But I'm new to gay dating, so I don't know.

A couple of minutes went by without any messages from Kent. Aaron checked his newsfeed again. He was about to sign off when another message from Kent popped up.

You doing anything tonight?

Not really.

Wanna come up here for dinner? Nothing fancy, just hang out and talk.

Sure! What time? What can I bring?

6:00. Nothing. We've got everything we need. Maybe a bottle of wine.

White or red?

How about red?

Cool. See you then.

C-ya.

Kent disappeared, so Aaron signed off too.

Dinner and Dirt

Saturday, June 4, 2016

Aaron arrived at Kent and Justin's apartment promptly at 6:00. As he was walking toward their front door, a car pulled into the parking lot and parked in front of the building across from theirs. Aaron glanced over and saw Petunia get out of the car. Petunia waved and called out, "Heading to a party, are we?"

*No, **we** aren't, **I** am,* Aaron thought. "Just dinner with Kent and Justin."

Petunia feigned indignation. "And *I* wasn't invited?"

Aaron shrugged. "Hey, I didn't make up the guest list." He reached Kent and Justin's door and knocked, hoping they would let him in quickly. Thankfully, they did.

After hellos and hugs, Aaron said, "I just ran into Petunia. Don't be surprised if you get a call from him, trying to invite himself over."

Justin made a quick brushing-off gesture with his right hand. "I can handle it if he does."

Kent said, "He's just being the drama queen he is. We're used to it."

Aaron handed the bottle of wine to Kent.

Kent said, "We're having chili tonight. This Merlot will go great with it. Have a seat at the table, and I'll carry the pot over." He turned to Justin. "Sweetheart, would you slice the cornbread, please?"

After the meal was underway, Aaron asked, "So, how was your trip to Austin? Did you get Jeremy all settled in?"

Justin said, "It was a long-ass drive. Fifteen of the longest, most boring hours I've ever spent in my life. Have you ever driven across west Texas?"

Aaron replied, "No, just the panhandle. I came in on I-40 when I moved here from Ohio. But that was pretty boring, too."

Justin said, "Anyway, Austin is nice once you get there. We didn't get to see much because we were unloading the truck and helping him unpack. We wanted to fly back in time to make it to work on Tuesday. But I'd love to see more of it, as long as we can fly there."

Kent said, "Jeremy's apartment is nice. It's in a new complex with a gorgeous pool and a gym, and lots of restaurants and stuff close by."

Aaron said, "Sounds like he's pretty well set."

Kent said, "Yeah. He's excited about starting his new job and exploring his new town–"

"And new men!" Justin interjected.

"But part of him is sad about leaving Phoenix behind – the band, his friends…"

Justin finished Kent's sentence. "And you."

Aaron said, "What? Really?"

Kent said, "That's right. Your name came up a few times. Did you feel your ears burning?"

Justin said, "He likes you. He thought you were really nice."

Kent said, "He said it would have been nice to get to know you better. But the wheels had already been set in motion for his move, and he felt it was the right thing for him to do."

Justin said, "But I understand you two spent some, shall we say, *quality* time together."

Aaron blushed. *I thought we weren't supposed to talk about having sex with other people.* "Yeah, I guess you could say that. And… well, he was my first time."

Kent and Justin smiled mischievously. Aaron guessed they already knew that.

Kent said, "And apparently, you were a first time for him too."

"He told you that?"

They nodded. Kent said, "You made quite an impression on him."

Justin said, "And it looks like you're making an impression on Ryan, too."

"Well, kinda. I don't know. That's one reason I'm glad you guys invited me here tonight. I'm not sure what's going on, or if I'm doing the right things. I mean, we seem to be into each other and everything, but I'm not sure whether I should be going faster or slower, or how interested he is, or anything like that."

Kent said, "So, may I ask? Have you guys spent the night yet?"

"No! That's what I'm wondering about. I want to, but it's like he's pushing back. I mean, I know it's only been two and a half weeks, so maybe that's too soon. But, like, here's a good example. When Jeremy and I went hiking on South Mountain a few weeks ago, we were really hot afterward so we got in his pool – naked. And it wasn't even for sex, but I thought, you know, we're both guys. So what? And then the next time I went over, we got in his hot tub – naked. And that's when stuff started happening. But this morning, after Ryan and I went running, we were all hot and sweaty, so we got in his pool – with swimsuits. He specifically said, 'Bring your swimsuit.' And he was wearing these big-ass board shorts that went down to his knees. So if he's interested in me, why didn't he want us to get naked? Does he have a little dick or something? I mean, I don't really care, but–"

Justin cut in. "Oh, no. He *definitely* does not have a little dick."

Aaron looked puzzled. "How do you know?"

Kent replied, "We've seen it. Up close and personal."

Justin added, "*Very* personal. And *very* up."

Aaron still looked puzzled.

Justin said, "Remember how we met him on a gay cruise three years ago? Well, we hooked up with him."

Aaron's eyes bugged out. "But… you're a couple."

Kent said, "We have an open relationship. We love and trust each other completely. We're very secure as a couple and we know we want to spend the rest of our lives together. But we like a little variety now and then. We're totally honest with each other. We never do anything behind the other one's back. We only do it every now and then, and only when we know there's no chance of any emotional attachment."

Justin said, "So yeah, we did it with him. And let me tell you, it's *huge*."

Kent said, "*HUUUUGE*. I mean, we both love to bottom and we can usually take whatever comes along–"

"–Literally–"

"–but that… *That* was a challenge."

Aaron was stunned, both about Ryan's ample endowment and that Kent and Justin had sex with him. He wondered how much he should say, but obviously, Kent and Justin had no issues with discussing personal matters. "So… since you know I've had sex with Jeremy and, well… I'm no expert, but I thought his dick was kinda big, or at least thick. And it was all I could do to take that."

Kent said, "And for your first time, no less."

Justin said, "Yeah, he does have a thick one. It's thicker than Ryan's. But with Ryan, it's more about length than girth."

Aaron said, "So wait a minute… You guys have had sex with Jeremy too?"

Justin said, "Yeah, just last weekend. Sort of a housewarming celebration, you might say."

Kent added, "He let us sleep on his queen-size bed and he was going to sleep on the couch, but we all ended up on the bed. Since he's not in the band anymore, he lives in Austin, and he's a free man now, we thought, why not?"

"So… how do guys learn to take dicks up their butts? Especially big ones?"

Justin said, "Well, practice, for one thing. The more you do it, the easier it gets. You learn to relax more."

Aaron said, "Yeah, but I'm already dating Ryan. And I hope we start having sex sooner rather than later. I don't want to go out and sleep with a bunch of other guys now just to get ready for Ryan."

Kent asked, "Have you guys actually said you're dating yet?"

Aaron said, "No. So far, it's just been like 'I had a good time. When do you want to hang out next?' I guess what I'm wondering is, when guys start seeing each other, when's the right time to start having sex? How do you bring it up?"

Justin said, "Pun intended, right?"

It took Aaron a moment, but he got it. "Yeah, right."

Kent said, "Well, it depends. Guys are different. Some guys want to jump in bed right away and others want to get to know each other first. Still, I'd say by the fourth or fifth date."

Justin nodded. "Yeah, that seems about right."

Kent asked, "Have you talked about it yet?"

"No. It's like, I'm so new to being gay I don't know how guys are supposed to do things. And to be honest, I'm a little intimidated by him. I mean, he seems so perfect in so many ways. I'm kinda surprised he's even interested in me. So I don't want to say or do anything that might mess things up."

Justin said, "Sounds like you're letting him drive the car where this is concerned."

"Yeah. Where everything is concerned, really."

Kent said, "Well, you should be an equal part of this relationship. If he's interested in you, that means he sees things he likes about you. You need to talk about what he wants and what you want, then find common ground. That's what relationships are all about – some give and some take. And getting things out in the open."

Justin said, "And don't sell yourself short. You've got a lot going for you."

Kent said, "Okay, so here's my advice. And you can take it or leave it. Give it a week or two after he gets back. If he starts getting more interested in you sexually, great. If not, then talk with him about it. I know it will be kind of awkward, but being able to talk about uncomfortable things is one of the skills you need for a good relationship."

"Yeah, that sounds like a good plan." Aaron thought for a moment. "So, based on what you've seen, does he hook up with other guys much?"

Kent said, "I don't know. We mostly see him in the running club and sometimes in the hiking club. We get together for dinner once in a while. So we don't know much about his day-to-day life. But he's never talked about it."

Justin said, "Just like he doesn't talk much about a lot of things."

Kent said, "Still, I don't think I've ever seen him with a boyfriend or heard him talk about one. So yeah, I'd say he probably doesn't hook up much, if at all. He doesn't seem like the type."

Aaron said, "Okay. So maybe he doesn't want to rush into having sex."

Kent said, "That wouldn't surprise me. But like I said, if it doesn't start happening pretty soon you need to talk about it."

Justin said, "You know, maybe he's holding off until he gets back from Argentina. He's visiting that guy he used to live with, right? That hunky ginger he was with on the cruise?"

Aaron said, "Yeah. Ted."

Justin said, "I'll bet you anything he's getting some while he's there. Then after he gets back, he'll get more serious with you."

"You really think so?"

Kent said, "Honey, Ted is *hot*! A total stud puppy. Man, I'd travel halfway around the world to get some of that."

Justin said, "Not to mention him wanting some of Ryan."

Aaron said, "I saw some pictures of him on the wall at Ryan's. He's definitely good-looking. And they seem pretty close."

Justin said, "And there you have it."

"Well, okay. I mean, yeah, we haven't committed to anything yet. But still, I don't want to go out and sleep with a bunch of guys just to get more experience with sex. I'm only interested in him."

Kent said, "Well then, another option would be to get a dildo and practice on that."

"Are you serious?"

Kent said, "Yes, I'm serious. Why not?"

"So where would I even go to get one? How would I know what to get?"

Kent said, "They have stores for that. For example, the Pleasure Palace. They have several locations around town. You live in Tempe, right? I think there's one on West Elliot."

Justin said, "As to what to get, well… get one that looks slightly larger than you could handle now. And get some lube and condoms while you're there."

Kent said, "We have a few. We're both bottoms. I mean, we'll top for each other, but a lot of times when we get together with someone else, it's so they'll fuck us. And sometimes we play with toys."

Aaron was speechless as he tried to process all this new information. Kent and Justin glanced at each other and communicated with their eyes.

Justin said, "C'mon, we'll show you what we have."

They led Aaron back into their bedroom and over to a dresser on the other side of the bed. Justin opened the third drawer and moved a few towels aside. He pulled out an 8-inch specimen and said, "Something like this would be a good start." Next, he pulled out a dildo that looked to be about 18 inches long and had a head on each end. "We have a lot of fun with this one." Aaron stared in amazement. Then Justin pulled out a box that was about three inches wide, three inches deep, and twelve inches tall. The box had an illustration of some guy who looked like he could be a younger version of Ryan with the words, 'Luke Loadstar Celebrity Dildo.' Underneath, in smaller letters, it proclaimed, 'Molded directly from the legendary porn star's giant cock.'

Aaron asked, "Who's Luke Loadstar?"

Kent said, "A gay porn star. He was really big – pun intended – six or eight years ago. I don't think he's doing porn anymore."

Justin reached into the box and pulled out a dark red velvet bag with a gold drawstring on top. He loosened the drawstring and pulled out an 11-inch lifelike latex dong. It looked almost real, complete with veins and natural coloring. Justin held it by the balls and wagged it in Aaron's direction. "This bad boy is a lot like what Ryan has."

Aaron stared at the massive mound of molded latex in front of him. He couldn't imagine that going into him – or anybody, for that matter. "Uh… Are there really guys with dicks that big?"

Kent said, "Yep. A small percentage, but they do exist. And they're in hot demand as porn stars."

Justin said, "If you can take this, you'll be able to handle Ryan."

Aaron looked terrified.

Kent said, "Start with the other one. Take your time, go slow, breathe deeply, and relax. Once you get comfortable with the smaller one, then try the larger one."

Justin added, "Use plenty of lube. And don't feel like you have to get every inch in. You probably can't. It's more about the thickness. Just do as much as you can, and you'll be okay."

Kent said, "And you can fuck him, too. He's versatile."

Justin said, "And besides. It's not so much about the specific things you do. Guys can do all kinds of things with each other. What you do isn't as important as the connection you're making. It's all about the intimacy, the deep personal connection."

Aaron thought, *It'll be a deep connection, all right.*

Kent feigned shock and said to Justin, "Did those words really come out of your mouth? Who are you, and what have you done with my slutty husband?"

Justin chuckled and said, "I know, right?" He put the immense, lifelike dildo back in its velvet bag and tightened the drawstring. He picked up the eight-inch dildo and extended them both toward Aaron. "Here. Use them with pride. Open yourself up to new experiences! Literally."

Aaron took them hesitantly.

Kent said, "We want them back at some point, but there's no hurry. Keep them as long as you need to."

Justin said, "And they're dishwasher safe, top rack. Just sayin'."

Aaron said, "Uh… thanks, I guess."

Kent said, "Oh honey, you'll thank us later."

Justin added, "So will Ryan."

Aaron thought, *I'm not about to tell Ryan I borrowed dildos from Kent and Justin. I can't believe I'm even doing this. I'm standing in a gay couple's bedroom talking about butt sex. A gay couple with an open relationship. And they're loaning me two of their dildos.*

For an awkward moment, nobody said anything. Then Aaron said, "Well, guys, I should probably be going. Thanks for the excellent dinner and the advice and, uh… this."

They left the bedroom and walked back out toward the living room. They exchanged goodbyes and hugs. As Kent was about to open the front door, Aaron remembered Petunia lived across the parking lot. "Do you have a bag I could put these in? Preferably not a clear one."

Justin smiled. "Sure." He looked in their pantry and found a brown paper grocery bag.

Shocking News

Sunday, June 12, 2016

This was Aaron's weekend to work. Since Ryan was in Argentina, it was just as well that he spent the weekend working rather than having time off with nothing to do.

After work, Aaron contemplated what he wanted to eat for dinner. Ryan's tradition of cooking a nice meal on Sunday evening was a good idea. He'd rather be eating Sunday dinner with Ryan, but eating alone had not stopped Ryan from honoring his tradition. So Aaron walked over to Food World and picked up a steak, a container of mashed potatoes, a bag of salad, a package of frozen garlic bread, and a bottle of red wine. He returned home and grilled the steak on the communal grill in the courtyard outside his front door.

Half an hour later, he was enjoying his meal at his kitchen table. As he ate, his thoughts wandered. *Man, this is delicious! I'm pretty good at grilling if I do say so myself. I need to grill steaks for Ryan sometime. I wonder if he'd be okay with having Sunday dinner here every now and then. Or maybe I could take steaks up to his place. He's got that nice barbecue island on his patio. We could spend Sunday afternoon in the pool, and maybe even have sex in it like Jeremy and I did. Then finish it off with a steak dinner. That would be just ... perfect.*

God, I've only known him for three weeks. We've only even seen each other, what? Six times? I can't believe I'm so wrapped up with him. It's kinda like I was with Jeremy, but even more intense. I really need to slow down. But... I can't help it!

As he ate another bite of steak and washed it down with a sip of wine, he thought, *I wonder if he and Ted have been screwing all week. Probably so. Kent and Justin seem to think they would. It makes sense. And it kind of bugs me. I know, we've only been seeing each other for three weeks and we haven't made any commitments, so it's not like he's cheating on me. So why do I feel like he is?*

I wonder if Ted can fit it all in. What if we get to that point and I can't?

Will he still be interested in me? God, if he thinks I'm lame in bed, especially after he and Ted have been having hot sex for two weeks… I don't even want to think about it.

But it was all Aaron could think about.

He ate the last bite of steak, cleared the table, and put the dirty dishes in the dishwasher. He poured another glass of wine, carried it to his desk, and turned the computer on.

He checked his email first. To his delight, there was an email from Ryan with attachments.

Hey Aaron,

Having a great time in Buenos Aires. It's an amazing city. So much beautiful architecture. And great food!

Ted lives in an area called Recoleta. It's charming – almost European. Tree-lined streets, sidewalk cafes… I could so live here! We've been to a couple of amazing art museums.

We're in Uruguay for the weekend. The capital, Montevideo, is right across from Buenos Aires. It's beautiful too! Today, we're in Punta Del Este. It's this cool beach town where a lot of rich people go for vacation. Lots of great art and food here, too! You'd love it.

I attached a couple of pictures. One is a selfie of me and Ted in front of Casa Rosada, the presidential palace. The one of me on the beach in front of the giant white hand coming out of the sand is in Punta Del Este. I've got lots more pictures I'll show you when I get back.

On Tuesday, we're going to fly over to Mendoza for a couple of days. That's the wine region in the western part of Argentina. Looking forward to some good wine tasting!

Enough for now. We're about to head out for dinner. Take care, and I'll see you when I get back. I'm looking forward to your concert!

Big hugs,

Ryan

Aaron clicked on the first picture to open it. Ryan and Ted were standing close together, almost head-to-head, with Casa Rosada in the background. They were obviously happy and comfortable being that close. It reminded him of the picture of him and Jeremy on South Mountain.

He opened the second picture. The sculpture of the giant white hand emerging from the sand was clever. There were dozens of other beachgoers in the picture, all trying to get a good picture of them with the hand. Ryan was wearing sunglasses, a tank top, and sandals. But what struck Aaron most was his swimsuit. He wasn't wearing the oversized board shorts he wore in the pool last weekend. He was wearing a skimpy swimsuit with high-cut sides and a generous pouch, which he filled with no problem. Aaron looked at some of the other men in the picture. Ryan's swimsuit wasn't out of place, but it was certainly the sexiest one in the picture. He spotted a few other men and women looking in his direction. He wondered what Ted was wearing. According to Kent and Justin and the pictures on Ryan's wall, Ted had an impressive physique. He probably looked great in a brief swimsuit, too.

Aaron closed the pictures and the email. He needed time to think about how he would respond.

He opened Facebook. His newsfeed was filled with shocked, stunned, and angry reactions to a shooting that had taken place at a nightclub in Orlando. He opened CNN and read the story. A gunman had killed 49 people and injured 53 others in the Pulse nightclub. It was a gay bar.

Aaron was overcome with sadness and horror. Sadness for the victims and their families. Horror at the realization that someone walked into a gay bar with the intent of murdering the patrons. He was rational enough to know that it could have been a school, a workplace, a concert, a church, or a movie theater. But as more information about the shooter came to light, it appeared that his hatred of LGBT people was the motivation for his crime.

Aaron thought, *You know, that could happen here. A homophobic gunman could walk into Raise! the Bar any time with an AR-15 and spray the place with bullets.*

I've cut off contact with my parents because they can't accept that I'm gay. I met a great guy, but then he moved away. Now I've met another guy I can't stop thinking about, but he's in Argentina fucking his buddy from college. And he doesn't seem interested in doing that with me.

This gay thing isn't so great after all.

Music to His Ears

Sunday, June 19, 2016

The next Sunday morning, Aaron drove to the Maricopa Cultural Center with his trombone and a garment bag with his tux. Throughout the dress rehearsal, Aaron couldn't stop thinking about where Ryan was. During the break, he checked the progress of the flight on his phone. *It says the flight from Atlanta to Phoenix is on time, but is he on it? What if he's so exhausted from the overnight flight that he skips the concert? What if he says he's too tired to have me over for dinner?*

When they broke for lunch at noon, Aaron checked his phone again. There was a text waiting for him from Ryan.

Made it home! Can't wait to see your concert — and you!

Whew — relieved! How are you holding up?

Okay. Kind of tired. Got some sleep on the plane. I'll be okay after I get more caffeine in me.

Cool. Meet me in the lobby afterward.

Looking forward to it!

Me too. Gotta run and grab lunch. C-ya soon!

Aaron put his phone back in his pocket. Everything was going according to plan. Ryan seemed genuinely excited about coming to the concert and seeing Aaron again.

***

The concert was Aaron's first performance since his senior year of college six years ago. He realized he missed the adrenaline rush of performing in front of a live audience.

The jazz ensemble opened the second act and played four songs. Aaron hung around backstage and listened. They sounded great. Aaron had no idea how they compared to Ryan's high school and college bands, but he hoped he was enjoying it. Then the wind ensemble returned and finished the concert.

Afterward, Aaron put his trombone away and headed out to the lobby to meet Ryan. Since Ryan was 6' 6", he was easy to spot. He was talking with Colin, the jazz ensemble director. Both men were smiling and having an enthusiastic discussion. Ryan glanced over and saw Aaron approaching. He turned back to Colin, exchanged a few more words, then shook his hand.

Ryan turned toward Aaron and grinned. When he reached Aaron, he threw his arms around him and swept him several inches off the floor. With their faces at the same level, Ryan planted a kiss on Aaron's lips. Aaron was starting to slide down through his tux, so Ryan set him down.

Ryan said, "Nice job! You guys sounded great!"

"Thanks! I thought it went pretty well."

"That was better than 'pretty well,' that was excellent! Seriously! I had no idea what to expect. But I am truly impressed!"

"Yeah, so was I when I heard them back in March."

Ryan took a step back. "Look at you! All dapper in your tux. You look so handsome!"

Aaron blushed. "Thanks. I've never had to play in a tux before. It's not what I would choose, but it's what they do."

"Well, you look nice. And you sounded even better!"

"Thanks. I see you were chatting with Colin."

"Yeah! That jazz ensemble kicked ass! I asked him to keep me in mind next time they have an opening for a trumpet or they need a sub or something.

He said they're starting back up on July 11 and asked if I'd come to the rehearsal."

"That's great! They'll be lucky to have you."

"I can't wait. But of course, I'm going to need to start practicing again. If I hit it every day, I might sound okay by then."

"I'm sure you'll do fine."

"And I'd like to play in the wind ensemble too. That is, if it's okay with you."

"Of course, it's okay with me! It's not like you need my permission anyway."

Ryan smiled. "It's wonderful to see you again. I thought about you a lot. We'd go to all these great places and I'd think, 'I'll bet Aaron would like this.'"

"Really?" Aaron couldn't tell if Ryan was serious or if he was blowing smoke up his ass. Maybe he was trying to make nice after spending two weeks fucking another guy.

"Really. It was a great trip. I saw a lot of cool stuff and it was great to see Ted again, but it's nice to be back home."

"Good. I'm glad you had a nice time."

Ryan asked, "So, are we still on for dinner?"

"Yeah. I'm up for it if you are. I know you're probably tired, so if you'd rather not…"

"I'm fine. See you in, what, about an hour and a half?"

"Yeah. Or maybe a little less. I'll get there as quickly as I can."

"Cool." Ryan gave Aaron another big hug, then he kissed him and turned to go.

***

At 6:30, Aaron arrived at Ryan's house. He had perspired heavily while loading and unloading the instrument truck on the hot June afternoon. Oh well, there was nothing he could do about it now. He rang the doorbell.

Ryan answered with a big smile and swung the door open for Aaron to enter. He started to give Aaron a hug, but Aaron put up his hand and said, "I'm all hot and sweaty from unloading the truck."

Ryan gave Aaron a big hug anyway. "That's okay. I like my men hot and sweaty."

"I don't smell very good either. Sorry."

"Don't worry about it. It doesn't bother me. I'm a runner, so I'm used to it."

Ryan led Aaron to the back patio. As before, jazz played softly from speakers that seemed to be everywhere. The tantalizing smell of grilling meat permeated the air. Ryan lifted the lid of the barbecue and a cloud of gray smoke escaped. He said, "I stopped and picked up a couple of steaks on the way home. I hope that's okay."

"Of course! I love steak."

"How do you like yours cooked?" Ryan asked as he grabbed a pair of tongs and flipped the steaks. The juices from the steaks set off a fresh round of sizzle.

"Medium or medium well. Whatever. As long as it's not raw or burnt, I'm good."

"Medium it is!" Ryan lowered the lid and led Aaron back inside. "Since it's hot out, I thought we'd eat inside." Ryan had set two places at the table in his dining room. There were salads at each place setting and several bottles of dressing in the middle of the table. There were also two candles waiting to be lit. Ryan said, "So I brought a bottle of Malbec back from Mendoza. I thought it would go well with the steak. How does that sound?"

"Fine, but you don't have to open it just for me. Why don't you save it for a special occasion?"

Ryan shrugged. "This occasion is special enough. A lot of people save things for special occasions and they end up hanging onto them for years. I like to find special occasions as I go along. Any occasion can be special if you decide to make it that way. Besides, you can buy wines from Argentina in the stores here."

Aaron remembered the bottle of Chardonnay he had kept in his refrigerator for over a year. "Yeah, you're probably right."

Ryan uncorked the bottle and poured a few ounces into their wine glasses. He handed one to Aaron and said, "To playing music again!"

Aaron smiled and clinked his glass. "To playing music together!" He took a sip. It was rich and full-bodied. It would, indeed, go well with steak.

Ryan swirled his glass, inhaled the aroma, then took a sip. "Mmm, mmm. That is so good. Let me tell you... the beef they have in Argentina and Uruguay – oh my God, it's so good. They're big meat eaters down there. Good luck finding something to eat in a restaurant if you're vegan."

"I wonder if they die early from high cholesterol."

"I dunno. But then, the wine might help with that. Like most other places, people get more exercise than we do here. They walk a lot more."

Ryan went back outside to check on the steaks. He returned with a plate in each hand. The steaks looked like they were grilled to perfection. Ryan opened the oven, pulled out a small pot of mashed potatoes, and scooped some onto each plate. He reached into the oven again and pulled out a basket with several slices of garlic bread wrapped in cloth. He asked Aaron, "Would you carry this over to the table, please?" Ryan carried their plates into the dining room and set them down on the placemats. He went back to the kitchen, topped off their wine glasses, then carried them into the dining room. Then he lit the candles. "Have a seat!"

Aaron let Ryan do most of the talking. Ryan was effusive in his praise of the concert, and he was excited about joining the bands and playing his trumpet again. Then he got onto talking about the trip. He talked a lot about the places they went, but not much about Ted. Finally, Aaron asked, "So, how was Ted?"

"He's fine. He said he likes Buenos Aires okay as a place to live for a year or so, but he wouldn't choose to live there permanently. He liked London and Berlin better, even though in a lot of ways Buenos Aires seems like a European city."

"Does he know where he's going to go next?"

"No. He's got another year to go there, so it's too soon to be planning his next move. A lot depends on what assignments will be available in a year. He wants to go to someplace in Asia, like Japan or Singapore."

"Cool. Why do you think he likes to wander around so much?"

"Basically, he doesn't want to live in the US. He doesn't like the political situation here, or the gun culture, or all the right-wing religious groups. And the expensive healthcare. We talked about that several times when we lived in LA. I have to say, I see his points."

"And it's better elsewhere?"

"He seems to think so. Although the government situation isn't that great in Argentina. Their economy has a lot of problems. That's the main reason he wouldn't stay there."

Ryan took a few bites of food and sips of wine while he thought about what he wanted to say next. "I think there's something deeper, though. He's a loner, and he never feels like he really belongs wherever he is. I get the impression he believes there's a promised land out there somewhere, and he wants to explore the world until he finds it."

Ryan took another bite, then continued. "And that's not necessarily a bad thing. At least he gets to experience other cultures, whether or not he finds his promised land. Or promised man, if that's what it really is. But I think this is a classic case of 'No matter where you go, there you are.'"

Aaron said, "Sounds like he's traveling the world looking for something, but that something is himself."

"Yeah, that's a good way to put it. Anyway, he seems to be happy with this plan for his life, at least at this stage."

"Do you think he'll settle down someday?"

"Yeah, probably. But who knows? I don't even think he knows."

Aaron decided to ask a question that had been on his mind for at least two weeks. "So, were you and Ted ever boyfriends?"

Ryan put his fork down. "Do you mean have we had sex or were we dating each other?"

"Dating. Boyfriends. Like, maybe you'd spend the rest of your lives together."

"No. It's funny. When I first met him, I fell for him – hard. It was physical at first. We went running one day soon after I moved in, and when he took his shirt off... oh my God! He has, like, the most perfect body you've ever seen. And he's handsome – a totally good-looking guy. And he's really nice. I totally fell for him. He picked up on it, so we talked about it. He said, first of all, I was too young. He has this rule where he won't date anyone who's younger than half his age plus seven. And at the time, he was 25 and I was 17, so he thought I was too young for him. Plus, he said there was an unwritten rule in the house we lived in that the guys wouldn't have sex with each other. I could see how that could lead to some big drama if it didn't work out. So yeah, nothing happened with that. And he was probably right. I had only been out of the closet for a couple of months at the time. I was still figuring out the whole gay thing. And with everything else going on, it wasn't the right time for a relationship anyway. But we became really good friends. We spent a lot of evenings in the hot tub or the pool together drinking wine and talking about life. We bonded. It's like we 'get' each other, you know what I mean?"

"Yeah, I guess. So does that mean you've never had sex with him?"

"Not while we were living together in the house. He moved out after he graduated and for a couple of years, he had an apartment in LA. We'd hang out every now and then. When I turned 21, he took me out for an expensive dinner at this place on the beach that overlooks the ocean. It was super nice. Probably still one of the best meals I've ever had in my life. After dinner, we went for a walk on the beach, then we went back to his apartment and… well, let's just say we celebrated my birthday in our birthday suits. We weren't living in the house together anymore and since I had just turned 21, I satisfied his half-your-age-plus-seven rule. So yeah, we've done it a few times. But to get back to the question about dating or a relationship, we actually talked about that on the last night of the gay cruise we went on – the one where I met Kent and Justin. We agreed that we both want different things in our lives. And while we love each other on a certain level, we aren't the best match for each other in terms of a relationship."

Aaron didn't say anything more. He had already pried enough, and he didn't feel comfortable asking about what happened during Ryan's visit with Ted. It seemed pretty obvious. And there was one thing Ryan said that stuck in his mind: 'I had only been out for a couple of months at the time, so I was still figuring out the whole gay thing, and with everything else going on, it wasn't the right time for a relationship anyway.' Aaron thought, *I've only been out a couple of months. The way he fell for Ted sounds an awful lot like the way I'm falling for him. Maybe he thinks I'm so new to being gay that I'm not ready for a relationship yet.*

After a few moments of silence, Ryan asked, "So, is everything okay? I can tell you have something on your mind."

"Yeah. It's been a long day, with the dress rehearsal and the concert and then loading and unloading the instrument truck. It was a great day, but now I'm mentally exhausted. And the wine is mellowing me out a bit."

"I know what you mean. After my long flight home and the concert and the big meal, I'm fading fast. I'll probably want to call it an early evening. But it seems like something else is on your mind."

Aaron said, "Well, at various points during the day, I was thinking about the shooting. I mean, I'm probably overreacting, but it's been on my mind a lot."

"Shooting? What shooting?"

"Oh, didn't you hear about it? Last weekend, some guy went into a gay bar in Orlando and shot 49 people and injured 53 others."

"OMIGOD, no! I didn't hear about that! Of course, I was down in Argentina, or I guess it was Uruguay at the time. But seriously… that's awful!"

"Yeah. Since then, I've been on edge. Like last Thursday night when we went to Raise! after band, I kept thinking, what if some guy walks in the door and starts firing an AR-15 around the room? And even at the concert today, somebody could walk in and shoot everyone in the auditorium. It's like, now I'm afraid to be gay in public – at least in large groups."

Ryan said, "I see what you're saying. And yeah, it's scary. But the thing is, it's all so random. It could happen at any place, any time. So I figure, you shouldn't live your life in fear of something like that happening. That's no way to live. If some militia group announced they were going to go around murdering gay people in crowds, that would be one thing. But so far, this was only one guy who was probably mentally ill."

"Yeah, I know. That's the rational way to look at it. But sometimes our feelings aren't rational."

"True. And you know, this is one of the main reasons Ted wants to live someplace else. Most other places don't have all these mass shootings like we have here. They don't have half the population arming themselves to the teeth."

"He's got a point. Well, anyway, you asked, and that's what's been on my mind."

"Fair enough."

They were both through with dinner, so they got up and carried the dishes into the kitchen. Ryan said, "I'll take care of these later. I hate to kick you out, but I need to turn in early. If I can get ten hours of sleep, I should be okay at work tomorrow."

"I understand. Thanks for dinner. It was great. And thanks for sharing the Malbec with me."

"My pleasure. Thanks for coming up. And I really enjoyed the concert."

"So… sushi on Wednesday?"

"Sounds great. I'll look forward to it."

Ryan took a step toward Aaron. They wrapped their arms around each other and kissed for about ten seconds. Then Ryan stepped back with a satisfied smile on his face. He led Aaron to the front door and they exchanged another quick kiss and said goodbye.

Ryan's First Rehearsal

Thursday, July 7, 2016

Desert Pride took a couple of weeks off following their June concert. Tonight was the first rehearsal for their September concert. Aaron was thrilled because Ryan would be there. They'd have something to do together, and he couldn't wait to have his friends meet his new catch.

Ryan had mixed feelings. He was excited about playing his trumpet again. He had been practicing almost every day since the band's concert on June 19. He, too, viewed his participation in the band as a shared activity with Aaron. But he was nervous about meeting a new group of gay people.

He auditioned for Lee, the director, before rehearsal. His intensive practice paid off. Lee assigned him to first chair.

As was his custom, Lee asked the new members to stand and introduce themselves. When Ryan's turn came, he stood and said, "Hi. I'm Ryan Robertson. I'm thrilled to be playing again. I haven't played my trumpet since I graduated from college four years ago, and I didn't realize how much I missed it. So, I apologize in advance for all the wrong notes you're about to hear. Anyway, I want to thank Aaron for inviting me to your concert last month and for encouraging me to join. I'm really forward to it." He turned and smiled at Aaron, who was seated in the row behind him.

Aaron smiled back. He thought, *It would have been nice if he said 'my boyfriend Aaron,' but oh, well. At least he gave me a shout-out.*

In the French horn section, Petunia leaned over to Kent and whispered, "Is that who I think it is?"

Petunia was unaware that Kent already knew Ryan from the gay cruise and the running club, much less that Kent and Justin had slept with him. Kent glanced at Petunia and shrugged.

Petunia whispered, "I swear that's Luke Loadstar. If that's him..." Petunia put one of his hands between his legs and curled his fingers around an imaginary penis, then slid his hand about ten inches away from his crotch.

Kent whispered back, "I don't know." He looked forward, hoping

Petunia would let it drop.

Petunia pulled out his phone and opened the browser. He searched for an image of Luke Loadstar, then showed a naked picture of him to Kent. "Yes, I believe that's him."

Kent waved him away, knowing it was inappropriate for Petunia to be showing dick pics on his phone during rehearsal. He whispered, "Put that thing away."

"I know where I'd like to put it."

Kent rolled his eyes, then turned away from him.

***

After rehearsal, Aaron convinced Ryan to come out to Raise! the Bar with him. Ryan was reluctant, but Aaron said, "Come on! That's where you really get to know the other people in the band. Rehearsals are nice and everything, but this is where the socializing happens."

"Okay. Maybe for one drink."

"It's two-for-one on Thursday nights."

"Well, we'll see how it goes. I may or may not have that second drink."

Ryan followed Aaron to the bar, and they found parking spaces next to each other. They entered the bar and Aaron asked, "What do you want? It's on me."

Ryan asked, "What's good?"

"Their Long Islands are good. Not as good as yours, of course, but pretty good. So are their Aperol Spritzes."

"I'll try the Aperol Spritz."

Aaron bought their drinks, then led Ryan toward the band's usual table at the back of the bar. Along the way, someone called out, "Luke!"

Ryan grimaced and stared straight ahead.

Aaron didn't pay any attention. He didn't know anyone named Luke.

When they arrived at the table, it soon became clear to Petunia that Kent and Justin already knew Ryan. He leaned into Justin and whispered, "Do you know that guy?"

Justin wasn't a member of the band, so he wasn't at rehearsal. "He's in the running club we belong to. We met him on a gay cruise a few years ago."

"Ahhh… And his name's Ryan? Or is it Luke?"

Justin wasn't sure how to reply, but Kent overheard this exchange and turned toward Petunia. He glared at him and said, "Don't you dare say a word about that to Aaron or anybody else. Seriously. Don't."

Petunia said, "I wonder if he knows."

"I don't know, but that's between him and Ryan. That's his story to tell, not yours. You keep your mouth shut."

Petunia started to say something, but Kent cut him off. "Drop it." Petunia could tell from Kent's stern look that he meant business. He let it drop.

Half an hour later, Ryan had relaxed and was enjoying socializing with his bandmates.

Aaron asked, "Would you like me to get the second drink of our two-for-ones?"

Ryan said, "Sure, why not?"

When Aaron returned with their drinks, the conversation had turned to Pride parades and festivals. Ryan asked, "June was Pride month. Did Phoenix have a parade?"

Rob replied, "Ours is in April. It's too hot in June. Our band marches in the parade each year. That was right before Aaron joined."

Aaron asked, "What's it like? Do a lot of people show up?"

Rob said, "It's not bad. I'd say a few hundred people show up to watch it. Maybe a thousand. There's probably about as many people in the parade as there are watching it."

Stephen, the trombone player, said, "It's nothing like LA, Palm Springs, or San Diego. Man, their parades and festivals are huge!"

Rob said, "Yeah. Palm Springs Pride is in November. It's too hot in summer there, too. Some of our people go march with their band."

Justin said, "San Diego's is in July. Hold on a sec…" He pulled out his phone and did a quick search. "It's next weekend. July 15th through 17th. We ought to go!"

Kent said, "That would be fun, but where would we stay on such short notice? I'll bet every hotel within twenty miles is booked."

Justin said, "Yeah, we may have to stay a little farther out, but we could drive in. Who's up for it?"

Rob said, "I've been there several times, and it's a lot of fun. But I already have plans."

Stephen said, "Yeah, me too. Maybe next year, when we can make plans farther in advance and find a place to stay in Hillcrest."

Aaron turned to Ryan, "Wanna go? It's my weekend off. Sounds like fun!"

Ryan said, "I don't know. I went to LA's a couple of times. It's a sea of people everywhere. I really don't like large crowds."

Aaron said, "Yeah, but it would be something for us to do together. And I've never been to San Diego."

Ryan didn't want to go, but he didn't want to disappoint Aaron either. "Let me think about it. I'll have to check my work schedule. I'm not sure if I can get off next Friday."

Justin turned to Kent and asked, "Can you take next Friday off? I think I can."

"Yeah, I think I can too, but let me check my work schedule in the morning."

Justin started searching for hotel rooms on his phone. After a couple of minutes, he said, "Okay, so here's the deal. Everything near Hillcrest is sold out. We can stay in one of the hotels near the airport for $245 per room per night. There's an Econo-tel in Chula Vista for $129, but it's ten miles away. So, what's more important, price or distance?"

Kent said, "I dunno… neither of them sounds appealing. Maybe we ought to wait until next year and plan further in advance. Or go to Palm Springs in November."

Aaron was clearly disappointed. They spent another half-hour at the bar, then went their separate ways.

On the way home, Ryan tried to think of how he could make next weekend happen for Aaron. Then he remembered the four guys from San Diego he met on the gay cruise in 2013 – the one where he met Kent and Justin. He dated one of them, Kevin, for a few months after the cruise. But they decided that long-distance dating wasn't going to work out. Kevin now had a partner named Chase and they owned a house together. Maybe he could ask a favor.

When he got home, he checked out the website for San Diego Pride to learn more about what would be happening. He glanced at the list of entertainers who would be performing on the festival stage. He lit up when he spotted a familiar name – Whitney Austin.

Oh my God! he thought. *Darnell's going to be there! It would be great to see him again and see his show.*

Now Ryan felt more enthusiastic about going to San Diego. He sent Kevin an email asking if they might be able to accommodate four house guests for the weekend.

Then he shut off his computer and went to bed.

***

The next day, Ryan checked his email. Kevin replied and said he and Chase would be happy to host Ryan and his friends.

Ryan texted Aaron, Kent, and Justin:

> Good news! A friend of mine in San Diego is willing to let us stay in their home. I can't get off on Friday, but you guys can go on Friday morning and I'll leave as soon as I can after work.

A few minutes later, Kent texted back:

> Dude, you're awesome! Thanks for setting that up!

> I found out that my dear friend Darnell is going to be performing on Saturday afternoon. He's a drag queen named Whitney Austin. He's amazing. He sings with his real voice, and it's incredible. So I will want to see that.

Justin replied:

> Wasn't he on that cruise? I'm really not into drag queens.

Hey, I'm making it possible for you to go. You're going to be at the festival anyway. At least do me this one favor. I promise you'll love it.

A Curious Gesture

Thursday, July 14, 2016

On Thursday, as the band members were heading out to the parking lot after rehearsal, Petunia asked Aaron, "Are you coming out to Raise! for a drink or two?"

"Sorry, not this week. I'm leaving tomorrow morning for San Diego, so I've got to go home, finish packing, and turn in."

Petunia pressed a button on his remote and the trunk popped open. He placed his French horn case in the trunk and pulled out a light brown mailing envelope. "Here's a little video you might enjoy watching. I think you'll find it very … *informative*."

Aaron took the envelope, reached in, and pulled a DVD out far enough to read the title, *The Boys of Breckenridge*. On the cover were several very handsome men at a ski resort, bundled up in heavy jackets, scarves, and gloves. Aaron looked perplexed. "A video about skiing?"

Petunia pushed the video back into the envelope. He patted Aaron on the side of his face and said, "You're cute. Just watch it. It should be … *eye-opening*." Petunia turned to get in his car. "See you next week."

Aaron stood there for a few seconds, wondering what prompted this. He put his trombone and the light brown envelope in his trunk, then drove home.

Black's Beach

Friday, July 15, 2016

On Friday morning, Kent and Justin picked Aaron up at his apartment at 8:00 a.m. and began their six-hour drive to San Diego. Justin paired his phone with the car's sound system and assumed DJ duties. He played an assortment of Lady Gaga, Madonna, Cher, Abba, and dance club mega mixes, most of which Aaron didn't recognize. They engaged in very little conversation except during their lunch stop in Yuma. While Aaron didn't find the music objectionable, the constant rhythmic thumping grew tiresome after a few hours.

Their first stop was Black's Beach, near La Jolla. They descended the long, winding pathway from the parking lot and walked north until they reached an area where the only beachgoers were gay men. Given what he had been led to expect, Aaron was surprised that only about half of the men were naked.

They walked the entire length of the gay area, ostensibly to look for the ideal spot to claim for themselves. *What's the big deal?* Aaron thought. *Just pick a place.*

Once they reached the end, they turned to go back. Kent said, "Okay, we've seen everything. What looked good to you?"

Justin replied, "Mmmm… Quite a few of them looked good. So many men, so little time!"

Kent said, "No, you horn dog. I meant where's a good place for us to sit down?"

Justin replied, "I saw plenty of places where I'd like to sit. But how about next to that group of hunks we walked past near the beginning?"

Aaron thought, Oh, I get it. They weren't looking for a spot to claim on the beach as much as they were checking out all the other guys. Do people actually have sex down here?

They retraced their steps, taking in the sights a second time. It seemed to Aaron that more of the guys had taken off their shorts.

They set their towels and backpacks down about ten feet away from the group of hunky men Justin had referenced. Kent and Justin removed their shoes and tank tops, and Aaron followed suit. He took a little more time so he could see whether Kent and Justin were going to remove their shorts. Not surprisingly, they did. Aaron decided he should do likewise.

They sprayed each other with sunblock, then sat down on their towels. Kent said, "Make sure you spray all over. You don't want to spend Pride weekend with a burnt weenie."

Some of the men they passed on their journey were lying on their backs or stomachs to work on their tans. Others sat and read books – or at least held books and appeared to be reading. Kent lay on his stomach with his head toward the ocean. He rested his chin on his folded arms so he could watch the passersby from behind his sunglasses. Justin was less subtle – he sat facing the ocean leaning back on his hands, legs spread and package in full view. Aaron decided to lay on his stomach like Kent.

Justin said, "This is a good spot. We can see practically everyone who comes along. The farther down you go, the fewer people you'll see."

To Justin, this was clearly a meat market. To Kent, it was more of a place to see and be seen. To Aaron, it was a peaceful respite from the last six hours of thumping dance music. Plus, there was something liberating about being naked in a crowd with other gay men. He felt free.

Aaron watched the passing men for about twenty minutes. Then a man about a hundred yards away caught his eye. He looked to be about 6' 4", with wavy light brown hair. He was walking with another guy. The tall one smiled as he and the other guy exchanged a few words, probably about picking a spot. Aaron couldn't take his eyes off the taller one. As he got closer, Aaron realized why he was so drawn to this guy. He looked enough like Ryan to be his brother.

Aaron wondered, *Maybe he **is** Ryan's brother! Ryan said he had a brother who was eight years younger than him. Hmmm… that would make him 18, give or take, so he could be this tall now. This guy looks more like he's in his mid-20s, though. So it's probably not Ryan's brother. But he sure looks like him.*

When the guy was about 30 feet away, Aaron whispered to Kent and Justin, "See that tall guy coming this way? Who does he remind you of?"

Kent said, "Yeah, no kidding. Does Ryan have any brothers or cousins?"

Justin said, "I wonder if he's hung like Ryan."

Kent said, "It figures you would say that."

Justin replied, "Oh, come on. I just said what you thought."

Aaron wondered that too, although he wasn't going to say anything. He still hadn't seen Ryan naked yet, so he had to rely on what Kent and Justin had described.

By this time, the Ryan look-alike had passed. Justin turned to Aaron and said, "So here's what you should do. Wait about five minutes for them to get settled in. Then take a stroll up and down the beach and enjoy the scenic view."

Aaron thought, *I might just do that.*

An hour later, Kent glanced at his watch and said, "It's almost 4:00. We should get going."

They stood up and started folding their towels. Justin said, "Hey, let's take one more walk up and down the beach before we put our clothes back on."

Kent said, "You've already done that, what, four times? Come on, the sausage fest is over. Kevin and Chase are expecting us at their place between 4:30 and 4:45, and who knows what the traffic will be like? And we want to get to happy hour at the Sky Bar before it gets too crowded."

Justin heaved a dramatic sigh and put his clothes back on. Kent said, "Yeah, I'm such a buzzkill. Well, get over it. We have a busy weekend ahead of us, and it will be wall-to-wall men the entire time."

They stuffed everything into their backpacks and hiked up the steep path back to the parking lot.

The Sky Bar

Friday, July 15, 2016

At 4:35, Kent pulled up to an attractive house at the end of a cul-de-sac in the Kensington neighborhood. Kent, Justin, and Aaron pulled their suitcases out of the trunk and carried them up to the front door. Kent rang the doorbell.

A moment later, Kevin answered. "Hi, guys! Welcome! Come in!" They entered the living room and set their luggage down. Kevin hugged Kent and Justin and said, "Great to see you guys again."

Aaron stepped up and shook Kevin's hand. "Aaron. Nice to meet you. Thanks for allowing us to stay here."

Kevin said, "My pleasure."

An older man, who appeared to be about 50, entered the living room from the hallway.

Kevin handled the introductions. "Guys, this is my partner, Chase. Chase, this is Justin and Kent. They were on the same Amsterdam-to-Barcelona cruise my friends and I were on back in 2013. That's where I met Ryan. Then we all went to the resort in PV later that year." Justin and Kent stepped forward and shook Chase's hand. "And this is Aaron." Aaron shook Chase's hand.

"You're Ryan's new boyfriend, right?"

"Something like that. We've been hanging out a lot, but we haven't put a label on it yet."

Chase furrowed his eyebrows but didn't say anything.

Kevin said, "Let me show you to your rooms." He led Kent, Justin, and Aaron down the hallway. He stopped at one of the side bedrooms and said, "This is our guest bedroom. Kent and Justin, you'll stay here. Why don't you put your suitcases inside, then let me show you the rest of the house?" Kevin then led them to the kitchen. The kitchen and breakfast nook faced toward the back of the house. A long wall of windows provided a spectacular view of a wooded canyon, and beyond that, a row of houses on the next ridge.

Kevin led them down a staircase to a large family room. The house was built on the side of a hill, so while it appeared to be a one-story house from the street, there was another level below the street. Kevin pointed to a hide-a-bed that had been opened and freshly made. "Aaron, this is where you and Ryan will sleep. There's a full bathroom over there. There's also a kitchenette with a mini-fridge in case you want water or soda or something. Help yourself." Aaron set his suitcase down next to the bed. "Let me take you outside."

Kevin led Aaron, Kent, and Justin through a sliding glass door onto a patio. There was a barbecue grill, a fire pit, a variety of tables and chairs, and light strings crisscrossing the patio overhead. The patio also afforded a lovely view of the canyon through a clearing in the trees. "We're having a little get-together here on Sunday afternoon for about 20 of our friends. Of course, you're welcome to be part of it if you want. The festival will still be going on, so do whichever you prefer."

Aaron said, "Wow. This is really nice!"

Kevin replied, "Thanks! It's our little corner of paradise." He led them back inside. "You guys probably want a few minutes to change and freshen up, but let's try to leave at around 5:00."

Everyone nodded, and Kevin, Kent, and Justin went back upstairs. Aaron lifted his suitcase onto the bed, opened it, and selected the clothes he would wear for the evening. He thought, *Hmmm. Finally, we get to sleep together. I wonder if anything's going to happen.*

***

At a few minutes past 5:00, the five men climbed into Chase's SUV, with Aaron, Kent, and Justin scrunched together in the back seat.

Fifteen minutes later, they arrived in Hillcrest. Cars lined the streets everywhere, but Chase turned down a side street at the right moment. A car was pulling out, so he quickly pulled into that space.

Kevin and Chase led the others to the Hillcrest Inn, a plain brick six-story hotel located near Balboa Park. There was already a line of at least 80 people wrapped around the hotel's parking lot. Justin's eyes popped open wide. "Is that the line to get in? Shit!"

Kevin led them to the end of the line and said, "You guys wait here." Then he ran off around the side of the building. Two minutes later, he reappeared at the corner of the building. Aaron and Kent saw him first. He was frantically waving for them to follow him. The others looked at each other and shrugged. Chase said, "Come on, let's go."

They left the line and walked over to the corner of the building where Kevin was standing. He led them around to a service door at the back of the hotel. There was a stairway inside the door. They walked up six flights of stairs to a door at the top. They emerged into a large room with wall-length glass windows facing north and south. The east end of the room opened onto a large open rooftop patio.

The indoor room was fairly full, but Aaron could see the outdoor area was filled with men packed like sardines. Aaron walked over to the south windows and looked out. The line in the parking lot below had reached the street. He could see the guys who had been ahead of them, only a little farther forward than they were when his group left the line. He estimated they had a twenty to thirty-minute wait ahead of them. He turned around and rejoined his friends, who were now in line at one of the bars. Chase said, "Their Cape Cods are really good. The first round is on me!"

The bartenders were impressively efficient, and the group had their drinks in less than five minutes. Kevin said, "Let's see if we can find a place outside." He led the group as they snaked their way through the crowd to an open spot near a rail, and they crowded into it. This vantage point afforded them a breathtaking view of the downtown San Diego skyline. Off to one side, they could see Balboa Park. A few minutes later, a jet flew between them and the downtown buildings. It seemed dangerously low to the ground. "Jesus Christ!" Aaron exclaimed. "Is it going to crash?"

Kevin laughed. "No. But it looks that way, doesn't it? The airport's right over there. That's their regular flight path. It's kind of cool to watch, isn't it?"

Ten minutes later, most of the guys had finished their drinks and were ready for a second round. Aaron said, "I'll buy this round. Justin, would you come along and help me carry them?"

Kevin said, "We'll stay here and hold the spot."

Aaron and Justin worked their way through the crowd toward the outdoor bar. Justin said, "Jesus, look at that line. I'll bet the line inside is shorter." They went back inside and, sure enough, the line was noticeably shorter.

As they were waiting, the elevator door opened and a group of new arrivals entered the room. Aaron said to Justin, "Look! I think that's the same tall guy we saw at Black's Beach earlier. You know, the one who looks like Ryan."

Justin turned to his left to get a better look. "Yeah, I think you're right. And he's with the same guy. Do you think they're partners?"

"Hard to tell if they're partners or just friends."

"So did you go up and talk to him when we were at the beach?"

"Nah… I felt like it would be weird to walk up to a naked guy I don't know and say something."

"Well, he's not naked now."

"True. Still, what would I say? 'Hey, you look like this guy I'm seeing. Are you related?'"

"Sure. Why not? That's actually a good pickup line. And it's true. Do you have a picture of Ryan on your phone?"

Aaron thought for a moment. "I don't think I do. Let me check." Aaron got out his phone and scrolled through his pictures from the past couple of months. "Nope."

Justin got out his phone and scrolled through his pictures. Finally, he said, "I've got one we took when we were at that resort in PV a couple of years ago. I'll send it to you."

"Thanks."

"So, did you get to see that guy naked on the beach?"

Aaron nodded. "I didn't get a real good look 'cause I didn't want him to see me staring at it."

"Does he look like Ryan down there, too?"

Aaron rolled his eyes. "I wouldn't know."

"You mean you guys still haven't done it?"

"No! And it's driving me up a wall. Like, what is he waiting for? I mean, if he just wants to be friends, that's okay, but I want to know so I can manage my expectations."

"Totally. If you're not boyfriends, there's no reason why you shouldn't be having a lot of fun this weekend."

Aaron hadn't thought about that. He looked around the room. There were fuckable men everywhere.

Justin said, "Well, you're going to be spending six hours in a car on Sunday, so maybe you should talk about it then."

"Yeah. And we're sleeping in the same bed tonight and tomorrow night, so maybe something will happen."

They reached the bar. Aaron ordered five Cape Cods, then he and Justin worked their way through the crowd carrying the drinks. They passed the tall guy who looked like Ryan. He glanced at Aaron and made eye contact. They smiled.

Aaron and Justin reached the others and gave them their drinks.

A few minutes later, three of Kevin's friends Derek, Stephen, and Zach emerged from the elevator and joined the group. They also knew Kent and Justin from the cruise and the resort in PV, so Kevin introduced them to Aaron.

Kevin said, "What took you guys so long?"

Zach replied, "The line! It took us 40 minutes to get up here. Man, this place needs a larger elevator."

Kevin said, "You don't know about the back stairs?"

"Are you shittin' me? Why didn't you tell us?"

"I thought you knew."

Aaron kept looking at the tall guy and looking away whenever the guy looked in his direction. Fuck it, Aaron thought. Ryan and I aren't boyfriends yet. We haven't had sex. We haven't made any commitments. I'm a free man. If we do end up getting together, this might be my last chance to have some fun.

Aaron turned to the others and said, "Guys, if you'll excuse me, I'm going to go ask that tall guy if he's related to Ryan."

As Aaron approached the tall guy and his friend, he thought, *Am I really doing this? Will he mind being interrupted by a stranger? What am I going to say that doesn't sound like a cheesy pickup line?*

Despite his mental hesitation, his feet carried him right up to the two men. "Excuse me, but uh… I know this is going to sound weird, but…" He looked up at the tall guy. "You look like this guy I know back home. Like, you could be brothers."

The tall guy smiled. "Sorry, but I don't have any brothers." The tall guy and his friend glanced at each other. "But just for grins, do you have a picture of him?"

"Yeah. Here, can you hold this?" Aaron handed the tall guy his drink, then pulled his phone out of his pocket. He opened the text from Justin and tapped the photo to enlarge it.

"Damn! He does look like me!"

Aaron showed the picture to the other guy. "Yep. I'd think it was him."

"That's uncanny."

Aaron said, "Maybe he's related to you somehow."

The tall guy said, "Where's he from?"

"He lives in Scottsdale now. But he's originally from Kansas."

"You know, I have an uncle who lives in Kansas, at least he used to. My folks aren't in touch with him. He's some right-wing fundamentalist minister, and my family isn't into that at all. So he and my family kind of went their separate ways a long time ago. Anyway, if he has any kids, they would be my cousins. But I've never seen them."

"What's your uncle's name?"

"Brad Bauer."

"Nope. My friend's name is Ryan Robertson. So, I guess not."

"Oh, well, So what's your name?"

"Aaron Bradbury. And you?"

"I'm Brady Bauer. This is my friend, Andy Fox."

They shook hands. Aaron said, "So, you guys are friends. I thought you might be a couple."

Andy said, "Nope, just besties. Besties with benefits."

Well... okay, Aaron thought. "Do you guys live here?"

Brady said, "No, we live in Seattle. We came down for the festivities. And how about you?"

"I live in Tempe. I'm here with a few of my friends."

Andy said, "Yeah, I think I saw you and that guy you were carrying drinks with at the beach this afternoon with one other guy."

Aaron said, "Yeah, I saw you too."

Brady said, "Oh. So you've seen us naked?"

Aaron had, but he didn't want this to get awkward. "Uh... actually I saw you when you first arrived as you walked past us."

Brady said, "Ahhh." He glanced at Andy, who nodded. "Well, would you like to see us naked?"

Aaron did not see that coming. *Are they saying what I think they're saying?* "Well, uh... You mean now? Uh... where?"

Brady said, "We're staying here at the hotel. Our room is on the fourth floor."

"Well, uh..." He looked in the direction of his friends. There were too many other guys in the way, so he couldn't see them. His head was spinning.

What should I do? Can I leave my friends for that long? What if they want to go, and they come looking for me and can't find me? He said, "Hang on a sec." He tapped his phone to reply to Justin's text. He whispered into the phone,

> How long are we staying here?

A moment later, Justin replied,

> At least an hour. Go for it, dude!

Aaron turned to Brady and Andy and said, "Let's go."

***

When Aaron returned to the Sky Bar to rejoin his friends, the crowd had thinned out. Aaron wondered whether there would be time to get another drink, but Chase said, "We should get going. Our dinner reservations are for 7:30, and I have no idea what traffic or parking will be like."

No one said anything about Aaron's disappearance.

Aaron Spreads His ... Wings

Friday, July 15, 2016

After dinner, Chase wanted to return home, but everyone else wanted to head out to the bars. So after dropping Chase off, Kevin, Kent, Justin, and Aaron headed back into Hillcrest. Derek, Stephen, and Zach drove directly there.

Kevin led them to Fort Dicks, a large bar with multiple rooms, the largest of which held a dance floor. The place was packed. Up to this point, Raise! the Bar and the Sky Bar were the only gay bars Aaron had ever been to. Fort Dicks was easily five times larger. They spent their first fifteen minutes wandering through the various rooms and the outdoor patio. It was a nice evening and the patio was cooler and quieter than inside, but it was also where the smokers hung out.

Aaron, Kevin, Kent, and Justin worked their way onto the crowded dance floor. The music was deafeningly loud and lasers were putting on a spectacular light show. There wasn't much room to actually dance, so most people were just rocking and bobbing in place. People brushed up against each other constantly, but no one seemed to mind.

Despite the high volume and minimal personal space, Aaron was having a blast. The entire spectacle enthralled him. Even though he had a long day, the energy of the dance floor was a shot of adrenalin. He had never seen so many gay men in the same place. He scanned the crowd, admiring the scenery. There was eye candy everywhere.

Kevin, Kent, and Justin had been to large gay dance clubs many times before, so the experience was not novel to them. After about twenty minutes, Kent signaled for a break. They carved a path through the crowd and retreated to one of the quieter rooms. Kevin said, "We've been here half an hour, and we still haven't seen the other guys." He texted Zach to let them know which room they were in.

After ordering drinks, Aaron said, "Wow! This is totally amazing! I had no idea places like this even existed! Is it like this every weekend?"

234

Kevin said, "Not like this. It's Pride weekend, so everyone comes out. Plus, there's a lot of people who come from other places – like you guys."

Derek, Stephen, and Zach came in from the dance floor and met up with the others. They stood around making small talk. No one made any attempt to hide the fact that they were checking out the crowd.

Kent said, "Did you see the go-go boys dancing on those little platforms?" Everyone nodded. "That good-looking well-built Latino guy – I think I've seen him in pornos."

Justin said, "Yeah. What's his name?"

Derek said, "Juan Knight. I have some videos he's in."

Justin said, "Yeah, that's it. Well, I'd spend Juan Knight with him anytime he wants."

Kent rolled his eyes. "He's a total bottom. Why would he be interested in you?"

Justin replied, "Bitch. I'm versatile. I'd do whatever he wants."

Kent said, "Right. Besides, he's had so much shoved up his ass he wouldn't feel you when you entered."

Justin replied, "Speak for yourself, thimble-dick."

Kent said, "He took three cocks up his ass at once in *The Boys of Breckenridge*. Fucking him would be like fucking the Holland Tunnel."

Aaron's eyes popped open. He couldn't conceive of anyone taking two cocks at once, let alone three. He was having enough of a challenge with the huge dildo Kent and Justin loaned him. He fervently hoped they wouldn't say anything about that. *Wait a minute. Wasn't The Boys of Breckenridge the name of that video Petunia gave me last night?*

Derek laughed at Kent and Justin's banter. "So I assume that means you guys are open."

Kent said, "Yeah, we play around every now and then. Mostly when we're away from home, like on a gay cruise or something."

Justin said, "Or here." He winked at Derek.

Kent asked Kevin, "What about you and Chase?"

Kevin said, "We have sort of a 'don't ask, don't tell' agreement. Chase is almost 20 years older than me and let's just say he doesn't want it as often as I do. So as long as I'm giving him everything he wants, he doesn't care if I get a little extra every now and then. And of course, I'm safe. He'd rather not hear about it, and I don't abuse the privilege."

Justin said, "Well, this place is an all-you-can-eat buffet and I'm starving."

Kent rolled his eyes and the San Diego guys all laughed.

Aaron wondered, *Are these guys really that promiscuous?* He turned toward Derek, Stephen, and Zach and said, "Are you guys single or are two of you a couple, or what?"

Zach said, "We're all single. The four of us used to go on gay cruises together. That's where we met these guys and Ryan."

"So, if you don't mind me asking, have all you guys, you know..."

Kevin said, "...slept with Ryan? No, I'm the only one who's had that honor."

Stephen said, "Yeah. Selfish bitch wouldn't share."

"Damn right. Besides, I don't think he wants to be shared." He turned to Aaron and said, "He's really nice. We tried long-distance dating for a couple of months after the cruise. He came here a couple of times and I went to Scottsdale once. We went on a week-long gay resort vacation in Puerto Vallarta. But we decided long-distance dating wasn't going to work, and I met Chase not long after that."

Aaron thought back to a few moments ago when Kevin was talking about his relationship with Chase. 'He doesn't care if I get a little on the side every now and then.' *Was he hoping to get a little – or, more accurately, a lot – with Ryan this weekend?*

Justin said, "Damn. Juan Knight sure had a lot of dollar bills stuffed in his thong."

Derek said, "Well, he's a porn star. He probably gets attention everywhere he goes."

Zach said, "It doesn't look like he minds it."

Aaron asked, "Can he really, you know... take three dicks?"

Derek said, "And more." He held up a hand. Aaron's eyes popped wide open.

Zach moved closer to Aaron and motioned for him to take a couple of steps away from the others. He said, "Seems like you're kinda new to the gay thing. At least where porn is concerned."

Aaron replied, "Yeah, I just came out about three months ago. This whole weekend has been unbelievable so far. Like, I had never been to a nude beach until today. I didn't know so many gay couples had open relationships. And I guess I'm pretty naïve about what gay guys do together."

"Have you done it with a guy yet?"

"A few times. About two months ago, there was this guy I met in the band I play in. We did it a few times, but then he moved away." Aaron paused. "And uh... there was earlier today."

"So you and Ryan haven't done it yet?"

"No! We've been seeing each other for almost two months now. I don't know whether to call it dating or just hanging out or whatever. He acts like he's into me, but he keeps avoiding spending the night or doing anything physical. So I figured, we haven't made any kind of commitment to each other yet, so I'm gonna have fun this weekend."

Zach nodded. "Well, you're a nice guy and you're good-looking. I don't know what's holding him back."

"Do you really think so?"

"Of course! You're actually pretty hot. Hell, I'd do you."

I'd do you, too. Do you think...? What about all the others? What about transportation? I'm kinda dependent upon Kevin. His house is way too far to walk. How could we make this work?

Derek turned toward Aaron and Zach and motioned for them to rejoin their group. "It's too crowded and noisy here. We're going back to my place. I've got some vodka and Jack Daniels and we can pick up some beer and soda on the way. Maybe we'll watch Juan Knight in action!"

It seemed to Aaron like everyone else had decided this was what they were going to do. He couldn't think of any way to say he and Zach had other plans.

After they left the bar and were heading toward their cars, Zach pulled up next to Aaron and gently tugged his arm. They dropped back and let the others pass. Then he whispered, "So... do you wanna go with them or would you rather come home with me? There's no wrong answer."

"You. But could you drive me back to Kevin's house afterward?"

"Or you could spend the night."

Aaron seriously considered it. *It would be nice to fall asleep in his arms and wake up with him, like that one night with Jeremy. Then maybe do it again in the morning. And he's so nice. But... there's Ryan. Ryan will arrive between 11 and 12. What's he going to think if I stay out all night? Should I even care?*

Aaron said, "That would be nice, but I should probably get back by midnight."

"Okay." Zach took a few quick steps and caught up to the others.

"Hey, guys. We're going to call it a night. Okay?"

Kevin said, "Yeah. I'm gonna pass, too. I've got some stuff to do around the house before our party on Sunday."

Derek said, "Whatever. Your loss, dudes."

Kevin said, "Will you guys make sure Aaron, Kent, and Justin get back home?"

Zach nodded. Stephen said, "Yeah, sure."

Kevin said, "Okay. Oh, and Ryan texted me earlier. He's running late and his new ETA is 1:00. I'll stay up until he arrives, but if you guys are still out whoring around, I'll leave a key under the mat. Have fun!"

Zach said, "See you guys at the parade tomorrow morning." He and Aaron turned to go.

Derek said, "Later, dudes." He turned to Kent, Justin, and Stephen. "Forget those losers. Let's get the party started!"

***

Zach ushered Aaron into his condo and locked the door behind them. Then he threw his arms around Aaron and started kissing him passionately. Within minutes, all clothes were off and they went at it non-stop for over an hour. Finally, they collapsed in each other's arms and basked in the afterglow for another twenty minutes.

***

After a quick stop to pick up beer, sodas, and munchies, Derek, Kent, Justin, and Stephen arrived at Derek's apartment. They made drinks for themselves and migrated into the living room. Kent and Justin sat on the couch facing the TV, leaving space for Derek between them. Stephen sat on the side chair.

Derek poured a bag of chips into a bowl and set it on the coffee table. Then he walked over to his video shelf, scanned his collection, and pulled out three pornos that starred Juan Knight. "All right, dudes. I've nominated three videos that have Juan Knight in multiple-person scenes. There's *Poolside Pleasures*; *Three's Company, Four's an Orgy*; and of course, the classic *Boys of Breckenridge*.

Justin said, "Everyone's seen *The Boys of Breckenridge*. I mean, it's hot and everything, but I want to see something new."

Stephen said, "And I've seen *Three's Company, Four's an Orgy*. How about *Poolside Pleasures*?"

Derek looked at Kent and Justin and said, "Agreed?"

Justin said, "Sounds good. Stick it in there." A second later, he added, "The video I mean."

Kent said, "I can't believe we're doing this."

Derek turned on his home entertainment system and inserted the DVD in the tray. He sat down between Kent and Justin and clicked the remote to start the video. Throughout the first two scenes, both three-ways, the guys amused themselves by providing color commentary and joking about what was happening on screen.

Stephen asked, "So what do you guys think? Did Aaron go home with Zach?"

Derek said, "Of course he did. They're probably fillin' the cream donut right now."

Stephen asked, "I wonder what Ryan's going to think when he finds out Aaron's been doing it with other guys."

Kent said, "For some reason, Ryan's been holding off on the sex. I think Aaron's tired of waiting around."

Derek said, "Maybe he's trying to make him jealous. You know, like, 'if you're not going to give it to me, I'm going to get it someplace else.'"

Kent said, "I don't know, but it's not our place to tell him."

Derek said, "But..."

"No, seriously. This is between Aaron and Ryan. We need to stay out of it."

They turned their attention back to the video. As the scene progressed, there was less and less banter. A sense of awkward anticipation filled the room.

***

Finally, Aaron and Zach got out of bed. After taking turns in the bathroom, Zach said, "It's 11:30. We still have some time before you have to get back. Wanna hang out and talk for a while?"

"Yeah, that would be nice." Aaron found where his underwear had landed on the floor and put it back on.

Zach motioned toward the kitchen table. "Have a seat. Want

something to drink?"

"Sure. Coke, Dr Pepper, whatever you've got."

Zach pulled a 2-liter bottle of Coke from the refrigerator and set it down on the table. He filled two glasses with ice and set those down. He looked through his cupboards and brought out a box of crackers and a half-empty bottle of Jim Beam. He cut a few cheese slices into squares that would fit on the crackers, then sat down. "Sorry, it's not much. I wasn't planning to have company."

"That's okay, this is good. I'm more thirsty than hungry. Just a little to nibble on is fine."

The conversation flowed easily. Aaron told Zach about his experience with joining the band and coming out. Zach talked about growing up in Minnesota and how he ended up in San Diego. He told Aaron about how he, Derek, Stephen, and Kevin met Ryan and Ted on a gay cruise, and how it took Kevin almost a week to work up the nerve to approach Ryan. They compared San Diego and Phoenix and what they liked about each.

Aaron said, "This is my first time in San Diego. It's amazing! I could totally see myself living here."

"Yeah, it's nice. It's expensive, though. And sometimes traffic sucks. But overall, I like it. Sure beats West Bumfuck, Minnesota."

Aaron glanced at the time on the microwave and stood up. "Shit! It's 12:45. Ryan's going to be at Kevin's house any moment now!"

Zach stood up and said, "So, uh… just so I'm clear. Is this not supposed to have happened?"

Aaron said, "No, it's okay. I'm still a free man."

Zach said, "Okay, good. I don't want to get in the way of anything."

"It's cool. But I don't want to rub it in his face, either."

"I get it."

They headed back into the bedroom where the rest of Aaron's clothes were scattered on the floor. Before Aaron could bend down to pick up his shorts, Zach walked up beside him and placed his hand on Aaron's shoulder. Aaron turned to face him. Zach kissed Aaron lightly on the lips. "I'm really glad we got together tonight."

Aaron kissed him back. "Yeah, me too. It was really special."

They kissed again. Zach wrapped his arms around Aaron and pulled him forward so their chests pressed against each other. Aaron wrapped his arms around Zach. They kissed – more sweetly and tenderly this time, as opposed to the urgent, passionate kissing from before. They slid their hands up and down each other's backs. Aaron kept thinking, *Okay, this will be the last kiss. No, one more. Just one more. Well, maybe another minute.*

Zach slid both hands down inside the elastic of Aaron's underwear and cupped his butt checks. They could feel their hard cocks straining inside their underwear, pressing against each other. Aaron swiveled side to side so their cocks brushed back and forth, like swords still in their sheaths.

Zach whispered, "We're so bad."

Aaron whispered back, "Then why is it so good?"

Zach dropped to his knees. He pulled Aaron's underwear down to his ankles.

***

Back at Derek's apartment, Kent said, "It's 12:45. We'd better get back to Kevin's."

They put their clothes back on, and Justin said, "Hey guys, thanks a lot. That was hot."

Kent said to Derek, "Yeah, thanks for having us over." He turned to Stephen and asked, "Can you give us a ride?"

"Yeah, sure."

They all hugged Derek, then left.

When they arrived at Kevin's, the front door was locked. They assumed that meant Ryan had arrived. Kent looked under the doormat and, sure enough, there was a key. After he and Justin entered the house, he whispered, "Do you think we should bring the key in?"

"I don't know. Depends on whether Aaron is back yet."

"I guess we could sneak downstairs and take a look."

"Nah. Let's put the key back under the mat just in case."

***

As they lay in each other's arms, drifting in and out of blissful slumber, Aaron spotted the alarm clock. 1:56. He jostled Zach. "Now I really have to go."

"Can't you just stay?"

"I'd love to, but I really shouldn't."

They got up and put their clothes on. Zach grabbed his keys and his wallet and led Aaron out to his car.

They pulled up to Kevin's house at 2:20. Aaron leaned over and kissed Zach. "Thanks. I wish I could have spent the night."

"That's okay. It was wonderful."

"See you tomorrow at the parade."

"If I can drag my ass out of bed."

Aaron realized he was prolonging the inevitable, so he reached for the door handle. "Okay, well, good night!"

"Good night!" They exchanged one last quick kiss. "I'll wait until I see that you made it in okay."

Sure enough, the key was under the mat. Aaron waved. Zach waved back, then took off.

Aaron tiptoed down the stairs to the family room. Ryan was sleeping on the hide-a-bed. He had chosen the left side of the bed and was sleeping on his right side. Aaron got ready for bed as quietly as possible. As he was about to climb into bed, he wondered whether Ryan was sleeping naked or wearing underwear. He could see Ryan's bare shoulder above the sheet. He thought about lifting the bedspread enough to take a look but didn't want to risk disturbing Ryan. He left his underwear on.

242

Everyone Loves a Parade

Saturday, July 16, 2016

At 7:00 a.m., Ryan's phone alarm began chirping. He reached for his phone and silenced the alarm. He looked over his shoulder and saw Aaron lying in bed next to him. The alarm had not awakened him.

Ryan stood up and stretched. He was still tired after the long drive and only six hours of sleep, but he knew he needed to get moving. He stepped into the bathroom and took a shower.

When he emerged from the bathroom at 7:20, Aaron hadn't moved. Ryan got dressed, then sat on the bed next to Aaron and jostled him. "C'mon, sleepyhead, it's time to get up!"

"What… huh?" Aaron barely moved.

Ryan leaned down and kissed him on the cheek. "Time to get up. Kevin and Chase said we should leave for the parade at around 8:30 so we can find a place to park and get a good spot along the parade route. So you need to take a shower and get some breakfast."

Aaron yawned and stretched. He opened his eyes for an instant then closed them again to avoid the morning light. "Gimme another 15 minutes."

"Like that will make a difference. You must have been out pretty late last night."

"Yeah, I guess."

"You'll feel better once you get some caffeine in you. We've got an exciting day ahead of us!" Ryan leaned down and kissed Aaron's cheek again, then went upstairs.

Chase and Kevin were sitting at the kitchen table when Ryan arrived. Chase said, "I whipped up some scrambled eggs and bacon, and there are some pastries in that box over there. And there's coffee on the counter and orange juice in the refrigerator. Help yourself!"

Ryan replied, "Thanks! That's very kind of you." He served himself and sat down at the table with Chase and Kevin.

A moment later, Kent and Justin appeared. They served themselves breakfast and sat down.

Ryan asked, "So, what did you guys do yesterday?"

Kent said, "Well, first, Aaron and Justin and I went to Black's Beach for a couple of hours, then we came here at around 5:00."

Kevin said, "Then we all went to happy hour at the Sky Bar, across from Balboa Park. We met up with Derek, Stephen, and Zach there."

Justin said, "It was incredible! Wall-to-wall men! Plenty of hotties, too. And views all over the city! We watched low-flying planes come in and the early part of the sunset."

Chase said, "It's too bad you couldn't make it. You would have loved it."

Ryan said, "Maybe. I'm sure it was nice, but I'm not really into big crowds."

Kevin said, "Well, that's what you're going to be in for at the festival this afternoon."

Ryan said, "Yeah, I know. But I want to see Whitney Austin perform at 2:00. I'm going to meet up with Darnell after the show. You guys are welcome to join us if you want to."

Kent said, "Yeah, we'll at least say hi. But getting back to yesterday... After the Sky Bar, we all went out to dinner, then Chase came home but the rest of us went out to a dance club for a while."

Justin said, "It was packed! Man, you guys have a gay scene here! We don't have anything like that in Phoenix. We don't have a gayborhood like Hillcrest, either. Everything is spread out. We have gay bars, but nothing like that."

Kent added, "And nothing like the Sky Bar for happy hour."

Ryan asked, "So how late were you guys up?"

Kevin, Kent, and Justin all looked at each other. Kevin said, "I came home at around 10:30."

Kent said, "Justin, Derek, Stephen, and I stayed out until, like 12:45 or so. We got in shortly after you arrived."

That left Aaron. After an awkward pause, Justin said, "Aaron and Zach stayed out later. Zach must have driven him home."

Ryan said, "Speaking of Aaron, I'd better go make sure he's up. He was pretty zonked."

He scampered down the stairs to the family room. Aaron was sound asleep. Ryan stood by the side of the bed and jostled his shoulder. "Come on, man, get up!"

Aaron groaned and rolled over onto his back. "Do I have to?"

"Yes. Unless you want to miss the parade."

Aaron thought about it. Missing the parade in exchange for several more hours' sleep seemed like an appealing choice. But he knew he shouldn't. He pivoted so he was sitting on the side of the bed. He stretched and rubbed his eyes. "All right…"

"What were you doing out so late?"

Aaron took a moment to shake off his grogginess and compose his answer. "Zach and I were having a great time dancing and hanging out together." *Horizontal dancing, so to speak.* "I guess I lost track of time."

"Well, anyway… C'mon, stand up. They have breakfast and coffee upstairs. I'll make sure they leave some for you. It's 7:50. You've got 40 minutes."

Ryan walked back upstairs. Aaron debated plopping back down onto the bed but dragged his tired ass into the bathroom instead.

***

With six people to transport, they took two cars – Chase's SUV and Ryan's BMW. Ryan followed Chase to a neighborhood just south of Hillcrest. Parking spaces were already at a premium, but they were able to find two within the same block. They carried several collapsible lawn chairs and a cooler filled with water and soda to Sixth Avenue, then north a few blocks to Ivy Street. Kevin said, "Okay! Here's our spot. We sit here every year. It's less crowded. Up on University Avenue, the people are standing three or four deep!"

At 9:00 a.m. there were only a few people nearby.

Aaron asked, "What time does the parade start?"

Kevin answered, "Ten a.m."

Aaron said, "So we've got to sit here for an hour?"

Kevin replied, "Yes. But it's worth it to get a good spot."

Chase added, "Actually, the parade starts at the other end of Hillcrest. It'll get here 20 or 30 minutes later."

Shit, Aaron thought. *I could have stayed in bed another hour and a half.* He looked around. All the buildings came right up to the sidewalk. He spotted one house nearby with a small grass lawn. "Guys, I'm going to go lay down in the grass over there. Come get me when the parade gets here."

Over the course of the next hour, Derek, Stephen, Zach, and a few of Chase's friends arrived and joined the group.

Finally, at around 10:30, the parade reached the group. Ryan walked over to the small grass lawn and awakened Aaron.

The Finest City LGBT Youth Band was among the first units in the parade. Ryan said, "It's great that they have a marching band for gay kids. I wish they had that when I was in high school."

Aaron said, "Maybe we should start one in Phoenix."

Kent said, "The board talked about that once. You've got to be really careful with adults being around minors. The director and anyone else involved would need to get background checks."

Aaron said, "So? There's no reason that should stop us. There's an LGBT youth chorus, isn't there?"

Kent said, "Yeah, and it has, like, eight kids in it. We'd need more than that for a marching band."

Justin said, "Arizona isn't California. The right-wingers would say we're trying to recruit their children."

Ryan didn't say anything, but he started thinking about what it would take to form an LGBT youth band in Phoenix.

The LGBT marching band from Los Angeles came later. There were marchers from local organizations, politicians and drag queens perched on convertibles, and floats for local businesses.

After an hour, the parade showed no signs of ending. More convertibles, floats, and marching units kept coming. Aaron said, "I've never seen anything like this! San Diego's gay community must be huge!"

Zach said, "Yeah, we attract a lot of people from everywhere else in the country."

Chase said, "This parade has built up a reputation over the years."

A moment later, a float from Fort Dicks rolled into view. Dance music blared from speakers on a festively decorated flatbed truck. Go-go dancers in skimpy shorts danced and shook their goods.

Kent said, "You won't see a float like this in the Phoenix parade."

Derek called out, "Hey, look – it's Juan Knight!"

Ricky Montez turned to see who had called out his nom-du-porn. He spotted Ryan. He jumped off the end of the truck and came running up. "Ryan! OMIGOD! I can't believe it!" He planted a big kiss on Ryan's cheek and hugged him, not caring that he was drenched in perspiration. "How have you been?"

"Hey, Ricky! Great to see you again! Looking good, bro. You live here now?"

"Yeah. I'm doing a lot better now. I've got my life back on track."

"Are you going to see Whitney's show at 2:00?"

Ricky thought for a second. "Yeah, I can do that."

"Okay! See you there."

"Well, gotta run!" Ricky kissed Ryan again, then sprinted back to the float which was now 500 feet down the road.

Aaron was dumbstruck. "You know Juan Knight?"

Ryan said, "I know Ricky. That's his real name. He and I lived in the same house while I was in college. We were good friends."

"You used to live with a porn star?"

"I lived with a real person. Just like I didn't live with Whitney Austin, I lived with a real person named Darnell. They were my family."

The others silently decided they shouldn't comment on this topic.

***

Finally, the last unit in the parade, the Latte-loving Lesbians of La Mesa, passed. After that, an extended parade of spectators formed a massive pilgrimage to the festival grounds in Balboa Park.

Ryan said, "Man, I'm starving. Let's head back up toward Hillcrest and find someplace to eat."

Derek said, "Everything's going to be packed. Let's head on into the festival and get something from the food trucks."

Ryan said, "Those will be packed too. The crowd's heading that way."

Aaron said, "Well, if there's going to be a crowd either way, I say we head on into the festival!"

Ryan said, "I really don't want to eat junk food from a food truck."

Kevin said, "I'll go with you to find a place to eat in Hillcrest. You guys go on to the festival. We'll catch up with you later."

Stephen said, "Sounds like a plan. Text us when you get to the festival and we'll meet up."

Ryan said, "And remember, Whitney Austin goes on at 2:00. I hope you guys will join me, but I definitely want to be there."

Chase said, "I've been to enough festivals in my life. I'm gonna head home to get the house ready for tomorrow. You guys have fun!" He handed Kevin the keys to his SUV. "My friends can drop me off."

Everyone gave quick hugs to Chase and his friends. Then Kevin and Ryan headed north toward Hillcrest and the other guys joined the throng heading south toward the festival.

Old Friends

Saturday, July 16, 2016

Ryan and Kevin found a sandwich shop that wasn't too crowded. After waiting five minutes in line, they had their sandwiches, chips, and drink cups in hand. Fortunately, a table opened up and they immediately claimed it.

Ryan said, "Thanks for agreeing to come here with me."

"No problem. I'm not that big on food trucks either, and we wouldn't have anywhere to sit. And I wanted to catch up with you."

Ryan said, "Chase seems like a nice guy. And that's an awesome house you have! I love the view out the back."

"Yeah. That's a primo piece of real estate. He bought it when the market crashed in 2008. It was either a short sale or a foreclosure. Anyway, he got a screaming deal on it. It's worth twice as much now."

Ryan took a bite of his sub and ventured onto another topic. "I didn't know you were into older guys. Not that there's anything wrong with that, of course."

"I wasn't. It's not like I went out looking for an older guy. But I met him at a party and we chatted for a while, and we just kind of clicked."

"You seem happy together. Has the age difference ever been an issue?"

"Not really. I mean, he's not as much into the partying aspect of the gay community. Like going out for happy hour yesterday was fine, but he didn't want to go out dancing with us later. The parade was fine, but he's not interested in the festival. He says he's been to dozens of festivals, and after a while, they get to be the same."

"Yeah. I haven't even been to very many festivals and I feel that way. And same thing with the bars. I'm just not that interested."

Kevin said, "Being with Chase means less excitement but more stability. He has his act together more than those other guys. I mean, they're my friends and I like them, but I was ready to move beyond the bars and hooking up and all that. I was ready to settle down."

"Same here. I'm more of a homebody. I'd rather spend my money on a nice home that I can relax in and enjoy. And I'd rather have a few friends over than hang out in some noisy, crowded place surrounded by people I don't know. And those apps like Grindr? Totally not interested."

"That weekend back in 2013 when I came to visit you, I couldn't get over what a nice place you have. But now, I can't complain."

"No kidding! Your place is nice. So yeah, we're both very fortunate. Of course, you have a man to share it with, and I don't – not yet, anyway."

"So do you think Aaron might be the one?"

"I sure hope so. He's the nicest guy I've met in a long time – well, since I moved to Scottsdale, actually." Ryan realized how that comment might be received. "Present company excluded, of course."

Kevin laughed. "No offense. We would have made a nice couple. But I didn't want to move and disrupt my career and I know you didn't either. And then, of course, Chase came along."

"I hope we stay in touch and remain friends. But back to Aaron. In some ways, he reminds me of Chris, my old high school boyfriend. He's sweet, he's smart, and he's cute. He's not as much into jazz as I am, but he likes it. He's just started playing his trombone again and he joined the gay band in Phoenix. And they have a jazz ensemble, too. He convinced me to start playing my trumpet again. I'll be forever grateful to him for that."

"Didn't he recently come out?"

"Yeah, like about four months ago. And that's another part of his appeal. He's still kind of innocent, you know? Like, everything is new and exciting to him. He hasn't had time to become bitter and jaded yet."

Kevin laughed. "Is that it? We turn thirty and we become bitter and jaded?"

"Sometimes I feel like I am, and I'm only 26. It's hard to describe it, but when I'm with him, being gay seems new and fresh again. I was thinking about that during the drive here. I never had the chance to come out on my own terms. I had it thrust upon me quickly, and then I was in survival mode. Coming out wasn't an enjoyable experience for me, but now I'm experiencing it vicariously through him."

Kevin thought, I wonder how much I should tell him about Aaron's behavior so far this weekend. I probably shouldn't bring it up at all. Maybe I should come at this from a different angle. "How long ago did you come out?"

"The summer after my junior year, which would have been 2007. So, nine years."

"Okay, then. A while ago you asked whether the age difference between Chase and me was an issue. Even though you guys are about the same age, you've been out for nine years. You've had a wide range of experiences. He's just coming out now. Do you think that difference will present any problems?"

"I don't know. That's a good question. For one thing, he wanted to jump in bed right away and I wanted to take it slower. See, I've learned that if the relationship is all about sex right away, most of the time it never gets beyond that. Like when the hot sex wears off, what do you have left? I've met so many guys who are only in it for sex. And I really want this one to work out. I want our relationship to be based on more than just sex."

"I get that, but do you think he does? How old is he now?"

"Twenty-eight."

"Okay. So that's kind of late to be coming out. Emotionally, he's still a teenager where sex is concerned. He probably feels like he has a lot of catching up to do."

Ryan thought about what Kevin said. "So, what are you trying to tell me?"

"I'm trying to tell you he's newly out. He's just coming to terms with being gay. He wants sex! He may want a relationship too, but he wants sex. And if he isn't getting it from you, he's going to get it someplace else."

Ryan thought, *Aaron was out until at least 2:00 last night. Was he at the bars, or…?*

Kevin said, "It's not only about you and how you want the relationship to develop. It's about him too. He should have a say in how the relationship unfolds. And I can tell he's frustrated that you guys haven't had sex yet. So you need to get busy if you want to keep him."

"You mean he's told you guys we haven't had sex yet?"

"It's come up. And this was a telling moment. Yesterday, when he, Kent, and Justin arrived at our house, I introduced them to Chase. Chase said to Aaron, 'So you're Ryan's new boyfriend.' He said, 'Something like that. We've been hanging out together a lot. We haven't put a label on it yet.' And the way he said it, we could tell he was frustrated about it."

Ryan sat and contemplated this new information. They finished their lunches, so they got up, threw their trash away, and refilled their soda cups. They left the sandwich shop and started walking south toward Balboa Park. "I guess we should have a conversation about this on the way home."

Kevin said, "It's fine if you want to have sex with him tonight. I'm going to wash the sheets after you leave anyway. I've got some lube and condoms I can give you."

"Okay, thanks. We'll see how it goes."

"I'll put them under the bed. Which side are you sleeping on?"

"The left side."

"Okay."

They walked for a few minutes in silence as Ryan processed everything. He hadn't planned to have his first sexual experience with Aaron on a hide-a-bed in someone else's house, but maybe he should. He had been given permission. He put his arm around Kevin. "Thanks."

"No problem."

***

Ryan and Kevin arrived at the festival at 1:35. Whitney Austin was scheduled to go onstage at 2:00. Ryan wanted to get there early to get a good spot on the lawn in front of the stage. He texted Aaron.

> Hey! We just walked in the entrance. Where are you?

> Wandering around the booths.

> We're heading toward the main stage to get a good place to sit. Wanna meet us there at 1:45?

There was a pause. Ryan assumed Aaron was conferring with the others.

> Yeah, okay. Between 1:45 and 2:00.

Ryan sighed and put his phone back in his pocket.

Kevin and Ryan found a good spot to sit about thirty feet from the stage. They left a few feet between them and put their ball caps and drink cups on the ground a few feet on either side of them to stake out the area they were saving for the others.

Kevin said, "I remember that night on the cruise when you and I watched Whitney together."

"Yeah. During the day Ted and I and the four of you were all on the same tour of Seville, and then we had dinner together. You and I sat next to each other in the auditorium and held hands."

Kevin smiled at the fond memory. "And then that night was our first time. You and Derek traded places so you could be in my room with me and he could be in your room with Ted."

"Yeah, that was a great cruise. I haven't gone on one since. The resort in PV was the last gay vacation I've taken." Ryan paused for a moment. "Actually, the only other vacations I've taken were the times I went to see Ted in Berlin and Buenos Aires."

"How's he doing?"

"He's fine. He still likes moving from place to place every couple of years."

Kevin said, "I couldn't do that."

"Me neither. I mean, I see the appeal, and sometimes I think about getting out of the country, but I love my home too much. And my job's going well and I really like Scottsdale. But if Trump gets elected…"

"Oh, God. Don't even say that. But that'll never happen. Hillary's got a big lead in the polls. I mean, she's one of the most experienced presidential candidates we've had in our lifetime. He's never even held public office before. And he's so offensive. I don't see how he could win."

"Well, let's hope not."

Ryan glanced at his watch. 1:58. The stagehands finished clearing the stage from the band that had just performed. They brought out a microphone on a stand, a tall chair, and a small round table with a bouquet of roses and two water bottles. Ryan stood up and looked around. He saw Kent, Justin, Aaron, Derek, Stephen, and Zach enter the seating area at the back. He waved his arms so they could see him. At first, they just waved, as if standing in the back would be sufficient. Ryan motioned for them to come down and join them. They exchanged glances and a couple of them shrugged their shoulders. They made their way through the crowd and sat down on the grass. Aaron sat to Ryan's left, then Zach and Stephen. Derek sat to Kevin's right, then Justin and Kent.

The MC announced, "Ladieeeees and lesbians! You've seen her in P-town. You've seen her on Pacifica Cruises. You've seen her sensational YouTube videos. Now, on our very own stage, please put your hands together and welcome the one and only… Miss! Whitney! Austin!"

Energetic, thumping dance music started playing and Whitney Austin confidently glided onto the stage. Some people in the crowd clapped their hands over their heads and cheered enthusiastically, including Ryan and Kevin. Others politely applauded, waiting to see what all the fanfare was about.

Stephen called over to Ryan, "Isn't she the one that was on that cruise?"

Ryan nodded. While he, Kevin, Derek, and Ted had watched Whitney's show, Stephen and Zach opted to see comedians instead, saying 'we're not really into drag queens.' Apparently, they still weren't. Aaron didn't seem enthused, either.

After ten years as an internationally known drag performer, Whitney had honed every element of her humorous banter and stage presence to perfection.

While Ryan enjoyed Whitney's performance, he was filled with memories of living with Darnell for four and a half years in the house in Los Angeles. Darnell was just as flamboyant and fabulous in real life as he was performing as Whitney. Darnell taught Ryan the importance of being authentic and living life on your terms – honestly and without apology. Darnell possessed more strength of character than anyone else Ryan had ever met. He hoped he'd be able to say hi and talk for a few minutes after the show.

At one point, he locked eyes with Whitney. Whitney smiled but didn't miss a beat of her song. He couldn't tell whether Whitney recognized him or not.

Ryan was so caught up in the performance and his memories that he was oblivious to his immediate surroundings.

Aaron just couldn't get excited about the performance. *Why is Ryan so into this? It's just a guy dressed up like a woman. I mean, he's got a great voice and everything, but... how much longer is this going to go on?* He glanced at Zach. Zach looked at Aaron and smiled as if to say, 'Yeah, I know.' He wasn't getting into it either. Aaron wished he could telepathically send a message to Stephen and Derek saying, 'I'm so over this. Wanna go somewhere else?' He wondered if he could surreptitiously send them a group text.

A few people had left, but most of the crowd was now absorbed by the show. Whitney's pacing was perfect and she was building up to her dramatic final number. She always closed her show with 'The Greatest Love of All.' Today, she added something extra to her lead-in. "Folks, I'm so glad I had the opportunity to come to San Diego and be part of your special celebration. Nobody does Pride like San Diego!" The crowd cheered. "Thank you, thank you. You've been a fabulous audience. Now, I would like to dedicate my last song to someone very special to me who's sitting in the audience right now. I met him when he was still a teenager. He had just arrived in Los Angeles all by himself, having been forced to leave home because his parents couldn't handle the fact that he was gay. So there he was, on his own, alone in the big city. And by God's grace, he came to live with us. And I watched him grow from a scared, clueless high school kid into a proud, beautiful, successful man. I watched him endure bullying and humiliation and become stronger and better for it. And now… Oh my God, I can't believe he's here today. So this goes out, with all my love, to Ryan Robertson!" No one except their immediate group had any idea who Ryan Robertson was, but they applauded politely. "I love you, hon." The background music began and Whitney started singing, "I believe the children are our future…"

Aaron was shocked. At the parade, a porn star had come up and hugged Ryan. Now, this drag queen who was apparently relevant had dedicated a song to him. What Whitney said about Ryan arriving in LA alone after being forced to leave home left him stunned. There was obviously a lot about Ryan he didn't know.

After the show, Ryan eagerly made his way to the left side of the stage, where the steps were. The others straggled behind. He hoped to catch Whitney's attention. The backstage area was blocked off by crowd control barricades and monitored by two people wearing shirts marked SECURITY. There was a large white tent Whitney had disappeared into. Ryan asked the security guards, "Would it be possible to see Whitney Austin? We used to be housemates. I'm the guy she dedicated her last song to."

They looked at each other, and one of them said, "I'll go back to the performer's tent and see if she plans to come back out. What's your name?"

"Ryan Robertson. Thank you."

She walked back to the tent. A moment later, she returned and said, "She'll be out in a few minutes. Wait right here." By this time, the rest of the guys had arrived. Ryan turned around and saw Ricky heading toward him. He was wearing the skimpy, silky shorts he wore on the float in the parade, and he had put on a loose-fitting tank top that accentuated his impressive physique. They met and hugged each other.

Ryan said, "Ricky! Glad you made it."

Ricky said, "Yeah. I was a little farther back. I got there a few minutes after the show started, but you never turned around."

Ryan said, "Darnell – I mean Whitney – will be out in a few minutes. Let me introduce you to my friends." Of course, Ryan introduced him as Ricky Montez, not Juan Knight. He was unaware the others had seen Ricky go-go dancing at Fort Dicks the night before, wearing only a thong. Most of the others were thrilled to be meeting a porn star in real life. Neither Ryan nor Ricky could have known that last night, Stephen, Derek, Justin, and Kent watched Juan Knight taking multiple men in *Poolside Pleasures*. Stephen, Derek, Justin, and Kent had no idea *Poolside Pleasures* was shot at the house where Ryan, Ricky, Darnell, and Ted lived.

As they finished introductions, Darnell's voice rang out. "Darling!"

Everyone turned and looked. Whitney was hurrying toward the group as fast as she could, given that her stiletto heels were poking holes in the grass every step of the way. The security guard pivoted one section of the barricade enough to allow Whitney to pass through.

She hugged Ryan, then saw Ricky. "Oh my God! I had no idea you would be here too!" She hugged Ricky.

"Yeah. I live here now. You were *fabulous!*"

Whitney replied, "Oh, I know I was, but it's sweet of you to say so."

Ricky said, "Yes. Especially since you dedicated a song to him, but not me."

Whitney shot back, "Sorry, honey, but I don't have 'Bad Girls' in my repertoire."

Ryan and Ricky laughed. Everyone else was taken aback by that retort. They were unsure whether they should laugh, given that they didn't really know these guys.

Ryan introduced Whitney to his friends. After he finished saying each of their names, Whitney looked at Kevin and said, "You look familiar. Weren't you on the Amsterdam to Barcelona cruise?" Kevin nodded. "You two met each other there."

Kevin said, "You have a good memory."

Whitney said, "I watch out for my homies." She turned to Derek, "And you're the one who hooked up with Ted."

Derek said, "Guilty as charged."

"Oh, I can only imagine what you must be guilty of!" Everyone chuckled.

Ryan said, "Stephen, Zach, Kent, and Justin were on that cruise, too. Kent and Justin are now friends of mine in Phoenix, and they got me involved in a couple of groups back home.

Ryan handed his phone to Aaron and said, "Would you take a picture of us?"

Ryan and Ricky stood on either side of Whitney. She wrapped her arms around them and pulled them close to her face. The edge of her wig brushed against Ryan's face and tickled. Aaron snapped several pictures from different distances.

Whitney released Ricky for a moment and said to Aaron, "Now take one of the two of us."

Aaron said, "3… 2… 1…" and Whitney turned and planted a kiss on Ryan's cheek.

She let go of Ryan and turned to Ricky. "And now you." Aaron took another picture.

Whitney turned to the others and said, "Would anyone else like to have their picture taken with a celebrity?"

Most of the others weren't interested and wondered if they should say yes to be polite. Kevin said, "Yes, I would. How about one with you and Ryan?"

Ricky stepped aside and Kevin took his place. Aaron took a couple more pictures.

Several of the others wanted to have their picture taken with the legendary porn star, Juan Knight. But that wasn't being offered, and they knew they shouldn't take the spotlight away from Whitney Austin.

Ryan said, "Okay, I won't hold you up while we hang out and reminisce about the good old days. Why don't you guys go enjoy the festival and I'll catch up with you later."

The others looked relieved to be dismissed. Aaron said, "How about if you meet us in the beer garden when you're done?"

Ryan said, "Cool. Or text me if you decide to do something else."

As they turned to go, Whitney called out, "Ta-ta, boys! Don't forget to check out my Facebook page and my YouTube channel!" They turned, waved, and went on their way.

As they walked up the hill toward the beer garden, Derek whispered to Justin, "I wonder if Juan Knight has a YouTube channel."

Justin whispered back, "Probably a PornTube channel." They both snickered.

The next act was set up on stage and about ready to begin, so Whitney said, "Allow me to escort you backstage. Let's find someplace quiet where we can talk." The security guards didn't make a fuss when Whitney led Ryan and Ricky through the gap in the barricade.

There were folding chairs in the tent, so Ryan and Ricky sat down. Whitney walked over to a cooler and returned with three water bottles. She sat down, pulled off her wig, and kicked off her stiletto heels. "Whew! It feels good to have those off. So how are you boys?"

Ricky went first. "I'm doing good. As you probably heard, things kind of got out of control a few years ago. What was it? 2012?" Ryan nodded. "I had a substance abuse problem and I wasn't willing to deal with it. Hal and Ryan tried to convince me to go into rehab, but I wouldn't, so Hal kicked me out. It was brutal at the time. I mean, I felt like my family had turned against me. But they were absolutely right. They were trying to get me to do what I needed to do, but I was too dumb to realize it. So I called my druggie friends Jorge and Carlo. They let me stay a couple of nights, but then they told me I had to move on. As it turned out, they were only my friends as long as I had money and bought drugs from them. Anyway, I called around to a bunch of my other friends and couch-surfed with a few of them, but I knew I couldn't keep doing that. And since I had HIV, I knew I couldn't work at any of the studios in town, so I didn't have any money coming in and I couldn't buy drugs. So I had to quit."

Darnell said, "Good for you, honey. I know that must have been rough."

"Oh, it was. But it was for the best. When I look back on it now, I was pretty stupid. I was spending money as fast as I was making it. All that clubbing, drinking, drugs, fancy meals, nice clothes – man, I thought I was living the life. But I wasn't saving any of it. And I didn't have health insurance, which didn't help when I found out I had HIV."

Ryan asked, "So what did you do?"

"Thankfully, the City of Los Angeles has free clinics that provide HIV meds to people who can't afford it. It hurt my pride to have to go there, but that was a real wake-up call. Then I moved to Palm Springs and did a few scenes for this company that pairs HIV-positive performers with each other. I did enough of that to have some money to buy food and rent a room and get health insurance through Obamacare."

Ryan asked, "So how did you end up here?"

"I decided to go back to school and finish up my degree, and there weren't any schools in Palm Springs I wanted to go to. I have a friend from high school I kept in touch with on Facebook. He teaches at San Diego State, so he said, 'Why don't you come here? You can room with me and go to school here.' So that's what I did. I got my credits from UCLA transferred, and now I'm one quarter away from graduating. On the weekends I do go-go dancing in the clubs just for fun – and the tip money."

Darnell said, "Wow! Congratulations! I'm really proud of you."

Ryan asked, "What are you majoring in?"

Ricky said, "Social work. I want to work with young people in underprivileged communities to help them stay off drugs and improve their lives."

Darnell said, "That's wonderful. Oh, honey, I'm so happy for you!" He leaned forward in his chair and gave Ricky a hug. Then he turned to Ryan. "And what about you, sugar?"

Ryan said, "I'm in Scottsdale now. I work at a company called Technovations. That's the place where I interned after my junior year. They do all kinds of work on cutting-edge technology, like stuff that isn't even ready to come to market yet. It's challenging, but exciting at the same time. And some of the people I work with are incredibly brilliant. I learn a lot just being around them."

Ricky said, "Cool. So what's the gay community like there?"

"I don't know. I don't get out much. Up until recently, I've been so focused on my job, I didn't have much of a social life. There are a few other gay people I know at work, mostly the guy I stayed with for my internship and some of his friends. And I belong to a gay running club that goes running every Sunday morning except during the summer. Kent and Justin, whom you just met, got me into that. But that's about it."

Darnell's expression was a mix of sadness and concern. "You mean you don't have someone special? You have everything in the world going for you. You're nice, you're smart, you're irresistibly adorable, you've got a good job–"

260

Ricky cut in, "And a huge dick."

Darnell glared at Ricky and continued. "Are all the gay men in Phoenix blind? I'm surprised no one has snatched you up and put a ring on that finger."

"Well, you know I'm shy. I really don't like crowds or bars. So I don't put myself out there very much. But that guy Aaron, the one with the curly hair who took our picture? I've been kinda interested in him. In some ways, he reminds me of Chris. But a few things have happened this weekend that kinda make me wonder."

Ricky asked, "Are you still playing your trumpet?"

"Funny you should ask. If you had asked me a month ago, I would have said no. When I moved to Scottsdale, I was so focused on work that I never took the time to find any bands to play in. And next thing you know, four years went by. But Phoenix has an LGBT band and Aaron plays trombone in it. Kent, one of the guys you just met, plays French horn. So Aaron convinced me I should start playing again and join the band. And they have a jazz ensemble! Now I've been to a couple of rehearsals for each band. So, thanks to Aaron, I'm playing again."

Darnell said, "See? Sounds like you need to keep this one."

"We'll see. But what about you?"

Darnell said, "I'm good. Atlanta's good. I'm working at an LGBTQ+ medical group I like a lot and I'm building up my practice."

Ryan asked, "How about your mom and your sister?"

"My sister's doing great. She graduated a couple of years ago and got a good job and now she's engaged. So everything's good there. Mama… well she's kind of going downhill. She hasn't been the same since Dad died. She was staying with my sister, but when things got serious with her boyfriend and they moved in together, we moved Mama into an independent living community. At first, she hated the thought of going into a place like that, 'cause it was like, okay, this is the beginning of the end. But she likes it now. She's made a bunch of friends and there's stuff for her to do and her needs are being met. So yeah, she's where she needs to be. We visit her a lot and take her out places."

Ricky said, "And how's it going for Whitney Austin?"

Darnell sighed. "Well, Whitney doesn't get out as much as she used to. Now that I'm working full-time, summer in P-town is out. I flew out here on Friday night, and I'm flying back home later today. I only get two weeks of vacation a year, so that means I can only do two Pacifica events. So I do their Med cruise in the summer and their resort in PV in November. But I'm starting to think maybe I want to do other things for vacations instead of performing on gay cruises. I mean, it's fun, but it's work. So going forward, Whitney is going to limit herself to local events like charity banquets and fundraisers."

Ryan said, "And like you just told me, you need a social life, too. Are you seeing anyone?"

Darnell perked up. "Well, as a matter of fact, I am!" He walked over to his costume suitcase and pulled his phone out. He pulled up a photo as he walked back to his chair. He held the phone out so Ryan and Ricky could see it. "His name is Raythan. We met at a Christmas party last year, and we've been seeing each other for about six months now."

Ricky said, "Oooo, gurrl! You got yourself a hot one!"

Darnell grinned proudly. "I know, right? And he's smart. He's a financial advisor. And he's really sweet. And… well, he's really good for me, if you know what I mean." Darnell's coy smile said it all.

Ryan said, "And I'm sure you're good for him, too. He's the lucky one."

Darnell smiled and feigned bashfulness. "Well, I haven't heard any complaints."

Ryan said, "Wow. It's hard to believe how much has happened in the last four years."

Darnell said, "I know, right? Seems like ages ago that we were all living in that house together."

Ricky said, "Those were good times, though."

Darnell said, "They sure were. Sometimes you don't really appreciate something until it's gone."

Ricky said, "And not just the house. Hal. God, it's so sad that it had to end like that."

Their celebratory mood turned somber. Darnell looked like he might start to cry.

Ryan said, "You know, I did appreciate it at the time. I knew how lucky I was. I think back on that day I arrived in town and went to the LGBT Youth Project. I just happened to meet Hal, and he just happened to have a room available. If it had been any other day, none of that would have happened. I could have easily ended up homeless. Who knows what would have happened? I mean, you guys literally rescued me. You taught me so much.

You opened my eyes to so many things. Most of all, you loved me after I had been rejected by my parents. We were a family."

Darnell said, "Amen, brother."

Ricky said, "Same here. You guys were more of a family to me than my own."

Darnell said, "I wonder what Ted is up to these days."

Ryan said, "Actually, I saw him last month. He's in Buenos Aires now. I went to visit him for a couple of weeks. He moved to London first, then Berlin, and now Buenos Aires."

Ricky said, "How does he like it? And is he seeing anyone?"

"He likes his job and being able to move from one place to the next. He doesn't like Buenos Aires as much as London or Berlin, but it's fine for a while. As for seeing someone, I don't think so. He didn't mention anyone. I don't think a relationship is a priority for him at this point in his life. If he met someone he liked, it would only last until his assignment was up."

Darnell said, "I'm surprised you two didn't end up together. I always knew you had a thing for each other."

"Was it that obvious?"

"Uh-huh."

"We're bonded pretty tight, that's for sure. But you know, I think that happened because he took a relationship off the table right away. It's like we became better friends because we knew we weren't trying for a relationship. Besides, I want to have a nice comfortable home and he wants to live all over the world. That's one thing I learned about living in our house. I want to have a nice place to come home to. I'd rather spend money on that than a lot of other things."

Darnell said, "Well, I'd better change out of this gown and get ready to go. I have to be at the airport by 5:00. But it's been so wonderful to see you guys again and chat for a bit."

Ricky said, "Yeah. We need to always stay in touch."

Darnell asked Ryan, "Did you finally join the modern world and get on Facebook?"

"Nope. I still have no interest in social media. But I'll upload those pictures to my Google Drive and send you guys the link. Let me make sure I have your phone numbers and email addresses." They pulled out their phones and updated their contacts. Ryan said, "I'll send you Ted's contact info too."

Darnell asked, "Is it okay if I post the pictures on my Facebook page?"

Ryan said, "Yeah, sure. I think my family gave up on looking for me a long time ago."

They hugged and kissed each other, then said goodbye.

***

As Ryan walked toward the Beer Garden, his mind was flooded with memories of the times he shared with Darnell, Ricky, Ted, and Hal for five years. He barely saw anything that was happening around him. He was jolted from his nostalgia when a voice called out, "Ryan! Hey, Ryan!"

Ryan turned around and saw a young man hurrying toward him. He recognized him from his senior year of high school and freshman year of college. His face had matured, his hair was starting to recede, and he had put on ten or fifteen pounds. "Well, if it isn't Jordan Harrington."

Jordan reached Ryan and threw his arms around him. "Oh, man! It's so great to see you again."

Ryan wasn't interested in being hugged by Jordan, but he didn't push him away. "You are literally the last person I would have expected to see here. What are you doing here?"

Jordan said, "I'm enjoying the Gay Pride festival. Duh! But yeah, I get it. Back when we parted company, I was still trying to convince myself I wasn't gay."

"You had me fooled."

"Really? I thought you had figured it out. So anyway, whatcha been up to? Do you live here now?"

"No, I live in Scottsdale."

"I'm in Long Beach. I'm staying at the Hillcrest Inn."

"Okay, well, I'm on my way to meet some friends. It was nice running into you."

"Totally. Hey, can I get your phone number? Maybe we can talk sometime."

Ryan had no interest in getting back in touch with Jordan, who had tormented him during their senior year of high school. Jordan befriended Ryan during their freshman year at UCLA, but then abruptly cut that off. But he was too nice to say no. They exchanged numbers. Then Ryan said, "Later, man. Enjoy the festival."

"You too!"

Ryan turned and resumed his journey to the beer garden.

So Many Men

Saturday, July 16, 2016

At a few minutes before 8:00, the group arrived at Burger Betty's for dinner. When Ryan made the reservation a week ago, he was planning to treat Kevin and Chase to dinner to thank them for hosting, along with Aaron, Kent, and Justin. But as the weekend progressed, it became obvious that Zach, Stephen, and Derek were part of the package too. Ryan decided it would be awkward to exclude them from dinner. He called Burger Betty's, and they reluctantly agreed to increase the reservation from six people to nine. This meant the group had to wait a little longer to be seated.

At 9:45, they finished dinner and Ryan paid the check. As they were heading back to their cars, Derek said, "So what's next? You want to go back to Fort Dicks or check out someplace else?"

Justin said, "They're having a foam party called Studs in Suds at the festival. I wanna do that."

Aaron asked, "What's a foam party?"

Stephen said, "They set up an area where they have several machines that shoot out foam. It's like a giant bubble bath. They have a DJ, so it's like a big dance but with foam everywhere."

Aaron asked, "Don't you get wet?"

Stephen said, "Just kind of moist. And a lot of guys only wear shorts or underwear. It's pretty wild!"

I'll bet it is, Aaron thought.

Justin added, "And when he says you'll get moist, he's not kidding!"

Ryan leaned in toward Aaron and lowered his voice. "I was hoping maybe we'd go home and…"

Aaron said, "Aw, man, I'm not ready to go home yet. It's only 10:00." *And besides, if I play my cards right, I might be able to score another round with Zach.*

The last thing Ryan wanted to do was dance in a mob of intoxicated, horny guys in his underwear. He knew how that would turn out. "Okay, well, why don't you go for a little while and see what it's like? But try not to stay out too late, okay?" He smiled as he said it and winked, trying to convey a suggestion. Aaron didn't pick up on it, but Zach did.

To Aaron, Ryan sounded like a nagging parent. *Fuck that. Who goes home at 10:00 on a Saturday night when there's all this going on?*

Kevin gave Kent his house key. Aaron rode to the festival with Kent and Justin, and the local guys rode in Derek's car. Ryan rode home with Kevin and Chase. On the way, he checked his phone. A message from Jordan had come in at 8:32.

Ryan wasn't sorry and he had no interest in getting together with Jordan for 'eggplant' or anything else.

A few minutes later, Jordan replied.

Ryan thought, *Yet another reason I'm glad I didn't go.*

When they got home, Chase said, "It's a lovely evening. Would you like to enjoy some wine with us on the back patio? I can light a fire in the fire pit."

Ryan said, "Yeah, that would be nice. Thanks!"

Kevin said, "I'll get some crackers and cut up some cheese."

Ten minutes later, they were seated around a small round table sipping wine and eating cheese, with the fire crackling a few feet away.

Ryan said, "This is really nice. I can't thank you guys enough for being such great hosts."

Chase said, "Our pleasure. And thanks again for treating us to dinner. With nine guys and all the drinks some of them ordered, I'll bet that was a pretty hefty check."

"Yeah, it was more than I planned for, but it's cool. I can afford it. I wanted everyone to have a good time."

Chase said, "You were lucky to get into Burger Betty's during Pride weekend. We could have gone to someplace away from Hillcrest and there wouldn't have been such a crowd."

"Yeah, but I really wanted to go to Burger Betty's. That place is kind of special to me." Ryan relayed the story of how Russ Simonton, his grocery store boss in Kansas, had taken him to Burger Betty's in Kansas City on the night he left home. He talked about the special occasions he had celebrated with his housemates at the location in West Hollywood. He said, "They don't have one in Phoenix. So I wanted to go to the one here this weekend."

Kevin said, "I enjoyed seeing Whitney Austin. She sounded better than ever."

"Yeah, I haven't seen her perform since the cruise. I'm really happy I got to catch up with Darnell and Ricky after the show. They were more than just housemates; they were my brothers for five years of my life. I mean, life goes on and we've all gone our separate ways. But it was nice to see them again."

Ryan regaled them with stories from their years of living together in the house. Kevin and Chase talked about how they met and fell in love, and they all talked a little bit about their jobs. The conversation flowed freely for over an hour.

***

When Aaron, Kent, Justin, Zach, Derek, and Stephen arrived at Studs in Suds, it was already in full swing. Aaron couldn't tell how many guys were there since it was dark and the foam was obscuring the view. But it had to be at least a couple hundred.

They took their shirts off and tucked them into the waistbands of their shorts. Soon they were dancing with the masses in the center of the crowd. Some of the others were also wearing shorts, but the majority were dancing in their underwear or skimpy swimwear.

Derek leaned into Justin, Zach, and Aaron and shouted over the dance music, "Man, I wish we had left our shorts and shirts in the car!"

Justin said, "We could take them back now. It would only take five or ten minutes."

Derek motioned to Kent and Stephen and the six of them worked their way to the edge of the foam pit. Derek said, "We don't all have to go. I can take all the stuff for my guys."

Aaron and Kent looked at Justin. Justin said, "Oh, all right. Give me your stuff and I'll take it to the car."

The guys handed their shorts and shirts to Derek and Justin. Aaron, Kent, Zach, and Stephen made their way back into the foam and resumed dancing, clad only in their underwear and shoes. Derek and Justin rejoined them a few minutes later.

Aaron thought, *I seriously can't believe I'm doing this. Three months ago, this would never have entered my mind.*

As they danced, the crowd naturally shifted. Other guys worked their way into their space, but Aaron made sure he was always dancing across from Zach. He was totally enjoying the foam party and hopeful about how the night would progress. He wasn't sure what the other guys had in mind for later in the evening, but he knew what he wanted.

A cute blond guy in his mid-20s worked his way into their cluster. He seemed to be alone. Although he tried to be nonchalant about it, Aaron could tell he was checking everyone out. Aaron stayed close to Zach. He was not about to let this little blond twink work his way between them.

Derek was more interested in getting his attention. They made eye contact and Derek smiled. "Hi. I'm Derek."

Twinkie Boy smiled back. "Jordan." As he danced, he moved a

few inches closer to Derek. "Are these your friends?"

"Yeah."

"Nice."

They kept dancing, both wondering what to say next. Jordan was dividing his attention between Derek, Aaron, and Zach.

Derek said, "Are you here with friends or a boyfriend or anything?"

"Nope. By myself. I came down from Long Beach for the weekend."

"Are you driving back tonight?"

"No, I have a room over at the Hillcrest Inn."

"Ahh. We were there for happy hour yesterday."

"Yeah, I think I saw you guys."

A fresh blast of foam made its way to the group. Justin moved in close behind Jordan and brushed his bulge back and forth across Jordan's butt. Jordan pushed his butt backward and ground it into Justin's crotch. Stephen and Kent moved closer, watching the developing situation with interest and curiosity.

Aaron was interested in only one man, and it wasn't Jordan. He glanced at Zach, wondering what he was thinking now. He moved a few inches closer to Zach. With the new foam as cover, he contemplated whether a wandering hand might be well-received.

Rather than go right for his package, he placed his hand on Zach's side. Zach looked at him and smiled. Aaron leaned forward and gave Zach a quick kiss on his cheek. He hoped that would send a message to Jordan.

They danced for another ten minutes. Jordan had integrated himself into the cluster of Derek, Justin, Kent, and Stephen, and they all seemed fine with that. Aaron tried to steer Zach a little farther away.

Aaron glanced over and noticed a brief conversation taking place. Then Derek took a few steps over to Aaron and Zach and said, "We're heading over to Jordan's room at the Hillcrest Inn. Are you coming too?"

Aaron and Zach looked at each other. Zach looked like he was seriously weighing his options. Aaron shook his head just enough that he hoped Zach would get the message. As he waited for Zach to answer, he glanced at the others. Jordan was flashing an optimistic smile that said, 'Four would be hot. Six would be even hotter. C'mon!'

Aaron leaned into Zach and whispered, "I'd rather go home with you."

Zach thought, *But what about Ryan? He wasn't here last night, but he's at Kevin's house right now, hoping Aaron will come home. If I say no, he'll probably go with them. Maybe I'll be able to talk him out of it. At least I'll get him home earlier.*

Zach looked at Aaron, then he looked at Derek and the others. He said, "Nah, I think I'll pass."

Aaron breathed a sigh of relief.

Derek said, "Okay, whatever. But you need to come and get your clothes out of my car."

The group left the foam party, returned to their cars, and put their clothes back on. The four that were going with Jordan to the Hillcrest Inn decided it was close enough to walk, and it wouldn't be worth the bother to try to find parking places closer to the hotel.

When they reached the hotel, Aaron and Zach continued walking to his condo, which was another 15 minutes away.

Aaron felt exuberant. Dancing in his underwear with hundreds of other gay men at a foam party was the edgiest thing he had ever done. Everything about the weekend so far had exceeded his wildest expectations. Coming out had been liberating, but this weekend was introducing him to a whole new world of self-affirmation, freedom, and hedonism he could never have dreamed of a few short months ago. And it was only going to get better!

After the wonderful experience he shared with Zach last night, he was eagerly anticipating their encore. He glanced at Zach. Zach wasn't radiating excitement and joy as Aaron was. He seemed like he had a lot on his mind.

Aaron reached over and held Zach's hand. *Why not? It's Hillcrest! It's LGBT pride weekend!* Zach seemed surprised by this gesture. Aaron said, "Whatcha thinkin' about?"

Zach looked straight ahead. He had a serious expression on his face, like he was trying to make a difficult decision. Finally, he released his hand from Aaron's and said, "I don't think this is a good idea."

"Huh? Why not?"

Zach stopped walking and turned toward Aaron. "Okay, look. Last night was great and everything, but in hindsight, I don't think it was such a good idea. You've got a boyfriend. Maybe you're not officially boyfriends yet, and maybe you haven't explicitly committed to being monogamous yet, but that's where it's heading. I can tell that's what Ryan wants. It was obvious by the way he looked at you and acted around you all day."

"Yeah, maybe, but as you said, we haven't committed yet. I'm not sure where things are heading with us, but even if we end up being boyfriends, we're not there yet. This weekend might be my last opportunity to have fun before I settle down."

"You make it sound like settling down isn't going to be fun. If you would rather be out partying and having sex with other guys than spending the evening with Ryan, then you should probably reconsider whether you really want a relationship."

"He could have come with us, but he chose not to."

"Yeah, but did you see the way he looked at you when he said, 'Don't stay out too late?' It was obvious what he had in mind. So yeah... If you want to get laid tonight, it should be with Ryan, not me."

"That's my choice to make."

"Yeah, but I have a choice in this matter, too, and I'm choosing not to. Yesterday was one thing. Ryan hadn't arrived yet. But he's here now, and I saw how he looked at you and how much he cares about you and wants you. So no – I'm not going to take you home. I'm going to drive you back to Kevin's house."

Aaron stood still for about five seconds. "No, you're not. If that's the way you feel about it, I'm going to the hotel with the other guys." He turned and started walking back toward the Hillcrest Inn. When he got there, he texted Justin and asked what room they were in.

He wanted a piece of Jordan, too.

***

At around 11:30, Chase said, "Well, I need to turn in. We have a big day ahead of us tomorrow with the party in the afternoon. We still have a lot of work to do to get ready."

Ryan said, "What can I do to help?"

Chase said, "Nothing. Don't worry about it. You're our guest."

Ryan said, "No, seriously. I don't mind a bit. I can't speak for the others, but I'm happy to help in any way I can."

Chase said, "That's very kind of you. But let's deal with that tomorrow. I'm heading for bed." He stood up, walked over to Kevin, and gave him a kiss. "Good night!"

Kevin stood up and hugged him. He kissed him and said, "I love you."

"I love you too." Chase walked to the door. He turned around and winked at Kevin, then disappeared inside.

Kevin picked up the wine bottle and divided the remaining wine between his glass and Ryan's.

Ryan said, "He's really nice. You guys are so sweet together."

"Yeah, he's pretty special. In spite of our differences, we make it work. We just kind of 'get' each other, you know?"

"I can tell. I'm glad you found each other."

Kevin decided to address the elephant in the room – or on the patio, to be more precise. "I'm sorry it didn't work out for you and Aaron tonight."

Ryan sighed. "That's okay. That time will come." He paused. "Or not."

A moment passed. Ryan's hand was resting on the table next to his wine glass. Kevin reached over and placed his hand on top of Ryan's. "He has no idea what he's missing out on."

Ryan forced a weak smile.

Kevin said, "I really enjoyed the times we had together. And not just the sex."

"Yeah, me too. But I'm glad you found Chase."

Kevin paused while he decided what to say next. "Yeah, we're very happy together. As I said earlier, I appreciate the stability, even at the expense of a little excitement."

"Yeah, I know what you mean. I'll take stability over excitement any day. Maybe I should try to find an older guy. There have been several older guys in my life who have been really important to me. I didn't think about any of them in romantic terms – well, except for Ted, of course. Aaron's cute and everything, but we're not on the same level when it comes to maturity."

Kevin said, "Still, there's something to be said for youthful energy." Kevin's hand was still on top of Ryan's. He gave his hand a little squeeze. "I mean, things are good with Chase. But… well, if I can be honest, I don't always get it as often as I'd like. Things have changed for him as he's gotten older, and... well, let's just say most of the time I'm the top, if you get what I mean. And while I like being a top–"

"And you're very good at it, as I recall."

"Yes, well… I guess what I'm saying is I don't always get everything I want."

Ryan wondered, *Is he trying to say what I think he is?* He glanced at Kevin, who was gazing at him with a hopeful look on his face. *Okay, this is ... interesting. And awkward. What should I say? What if I'm misreading him?*

Kevin squeezed Ryan's hand again. "I put the condoms and lube under your bed this afternoon before we left for dinner."

Well, that clears that up – I think. "Are you suggesting..."

Kevin smiled and nodded.

"But… what about Chase?"

"Remember yesterday at lunch when I told you about our agreement?"

"But right here in your house?"

Kevin nodded. "Did you see the way he looked at me when he kissed me and how he winked at me before he went inside? That was him telling me it's okay. Like I said, we 'get' each other."

Oh, God. What should I do? I want to, but… he's got a partner. I suppose that's between them, but…

"But what if Aaron comes home while we're… you know… in the act."

Kevin sighed. "Honey, he's out there looking for someone to hook up with right now. It's not yet midnight. He'll be out for another couple of hours."

"You mean he's…"

"Yes. I hate to be the one to break this to you, but he hooked up with a couple of guys at the happy hour yesterday afternoon. And he hooked up with Zach last night. And I could tell he was hoping for more tonight. They went to a foam party, for Christ's sake. Hundreds of guys wearing nothing but underwear or thongs. Gee, where could that possibly lead? Face it, Ryan. He's a kid in a candy store, and this weekend it's all you can eat. He isn't going to come home and get it with you."

Ryan's heart sank. *Obviously, Aaron is not boyfriend material. Either that, or he wants to have an open relationship and, well… no thanks. And if he'd rather hook up with someone else than be with me, what am I holding out for? I care about Kevin and it would be hot… but he has a partner. But it's all right with them.* "Sure, why not?"

Kevin stood up and put the cover on the fire pit. He and Ryan picked up the glasses and plates from the table and carried them inside. Then they headed downstairs to the hide-a-bed in the rec room.

When they reached the side of the bed, they wrapped their arms around each other and started kissing. The temperature rose quickly. Soon they removed each other's shirts and kicked off their shoes. As their tongues explored each other's mouths, they pressed their bare chests and bulging shorts against each other and stroked each other's backs. Soon they were squeezing each other's buns and grinding their crotches. Then Kevin unbuckled Ryan's belt, unzipped his pants, and reached inside for the grand prize he remembered so well from the cruise ship and their two months of long-distance dating.

Ryan's emotions were pulling him in every direction. *I so want this right now – emotionally even more than physically. It's been months since I've had sex with anyone. I still care about Kevin, and Kevin still does it for me in that special way. It would be so hot! But I feel like I'm enabling Kevin to cheat on his partner, even though they have an agreement. I want wild, passionate, fulfilling sex with Kevin in the worst way, but I feel guilty about it.*

Kevin dropped to his knees, pulling Ryan's underwear and shorts down as he went. Yet, Ryan's cock was deflating. As Kevin was about to take Ryan's cock in his mouth, Ryan stepped back. "I'm sorry. I can't. I just can't. I'm sorry."

A tear fell from Ryan's eye and ran down his cheek. He pulled his underwear and pants back up. He sat down on the edge of the bed and buried his head in his hands.

Kevin sat down next to him and put his arm around Ryan's shoulder. "It's okay."

Between sobs, Ryan said, "I'm so sorry. It's not you. I feel awful. On the one hand, I want this so much. I know it would be great. But… I don't know… I don't feel right about it. I'm sorry."

Kevin tried his best to hide his disappointment. "Then we shouldn't do it." He leaned in and kissed Ryan's cheek. "It's okay."

Ryan put his arm around Kevin's shoulder. They turned toward each other and put their other arms on each other's shoulders. For a few minutes, neither of them said anything. They held each other until Ryan stopped crying.

Ryan said, "I'm sorry. I shouldn't have allowed us to get started and then let you down."

"It's my fault. I shouldn't have come onto you."

"No, that's okay. I think we both wanted it, on one level."

"Well, I guess I should go." Kevin started to get up.

"Wait."

Kevin sat back down.

"Can I hold you for a few minutes?"

Kevin nodded.

Ryan moved further onto the bed, pivoted, and laid down. Kevin laid down next to him. They held each other and for a few minutes, neither of them spoke. Finally, Ryan said, "Am I fucked up or what?"

"What do you mean?"

"When I was living in LA with Ricky, the guy you met earlier this afternoon – you know, Juan Knight – one time he said there's having sex and there's making love. And it's okay to just have sex sometimes. Intellectually, I know that's true. And with Aaron, whatever he might be doing right now, I know he's just having sex. I wanted to wait until we had reached the point where we would be making love. And for us here tonight, I don't know… I suppose it's somewhere in between. I mean, I still love you as a good friend and I still think you're hot. When we first hooked up on the cruise ship, I knew we were just hooking up, but there was a spark there, you know? And when we were dating it was more like making love because we were trying to build a relationship. Tonight, it would have been just recreational, but yet there's still some feeling there. And the fact that you're in a relationship with another guy and I'm hoping something works out with Aaron makes it too weird. I don't know… why can't I just have sex for the hell of it and enjoy it for what it is?"

Kevin paused, knowing he needed to say exactly the right thing now. "Maybe because you're such an uncommonly decent guy."

Ryan gave Kevin a gentle squeeze. "That's nice of you to say."

"No, seriously. You are."

"Then I guess what they say is true – nice guys finish last."

"Oh, come on. Don't talk like that."

A moment went by, then Ryan said, "I guess what I crave is lovemaking. I don't want to just have sex."

Kevin thought about it for a moment, then said, "That's beautiful. It shows what kind of person you are."

"Yeah, the kind of person who rarely gets laid."

Kevin chuckled. "There's that."

"And something else. No offense, but I just can't get into open relationships. I guess they're okay for some people, but not for me. It seems to work for you and Chase. In your case, it solves a problem. Kent and Justin have an open relationship and they seem to be okay with it. I don't know. I guess it gets back to the whole thing about making love or having sex. And I wonder where that leaves Aaron and me."

"Well, I guess you two have a lot to talk about."

"And a long drive home tomorrow in which to do it."

They held each other for a few more minutes.

Kevin said, "This is nice."

"Yes, it is. Thanks. I feel a lot better now."

"I think what you needed tonight was intimacy, not sex."

"Exactly."

"I think a lot of times when people hook up, what they really want is intimacy."

"You're probably right." Ryan sighed. "I wish we could spoon together all night like we used to."

"We can."

"No… Aaron will come back at some point. I assume, anyway."

"I guess you're right. I should probably go back upstairs, then."

They got up, and Ryan opened his arms.

Kevin stepped into his arms and they hugged.

Ryan whispered, "Thanks."

Then Kevin picked up his shirt and shoes and went upstairs to his room. Ryan brushed his teeth, stripped to his underwear, and went to bed.

Sunday in the Suburbs

Sunday, July 17, 2016

Aaron, Justin, and Kent arrived at Kevin and Chase's house at 2:30 a.m. When Aaron tiptoed downstairs, Ryan was sound asleep. As he climbed into bed, he looked at Ryan. He was too tired to think about the current state of their relationship, if it even was one, much less about their future. He promptly fell asleep.

***

The next thing Aaron knew, he was being jostled by Ryan. "Time to get up. It's 9:00."

Aaron barely stirred. He really wanted to sleep for several more hours.

Ryan said, "There's coffee upstairs. Chase made scrambled eggs and bacon, and there are some cinnamon rolls. C'mon."

Aaron yawned. "The party isn't going to start until 2:00, so why can't I sleep a while longer?"

"All right, whatever. But it's going to get noisy when we start setting up for the party."

***

Aaron finally got up at 10:45. He could hear chairs and tables being set up on the patio outside and people talking upstairs. He got up, took a shower, and got dressed. By the time he made it upstairs at 11:15, breakfast had been cleared away. Chase and Ryan were arranging hors d'oeuvres on plastic platters. Kevin was out on the patio.

Without looking at Aaron, Ryan said, "It lives."

Chase said, "There are still a couple of cinnamon rolls in that box over there. You can finish them off if you want to."

Aaron was starving. He ate the remaining cinnamon rolls. Chase,

Kevin, and Ryan seemed too absorbed in their tasks to pay much attention to him. That was okay. He wasn't ready to be sociable yet. "I'm going to walk over to Burger Palace on Adams Street and get something to eat."

Ryan said, "Later."

Aaron knocked on the guest bedroom door to see if Kent and Justin wanted to go, but there was no answer. As he walked out the front door, their car was gone. Just as well. He felt like being alone for a while.

***

At around 2:00, guests started arriving. Many of them were in their 40s. It was a mixed crowd – straight and gay, men and women. Everyone seemed comfortable around each other, like other people's sexuality was totally irrelevant. The people were nice and the food was plentiful and delicious. Light jazz played softly from a boom box near the food table. Aaron assumed most of the guests were Chase's friends, although Derek, Stephen, and a few others their age were there. Zach did not come.

Ryan spent most of his time in Chase's orbit and mingled easily with the older, more diverse guests. Aaron recalled Ryan saying he was shy and didn't like to be in crowds, but he seemed comfortable today. In fact, he seemed to be having a great time. Ryan seemed more interested in getting to know the other guests than hanging with Aaron.

At around 4:00, Derek and Stephen beckoned Aaron into the rec room. Derek said, "This party's lame. We're heading over to the T-dance at Fort Dicks. Wanna come?"

Aaron thought, *That would be so much more fun. These people are dull compared to the high-energy crowd that will be at the T-dance. This is boring, and I don't want the weekend to end on such a mellow note.* "Sounds great. Let me ask Kent and Justin if they want to go."

Aaron found Kent and Justin at the far end of the patio. He whispered, "Derek, Stephen, and I are going to blow this joint and head over to the T-dance at Fort Dicks. Wanna join us?"

Kent looked at Justin, then turned to Aaron. "Do you really think that's a good idea? Kevin and Chase were generous to let us stay here. It wouldn't look good to blow off their party."

"We're not blowing them off. We stayed for a couple of hours. But come on, this is boring."

"You've done plenty of partying this weekend. Besides, Ryan wants to leave at six. By the time you got there, you'd have to leave at 5:30 to get back here on time. Is it worth it for only an hour?"

Aaron sighed. "Yeah, I guess you're right."

Kent said, "You can force yourself to be sociable for two more hours. Besides, we might want to stay here again next year."

Aaron returned to the rec room and said, "I think it would be better if I stayed. You guys have fun."

Aaron wandered over to the food table, grabbed a fresh paper plate, and selected some more food. He wasn't hungry but grazing gave him something to do. Besides, they might not stop for dinner on the way home, so this could be it.

Ryan was talking with a small group of people near the edge of the patio that faced the canyon. Aaron wandered up and worked his way into a spot next to Ryan. Aside from Ryan, there were two women, Chase, and two gay men who were presumably a couple. Aaron couldn't tell whether the women were lesbians or straight, but in either case, they seemed comfortable in this crowd.

Ryan was saying, "But if Prop 60 passes, most of the industry will move out of California. It will have a huge economic impact, especially in the San Fernando Valley."

One of the gay men said, "They'll figure out some way around it. Besides, how are they going to enforce it? Are they going to try to track every scene that's being shot somewhere and send an inspector to make sure they're wearing condoms?"

The other guy said, "Well, they'll know when the video comes out."

Chase said, "Yeah, but how would they know whether the scenes were shot in California or someplace else?"

One of the women said, "Why don't they just go back to wearing condoms? It's safer for the performers, it sends a better message to the audience, and they wouldn't be breaking the law."

Ryan said, "Because nobody will buy it. They tried that for a while, and for a few years, most of the studios used condoms. But a few didn't, and they made all the money. They actually advertised they were doing bareback porn like it was a selling point. And as it turned out, it was. They eroticized it. They made it seem hotter and more edgy. And people bought it. Porn is all about selling fantasy. Nobody fantasizes about using condoms. They fantasize about not using them. Now, everyone's ditched the condoms."

The other gay man said, "Besides, now they have PrEP, so you can have sex without condoms and not get HIV."

Chase said, "Yeah, but that doesn't protect them from syphilis, gonorrhea, chlamydia, or anything else."

Ryan said, "True, but those are treatable. There's still no cure for HIV."

The other woman said, "Really? You mean after all these years there's still no cure for AIDS?"

Chase said, "Nope. Fortunately, the drugs they have now are so good that for most people, their viral load is undetectable. But you still have to keep taking the drugs, and they're still expensive."

Aaron wondered how they had gotten onto this topic. *Does Chase have HIV? And why does Ryan know so much about condoms in porn?*

Having exhausted this topic, Ryan said, "Everyone, I'd like you to meet Aaron. Aaron, this is Chad, Wayne, Claudia, and Monica."

"Nice to meet you."

Chad asked, "How long have you two been dating?"

Aaron knew what he wanted to say, but he decided to let Ryan take this one.

Ryan said, "We met back in May. May 21st, if I remember correctly. So it's only been a couple of months."

Ryan actually remembers the date we met? That's sweet.

Claudia asked, "How did you meet?"

Wayne grinned. "Wait! Let me guess... Grindr."

Ryan chuckled. "No, we met in a gay running club. The other guys we're here with, Kent and Justin, help run it. I've been running with them for a couple of years now, and then one day, Aaron showed up."

Chad said, "And the rest, as they say, is history."

Ryan said, "Well, kinda. Anyway, Kent also plays in Phoenix's LGBT band, and Aaron joined it this past spring. So when they found out he likes to run, they invited him to the running club."

Monica said, "I didn't know there was an LGBT band in Phoenix." Her inflection implied, 'I thought Phoenix was too backward or too conservative for that.'

Aaron said, "Yeah, actually they've been around since 2010. There's, like, 50 people in it."

Monica looked surprised. "Really!"

Ryan said, "One of the many great things about meeting Aaron is that he talked me into playing my trumpet again. I hadn't played it since I left college. They also have an LGBT jazz ensemble, which I totally love."

Chad said, "Well, you guys seem to have a lot in common. I hope it works out well for you."

Ryan put his arm around Aaron's shoulder and squeezed gently. "Yeah, I hope so too."

Aaron smiled. He wasn't sure what he should say.

Aaron stayed with Ryan for the rest of the party. The conversational groupings gradually shifted, so he ended up spending time with most of the others. He didn't have much to add to the conversations, but he smiled and tried to appear interested.

He thought a lot about Ryan. *I'm seeing a totally different side of Ryan today. He can actually open up and have intelligent conversations with people he's just met. Everyone else seems to be fascinated by him. He was kind of cold to me this morning, but I guess I can't blame him. God, I hope he doesn't find out how much fucking around I did this weekend. I wonder if Kent or Justin will tell him. Maybe I can get to them first.*

The Long Ride Home

Sunday, July 17, 2016

At around 6:00, Ryan whispered into Aaron's ear, "We'd better get going. We have a six-hour drive ahead of us and we both have to work in the morning."

They said goodbye to Kevin and Chase and everyone else who was still at the party. They loaded their suitcases into Ryan's BMW and began their journey east on I-8.

Aaron was sorry to see his action-packed weekend come to an end, but he had more fun than he ever dreamed possible, in ways he never dreamed of. "Oh, man! What an awesome weekend! I don't think I've ever had so much fun in all my life!"

"Yeah, you were constantly on the go."

"And to think, only four months ago, I didn't realize I was gay. If I had known being gay was so much fun, I would have come out years ago!"

"Life can change quickly, that's for sure. But did you have any idea you might be gay back when you were in high school or college?"

"Yeah, kinda. There were a couple of times in my sophomore year when my roommate and I fooled around a little bit. But I was busy with other stuff, like marching band and studying and all that. I just didn't want to deal with it. I thought if I ignored it, it would go away. Or maybe I hadn't met the right girl. Besides, I knew Mom and Dad would flip out."

"So you were happy enough with the status quo and you didn't want to rock the boat."

"Yeah, basically."

Ryan said, "Let's say you came out when you were a sophomore. How would your life have been different between then and now?"

"I don't know. I've never thought about it until now."

"Right. You don't know how your friends would have reacted. Maybe you'd have had different friends. Maybe you'd be in a relationship now. And because of him, you might not have moved to Arizona or you might have moved someplace else. Your life might have taken a completely different path."

Aaron thought about that for a moment. "Yeah. Who knows how it would have turned out? And I might never have met you."

Ryan didn't say anything to that. After a few moments, he said, "You never know how a decision you make one day might totally change your life. It's like every time we come to a fork in the road, we have to choose whether to go left or right. It may not seem like a big decision at the time, but you never know whether the two roads will come together again or they'll take off in completely different directions. You'll never know what might have been down that other road. But there's no point in wasting time thinking about it. It's not like you can go back and choose the other option instead. You just have to move on and make the best of the decision you made."

Aaron asked, "Have you ever had one of those times when you had to pick one road or the other, and it changed your life?"

"Yes, of course."

"What would you say was the biggest one?"

Ryan sighed. "I'd rather not talk about it."

"Why not?"

"It was quite traumatic at the time. I've gotten over it and moved on, and I don't want to rehash it now. I'd rather leave it in the past where it belongs and look to the future." *Please, just let it go.*

Aaron sensed that he had reached a dead end on this conversation topic, so he shifted gears. "What was your favorite part of the weekend?"

After thinking only a few seconds, Ryan said, "Seeing Darnell and Ricky again. It brought back a lot of memories. It was nice to see Kevin again and get to know Chase. And I enjoyed the party this afternoon. It was more chill – just people hanging out and talking. I like that a lot more than going out to festivals and bars and stuff."

Aaron waited to see whether Ryan would ask him what his favorite part of the weekend was. A few minutes passed. Finally, Aaron said, "Okay, here's a question. Let's say you could live anywhere you want. You'd have a job and you'd have enough money to live on. Where would you live?"

Without hesitating, Ryan said, "New Zealand."

"Really! Why New Zealand?"

"It's beautiful! My company has an office in Auckland, and I got to go there on a business trip for a month last year. I totally fell in love with it.

Auckland is gorgeous, with its harbors and all the sailboats. Wellington's nice, too. I spent two extra weeks there on vacation and traveled around and saw as much as I could. The countryside is filled with rolling green hills and charming towns. There's so much to see and do! There's even more on the south island I didn't get to. But most of all, the people are so nice. Everyone's friendly. The whole atmosphere is more relaxed and civil. And it's a lot safer – not like here where you have all this gun violence and religious nuts and right-wing politicians. God, if Trump gets elected, I might pack up and move."

"Well, I can't see him getting elected. Hillary's way ahead in all the polls."

"Let's hope so."

"But seriously – you'd leave the country and move to New Zealand if Trump got in office?"

"I might do it anyway, at some point. It resonated with me, you know? I felt like I belonged there; like I could really enjoy living there."

Aaron took a moment to process this. "Well, okay. I guess I wasn't expecting that. I was thinking in terms of places in the US."

Ryan asked, "So where would you like to live?"

"San Diego! I really liked everything I saw this weekend. I could so get into living there!"

"San Diego *is* nice. I came here a couple of times while I lived in LA. But it's expensive. It's not as bad as LA, but it's a hell of a lot more expensive than Phoenix."

"Really? I thought Phoenix was kind of expensive, at least compared to Ohio."

"I guess it depends on what you compare it to. I mean, Scottsdale seems expensive compared to the rest of Phoenix, but it's cheap compared to LA. So yeah… San Diego is beautiful and the weather's always pleasant. But did you see how much gasoline costs? And you should look into how much houses cost and what taxes are like. And keep in mind, every weekend is not going to be Gay Pride weekend. The day-to-day experience would be different."

Aaron said, "Okay, so no place is perfect. But there are plenty of good places to live in the US. Why would you want to leave?"

"It's a big world. There are lots of other places out there. This isn't the only option."

"Well, I'd like to visit other places on vacation, but why would you want to live someplace else? The United States is the greatest country on earth!"

"Is it really? Have you ever been outside the US?"

"Only once. We crossed over into Canada one time when we went to Niagara Falls."

"You should get out and see more of the world. Go to Europe and New Zealand and Australia. Visit Mexico and maybe South America. Maybe Japan or Thailand or South Africa. That might open you up to new possibilities. I want to travel to those places, and not just to see the tourist attractions. I want to get a feel for a place's history and culture. I want to get a taste of what day-to-day life is like for the people who live there."

Aaron thought about that for a moment. He and Ryan obviously weren't on the same page about where they would like to live. That raised other concerns.

Aaron said, "Okay, so you're saying you want to live in New Zealand or someplace else outside the US."

"I'm leaning in that direction, yes."

"So… what does that mean for us?"

"What do you mean?"

"Well, if we're going to be a couple, we kinda have to agree on where we want to live." Aaron glanced over at Ryan. He was staring at the highway ahead of them and didn't glance back.

After a tense moment of anticipation, Ryan glanced at Aaron and said, "We need to talk, and I guess now's as good a time as any." Ryan took a deep breath. "You're a nice guy and I've enjoyed hanging out with you and getting to know you. I like your exuberance and your positive energy. Part of it is, you're new to the whole gay thing. To you, it's fresh and exciting. That's one big difference between you and me. You're newly out and I've been out for, like, nine years. I've been through a lot, and for me… well, let's just say the novelty wore off a long time ago." Ryan paused to choose his next words. "This weekend, it became clear that you and I view being gay very differently. And while I like you and everything, this weekend I saw a couple of things that, uh… showed me that maybe we're not suited for each other well enough to be in a relationship."

"What do you mean?"

Ryan sighed. "Well, for example… Friday night, you didn't get home until sometime after 2:00. I don't know exactly when, since I was asleep. But

I remember waking up at 2:10, and you weren't there. Kent and Justin came back a little after 1:00. What were you doing during that extra hour?"

"Well, I was having a lot of fun dancing and being in the whole scene, you know? And I met this one guy and we danced for a while, then we hung out and talked about a bunch of stuff."

"The bars close at 2 a.m." Ryan paused. "Did you go home with him?"

Aaron debated what to say next. "Yeah… he invited me back to his place for another drink. And so we could hang out some more where it would be quieter." He decided not to mention that it was Zach.

"Did you have sex with him?"

Aaron debated whether he should lie, tell Ryan it was none of his business, or be honest. He opted to be honest. "Yeah, I did."

Ryan didn't say anything.

Aaron added, "We were safe."

"Well, that's good. And apparently, that's not the only sex you had over the course of the weekend."

Aaron froze. *Who ratted on me? How much does he know? How much should I say?*

Ryan said, "I'm not going to pin you down for details. But look. A moment ago you said, 'If we're going to be a couple...' But over the course of the weekend, you hooked up with several other guys. Is that the sort of thing you think is okay to do when you want to be in a relationship with someone? Or do you want to have an open relationship like Kent and Justin?"

Aaron was so flustered he didn't know what to say next – if anything. The more he thought about it, the more irritated he became. Finally, he said, "This is totally unfair. We haven't made any commitments to each other. We haven't even had sex yet. I want to, but you keep saying, 'Let's not rush into it.' Now, you're upset because I had sex with other guys and you're all butt-hurt like I cheated on you. So if we're not a couple yet and we've made no commitment to each other, then I should be free to have sex with other people. I mean, come on. Just last month you spent two weeks in Argentina with that guy you used to live with and apparently still have a hard-on for. You can't tell me you and he didn't fuck."

"We did. But I didn't go down there just to fuck him. I went down there to spend time with him and see Argentina. And besides, that's a little different than going out in a crowd and indiscriminately picking up guys."

"In a way, that's worse. You have a history with him. You two have an emotional connection. I was having sex with someone I just met. But regardless, both of us have had sex with someone else while we're somewhere in the process of becoming a couple."

"True, but my trip to Argentina was a month ago. We're farther along on our journey now."

Aaron sat and stewed. *This is so unfair! It seems like there's a double standard here.*

Ryan said, "And besides, if you had stayed at the house last night, you and I could have done it then. Kevin even put condoms and lube out for us."

"How was I supposed to know that?"

"I was trying to give you hints, but you seemed more interested in going out."

Aaron thought back to the moment last night when Zach told him the same thing. "Well, okay. But it's not fair for you to hold it against me because I did. You're the one who's holding back on being a couple, not me. Hell, I would have made a commitment to you in a heartbeat. But we're not there yet, and that's because of you."

They rode for a few miles in silence. Then Ryan said, "You're right. We haven't made a commitment yet, so it's not fair for me to get upset because you had sex with other guys. And yes, I'm the one who's been holding back on that. I realize you just came out a few months ago, and you're eager to get laid. I can't blame you for wanting to sow your wild oats before you settle down with someone."

"I'd do all my wild oat sowing with you if you'd let me. I'd much rather have done it with you than with those other guys. I'll probably never see them again."

"Really?"

"Yes, really. I just said I'd make a commitment to you in a heartbeat. But you don't seem to want that yet."

"I guess I need to know that I can trust you. And this weekend was kind of a step back in that regard. Be honest. Would you have told me you slept with those other guys if I hadn't asked?"

"WHAT THE FUCK, MAN! You have no reason not to trust me. I could have just as easily told you I didn't have sex. But I chose to be honest with you, and now you're giving me shit. And I've never lied to you about anything else. So how dare you tell me that I'm not trustworthy! And besides – what about you? If I ask you anything about your parents, or why you left home, all I get is, 'That's too painful for me to talk about. That's in the past, and I'm only interested in today and tomorrow.' Well, how the hell am I supposed to trust you when there's so much about your life you won't talk about? So much of your past is a big black hole. Trust works both ways, Ryan. You need to trust me enough to tell me sensitive things and trust that I'll handle them with care." Aaron paused. "So don't talk to me about trust."

Aaron thought, *Okay, I've said enough. Maybe I've said too much. I've probably blown it. But if he's going to hold me to a double standard about having sex with others, that's not fair. And if he can't trust me when I've done nothing wrong, well... maybe this won't work out. Maybe he's not the right one. Maybe he's not so secure and confident after all. Maybe he's too fucked up. In any case, this is getting too hot. I need to calm down.*

Ryan thought, *He's right. I've been holding back on him. We haven't made a commitment, so he had every right to go out and hook up with other guys. I can't hold that against him, as much as I wish he hadn't. But still, it seems like he wants me. Maybe he's too new to all this to know what he really wants. And the trust thing. He's right. I have no reason not to trust him. The problem isn't that he's untrustworthy, it's that I'm afraid to trust.*

Twenty minutes passed as they rode in silence, each of them processing their feelings and contemplating what, if anything, could be done to salvage this situation.

Finally, Ryan said, "There's a rest area up ahead. Wanna stop?"

"Sure."

After they used the restroom and were heading back to the car, Ryan said, "Would you drive for a while? I can take over again if you start to get tired."

"Okay."

Ryan handed Aaron his keys. This would be the first time anyone else drove Ryan's prized BMW since he bought it from Ted.

Once they were back on the highway at cruising speed, Ryan spoke. "Okay, I've been thinking about everything, and you're right. First, you're right that we haven't made a commitment yet, so you're free to have sex with others. I was wrong to get upset about it and hold it against you. Second, you're right that I need to trust you. You've done nothing untrustworthy up to this point. You're right that I should be able to trust you enough to tell you things from my past I'd rather not talk about. If we're going to be a couple, you need to know these things. So, here goes. I guess I should start at the beginning.

"I was born in Tulsa, Oklahoma, but my parents moved to Prairie Village, Kansas when I was little. It's a suburb of Kansas City, right across the state line. So for all intents and purposes, I lived there my entire life. Well, up through the summer after my junior year of high school, but we'll get to that. My dad was the head pastor of a huge mega-church. He was really religious and conservative, and so was my mom. That church was everything to him. He built it from a small church with a few hundred people to the largest church in Kansas. They built this huge sanctuary that looks more like a big concert hall or theater venue. It has a huge stage, lighting, sound system… everything. It seats, like, 3,000 people. Shortly before I left, my father got a contract to start writing books. He had big dreams of being a nationally-known televangelist, with a TV show and speaking tours and all that shit. Anyway, he was so wrapped up in his church he never had time for me and my little brother, Brandon. Like, he never participated in Scouts like some of the other boys' fathers did. He never came to my concerts or track meets. He thought raising kids was the woman's job. Like I said, he was really conservative. My mom was a good mother and I know she loved me. She did her best to raise me and Brandon and still be a supportive wife to my father. But she bought into all the conservative church bullshit, too.

"And then there's Brandon. Brandon is eight years younger than me, but we were really close. In some ways, I kind of filled in the gaps my father left. I played with him and we talked about stuff – all kinds of stuff he knew he couldn't ask Mom and Dad about. And he'd always come and listen when I played my trumpet. God, I love that little guy." Ryan started sniffling. He wiped away a couple of tears.

"I miss him so much. Anyway, up through eighth grade they made me go to this little private Christian school. But starting in ninth grade, I got to go to the public high school. And that's where I met Chris. I'll never forget the first day of band camp. I was scared and I didn't know anybody. I had no idea if I'd be able to make friends and fit in with all the other kids who already knew each other. Chris saw me standing off to the side and he came up and introduced himself. Then he introduced me to all his friends, and they became my friends too. So high school was great. We had a great marching band and symphonic band and jazz ensemble. I mean, we were really good. During my sophomore year, I was recruited to be on the track team because I'm tall and I have long legs, which meant I could do well with the hurdles and the long jump. Chris joined the track team with me. We'd run together all the time and we practiced our instruments together. He played alto sax. I had some jazz play-along CDs, where they have a piano, bass, and drums that play backgrounds so you can practice improvising solos. I still have those. Maybe you and I can practice together if you're interested in playing jazz. But anyway, he'd come over and we'd jam together, and Brandon would sit and listen to us. Chris was the best friend I could ever ask for. We did everything together. We'd go to the mall and hang out. And we used to go to this place called Slush Fun. We'd sit in the car and drink slushies and eat junk food and make jokes and talk about all kinds of things. We were so close. And we talked about going to college together, like maybe UCLA.

"Remember me telling you about the time we went to the state championship track meet in Wichita and we spent the night in a motel?"

"Yeah..." Aaron certainly remembered that, and he remembered getting a hard-on in Ryan's pool while he was describing it.

"So not long after that, we started messing around with each other. We usually did it in Chris's bedroom when his parents and brother weren't home. Then there was this one time in June... We were at Slush Fun and we were talking and joking about all kinds of stuff, and we were getting horny. So Chris drove us to this out-of-the-way parking lot behind some building, and we started kissing. But then a cop pulled up and caught us. Fortunately, we were just kissing and we still had our pants on. If he had pulled up fifteen minutes later, he might have caught us fucking. Anyway, when he checked our driver's licenses, he recognized my name because he went to my dad's church. So he told my dad.

"So Mom and Dad freaked out, and they sent me to this so-called therapist Dad knew from college. This guy was a real piece of work. He used to be gay, but then he claimed he turned his life over to God, and that somehow made him straight. He got married and had three girls. He had a PhD in theology and started running this counseling practice where he tried to make gay people straight."

Aaron said, "Are you serious? Can they even do that?"

"Yep. Most states have no laws prohibiting gay conversion therapy. Besides, they can get away with it because they call it 'pastoral counseling.' He admitted he wasn't a psychiatrist. He was a minister. But people can do all kinds of shit in the name of religion. So anyway, this guy was totally creepy and pervy. He kept asking me questions like what I fantasized about and if I had been molested as a kid. Then he tried this thing where he'd hug me and cuddle me in his arms like a baby. Like that was supposed to make up for the attention I didn't get from my father."

"Are you shittin' me?"

"I shit you not. So I told Mom and Dad I wasn't going back for any more of that. So then Dad and this guy decided to send me away to some secret place in Alabama where it's like you're trapped there, and they try to convert you to be straight. It's like you're forced to live there and you can't escape. Anyway, they were making all these secret plans to force me to go there. But I found out about it the day before it was going to happen. So – oh, I didn't tell you this. I had a summer job at a grocery store, and my manager happened to be gay. So I had one person I could turn to. I told him about all this stuff while it was going on. And when I told him where they were planning to take me, he said I had two choices – either let them send me there or disappear. Of course, I chose to disappear. There was no way in hell I was going to let them take me to that place.

"So with my boss's help, I ran away. I had, like, an hour to decide what I wanted to take. I packed as much as I could into a couple of suitcases. Then my boss drove me to the bus station, and I took a bus out to Los Angeles."

Aaron said, "Oh my God… That's unbelievable. I can't imagine what it must have been like to go through all that."

"It was pretty intense. Oh, and when my dad found out I was gay, he grounded me, took away my phone, and told me I couldn't ever see Chris again. And he was going to send me to some lame-ass Christian school for my senior year, so I wouldn't have my friends or band or track or anything else."

"Did he actually think that was going to make you straight again?"

"Well, the so-called therapy was supposed to do that. And going to the Christian school would keep me straight, 'cause you know, the public schools are so liberal and godless. See, he thought I turned gay because of the bad influences I got at the public high school. He seriously thought Chris recruited me, and I never would have been gay otherwise.

"So that's how I ended up in LA. My boss from the grocery store used to live there. He told me to go to the Los Angeles LGBT Youth Project, and they'd be able to help me. So I went there as soon as I got into town. They hooked me up with an attorney because I wanted to get emancipated from my parents. As it turned out, since I was turning 18 in three months, it wasn't possible to do that. So I had to lay low and hope the police didn't find me before I turned 18. Thankfully, they didn't."

"So you were totally on your own? What did you do? Where did you live? How did you support yourself?"

"Well, I totally lucked out. That attorney was Hal, the guy who owned the house near UCLA and rented rooms to gay college students. He happened to have an opening, so he invited me to live there. The house was super nice and it was only $500 a month for the room. I lived there for five years until I graduated from UCLA."

"Yeah, you were lucky. You could have ended up homeless."

"Oh, believe me – I'm well aware of that. But I had saved around $3,000 from working at the church and the grocery store, and I had to work all during my senior year of high school and college. That meant I couldn't be in the marching band or have much of a social life. I was able to get a scholarship for college, but that didn't cover everything. But Hal and the other guys in the house were really nice to me and they supported me in all kinds of ways. Those other guys were Darnell and Ricky, whom you met yesterday, and Ted, the guy in Buenos Aires. They became my family. I mean, it still sucked not having my biological family anymore, especially Brandon. But I had those guys who loved me and accepted me for who I am."

"So you've had no contact with your parents since you ran away?"

"Nope, and I never want to. As far as I'm concerned, they're not even my parents anymore. I guess you could say I disowned them before they could disown me."

"That's pretty harsh."

"Maybe. But what kind of parents would do that to their own kid? Anyway, I'll never forgive my dad for what he did to me. He ripped me away from Brandon and Chris and all my friends at school. I didn't get to have the kind of college experience I hoped to have because I had to work. So, while I'm happy that you had such a great experience in Ohio State's marching band, I wasn't able to have that."

"What about your mom?"

"If it was up to her, I don't think they would have been so extreme. But she wasn't happy about me being gay, either. I remember the time we were in my dad's home office right after they found out, and he was saying I was grounded and I had to go to that Christian school next year and I could never see Chris again. I turned to her, but she was like, 'I agree with your father. I don't want you to be a homosexual either.' And she took Brandon to Tulsa to see our grandmother, to get him out of the house for when Dad and whoever else was going to take me to that place in Alabama. So she was complicit in all this. She took his side, not mine."

"Wow. That's awful."

"Now you know why I don't like to talk about my past. I mean, it happened and I had to deal with it and make the best of it. And I'm bound and determined to have a good life in spite of what they did to me. Living well is the best revenge, as they say. But I don't like to think about it. It puts me in a negative space like I am now. It's like picking open an old wound."

"I get it. But at least now I know why." Aaron reached over and held Ryan's hand. "Thanks for telling me all that. I really appreciate it. Now I understand why it's painful for you. I'll try not to bring it up."

"Thanks. I would appreciate that. And thank you for listening."

They rode for a while in silence. Aaron thought, *I see Ryan much differently now. I had no idea he's been through so much. It's a wonder he made it on his own in LA and graduated from UCLA. And in spite of everything, he's so successful now. All his hardship has made him a strong, determined person.* He glanced over at Ryan. He looked serious and a bit sad, but Aaron felt renewed admiration for him. Then he thought about what Ryan's parents did. *Maybe I've been too harsh with my parents. I don't really want to be cut off from them for the rest of my life. Maybe we can talk and work through this. Besides, I don't live under their roof anymore, so they can't force me to go to counseling or make me stop playing in Desert Pride.*

Ryan was thinking about whether there was more he should say to Aaron. *Being open with him about what happened with my parents went pretty well. Maybe this will too.*

Ryan said, "There's something else I want to talk about. I know I've been pushing back on this relationship thing – saying I want to go slow and all that. Well, there's a reason. To be honest, my heart's been broken a lot. Chris and I loved each other so much, and I thought we'd spend the rest of our lives together. As long as I had him, I could handle whatever else came along. But then, he got taken away from me. There was a guy I dated for a few months at the high school in LA where I went my senior year. I didn't expect that one to work out, but he dumped me in the worst possible way. Then in college, I dated this Mormon guy for almost a year. He wasn't Chris, but I thought he and I could make it work. I was even ready to take a job in Utah after I graduated so he and I could be together. Then he told me he got engaged to the girl he dated in high school and he was going to go back into the closet and marry her. He was just using me for sex all along. And there have been a couple of other times I've been interested in someone, but it turned out they only wanted me for sex. So that's why I've been hesitant about having sex right away. I want us to get to know each other and love each other for who we are, not get carried away by sex. With a lot of couples, sooner or later the hot sex dies down, then they discover they don't have that much else in common. And it's because they didn't take the time to become friends first. Chris and I were already best friends for three years before we started having sex. And with Ted, I wanted to have sex with him so badly at first, 'cause he's like one of the hottest men I've ever seen in my life. But he made it clear up front that wouldn't be happening, so we became really close friends instead. And I value that more. We started having sex three years later after he moved out and got his own place. But by then it was different. It was more like friends with benefits. So anyway, that's why I'm so careful about getting involved with anyone. I've lost so many people I love. I don't know if I can handle another heartbreak. Well, I could handle it, but I don't want to go through it again. I guess I'm kind of broken."

"Wow. I'm really sorry. I may not be Chris, but I still think you and I could make a great couple. And for the record, I don't think you're broken."

"That's nice of you to say."

"I mean it. So, have you tried contacting Chris?"

"Yeah, we got back in touch during our freshman year. He went to the University of Maryland. We had three Skype calls and kinda brought each other up to date. But he had a boyfriend he met in the marching band there, so that meant we couldn't spend our lives together like we had dreamed of. We still send each other emails once in a while. Last I heard, he and his boyfriend are still together, so they've been a couple for almost eight years now. They live in DC and he works in some senator's office. Anyway, our lives have gone off in different directions and he has his partner, so I've given up hope that he and I will ever get together again."

After a few minutes, Aaron said, "Do you worry that you may never find someone as good as Chris again?"

Ryan didn't answer right away.

Aaron said, "I mean, I can't be Chris. I can only be me. I don't even know this guy, but it sounds like I have pretty big shoes to fill."

"Yeah, I hear what you're saying. It's not fair to expect you to be Chris. And who knows? It might not have worked out with him. He and I would have had problems sooner or later. I'm human and I have faults, and so does he. Anyway, to be honest, you're the first guy in a long, long time who I thought was relationship material. You remind me of him in a lot of ways. You both have this positive vibe, like you're happy in the moment and excited about discovering new things. Remember me telling you about the time Chris took me to the gay pride festival in Kansas City? He was all excited about checking out every booth and organization, being around gay people, and the whole gay community thing. You were the same way this weekend. You're a musician and you like jazz, so that's a big plus. You even look kinda like him. You're cute and – how do I say this? – you obviously have a healthy appetite for sex."

"Yeah… if you'd ever let me."

"Well, speaking of that… okay. We can start having sex. Not tonight – it'll be late by the time we get home and we're both tired. But soon. I'm willing to move forward with dating. I'm willing to give the relationship thing another try. I'm willing to trust you with my heart." Ryan paused. "But please. If things don't work out and you decide you don't want to continue, please be kind. Please let me down gently."

Aaron was ecstatic. "Okay. But I have no intention of letting you go."

Aaron put his hand on Ryan's thigh, and Ryan placed his hand on top of Aaron's. Aaron checked the mirrors and saw that there weren't any cars close by. He leaned over and gave Ryan a kiss on the cheek.

They rode in silence for a while, grateful they had been able to talk through some of their issues and come out stronger for it.

There was a rest area approaching, so Aaron said, "Can we stop? I have to pee again, and you can take over driving. I'm starting to fade."

Ryan said, "Sure. And I have an idea. I know you have long days on Monday and Tuesday, but why don't we do sushi at my place this Wednesday? We can have a nice, romantic evening and you can stay over. I still have to be at work by 9, but you're off on Thursday."

"That sounds wonderful."

Detective Work

Wednesday, July 20, 2016

Wednesday morning, Aaron sprang out of bed at 7:30 a.m. without the aid of an alarm clock. For the past two days, all he could think about was the evening that lay in store for him.

As he enjoyed an energetic run along the canal, he fantasized about all sorts of possible scenarios.

Wouldn't it be sweet if we ate our sushi by candlelight?

Maybe after dinner, we'll get in the pool – naked, finally! We'll gently kiss each other as I wrap my arms around his shoulders and my legs around his waist.

After a half-hour of passionate kissing, he'll lead me through the door from the patio into his bedroom. Or maybe we'll do it right there in the pool!

Or maybe the moment I walk in the door, he'll wrap his arms around me, kiss me passionately, and we'll do it right there in the living room!

He took a shower and ate breakfast, then sat down at his computer. After he checked his email, he opened Facebook. He had friend requests from Kevin, Chase, Derek, Stephen, Brady Bauer, Andy Fox, and Jordan Harrington. He spent an hour traveling back on their timelines, learning more about each of them. Jordan Harrington went to UCLA at the same time as Ryan. He wondered if they knew each other.

As he scrolled through Brady's photos, he couldn't get over how much he looked like Ryan. He remembered Brady said he had an uncle who was a right-wing minister somewhere in Kansas. He clicked over to Brady's Family and Relationships page and saw that his father's name is Bruce Bauer. He clicked on his father's page and discovered that he was originally from Tulsa, Oklahoma. He recalled Ryan saying he was born in Tulsa and his grandmother lived there.

All these coincidences piqued Aaron's curiosity. He opened a search window and typed 'Rev Robertson Prairie Village.' Nothing came up. He tried several variations, such as Reverend and Pastor. Nothing. He tried changing the city to Overland Park and Olathe. Still nothing.

He searched for 'largest churches in Prairie Village,' then visited each of their websites. When he visited the Eternal Savior Christian Church's website, he saw that their pastor was Rev. Brad Bauer. Then he remembered Brady telling him that was his uncle's name. *I wonder if all the men in their family have names that start with B-R.* He searched for the largest churches in Overland Park and Olathe. None of them listed Rev. Robertson as their pastor. *Oh, well. He must have moved someplace else.*

Aaron glanced at the time in the lower right corner of his screen. 11:45. He had spent the entire morning on his computer. He decided to break for lunch.

As he ate, he kept going over all the new information he had discovered. *There were too many coincidences. The Tulsa connection. Brady's uncle and Ryan's father both being fundamentalist pastors at churches in Prairie Village.* Aaron tried to recall everything Ryan had told him about himself. He remembered Ryan saying he and Chris had been on their high school's track team together. They spent the night together in a motel room in Wichita when their team went to the state championship track meet.

Aaron finished his lunch and returned to his computer. He returned to Eternal Savior Christian Church's website. There was a drop-down menu for Our Staff. He clicked on the page for Rev. Brad Bauer. Rev. Bauer resembled Ryan, so he could easily be his father. He discovered that Rev. Bauer received his degree from Oral Roberts University. Aaron chuckled at the name. Then he thought, *Wait a minute. Where is that?* He searched for Oral Roberts University. It was in Tulsa, Oklahoma.

Aaron's mind was racing. *What year did Ryan graduate from high school? He's two years younger than me and I graduated in 2006, so that would mean he graduated in 2008.* He opened another search window and typed 'Kansas state championship track meet 2008.' It was a long shot, but it was worth a try. Sure enough, there was a page that listed the results of that year's state championship track meet. There were no athletes from Prairie Village High School named either Ryan Robertson or having the last name Bauer. For a moment, Aaron was stumped. Then it hit him. Wait a minute! He said that was after his junior year. He changed his search criteria to 2007. As he scanned the results, he saw that Bryan Bauer won first place in the 300-meter hurdles. He kept reading. Bryan Bauer showed up again in the 4x440 relay, finishing third. That's right! Those are the events he told me about that day we were in the pool. The other three guys on the relay team were Clayton Crockett, Trevor Zimmerman, and Chris Robertson.

Chris ... Robertson.

Aaron stared at his computer, stunned. He couldn't recall that Ryan had mentioned Chris' last name, but ... Robertson.

Aaron searched Facebook for Chris Robertson. Being such a common name, there were dozens of Chris Robertsons. He scrolled through the list, opening any possible matches in new tabs. Finally, he found one who lived in Arlington, Virginia, and whose picture looked like he could be in his mid-20s. He opened that page. There was a profile photo of a cute young man with wavy black hair and a cover photo of him and another guy taken at EPCOT Center. Most of the information in the About section wasn't publicly visible, but it listed his hometown as Prairie Village, Kansas. Aaron scrolled down his newsfeed. There wasn't much aside from periodic changes to his profile photo and cover photo.

Oh, well, Aaron thought. I don't know why I'm going down this rabbit hole. It's not like I'm going to contact him or anything. I've wasted enough time on this. Obviously, he changed his name for some reason. But why didn't he tell me? Last Sunday on the ride home, I thought he told me everything. Apparently not.

Aaron was about to wrap up his detective work, but he decided to try one more thing. He opened a search window and typed 'Bryan Bauer Prairie Village.'

The first result was a link to the 2007 state championship track meet he had already visited. The second result was an article on the website of the Prairie Village Post.

Local Pastor's Son Missing

Friday, July 27, 2007

Bryan Bauer, a student at Prairie Village High School, was reported missing on Sunday, July 22. He is the son of Rev. Brad Bauer, pastor of Eternal Savior Christian Church, and his wife Brenda. Bauer, 17, was last seen at approximately 1:00 p.m. on Saturday, July 21. Police are investigating the matter but have uncovered no clues as to his whereabouts.

In a statement to the Prairie Village Post, Rev. Bauer

claimed, "We have reason to suspect he has been kidnapped by a homosexual organization known for abducting, recruiting, and exploiting children. There is no other explanation for why he would suddenly disappear without warning." When asked, Rev. Bauer confirmed that no ransom note or other communication from any such organization has been received.

Police detective Susan Wagner noted that there were no signs of a struggle or forced entry at the Bauer home. She stated that Bryan "appears to have left voluntarily, with two suitcases and a small assortment of personal possessions. We are closely coordinating our efforts with the Kansas Bureau of Investigation and the National Center for Missing and Exploited Children. A nationwide missing child campaign is being launched."

Bauer resigned from his job at Price Cutter grocery store on Saturday. No reason for his resignation was reported.

Detective Wagner believes that Bauer is no longer in the Prairie Village area. Police have no leads at this time. Any tips or information regarding Bryan Bauer's whereabouts should be directed to Detective Susan Wagner at the Prairie Village Police Department, 555-PVPD.

The article was accompanied by a grainy, low-resolution photo of Bryan. Aaron stared at the photo. Ryan was enviably handsome now, but as a teenager, he was a heartthrob. He looked so sweet and cute. Aaron tried to imagine what it must have been like for this adorable teenager to leave his whole life behind and run away from home, and what it must have been like to arrive in a large unfamiliar city all alone.

Now it makes sense why Ryan changed his name. *But why didn't he tell me? Maybe he forgot. Oh well, it's not that important, and I'm sure there are many other details he left out.*

Aaron closed all his browser tabs and got up from his desk. He decided to practice his trombone for a while since it had been almost a week since he played it.

When he went to get his horn, he saw the envelope with the DVD next to the case. After everything that happened in San Diego, he had forgotten about it.

He blew his horn for about a half hour, put it away, then pulled the DVD case out of the envelope. He looked at it some more. It was a gay porno.

Why did Petunia loan this to me? He turned it over and scanned the names of the sixteen performers. One of them was Juan Knight, the guy who had jumped off his float and hugged Ryan during the parade, and who lived in the same house as Ryan. The name Luke Loadstar made him chuckle. *Is that really someone's name? But wait... that sounds kind of familiar.* He thought for a moment. *Oh, yeah... the dildo Kent and Justin loaned me... it's supposed to be a replica of his cock.* He turned on his TV, inserted the DVD into the DVD player, and sat back to watch.

The movie opened innocently enough. It began with a mountain scene with several inches of snow on the ground. A bus pulled up in front of a large, luxurious chalet. About a dozen guys filed out of the bus, fetched their skis and suitcases from the bus's underbelly, and headed towards the chalet while engaging in friendly banter.

In the blink of an eye, the scene changed. A couple of guys were sitting in front of a warm, cozy fireplace. After a few lines of stilted, unconvincing dialog, clothes started coming off. One guy went down on the other. Aaron continued to watch with interest as the scene progressed from oral to anal action. Aaron couldn't help but wonder, *Why did Petunia loan me this video? Does he loan pornos to all his friends?*

The next scene began with three guys in an outdoor jacuzzi. The darkness and the churning water hid their bodies below their shoulders. All the guys were pretty hot, but Aaron's attention was drawn to the young, cute, blond fellow. The blond chuckled at something one of the other guys said, revealing an adorable, easy-going smile that reminded him of Ryan.

After a moment, the blond raised himself up out of the water. He was slender and well over six feet tall. He sat on the edge of the jacuzzi, revealing a fully erect, impressively large cock. It was easily nine or ten inches long. One of the other guys approached and took the first few inches into his mouth. The tall blond moaned a few times, then said, in a deep, rich voice, "Yeah, that's it. Just like that." He sounded exactly like Ryan.

Aaron sat there stunned as the scene progressed from sucking to fucking, and concluded with a round of messy climaxes. Whoever used that jacuzzi next would be immersed in more than just bubbles.

This movie was informative, indeed.

Aaron reached for the case and looked at the fine print on the back for a copyright date. 2010. Yes, the guy in the scene was easily what Ryan would have looked like six years ago.

Aaron scanned the names of the performers. *No mention of Ryan Robertson anywhere. But of course – why would anyone use their real name for starring in porn?*

The next scene had already gotten underway, but Aaron's mind was racing elsewhere. He grabbed the remote, pressed pause, and headed for the computer with the DVD case in hand.

Aaron opened up a browser winder and typed the first name, Jason Chandler, into the search bar. The search produced way too many results, so he tried 'Jason Chandler gay porn star.' That search produced dozens of results as well, collectively revealing all the movies Jason had starred in and plenty of pictures. *Nope, that's not Ryan.*

Next was Neil Downe. *That's clever. I wonder if there's a porn star named Ben Dover.* That was also not Ryan.

Aaron discovered there were several websites with porn star directories.

Next was Luke Loadstar. Bingo. That was Ryan. His page on one directory listed dozens of titles. Another page stated that he had also performed in straight porn videos using the name Max Hadron. A search on Max Hadron revealed another dozen or so titles.

Aaron scrolled through all the pictures – video cover images, face photos, naked photos, and action photos. Some scenes were available online.

Aaron was stunned. Questions were racing through his head.

How many people has he had sex with?

What diseases has he had? What does he have now???

How could this man who seems so honest and decent have made dozens, if not hundreds, of sleazy porn videos? He was raised in the church and his father was a minister, for Christ's sake.

Was he ever going to tell me?

Then he had another thought. *The dildo. I've been fucking myself with a dildo made from Ryan's cock. God, that's actually funny. At least now I know I can take it. But... Knowing what I know now, do I even want to? Do I even want to see him again? Shit, I talked him into joining the band. I'm going to see him every week.*

Wait a minute! Surely, Kent and Justin must know about this. Why didn't they tell me when they loaned me the dildo? And why did they have it? They've been to bed with him before. Maybe that's why.

The more all these thoughts swirled in Aaron's head, the less he could make sense of it. I can't even believe this is true. *But wait... What if it's not? You know, Luke Loadstar could be that guy in Seattle I hooked up with last weekend. He looks an awful lot like Ryan, and he's big enough he could be the guy in the video.*

Aaron launched Facebook and opened a message window to Brady Bauer. Then he thought, *Wait. Am I actually going to send this guy a message and ask if he's Luke Loadstar?* He stared at the screen for a few seconds. *Yes, I am.*

> Hey Brady, it's Aaron Bradbury, from last weekend.
> Thanks again for the great time!
> I know this is kinda weird, but have you ever been in pornos? I just saw a video with a guy who looks exactly like you.
> If you'd rather not answer, that's okay. I totally get it.
> Thanks!

He thought about telling Brady he had found his cousin but decided that could wait for a later message. He pressed Send.

Then he opened a message window for Kent and Justin.

> Hey guys, I hope your week is going well. What was the name of that porn star on the box of that dildo you gave me? Thanks.

Out of morbid curiosity, Aaron watched the rest of the video. Among other things, he watched in disbelief as Juan Knight accommodated more than he imagined was humanly possible – including Ryan. He remembered the guys at Fort Dicks saying he had taken three cocks and a hand. He couldn't believe it at the time, but he watched it happen with his own eyes. He had no idea humans were capable of such things. *Is this common practice among gay men?*

When the first disc finished, he checked Facebook. He had responses. He opened Brady's first.

> No. Sorry to disappoint you. It's not the first time someone has asked. There's some guy named Luke Loadstar who looks a lot like me, and people mistake me for him all the time. I've gotten some action from it, so it's all good. I think he's got a couple of inches on me, though. LOL.

Aaron wondered whether he should tell Brady more, but decided to wait and think about it first. Then he opened the message from Justin.

> Luke Loadstar. Have you had any luck with it? 😊 😊 😊 😊 😊

Aaron was not in a laughing mood. He wanted to say, 'You knew! Why didn't you tell me?' But he would deal with them later.

Aaron reached for his phone. *No, wait,* he thought. *I need some time to think this through. And this is a discussion that should be had in person. Tonight.*

The Truth Will Set You Free

Wednesday, July 20, 2016

Aaron was seething with anger as he drove north on Loop 101 toward Ryan's home in Scottsdale. *How could he not tell me about this? And how could he have done porn in the first place – and so much of it? How could I have misjudged him so badly? How can he seem so nice and wholesome, yet be so sleazy? And what about Kent and Justin? They knew. Why didn't they tell me? And loaning me that dildo – was that some kind of crude joke or something?*

Aaron rehearsed what he was going to say and when he should say it. *Should we have dinner first and talk about this afterward? No, I don't think I'll be able to remain calm and act like nothing's wrong. I should confront him as soon as I walk in the door. Get it over with and leave.*

Aaron pulled into Ryan's driveway. He shut the car off, closed his eyes, and took a few deep breaths. *Relax. Stay calm. Try not to get angry.* He got out of his car and started walking toward the front door – probably for the last time.

Ryan opened the front door as Aaron approached. As soon as he was inside, Ryan gave him a big hug, which he barely returned. Ryan kissed him on the lips, but Aaron couldn't bring himself to muster much of a kiss in return.

Ryan said, "What's wrong? Did you have a bad day? Was traffic bad on the way here?"

"We need to talk."

They walked over to the couch and sat down. They sat angled toward each other, about a foot apart.

Aaron said, "Hmmm. Where to start?" He looked at Ryan sitting in front of him looking baffled and concerned – and handsome. He couldn't remember the opening he had rehearsed. "Okay, let's start with this. So, remember on the way home from San Diego, you were telling me about your father being a minister? Well, I was curious, so I went online and tried to search for his church. And you know what? I couldn't find any churches in Prairie

Village or Overland Park or Olathe that had a pastor named Rev. Robertson."

Ryan looked startled. He smiled nervously. "Oh, yeah. That's because Robertson isn't his name. I guess I didn't tell you this, but when I moved to Los Angeles, I changed my name so it would be harder for them to find me. Actually, I had to wait three months until I turned 18. But yeah, I changed my name."

"What was your previous name?"

"Why do you want to know? And why were you looking for his church? Were you going to contact him and tell him where I am?"

"No. I was just curious. I like to look stuff up on the internet. You must admit, you're quite the man of mystery."

Ryan looked uncomfortable. He didn't say anything.

Aaron said, "Okay, so you changed your name. Why did you pick Ryan Robertson?"

"I thought it was a cool name. I liked the sound of it – the way it alliterates. It has a nice ring to it."

"Any other reason? Is there anything significant about it?"

Ryan figured Aaron probably knew the answer. "Well, yeah. That was my boyfriend Chris's last name. At the time, I hoped we'd be able to get back together. Then when we got married, I'd already have his last name. But obviously, that didn't work out."

"Okay. So, uh… Have you had any other names?"

"Just the one I was born with and the one I have now."

"Really. So... Bryan Bauer and Ryan Robertson. Did I get that right? Bryan Bauer?" Ryan nodded. "You seem to have a thing for first names and last names that start with the same letter. Are you sure there haven't been any others?"

"No other legal names, no. Why are you asking me all these questions? I feel like I'm being interrogated. What the fuck is going on here?"

"You're sure there aren't any other names you've used here and there?" He paused to allow Ryan to answer. He didn't. "Like maybe, uh… Luke Loadstar?"

"What the fuck? Okay, so you found out I used to do porn. So if you already knew, why were you grilling me with questions?"

"I wanted to give you one last chance to tell me. When we were driving home, I said I felt like there were a lot of things you weren't telling me about yourself. So you told me all about you and Chris getting caught kissing, what your father did to you, why you had to run away from home, and how you lived in that house near UCLA. So I thought, great, you've opened up to me. Now I can trust you. But then I find out about all this and obviously, there's still a lot you've been hiding from me."

"I think I told you quite enough for one day."

"Were you ever going to tell me?"

"Yeah, I guess, at some point."

Aaron was becoming more agitated. "Don't you think that was a pretty important detail to leave out?"

"That's all in the past. It was just a job. I haven't done porn since I left UCLA. I don't need to anymore. I have a job that pays well. I have no desire to ever do porn again. So no, I don't think it's important now. That's not who I am today, tomorrow, or for the rest of my life. It wasn't even who I was back then."

"So why did you do it? I mean, what kind of person does that stuff? What does that say about you?"

"I did it because I needed the money. That's the only reason. I was busting my ass at a grocery store for $10 an hour, and I could only work part-time because I was going to school. The room at Hal's house cost $500 a month and I still had to buy food and clothes and pay for my cell phone. I was barely keeping up. And there was no way I was going to be able to afford college. So yeah, I did porn so I could survive on my own and go to a good university. I did what I had to do."

"You had other choices. You could have gone to a community college or something. You could have gone to school part-time and worked more. You could have taken out student loans like I did."

"Yeah, I thought about all that. And I wouldn't have received as good an education, it would have taken me longer, and now I'd be $50,000 in debt. As it is, I got a great education and I graduated with $100,000 in the bank. So in that regard, I made the right choice."

"Yeah, but it's dirty money."

"What are you talking about? It's perfectly legal and honest. You make it sound like I was selling drugs or something."

"You were selling your body, like a cheap whore."

"Well, first of all, at two to three thousand dollars a scene, I wasn't cheap. Second, being a whore is illegal. Making porn is not."

"Maybe not, but it's still sleazy."

"Sleazy is in the eye of the beholder. Funny how you think porn stars are sleazy, but that apparently didn't stop you from watching it. And speaking of sleazy, let's talk about your behavior this past weekend. How many guys did you hook up with?"

"Four. And that's four more than I would have hooked up with if I was getting it from you. But you have no room to talk about how many guys I've had sex with, which has been a total of five in my life. How many guys have you had sex with? Do you even know?"

"Like I said, it was a job. It's not like I wanted to have sex with them. Most of the time I didn't. They hired me to be an actor and play a part in a scene, and I did what they hired me to do. That's what you do in any job. You do the work they want you to do, and they pay you for it."

"Yeah, right. You were an actor. I think it's funny how porn stars think they're acting when all they're really doing is fucking."

"You better believe it's acting. I have to act like I'm attracted to the guy, or guys, that I'm doing a scene with. I have to kiss them and do whatever else with them, even though I'd never do it with them in real life. And I have to keep my dick hard the whole time. So yeah, it's acting. And consider this. What if I was in a crime movie and I was hired to play a killer who shot people? Does that make me a murderer in real life? Of course not. Same thing if I was playing a doctor or a cowboy or a politician or anything else. It's just a role I'm playing in a movie. It has nothing to do with who I am as soon as I walk off the set."

"Yeah, but they're fake bullets and it's fake blood and you're not really killing anybody. When you're in a porno, you're really fucking someone."

"Well, whatever. We're not getting anywhere here. That was a job I had a long time ago that I'll never have again. In real life, I'm a decent, honorable person. I want to fall in love with someone and have a monogamous relationship. I was hoping that would be you. The past is the past. I care about today and the future."

"Yeah, well I care about decency and honesty. And it seems you've done some very indecent things. But more importantly, you haven't been honest with me. You've been hiding it from me. Who knows if or when you would have ever told me? How can I trust you? How can I respect you?"

"If I had told you sooner, would it have made any difference? Seems like you're not going to be able to get past the fact that I used to be a porn star."

"No, probably not."

"Okay, look. Have you never done anything in your life you regretted later? Have you never made any mistakes? Like, if you've ever told a lie, does that make you a liar for the rest of your life? If you've ever stolen a candy bar from a store, does that make you a thief for the rest of your life? So I did porn, but that doesn't make me a porn star for the rest of my life. Look, we're human. We make choices we regret later. But that's how we learn and grow and become better people. If I didn't desperately need the money, I wouldn't have done porn. Don't forget, I was completely on my own. I had to pay for a place to live. I had to buy my own food and clothes. Did your parents help pay for your college? Did you have a place to come home to between quarters? Did they help you in other ways? Yes? Well, okay, then you weren't in my situation. So don't make judgments about me and the choices I made. You weren't walking in my shoes."

"Even if I was, I sure wouldn't have done porn."

Ryan sighed. He put his elbows on his knees and buried his head in his hands. Clearly, this was going nowhere. There was no resolution in sight. He had no desire to continue arguing. It was pointless. "Okay, so obviously this isn't going to work out. Too bad. It could have been wonderful. I really thought you were going to be the one." He sniffled and a tear ran down his cheek. "You have no idea what it's been like. I had Chris, but then I had to leave home and now he's with someone else. Then there was Cody, the Mormon guy, but he was just using me for sex before he went back home and married a woman. There have been several other guys, but they want to have sex with me *because* I was a porn star. Either that or they dumped me when they found out. I thought maybe you'd be different. I thought maybe you would love me for *me*. But I guess not. I guess this is going to end the same way as all the others." He sniffled again and wiped his cheek with the back of his hand. "I'll probably be single for the rest of my life, and I'm okay with that. I'm comfortable with who I am. I love myself. Maybe no one else ever will." Ryan stood up, signaling the obvious – it was time for the visit to end.

Aaron stood up. He couldn't think of anything else to say.

There were no hugs or kisses as Ryan opened the door. There was one more thing he decided to say. "I can't change the fact that I used to be a porn star. But you can change your perspective. If you and I are ever going to make it work, that's what will have to happen."

Aaron said, "Sounds like you're asking me to compromise my values. And that's not going to happen."

Aaron fumbled for his keys as he walked toward his car. Tears streamed down Ryan's face as he watched Aaron go. Aaron turned and said, "Oh, and just FYI… Last Friday in San Diego, I fucked your cousin."

Aaron got into his car and pulled the door closed. He turned the key in the ignition and shifted the car into reverse. He backed down the driveway and into the street, then sped away without looking back at Ryan.

Strangely, he didn't feel relieved to have that unpleasant confrontation behind him. He didn't feel satisfied that he had said what he wanted to say and accomplished what he set out to do. He felt sad.

Then he remembered what Ryan said on their drive home from San Diego. 'If things don't work out and you decide you don't want to continue, please be kind. Please let me down gently.' Oh well, so much for that.

As he turned onto the 101 freeway, his phone buzzed. *It's probably Ryan calling to beg me to come back. Well, I'm not going to do it, and I'm not going to check my voicemail while I'm driving. Or else he's calling to hate on me for dumping him or for fucking his cousin. Whatever… I'll listen to it when I get home.*

***

As Aaron approached his apartment, he stopped at Food World to pick up some sushi and sake. Eating $5 sushi on Wednesdays had been his tradition for almost two years. But in the past month and a half, it had become *their* tradition. Aaron put the sushi back. He knew he'd be thinking about Ryan with every bite. He decided to eat at the Chicago Pizza Company's buffet instead.

When he got home, he turned his computer on and set his phone down beside his mouse pad. Then he remembered someone had called and left a voicemail message on his phone. The call came from the 614 area code – Columbus, Ohio. Maybe it was one of his friends from Ohio State. At least it wasn't Ryan. Aaron listened to the message.

> *Hi Aaron, It's your Aunt Caroline. How are you, sweetheart? I hope you're doing okay. Anyway, I was calling to let you know that your mother's in the hospital. They discovered she has ovarian cancer, and they're going to*

operate on it tomorrow morning. They asked me to call and let you know. I guess they were having trouble getting through to you. Anyway, give me a call. I'm usually up until 11. Okay, well that's it. I love you! Bye.

Oh my God! Aaron thought. He pushed the icon to call his aunt.

"Hi, Aunt Caroline. It's Aaron."

"Oh, hi, honey. Thanks for calling me back."

"So where is Mom?"

"She's in Miami Valley Hospital in Dayton. They took her in this afternoon. Her surgery is first thing tomorrow morning."

"How serious is it?"

"Well, it's cancer, so it's serious. But they don't think it's spread. They plan to remove her uterus and ovaries, and they hope they'll get it all. Unless there are complications, she should come out of it okay."

"Do you think she'll want visitors?"

"It would mean the world to her if you came."

Aaron wondered how much his parents told Aunt Caroline about him being gay and their falling out.

"Okay. I'll get there as fast as I can. Thank you so much for calling, Aunt Caroline."

"You're welcome, dear. I love you."

"I love you, too."

Aaron hung up. He pulled up his parents' contact info and unblocked their number.

He called Charlie, the other pharmacist who worked at HealthPro. "Hi Charlie, it's Aaron. Hey, I just found out my mother's in the hospital in Dayton. Can you work my days tomorrow through Saturday? ... You can? Oh, thank God. Thank you so much! I'll work Thursday through Saturday next week for you. ... Okay, thanks. Bye!"

Fifteen minutes later, he had booked a flight to Dayton, reserved a hotel room, and rented a car.

The Prodigal Son

Thursday, July 21, 2016

Aaron spent all day Thursday en route to Dayton, Ohio. His flight left Phoenix at 8:30 a.m., but with the three-hour time difference and the two-hour layover in Charlotte, he didn't arrive at the Dayton airport until 7:15 p.m. He was starving for dinner, but he rushed straight to the hospital so he wouldn't miss visiting hours.

He had no idea how this was going to go.

At 8:20, he walked into his mother's hospital room. Her bed was cranked up so she was sitting upright. His father and grandmother were by her side. "Hi, Mom! Hi, Dad! Hi, Grandma!"

Martha lit up. "Oh, honey! I'm so glad you came! Come here and give me a hug!"

Aaron walked to the side of the bed, leaned over, and gave his mother a light kiss on the cheek as she wrapped her arms around him.

Ralph said, "Well. If it ain't the prodigal son."

Oh, please. Don't start shit now.

Aaron turned and glared at his father. "Yes, and when the prodigal son returned, his father rejoiced and threw a big celebration – complete with a fatted calf. So get busy."

Ralph said nothing else. He intended that remark as a good-natured jab, but Aaron clearly didn't take it that way.

His grandmother said, "It's so wonderful to see you! You're looking good. How was your flight?"

"Kinda long, and I had a two-hour layover in Charlotte, but I got here as quick as I could."

Aaron turned back to his mother, "So how did it go? How are you feeling?"

Martha said, "Well, I survived. They think they got it all. So I guess I'm doing okay, all things considered. They're going to keep me here two or three more days to keep an eye on me. Then no heavy lifting for six to eight weeks."

"Well, I guess that doesn't sound too bad."

There was a brief silence. Then Grandma said to Ralph, "I could use a cup of coffee. Would you please accompany me to the cafeteria?"

Ralph nodded, and the two of them left the room. Aaron sat down in the chair by the side of the bed. Martha said, "I'm so glad you came, honey."

"Me too. I'm sorry it took something like this to bring me to Ohio."

"Well, at least we weren't all gathering for a funeral."

"Yeah, I guess there's that. Still, cancer is pretty serious stuff."

"Oh, I know. I'm just thankful I got it where I did, and not someplace serious like my lungs or my stomach. They can take my uterus. It's not like I'm gonna need it anymore."

"Mommmm!" Aaron couldn't believe his mother was talking like this.

"Oh, honey, you might as well try to find a little humor in it. You've got to take it all in stride. You've got to deal with whatever life throws at you and try 'n' make the best of it."

"Yeah, I guess."

"And speaking of that... Honey, your father and I decided that we need to accept the fact that you turned out gay. It might not have been our first choice, but it's okay. You're our son and we love you no matter what. We want you to be happy. It's not up to us to tell you how to live your life, and we were wrong to try to do that." She extended her hand a few inches toward Aaron. Aaron gently held her fingers, so as not to disturb the IV that was stuck into the top of her hand. "Thanks, Mom. You have no idea how much that means to me."

"And honey, we want you in our lives. It hurt when you blocked our number. I realize I was being a pain in the rear, so I probably deserved it, but... well, we need to be able to get a hold of you when something comes up. Like this."

"I'm sorry, Mom. I shouldn't have done that. I've already unblocked you."

"Well, good. But you know, you blocking our number was a wake-up call for us. It got us thinking that maybe we had taken things a bit too far and we needed to back off. But the thing that really changed our minds was that terrible shooting down in Orlando last month."

"How so?"

"That guy walked into a bar and killed 49 people! Just 'cause he hated gay people. An' we were sittin' in church later that morning, and Rev. Fleming was sayin' how that was punishment from God for their sin – you know, for being 'practicing homosexuals' as he called it. He said they wouldn't have been killed if they hadn't been out in a gay bar that night. And how the 'homosexual lifestyle' should be called the 'homosexual deathstyle.' And I thought, now wait just a dog-gone minute. First, we've had all these other mass shootings, like those Christians who were shot in their church in South Carolina last year. He wouldn't be standing up there sayin' they were shot because they went to church. And it's ridiculous to think that God carries out His will by causing mass shootings. But then I thought, those poor people had families and friends and lovers. What if they were sitting in their churches and their preacher said their loved one deserved to get killed because it was punishment from God? How do you think that would make them feel? So I turned to your father and said, 'This is bullshit. Come on, let's get out of here.' And that's just what we did. We stood up right in the middle of his sermon and walked out. We're never gonna darken the doors of that place again."

"You quit going to church because of me?"

"Not because of you, because of the hatred. The intolerance. It dawned on me that everything he was sayin' wasn't Christian at all. So we found another church. It's a United Church of Christ. They say everyone is welcome in the house of the Lord, and that includes gay people. In fact, a lot of gay people worship there. And on the first and third Monday of every month, they have this Parents Support Network that meets there. It's for parents of gay 'n' lesbian kids. They share their stories and answer questions and provide support for parents like us who just found out their child is gay. So we've been going to that, and it's really helped us a lot."

"Wow, Mom, that's amazing!"

"We've only been going there for a month, but at least we've started the journey. And we have a whole new set of friends!"

"Oh, Mom, I'm so happy! Well, most important, I'm happy your operation went well and they think they got it all out. But I'm happy that everything's going to be fine between us again."

"Well, that makes three of us. Honey, we love you and we want to be part of your life. And I'm sorry about sending you all that stuff after we got home from our visit."

"That's okay, Mom. I forgive you. You were doing what you thought was right at the time."

"Thank you, dear. But what it comes down to is, we want you to be happy. And if you're going to be happy with a man instead of a woman, so be it. Speaking of which, are you seeing anybody?"

Aaron hesitated. "Well, that's kind of complicated. I met this guy a couple of months ago who totally rocked my world. But... well... a bunch of stuff happened and we kinda had an argument about it last night. So I don't think that's going to work out."

"Well, honey, I'm sorry. Sometimes people will impress you at first, but then later on you discover they're not so great after all. And don't feel like you have to jump on the first one you meet. But on the other hand, you can't go running just because you have an argument. Every couple fights from time to time. Lord knows, your father and I have had some doozies."

"Really? I don't remember ever seeing you and Dad fight."

"That's because we never did it in front of you. But you're never going to meet someone you never fight with. The trick is to learn how to work through your differences and come out stronger. The most successful couples aren't those who never fight, it's those who figure out how to solve their problems together. It's the ones who know they're going to stay together no matter what."

Aaron thought about that for a moment. "Yeah, I guess you're right. That makes a lot of sense."

Martha motioned for Aaron to lean in and she lowered her voice. "And you know what else? Make-up sex is the best sex there is!"

Aaron lurched back. "Mom! TMI! I can't believe you said that!"

"Oh, come on, honey. Get over yourself. It's part of life and part of a good marriage. We're grown-ups. We can talk about sex."

Aaron laughed. It dawned on him that his mother was treating him like a grown-up now.

Martha said, "So anyway, maybe this young man is the right one for you and maybe he isn't, but stick around long enough to find out. Give him a chance. Don't go running away at the first sign of trouble."

"Okay, I won't. Thanks, Mom."

Aaron's father and grandmother returned to the room. They chatted for a few minutes more, then Ralph said, "Well, it looks like visiting hours are almost over. We should let you get some rest."

Everyone said good night to Martha. On the way out the door, Ralph said, "Son, would you mind driving your grandmother back to her home in Piqua? I'm exhausted."

Aaron replied, "Sure, Dad. I'd be happy to."

Bradbury Family History

Thursday, July 21, 2016

Aaron led Grandma to his rental car and helped her in. Moments later, they were heading north on I-75 for the half-hour drive to Grandma's independent living home in Piqua, several miles north of Troy.

Grandma asked, "How do you like living in Arizona?"

"I love it, Grandma. I like not having the snow and ice to deal with."

"Yes, but how can you stand that heat in the summer? I remember one time when your mother and your Aunt Caroline were still girls, we took a trip out west. My word! It was like someone left the oven door open!"

Aaron smiled. "Yeah, well, you get used to it. And my apartment complex has pools, so that makes it nice."

"How's your job going?"

"Fine. It's kind of the same routine every day, but it's okay."

"How's my car holding up? Are you taking good care of it?"

"It's doing great. I don't put very many miles on it. My apartment is right next to the drugstore where I work. The shopping centers there have everything else I need, so I can walk almost everywhere."

"Sounds like a little old lady who only drives her car to church on Sundays. Except that's supposed to be me, not you. Don't you get out? Don't you have friends?"

"I do now. A few months ago, I joined a band, and since then I've made a lot of friends. It feels great to play my trombone again, too. So lately I've been driving a lot more to rehearsals and to visit friends."

"Is that the gay and lesbian band your mom was telling me about?"

Okay, so she knows. I wonder how well she's going to deal with this. Am I about to get a lecture about how evil and sinful being gay is? "Yeah, that's the one."

"Well, good for you. I'm glad you've found a band to belong to where you can make friends and have fun playing your trombone."

"Thanks." Aaron paused. "So I guess Mom told you about me."

"Yep, she sure did. She was all upset about it at first, but I told her she needed to get over herself. I said, 'So what if he's gay? He's your son. Do you love him unconditionally or not?'"

"Did you really say that to her?"

"I sure did. And she started giving me all this religious mumbo-jumbo from that damn church she and your father used to go to. And I said, 'Just stop. That's not how Jesus taught us to treat our fellow man. Love thy neighbor as thyself. Judge not, lest ye be judged. Let him – or her – without sin cast the first stone.' That shut her up."

Aaron was practically laughing. "Grandma, that is so awesome! Thanks for sticking up for me. And thanks for being so supportive. I wasn't sure how you'd react."

"Oh, come on. Just because I'm old doesn't mean I'm narrow-minded. Honey, I'm 80 years old. I've seen just about everything under the sun, and then some. I've lived through World War II and Korea and Vietnam. I've lived through JFK and Bobby Kennedy and Martin Luther King getting assassinated. I've lived through the McCarthy era, the civil rights movement, Watergate, 9/11, and on and on. I've been through every kind of conflict and plague known to mankind. And you know what? None of them were caused by gay people. Two men or two women loving each other is the least of my concerns. So what? Two people are happy and no one's getting hurt. Just stay out of other people's business and let people live their lives the way they want to."

"Wow, Grandma! You're amazing!"

"Oh hell, I'm not amazing. It's just good ol' common sense."

"Well, it seems like common sense isn't very common anymore."

"You can say that again!"

"Well, it seems like common sense isn't very common anymore."

"Oh, hush, Smarty-pants."

Aaron laughed, then said, "Anyway, Mom and I had a good talk tonight while you and Dad were out getting coffee. I think everything's going to be fine."

"So, if you don't mind me asking… are you seeing anybody? Is there someone special in your life?"

"Well, maybe, but maybe not. I met this guy a couple of months ago. He seemed really nice, smart, and very successful. And he's tall and good-looking, and we seem to have a lot in common. And we were getting along really well. I mean, so far so good, right? But the weird thing is, he didn't want to talk about his past. He'd always say, 'That's too painful, I'd rather not talk about it,' but, like, that meant there were all these things we couldn't talk about. So I finally got him to talk about some of it. As it turns out, his parents were really conservative and religious, and he had to leave home after they found out he was gay. And that meant he had to leave behind his brother and his boyfriend."

"That's terrible! I can certainly understand why he wouldn't want to talk about that. So what did he do?"

"He took a bus to Los Angeles. He was able to find a room to rent in someone's house, and he put himself through college."

"Good for him! Sounds like he has a lot of strength and determination."

"Yes, but I found out how he was able to support himself and afford college, and… well, it's not pretty. Let's just say I totally lost respect for him. And he didn't even tell me – I found out from someone else. So now I'm not sure if I can trust him."

"What was he doing? Selling drugs?"

"No, not that bad, but… he was performing in X-rated movies."

"Oh, dear…"

"I know, right? What kind of person does that sort of thing?"

"Someone who's desperate for money, which it sounds like he was. Maybe he didn't have any other choice."

"I asked him that, and he said he didn't. Anyway, whatever. That's what he did, and that's a deal-breaker as far as I'm concerned."

Grandma frowned as she thought about what to say next. "So, is he still involved in making pornography?"

"No, he says he quit doing that when he graduated."

"Do you think he'll ever do it again?"

"He says he won't. He said he only did it because he needed the money, and he doesn't need money anymore. He's got a great job at this high-tech company in Scottsdale. But here's another thing. He's only 26, yet he owns a beautiful house in Scottsdale and he drives a BMW. I mean, you should see his place! It's in a really nice neighborhood, and it has four bedrooms, and out back there's a pool and a hot tub and a barbecue island. I checked the value of his house on Zillow, and it was like $750,000 when he bought it! How can he afford that? Unless he's still doing porn."

"That does seem curious."

"Yeah. And then I look at my situation, and I have $30,000 in student loans and I'm living in an apartment. It's a nice apartment, and Tempe is nice, but it's like I'm two years older than he is, and he has so much more than I do."

"That, and you're driving your grandmother's old hand-me-down Toyota."

"Hey, I love that car, and I really appreciate it. I think of you every time I drive it."

"That's sweet. But it sounds like maybe you're a little jealous."

"I don't think it's jealousy so much as I feel unequal. Inadequate. Like, how can I keep up with that?"

"Honey, a relationship is not about keeping up with each other. It's about finding someone you really love and figuring out how to make it work. You both bring things to the relationship the other person benefits from. And they're not all money and possessions. So, do you love this guy?"

"Well, I thought I did, until I found out about this."

"So, just for the sake of argument, let's take him at his word. Let's assume he's not making pornography anymore. He has a good job and he makes a decent salary. It sounds like he's been through a lot of unpleasant things and has worked hard to get to where he is today. You said he has a lot of good qualities, and he's smart enough to see that you do too. So… what's the problem? What do you think the future will be like if you and he spend your lives together?"

"Well, he's doing pretty well on his income alone. I probably don't make as much as he does, but still… with my income added in, we'd be really comfortable together. But the problem is, he did some pretty sleazy and dishonorable things to get where he is. What does that say about the kind of person he is?"

Grandma sighed. "Well, I haven't met him, so I can't really say what kind of person he is. He sounds to me like someone who was dealt a rotten hand and played his cards the best he could. It sounds like he had to make some tough choices and do some difficult things just to get by. Maybe if he didn't do what he did, he wouldn't have been able to afford a college education – one that seems to be serving him very well now."

"Yeah, I guess…"

"And whether a relationship will last depends on a lot more than your combined income. It's how well you solve problems. It's about the dreams and goals you share and the future you build together. It's about forgiving each other when you make mistakes. And it's about appreciating your partner's good qualities and learning to overlook their faults."

Aaron couldn't think of anything else to say. Everything Grandma was saying made perfect sense. He couldn't refute any of it.

Grandma said, "Honey, maybe you need to overlook his past and evaluate him based on the person he is today. Let me give you a little bit of background on your parents. I don't know how much of this they've told you, but you're a grown man now and you should know. When I first met your father, I didn't like him at all. I didn't think he was good enough for your mother. You see, the first man your mother fell in love with was in med school. After he became a doctor, he'd be able to provide a very nice life for her. But then he got her pregnant, and next thing you know, he left her. He said getting married and having a child wasn't going to fit in with all the studying he had to do to become a doctor. Of course, if he wasn't ready to be a parent, then he shouldn't have been having sex with her, but people don't think that way. But anyway, she decided she was too young to be a mother and she wasn't prepared to raise a child by herself, so she had an abortion. I wasn't happy about it at the time, but I had to let her make that decision for herself."

Aaron was stunned. He had no idea his mother had gotten pregnant with another man before his dad came along.

"Then next thing you know, Ralph showed up. She met him at some bar in Dayton when he was home on leave from the Navy. I don't know what in the world she saw in him, but he kept writing to her. Every time he came home on leave, he would go out with her. I thought he was a crass low-life. He had no education to speak of, tattoos on his arms, and you should have heard some of the foul language he used!"

Aaron said, "Well, some things never change."

"Oh, it used to be worse. She told me he got gonorrhea from a prostitute he slept with when they went ashore in some foreign country. And I thought, oh great. *This* is the man you want to spend your life with? This is your Prince Charming? But after he got out of the Navy, he got a job at the factory there in Troy. And he cleaned up his act, sort of, and started being a responsible grown-up. And for all his other faults, he worshiped your mother. He really put her on a pedestal."

Aaron said, "Probably so he could look up her dress."

Grandma chuckled. "You got that right. Anyway, he worked and saved up his money until he could afford to buy her a diamond ring. And he had the decency to ask us for our daughter's hand in marriage. I mean, he could have just asked her. It's not up to us to say yes or no. It's her life. But it was a nice gesture. And I gradually came to see that he was, in his heart, a very decent man. He's always been faithful to your mother, as far as I know, and he's never mistreated her. He's always worked hard to provide for her and you. So yes, your father may be a bit crusty on the outside, but he's a good man on the inside. It took me a long time to see that."

Aaron was stunned by these new revelations. "I had no idea."

"He's done pretty well for you, too. He saved as much as he could for you to go to college. They could have spent that money on themselves and had a nicer house or nicer cars, or maybe taken some nicer vacations. But he wanted to make sure you had a better life than he had."

"Yeah, you're right."

"But my point is, either of them could have rejected the other one because of their past. When your mother got pregnant and got that abortion, that made her damaged goods as far as a lot of men were concerned. Trust me, it was different back then. And his sleeping with prostitutes and getting venereal diseases didn't make him very attractive to most women. But they saw the good in each other and overlooked each other's past mistakes. And I'd say they've had a happy marriage and a good life, at least in the ways that matter the most. And let's not forget – they raised a mighty fine son."

Aaron almost cried. He knew everything his grandmother said was true. And he realized he had taken a lot for granted throughout his life.

Aaron pulled into the parking lot of Grandma's retirement community. He said, "Thanks for the talk, Grandma. You've given me a lot of good advice. I've got a lot of things to think about."

"You're welcome, honey. Thank you for coming home. I know your mother and father really appreciate it. And I'm glad you've worked through your differences. Parents and their children shouldn't be separated."

"Yeah, I know. And thanks for everything you told me about how they met. I... I guess I see things a lot differently now."

"Good. And good luck with that young man. I hope it works out. But if it's not meant to be, at least learn what you can from the experience. Don't worry, you'll find someone. And make sure you hold out for the best!"

Aaron smiled. "I will, Grandma. Thanks! I love you."

"I love you too, sweetheart."

Aaron got out, walked around the car, and opened the door for his grandmother.

"Do you need any help getting inside?"

"No, I'm still able to make it from here."

They hugged. Grandma kissed him on the cheek, and he kissed her back.

Aaron said, "Bye! I love you!"

Grandma waved and walked into the building.

Aaron decided he needed to visit Ohio more often. Grandma was doing well now, but she was 80 and… well, you never know.

Father and Son

Friday, July 22, 2016

The next morning, Aaron slept until 8:45. He got up, showered, and availed himself of the free breakfast the hotel offered in a small room near the front desk.

He arrived at the hospital at 10:15. As he walked past the nurse's station on the way to his mother's room, he spotted his father in a small sitting area. He walked up and said, "Good morning, Dad. How's Mom doing?"

"She's okay. She says she slept pretty well, but she's still sore whenever she tries to move. The nurse's aide is in there now giving her a sponge bath and helping her to the toilet, so I thought I'd leave them alone for a little while."

"Okay. How much longer do you think it's going to be?"

"I dunno… probably 15 or 20 minutes. You wanna go to the cafeteria and get something?"

"Yeah, sure." Aaron had already eaten, but a nice big Coke or Dr Pepper seemed appealing.

After Aaron and Ralph purchased their drinks, they sat down at a table. Aaron had a few things he wanted to say to his father, but he wasn't sure how to start. He felt awkward, and it seemed like his dad felt awkward, too.

Ralph spoke first. "Son, I owe you an apology. I've been thinkin' back over some of the things I said while we were visiting you and, well… I said a lot of things I shouldn't have – you know, with you being gay and everything. Anyway, I'm sorry."

"That's okay, Dad. You didn't know."

"Well, I shouldn't have said those things anyway. I've learned a lot over the past couple of months."

"So have I. I've changed my thinking on a lot of things, too."

"Well, anyway… Lookin' back on it, I guess we bought into a lot of stuff that church was telling us. You know, you hear it in church, so of course you think it must be right. But you know, it changes things when you realize they're talking about your son. Anyway, your mother and I finally woke up to a lot of stuff, and we figured out that what they were preaching wasn't Christian at all."

"Yeah. Mom was saying the same thing yesterday. But I'm glad you and Mom changed your mind. I'm really sorry I cut you off. That was wrong. I should have left the lines of communication open."

"Well, I don't blame you. I know Martha was pestering you with all those emails and phone calls. We thought we were doing the right thing at the time, but it turns out we were wrong about the whole thing."

"That's okay, Dad. The important thing is we worked through it and we're back together again."

They smiled at each other, both relieved to get that out of the way.

Aaron took a good look at his father. He was older now. His hair was grayer and getting thinner. He had put on a few more pounds, and he looked haggard. Of course, the past few days had been rough on him, but still, he looked worn down.

Aaron thought back ten years, to when he was a senior in high school. Dad seemed more energetic back then, and more feisty. There was only a touch of gray coming in around his temples. He would have been 47 then, and now he's 57. What a difference ten years makes. Aaron recalled what his grandmother said last night. 'I think he's done pretty well for you, too. He wanted to make sure you had a better life than he had.'

Aaron asked, "How many more years until you retire, Dad?"

"Well, I qualify for it now. I can start taking my pension any time I want, but I can't start taking Social Security until I'm at least 62. So I reckon I've got five more years to go. But I hear they might be offering early retirement packages this fall, and who knows? I might take it. I'm sure as hell ready to get out of there."

"How did you like traveling in the RV? Do you think you and Mom might buy one after you retire and drive around the country?"

"I don't know. I think we'd be better off with a pick-up truck and a camper. The camper's not as big, but when you get somewhere, you can unhitch it and just drive the pickup truck around. With that RV, we had to drive it everywhere we wanted to go."

"Yeah, that makes sense."

"'Course, that all depends on how well your mother does after she gets through with this. And I'm startin' to slow down."

"It ought to be the other way around. You should get to do all the traveling and stuff you want to do in your 30s and 40s when you're young and you have the energy, then work from 50 until you die."

Ralph chuckled. "Yeah, ain't that the truth. You know, if I could change one thing, I wish we had traveled more when we were younger. I tell ya, doin' all that driving wore me out. That's something you oughta keep in mind. You're probably not gonna have kids. You should get out and travel while you're young. I know you work hard, but take your vacations! I've seen too many people work all their lives, then when they retire, they either they die within a year or their husband or wife does. Don't put off everything you want to do until you retire."

"That's great advice. Thanks, Dad." Aaron realized something was different. He and his dad were having a man-to-man conversation, not a father-to-son conversation. Those were never really conversations anyway.

While he was growing up, Aaron and his father had a tenuous relationship. They never fought outright and his father was never mean to him, but Aaron always felt like he wasn't the son his father had hoped for. His father was macho and coarse; he was gentle and sensitive. His father was blue-collar; and with a college education, he'd be white-collar. His father loved hunting and sports; he loved music and theater. Aaron knew his father loved him, but he couldn't remember if he had ever said so. Aaron saw his father differently now.

Ralph sat for a moment. Aaron could tell he had something else on his mind. He drank the last of his coffee and set the cup down on the table, and left his hands wrapped around the sides. He looked at Aaron for a second, then looked down at his empty cup. "I'm proud of you, son. I don't know if I've ever told you that, and I guess I should've. You've done real well for yourself. I was proud of you for making Eagle Scout and proud of you for making the Ohio State Marching Band. I was proud of you for going to college and gettin' your bachelor's degree and then goin' on to become a pharmacist. And now you've got a good job and you're making a nice life for yourself out in Arizona. I wish you had stayed closer to home, but I want you to be happy.

"And about the gay thing, well, like I said, I want you to be happy. I hope you meet someone real nice. When you have the right partner, you can make it through whatever life throws at you. I sure lucked out when I found your mother. I still can't believe I got her to marry me. I don't know what I would have ever done without her."

"Yeah, she's pretty amazing. She's been a wonderful mother."

"Which is lucky for you, 'cause I know I haven't been a real good father. I know they say that when a boy turns out gay, it's because he had a weak or absent father. So I guess that means–"

Aaron couldn't believe what he was hearing. "Dad–"

"–I didn't do a very good job. And I know, I'm not well-educated like you. I'm just an average guy who works in a factory–"

"Dad!"

"–but I did the best I could. And you turned out real good anyway–"

"DAD! STOP!"

Ralph finally stopped talking and looked up.

"Dad, stop talking like that! Dad, all that stuff about guys being gay because they have a weak or absent father is bullshit. That's been disproven over and over. You were a wonderful father! You worked hard so Mom and I could have a good life. You volunteered to help with my scout troop. A lot of the other kids' fathers didn't do that. You came to all my concerts. You came to my high school and college football games to see me marching in the band."

"Well, there was also the football game…"

"True. And you sacrificed a lot so I could go to college. I never really appreciated it back then, but I do now. I have a good life, because of you."

"Well, thanks, son."

Aaron and Ralph smiled at each other.

Aaron glanced at his watch. "They should be through with Mom now. Wanna head back up to the room?"

Ralph nodded, and they got up from the table.

"Dad…" Ralph stopped walking and turned toward Aaron. Aaron gave his father a big hug. "I love you."

For a few seconds, Ralph froze. He was never the type to hug other guys, especially not when there were other people around.

He quickly realized he didn't care. He hugged Aaron back. "I love you too, son. And I'm real proud of you."

Sorry I Missed Your Call

Friday, July 22, 2016

That evening in his hotel room, Aaron opened his laptop to catch up with the rest of the world. When he checked his email, he saw an email from Ryan. The subject read, 'Well, okay then.'

He opened the email and read it.

Dear Aaron,

Okay, I get the message. Obviously, you don't want to ever see or hear from me again. I won't leave you any more texts or voicemails, and this will be the only email I send. I thought you'd at least be decent enough to reply, but I guess you've decided to ghost me instead. That's so unlike you. I expected better. Oh well.

I have informed Lee that I won't be playing in Desert Pride any longer. I didn't tell him why. Since you don't want to have anything to do with me, it would be too awkward for me to be at rehearsals. I'm not giving up the jazz ensemble, though, since you're not in it. I will always appreciate you for convincing me to play my trumpet again.

I'm not angry anymore. I'm over that. But I'm sad and disappointed. You were the most promising guy to come along in at least eight years. I thought you were the one. But obviously, I'm not the right guy for you. I hope you find the right guy someday.

As I said, I won't contact you anymore. But our paths are bound to cross from time to time, and I hope we can at least be civil.

So long,

Ryan

Aaron was confused. He hadn't received any calls or texts. He picked up his phone and checked. Nothing. But then he noticed the little airplane icon in the upper right corner of his screen. *Shit! I forgot to turn off airplane mode after my flight yesterday!*

He turned off airplane mode, and text messages and voicemails began appearing.

He received three texts from Ryan.

Thursday morning:

> I'm really sorry about last night. Can we get together again and talk some more?

Thursday afternoon:

> FYI, I'm not going to band tonight so it won't be awkward for you to be there. I know you work Fri-Sat-Sun, but can we talk Saturday or Sunday night?

Friday morning:

> If you don't want to talk, that's okay. But please reply and let me know that, and I'll stop.

He received two voicemail messages from Ryan.

Thursday afternoon, 4:45:

Hey Aaron, this is Ryan. Listen, I wanted to let you know I'm not going to band tonight, so you can go and not worry about seeing me. I'd still like to talk sometime after we've both cooled down a bit. Maybe Saturday or Sunday night? We can get together or talk on the phone, whichever you prefer. If you want to wait a little while longer, that's okay. Just let me know. Bye!

Friday afternoon, 3:15:

> *Hi Aaron, it's Ryan. Hey look, I know we broke up and you're mad at me, and obviously, you don't want to see or hear from me again, but please don't ghost me. At least reply to this message or one of my texts to let me know you got them – please? I'm starting to get worried. Kent said you weren't at rehearsal last night. Has something bad happened? Please let me know you're okay. Bye.*

Aaron was mortified. He pressed the call-back icon and hoped Ryan would answer. At the same time, his head was spinning. *I don't even know what I'm going to say. If I get his voicemail, I'm just going to hang up until I decide–"* Then he heard a click.

"Hey, Aaron!"

"Uh, hi, Ryan. I just got your messages. Sorry for not calling you back sooner. I had to go to Ohio on short notice, and I forgot to turn airplane mode off when we landed. I just now turned it off and got all your texts and voicemails."

"Oh, thank God you're okay. What are you doing in Ohio?"

"Well, as I was driving back from your place on Wednesday night, I got a call from my Aunt. She said my mom found out she had ovarian cancer, so she was in the hospital to get a hysterectomy–"

"OMIGOD! Is she okay?"

"Yeah, she's doing fine. At least as well as can be expected. They operated on her yesterday morning, and they think they got it all. They're keeping her there for a couple of days, but she thinks they're going to let her go home on Sunday."

"I thought you weren't speaking to your parents."

"We worked through all that. Everything's great now. I'll tell you all about it when I get home. Anyway… Oh, Ryan, it's so nice to hear your voice! I'm sorry I didn't return your texts or your voicemails, but like I said, I didn't get them until just now. Anyway, I definitely want to get together and talk. I have so much I want to say!"

"Well, good. I've been doing a lot of thinking, and I have some things I'd like to tell you, too. When are you getting back?"

"I'm flying home tomorrow. My flight gets in at around 4:30, so I figure I'll be home at around 5:30 or 5:45."

"Would you like to have dinner? Wanna come up to my place?"

"I dunno. I kinda want to be home for a while. Would you mind coming to my place?"

"No problem. What time?"

"How about 6:30? That'll give me a little time to unpack and unwind and – shit. I'll need some time for dinner. How about 7:00?"

"I can bring some food, like maybe Chinese or pizza."

"Yeah, okay. So 6:30."

"Sounds good. I can't wait to see you!"

"I can't wait to see you too. Bye."

"Bye."

Aaron smiled. That went better than he expected. He was surprised at how good it felt to hear Ryan's voice.

So Much to Say, So Much to Do

Saturday, July 23, 2016

Aaron traveled with only a carry-on, so he didn't have to wait for his luggage. Still, it seemed to take forever to catch the parking lot shuttle, and for the shuttle to reach the stop closest to his car. Phoenix was experiencing a heat wave. At 5:15, it was still 115 degrees. Aaron's car was an oven.

He stopped at a convenience store and picked up a 44-ounce Super Sipper. By the time he got home, his Dr Pepper was two-thirds gone.

At 6:30 sharp, Ryan arrived at Aaron's apartment. His hands were full, so he kicked the door gently to knock.

Aaron opened the door and saw Ryan standing there grinning. He held a pizza box in one hand. A plastic grocery bag that contained what looked like a bottle hung from the same hand. His other hand was behind his back.

"Come in!" Aaron said.

"Can you take the pizza before I drop something?"

Aaron took the pizza box from Ryan's hand. It was a plain white box, so Aaron couldn't tell where it came from. He carried it into the kitchen and set it on the table. Ryan followed him in and set the white plastic bag down. "I thought a nice Merlot would go well with the pizza."

Aaron opened the pizza box. It looked a lot like the pizza Ryan made for Aaron the first time they had Sunday dinner together. "This looks amazing! Where did you get it?"

"I made it!"

"Seriously? I thought you would just pick something up along the way."

"I could have, but I thought, 'why not?'"

"But… the box…"

"I have some at home. I got them at a restaurant supply store. Sometimes when they have potlucks at work, I make a couple of pizzas and bring them in. It cooled off a bit along the way, so you might want to reheat it at 200 for five minutes."

Aaron turned and set the oven to preheat. When he turned back around, Ryan was holding a dozen red roses. He extended the bouquet toward Aaron.

Aaron looked genuinely surprised. "What the…? Really? Oh my God, that's so sweet!" Aaron took the bouquet from Ryan and smelled the roses. "Thank you! This is so nice! No one's ever given me roses." Aaron stood there holding the roses, at a loss for what to do next.

Ryan said, "Do you have a vase?"

"No. I've never needed one until now."

"Do you have, like, a pitcher or a large jar?"

Aaron took a quick mental inventory of everything in his cupboards. "I don't think so."

"I guess I could run over to Food World and buy one while the pizza's warming up."

Aaron spotted the Super Sipper cup in the trash can. "No, wait. I have an idea." He retrieved the empty cup. "This will probably work." He filled the cup half full of water and lowered the roses into the cup. He placed the cup on the table, centered along the side against the wall.

He stood back. They both looked at the roses in the makeshift vase and laughed.

Aaron said, "Not the most elegant sight, is it? God, I'm so tacky."

Ryan smiled. "It'll do in a pinch. And you're not tacky, you're resourceful."

Aaron still couldn't get over the fact that Ryan gave him roses. That, and he brought a homemade pizza and a bottle of wine. All this, after the way he had treated him on Wednesday evening. He turned and looked up at Ryan. Ryan was smiling at him. He wrapped his arms around Ryan and kissed him.

The oven beeped to signal that it had reached 200 degrees. Aaron looked puzzled. "I guess I shouldn't put the box in, right?"

"Probably not. You can put the pizza right on the rack. That's how I baked it."

Once he put the pizza in the oven, he opened the cupboard and took out two wine glasses. "At least I don't have to serve the wine in red plastic cups. There's some hope."

Ryan chuckled.

Aaron felt like a klutz as he struggled to cut the foil wrapper around the tip of the wine bottle. Then he awkwardly twisted the corkscrew into the cork. Fortunately, he accomplished the task without destroying the cork or breaking the bottle. When he finally poured the wine into the glasses, the pizza was ready. They teamed up to transfer the pizza from the oven rack onto his cutting board. He didn't have a pizza cutter, so he made do with his largest knife.

Aaron felt awkward and self-conscious. Everything he did seemed klutzy. Not having a vase, a pizza peel, a pizza cutter, or a tray to serve it on made him look uncultured and ill-prepared. Until Ryan came along, he never had people over for a meal. But he was deeply touched by Ryan's gestures, thrilled to be back in his presence, and nervous about the conversation they were about to have.

Ryan was anxious about their upcoming conversation too, but Aaron's nervousness put him at ease. His awkwardness was endearing. Ryan watched him with empathy. It was going to be a pivotal discussion for both of them, but he had a good feeling about it.

Aaron carried the cutting board with the pizza slices to the table. He was about to sit down, but Ryan said, "Hey."

He turned and looked at Ryan, and Ryan gave him a big hug. "You seem so nervous. Relax." They held each other for a minute. Aaron's tension gradually melted away in the comfort of Ryan's arms. *This is where I belong. Right here. So don't fuck this up.*

They finished hugging and shared a quick kiss. Then they sat down.

Ryan picked up his wine glass, but for once he was at a loss for what to say as a toast.

Aaron sensed that and said, "To us."

Ryan smiled. "To us."

They clinked their glasses and took a sip. Aaron said, "Delicious. You sure know how to pick good wine."

Ryan said, "I know how to pick good men, too."

"Really? After everything I said last Wednesday, I don't feel like a good man at all."

Ryan let that slide. They ate a few bites of pizza in silence, unsure of how to begin and waiting to see if the other one would go first. Ryan said, "So, tell me about your visit to Ohio."

"It was amazing. Well, okay, not really, because my mom had cancer and they just took her woman parts out. But she's doing well and she'll be fine. But it was amazing because my parents have totally come around. They're cool with me being gay now. I mean, they'd probably still prefer that I marry a woman and bring them grandchildren, especially 'cause I'm an only child. But still… They said they want me to be happy and they want us to be a part of each other's lives."

"That's awesome! What made them change their minds so quickly?"

"Believe it or not, it was the Pulse shooting in Orlando."

Ryan looked confused. "What did that have to do with it?"

"Mom said they were sitting in church the morning after it happened, and the preacher was going on about how that shooting was punishment for those people being gay."

"Man, that's fucked up. Last year, some guy killed a bunch of people in their church in South Carolina. Would he have said that was punishment for them going to church?"

"I know, right? Mom said the same thing. And she said, what about all the parents and partners and families and friends of the people who got killed? Is that the Christian response they should hear? So anyway, they actually got up and walked out during the sermon!"

"Wow… good for them!"

"Yeah. And now they're going to a United Church of Christ that welcomes gay people. They have a parents' support group that meets there, and Mom and Dad have been going."

"Yeah, they have one of those groups in Kansas City too. That day Chris took me to the Pride Festival, I talked with a lady there. I remember thinking my parents would never do that. So I'm glad yours did."

Aaron continued. "And the next morning my dad and I had a heart-to-heart talk. It was really good. He started saying this shit about how if he had been a better father, I wouldn't have turned out gay."

"What??? Where did that come from?"

"Oh, probably something he heard in his church about how boys turn out gay if their father doesn't pay enough attention to them."

"Boy, that sounds familiar. I don't think I told you this, but a few weeks before I left home, my dad's church hosted an event called Rescued Through Love. It was an all-day conference on a Saturday. They had these so-called experts talking to parents of LGBT kids. That was one of the things they said there."

"Oh my God, did they make you go to that?"

"Thankfully, no. But I ran the church's website, and Dad made me put a whole bunch of information from the conference on the website. You wouldn't believe some of the shit they said. But anyway, back to your father."

"Where was I? Oh yeah… So I told him he had been a wonderful father and that wasn't why I turned out gay. He helped out with my scout troop and he always came to my concerts and football games. He worked hard to provide for us and saved money for me to go to college. I never fully appreciated everything he did for us until now."

"Wow. You were lucky. My dad never did any of that stuff."

Aaron said, "You know, when I was growing up, I didn't think too highly of my dad. And let's face it, he's kind of crude and rough on the exterior. And he's more of a blue-collar guy and not very well educated. But on this trip, I saw him differently. He's human. He has his faults. But in his heart, he's a really good man. After all these years, he still worships the ground my mother walks on. He looked so worried and so worn down when I saw him in the hospital. And I came to understand he thinks the world of me too. He told me he's proud of me. He told me he loves me. I don't think he's ever said those things before. It's like, yeah, I knew he loved me, but to hear him say it meant everything. And I told him I was grateful for everything he's done for me and he's a wonderful father."

Aaron took a break from talking long enough to eat a few bites of pizza and sip some wine. He looked at Ryan. Ryan looked sad. He asked, "What's wrong?"

Ryan said, "I'm really happy for you. It sounds like you've built a whole new relationship with your parents."

"Yeah, but it's too bad it took my mom getting cancer for that to happen. I guess we woke up and realized that life is short and something could happen at any time. And we all realized we'd rather be part of each other's lives than be separated. And another thing. I could see they're getting older. My dad in particular. His hair is grayer and thinner, and he's gotten heavier. I can see he's starting to wear down. He's worked in a factory his whole adult life – well, after he got out of the Navy – and it's taken its toll."

Ryan thought, *I'm happy for him, but what about me? I'll never be able to reconcile with my parents like this.* "Well, I hope I get to meet your parents someday."

"Yeah, I'm thinking I should go home for either Thanksgiving or Christmas every year, and maybe for a few days in the summer. I want to see my grandmother more often, too. It would be great if you came! Oh, and speaking of my grandmother, I gave her a ride back to her independent living community after my first day there. She lives in a town called Piqua that's a few miles north of Troy. Anyway, Grandma and I have always gotten along great. She's a really cool lady. Like we have a bond. It's kind of hard to explain. Anyway, we had a nice talk on the way to her place. She told me a bunch of stuff about Mom and Dad I didn't know before. She said she didn't like my dad at first. She thought he was a crass low-life. He had no education to speak of, tattoos on his arms, and he used foul language. She thought he'd never amount to anything, and he wasn't good enough for my mother. And I guess he was kind of wild when he was in the Navy. He had sex with prostitutes when they were in port, and at least once he got gonorrhea."

"I can't believe she told you this stuff. I mean, I can't imagine my grandma ever saying stuff like this."

"Yeah, well she told me some stuff about my mother, too. Before she met my dad, she was dating this med student. And grandma was happy because that meant her daughter was going to marry a doctor. Anyway, he knocked her up and then left her. And she didn't feel like she could raise a kid on her own, so she had an abortion. Grandma wasn't happy about that, but at least she let Mom make her own choice."

"Okay, but I don't understand why she was telling you all this, and why you're telling me now."

"I'm getting to that. The point is, when Mom and Dad met each other, they both had things in their past that were, shall we say, less than desirable. I guess back in those days if a woman got an abortion, it was looked down upon more than it is now. But they fell in love anyway. They accepted each other for who they are and they overlooked the unpleasant things about each other's past. And they ended up having a good marriage and a good life together. And of course, they had me! So who knows? If they hadn't looked beyond each other's past, I probably wouldn't be here today."

Ryan looked like he still wasn't getting it.

"So Grandma and I talked about you, too, and why I got so upset when I found out you used to do porn. But when I told her your story, she said it sounds like you have a lot of strength and determination. You've overcome a lot of hardship to get where you are today. She said you were dealt a rotten hand and you did what you had to do to overcome it. And she said if I really love you, I need to overlook the unpleasant things from your past and focus on who you are today and the future you and I could build together."

Aaron reached across the table with both arms and held his hands open. Ryan reached out and placed his hands in Aaron's. Aaron closed his hands around Ryan's and looked him in the eye. "And that's exactly what I've done. I don't care that you used to do porn. You're a wonderful man, and I admire you for what you've accomplished and what you've overcome. I love you, and I want to live our lives together."

Ryan's eyes were moist. A tear formed in his right eye and started running down. He stood up, then Aaron stood up. They walked around to the side of the table and met each other halfway.

Ryan took Aaron's hands and said, "I love you too. And nothing would make me happier."

They hugged and kissed for at least two minutes. Then Ryan said, "Are you finished eating?"

There were a couple of half-eaten slices left, but they could wait. Aaron said, "Yeah… I can finish that later."

"You want any more wine?"

"I'm good for now."

"Then let's sit down on the couch. I have something I'd like to say."

Ryan led Aaron into the living room and they sat down close to each other. Ryan sat on the edge of the couch and turned to face Aaron.

"Over the past few days, I've been thinking a lot about us and how things have gone up to this point. And I realize I've made some mistakes. You and I have been approaching this thing differently. I know you wanted to start having sex right away and I wanted to go slowly and get to know each other first. We should have talked about it and come to an agreement that we could both be happy with. But instead, I forced what I wanted onto both of us. And that probably came across as not being interested in you either for sex or for a relationship. But really, I am."

Aaron said, "I understand. I guess I was pretty impatient. And horny."

"Yeah, I totally get that. But for me, well… relationships haven't gone well for me up to this point. As I told you on the way home from San Diego, every relationship I've tried has ended badly in one way or another. I've been hurt and taken advantage of a lot. And with you, well… I really wanted it to work out for us. And obviously, it was a mistake for me not to tell you I did porn. I guess I was hoping that if we built a solid relationship first, then when I told you, you would already know that's not really who I am."

Aaron scooted forward on the couch to be closer to Ryan. He put his hand on Ryan's knee and said, "I understand. Thanks for telling me all that.

Life's been pretty rough for you, hasn't it?"

"It's sure had its ups and downs. I've lost a lot. A lot of people I love have been taken away from me. But I'm grateful, too. A lot of people have been good to me, like Russ, my old boss at the grocery store in Prairie Village, and Eddie, the guy I stayed with during my internship. The whole experience of living in that house with Hal, Ted, Darnell, and Ricky was wonderful, even though we ultimately lost Hal. I learned so much from him, and he was so generous. I got a good education, and now I have a good job and a comfortable home. And I'm playing trumpet again, thanks to you. So I'm very fortunate in a lot of ways. I try to stay focused on that."

"That's one thing I love about you. In spite of everything that's happened to you, you still have gratitude. You always look at the bright side."

"Thanks. I try."

Aaron said, "There's something else I want to apologize for. I shouldn't have been so slutty last weekend. I know, we hadn't made a commitment yet, but still… I've never been in a situation where there were hundreds of gay men everywhere and it was so easy to get sex if you wanted it. And I just… well, I guess I got caught up in it and I didn't make the best choices."

"You were thinking with your dick instead of your brain."

"Yeah, that's one way to put it. And to be honest, part of the reason I did it was, I was frustrated with how things were going – or not going – between you and me. I was starting to think you weren't interested."

"Yeah, I get it. And like I said earlier, that's my fault for not talking with you about it."

"But still, I don't blame you for feeling the way you did on the ride home. Like, if I'm going to be that slutty, maybe I'm not the right guy for you."

"Don't worry about it. And if I had gone out to the bars with you, that wouldn't have happened."

"So how come you don't like to go to bars?"

"They're crowded and loud and I'm pretty shy and introverted. And, well… there's another reason I can tell you now. I don't want to be recognized. Some of the videos I'm in sold really well and being 6'6" makes me pretty recognizable. The few times I've been in bars, it never fails that someone will come up and hit on me. Or they'll try to engage me in conversation about the scenes I've done or just talk about doing porn, in general. Even at the festival last weekend, I could tell I was being pointed out. I'd rather not deal with it."

Aaron asked, "So does that mean you'd rather not come to Raise! the Bar with us after band rehearsals?"

"No, that'll be okay. I understand that's how you get to know the other people. That time we went after my first rehearsal was fun, although one guy called me Luke."

Ryan took a deep breath. "So, since we mentioned last weekend, I have one more question to ask. I know this might be kind of awkward and you don't have to answer if you don't want to. It's none of my business whom you've slept with."

"Okaaay…"

"Okay. So, as you were leaving my house on Wednesday night, you said you fucked my cousin. How did you know it was my cousin?"

"Well… I didn't, at the time. But we were at the happy hour at a rooftop bar at the Hillcrest Inn. It was only a couple of blocks from where we were watching the parade. Anyway, there was this guy there who looked just like you. Really… it was uncanny. Like he could have been your brother. I remember you saying you had a brother who was eight years younger, but this guy looked older than that. But anyway, I walked up to him and told him he looked like you and asked if you were his brother. I even showed him your picture. He told me he didn't have any brothers, but yeah, you look so much like him. So we started sharing information in case you might be related somehow. He lives in Seattle. I told him you were from Kansas. He said he has an uncle who's a preacher in Kansas, but his family's not in touch with him. I told him your name is Ryan Robertson and he said, no that's not it. But get this! His name is Brady Bauer. And he said his uncle's name is Brad Bauer. That didn't mean anything to me at the time, because I didn't know you changed your name until Wednesday. But anyway, he and I friended each other on Facebook. So on Wednesday, I started looking at his Relationships and Family page, and I saw that his dad's name is Bruce Bauer, and he's originally from Tulsa. Then I remembered you were born there.

"So I kept digging. I tried searching for Rev. Robertson in Prairie Village but I didn't find anything. Then I remembered you telling me about being on the track team and going to the state championships. So I searched for that, and I found a website with the results. And when I looked at the athletes from Prairie Village High School, imagine my surprise when I saw Chris Robertson. I didn't see anyone named Ryan, but I did see Bryan Bauer. Then it all clicked together. So I searched for churches with Rev. Bauer, and found your dad's church. So all the pieces fit. That's how I found out you changed your name and the guy I met in San Diego is your cousin."

"Wow… you did a lot of detective work. So, have you told this guy I'm his cousin?"

"Not yet. I wanted to ask you first."

"Okay. Thanks for not telling him. Let me think about it."

"Remember, his family isn't in touch with your dad. He said they were turned off by how right-wing he is."

"I'll keep that in mind. But… you said you fucked him."

"Yeah. He and his friend were staying in the hotel where the happy hour was. We went down to their room for a while."

"Just you and Brady, or…"

"Brady and his friend, Andy. They're besties with benefits, as they called it."

"So you've done a three-way."

"Yeah. It was actually pretty hot."

"So, are you going to want to…"

"No."

Ryan breathed a sigh of relief. He leaned over and kissed Aaron.

"Okay, so I have one more question. You said he looks just like me."

"I can pull up his Facebook page and show you some pictures."

"Maybe later. But, uh… how do I say this? Are he and I alike in other ways?" He glanced down.

"I wouldn't know. I haven't seen yours yet." *At least not in person. But I don't think this is the right moment to mention The Boys of Breckenridge or the Luke Loadstar Celebrity Dildo.*

Ryan smiled and looked at Aaron with a gleam in his eye. "Well, maybe it's time you did."

Aaron quickly stood up, and Ryan stood up a second later. Aaron grabbed Ryan's hand and led him into his bedroom. They were barely inside the door when Aaron spun around, threw his arms around Ryan, and began kissing him passionately. Within seconds, they were pulling off each other's shirts and unbuckling each other's belts.

Between kisses, Ryan whispered, "I love you" into Aaron's ear.

"I love you too." After a few more kisses, Aaron said, "You have no idea how much I want this."

"If you're like me… I think I do."

***

They collapsed into each other's arms, physically exhausted but basking in bliss. A couple of times, Aaron dozed off. But when he woke up he looked at Ryan's face and saw that his eyes were closed too. Finally, Ryan stirred. Aaron said, "That was incredible."

"Yeah, it was. I hope it was worth waiting for."

"Definitely. So, you wanna get up?"

"Sure. I need to pee. What time is it?"

"9:15. So, after we get cleaned up, you wanna go for a walk? Or we can watch something on TV."

Ryan thought about it for a moment. "Either would be fine. I'm not much of a TV watcher, but I'd enjoy snuggling and finishing off that wine."

"That sounds wonderful."

Ryan walked to the hall bathroom and Aaron used the master bathroom. After they were both out, Aaron asked. "So... can you stay over tonight?"

Ryan smiled, "Yeah, I'd love to. Maybe we can go someplace for brunch in the morning."

"I have to be at work at noon, but as long as we can be done by then, that would be nice."

"And do you want to come up to my place for dinner tomorrow night? Maybe we can get in the pool afterward."

"Sure. And can I stay over? I'd need to leave at, like, 7:15 to get to work on time."

"Yeah. I guess we need to start getting used to spending the night here or there." Ryan kissed Aaron, then squeezed his butt cheek. "Are you doing okay?"

Aaron knew what he meant. "Yeah. Actually, I am."

"You did a really good job with it. I mean, I know I wasn't your first, but... well, I know I'm pretty big."

Aaron smiled. "You were gentle and you went slow. I appreciated that." *Should I tell him about... Oh, hell. Why not?* "And, uh... you could say I've been training for the big event."

"What do you mean?"

Aaron opened one of his dresser drawers and pulled out the Luke

Loadstar Celebrity Dildo.

Ryan said, "Oh my God. Where did you get that?"

"Someone loaned it to me. I'd rather not say who."

"I think I can guess. Can I see it?"

Aaron handed the dildo to Ryan. He held it in front of his crotch. "They added an inch to it. I'm really pissed they did that. They're never big enough, I guess." Ryan gave the dildo back to Aaron.

Aaron smiled mischievously. "Maybe I'll stick this in you someday."

"I dunno… I'll have to think about that." Ryan enjoyed bottoming, but Ted's eight inches had been quite enough. On the other hand… "Well, I guess turnabout is fair play. Maybe someday. When are Kent and Justin expecting to get it back?" He paused. "Did I get that right?"

"Yeah. They said they were in no hurry. But just think… next time somebody tells you to go fuck yourself, you can."

Ryan rolled his eyes. Then he smiled. "I can anyway."

In a Relationship

Sunday, July 24, 2016

Aaron closed the pharmacy promptly at 6:00 and practically ran back to his apartment. He changed clothes, and he was about to run out the door to head up to Ryan's house for dinner. Then he remembered his mother was going to be released from the hospital today if her recovery was going well. He picked up his phone and called.

"Why, hello dear! How are you?"

"I'm fine, Mom. How are you?"

"Well, I must be doin' pretty good or they wouldn't have let me come home today."

"Oh, good! I was hoping today would be the day."

"Good thing you called now. I was going to go to bed pretty soon. Even though I did nothing but lay around in a hospital bed for the past four days, I'm still worn out."

"Well, get all the rest you need. How's Dad?"

"Oh, he's fine. He's happy to have me out of there and back home."

"I'll bet. Hey, I just want to give you one other little bit of news before I let you go. So… when I got back, Ryan – that's the guy I was telling you about – came over and we talked about a whole bunch of things and… well… we're back together again!"

"Oh, honey, that's wonderful!" She put her hand on the receiver, but Aaron could still hear her telling his father, "Aaron and his boyfriend got back together! Huh… what? Yeah, okay." She spoke into the receiver again. "Your father says congratulations! Here, let me put him on the phone. He wants to ask you something."

Ralph said, "Congratulations, son! I'm real happy for you. Now, make sure you're pickin' the best one you can find. Don't settle for just anybody. You need to hold out until you find someone who's going to be as good to you as your mother's been to me."

"I will, Dad. Trust me, Ryan's really special."

"Well, good. I want you to be happy. Now…" Ralph lowered his voice to almost a whisper. "So, there's something I've been wonderin' about… what do two guys do together anyway?"

Aaron heard his mother in the background say, "Oh, for heaven's sake, Ralph. Don't ask him that!"

Aaron couldn't even. But then, the perfect answer came to him. "Well, Dad… You know those things you wish Mom would do for you, but she won't?"

"Yeah…"

"That's what we do."

Ralph had to think about that for a second. Then he said, "Oh, you little son of a bitch!"

Aaron laughed out loud. "Dad, if you don't want to hear the answer, don't ask the question!" He could hear his dad laughing too. "And on that note… I need to get going. I'm driving up to Ryan's house in Scottsdale for dinner. Talk to you soon. I love you!"

"I love you too, son."

"And tell Mom I love her."

"Here, let me put her back on."

Martha said, "I love you, honey, and I'm real happy for you. I hope we get to meet him sometime soon."

"When I come home for Thanksgiving or Christmas, can I bring him with me?"

"Well, of course!"

"Thanks, Mom! I love you. Bye!"

Aaron glanced at his watch. Shit. It was already 6:35. He called Ryan.

After a couple of rings, Ryan answered, "Hey, hot stuff. What's up? We're still on for tonight, right?"

"Yeah, definitely. But I called my mom as soon as I got home from work. She was released from the hospital today and she's back home now. So we talked for a little bit. I just wanted to let you know I'm running a few minutes late. I'm heading out the door now."

"Okay, fine. Thanks for letting me know. And I'm glad she's back home."

"Thanks. So am I. Anyway, looks like I'll be there at about 7:00."

"I can't wait. Love you!"

"Love you too. Bye!"

***

When Aaron arrived, Ryan greeted him wearing a sexy tank top that showed off his broad shoulders and smooth chest. He wore thin, silky running shorts that didn't leave much to the imagination. Aaron wanted to pull them off right then and there.

They kissed. Aaron reached around, squeezed Ryan's buns, and pulled their bodies together. He ran his hands up and down Ryan's back as he kissed him some more.

Ryan smiled and stepped back. "Dinner's almost ready. Don't worry, we'll have lots of time for that." He winked and turned toward the kitchen. Aaron followed. "Hey, there's a bottle of wine on the counter. Would you take it outside and pour it into the glasses?" Ryan headed out to the back patio.

Aaron picked up the bottle and joined Ryan out back. Ryan had set a nice table, with a candle inside a glass cylinder to protect it from the breeze. A basket held several slices of warm garlic bread. Aaron poured the wine while Ryan retrieved two filet mignons from the grill. He placed them on their plates beside a mound of homemade sweet potato fries. He carried the plates to the table and set them down.

Aaron said, "Oh, wow… this looks amazing. You really went all out."

"Yeah, well… It's Sunday dinner. And this week, I wanted to do something a little special to celebrate us."

Aaron picked up his wine glass. "Well, then… to us!"

Ryan smiled. "To us!"

They clinked their glasses and took a sip. Then Aaron took a bite of the steak. "Oh my God, Ryan! This is delicious! I've never tasted steak with this much flavor. Did you put something on it?"

"I marinated it for a few hours. Just a simple mixture of lime juice, sherry vinegar, olive oil, steak seasoning, and a touch of garlic truffle powder."

"It's amazing. And the sweet potato fries. You made these yourself?"

"Yeah. I have an air fryer. I used to avoid fries because I don't stuff that's deep-fried in oil. But they cook up better this way and it's not nearly as bad for you."

"They taste great. And what's this sauce?"

"Remoulade. But I have ketchup if you would prefer that."

"No, no, I like this. This is like what they serve with those onion blossoms at Back Country Steakhouse." Aaron took a few more bites of his food. As he savored each bite, he basked in the ambiance Ryan had created – the candle on the table, the soft instrumental bossa nova playing on the outdoor speakers, and the serene white noise of the waterfall at the far end of the pool. Then he glanced across the table at Ryan – handsome, sexy Ryan, with whom he was now beginning a relationship. It was almost too perfect. As much as he was enjoying this experience, thoughts of inadequacy were nagging him.

Ryan took a sip of his wine and glanced across the table at Aaron. "Is everything okay?"

"Everything is perfect. Almost too perfect."

"What do you mean?"

"I don't know, it's just… Well, I guess I might as well put this out there. I don't know how to say this, but… Okay, so everything about this dinner is amazing. And you're amazing! I guess what's bothering me is, I don't know if I can live up to this. It's like… I can't cook like this. You have this beautiful house, and I have my crappy little apartment. I guess I feel pretty lame compared to you."

Ryan thought for a moment about how to respond. "Okay, well… First of all, it's not a contest. There's no need to compare ourselves to each other. We each bring things to the relationship. My life is a lot better now that you're in it, and I hope I can make your life better because I'm in it. And second, your apartment isn't crappy. It's nice. There's nothing wrong with it. And this house is nice and everything, but it's nicer when I get to share it with someone. Otherwise, it's just a bunch of stuff."

"Okay, but… I guess one thing I don't get is, how come you're only 26, and you already have all this? I'm 28, and I still have $30,000 in student loans I'm paying off. I feel like I'm so far behind you."

"But again, it's not a competition. For one thing, you went to pharmacy school, so you were in college for eight years, right? I only have a Bachelor's, so I got done in four. And you know why I don't have any student loans. And that causes problems for me sometimes. It caused problems for us, and it will always be something from my past that follows me around. And as for this house, well… that came at a price, too. Remember I told you Hal died a couple of months before I graduated? He left that house to me in his will. I couldn't believe it. I think he hoped I'd keep living there and rent rooms to gay college students like he did. But I had already accepted my job offer here, and I had to sell that house to pay off his debts. I still came away with over

$600,000. So that made it easy for me to buy a house here. But I only have this house because Hal died. I'd give it all up for him to be alive today."

"Oh, wow. I had no idea. I'm really sorry."

Ryan said, "Hal was an incredible cook. I learned a lot from him – not just about cooking, but about life. He was more of a father to me than my own dad."

"He must have been a wonderful man. I can tell how much he meant to you by the way you talk about him."

"He certainly was. But moving on… How are your parents?"

Aaron replied, "Well, Mom will have to take it easy for a few weeks – lots of rest and no heavy lifting. I told them we worked things out and we're back together again. They said they're looking forward to meeting you."

"I'm looking forward to meeting them too."

"It would be great if you and I could go there for Thanksgiving or Christmas."

"We should be able to do that. I guess that depends on your work schedule."

"Yeah. The pharmacy will be closed on Thanksgiving Day and Christmas Day, but not the days before or after. Charlie and I will work it out so that one of us works the days surrounding Thanksgiving and the other works the days surrounding Christmas."

"That sounds fair. Anyway, I can't believe they're so supportive now. Quite a change from a couple of months ago."

"I know, right?" Aaron thought for a moment. "Have you ever thought about reaching out to your parents? Maybe they'd like to be in touch with you again."

"Nope. Not interested. I'll never forgive my dad for what he did. And as long as he's still the pastor of that huge, right-wing church, he's not going to change his views about me being gay."

"True. But it's not like he can do anything about it now. He can't force you to go to that place they were going to send you. And what about your mother and your brother?"

Ryan sighed. "Yeah, it would be nice to see them again. But I don't see how I can be back in touch with them without having to deal with my dad. And besides, being gay was bad enough. What if they found out I did porn?"

"They probably wouldn't find out unless you told them. And maybe they'd forgive you like I did."

"Doing porn is nothing I need to be forgiven for, especially since the only reason I had to do it was because of what they did to me."

Aaron said, "You know, maybe you should try forgiving them. Forgiveness is a powerful thing."

"I seriously doubt they would ever apologize or ask for forgiveness. For that to happen, they would have to admit they did something wrong."

"But they can't do that if they can't even get in touch with you."

"Can we talk about something else?"

For the next few minutes, they ate in silence. Finally, Ryan said, "Okay, here's something. Earlier today I got an email from Chris. You know, my best friend from high school."

"Yeah. How's he doing?"

"Fine. Anyway, his partner is from Glendale. They're going to be coming here over Labor Day weekend for his partner's grandmother's 80th birthday. He wanted to know if we could get together at some point during their visit."

Aaron asked, "How do you feel about that?" *I'm not sure how I feel about that.*

"I'm all for it. It would be great to see him again in person."

"So did he mean just you and he getting together, or did he mean his partner, too?"

"He didn't say for sure in the email. But I'd like to do both. I'd like to visit with just Chris first. There are a few things I'd like to talk about, just to wrap up what happened in the past. And I'd also like to have the four of us get together. But that depends on how much time they'll have when they're here."

Aaron thought for a moment. "If his partner's parents live out here, don't you suppose they've come out here before, like for Thanksgiving or Christmas?"

"Yeah, probably."

"So I wonder why Chris has waited until now to set up a visit with you."

"I don't know. Things have been kind of weird between us since we got back in touch with each other in … let's see, that would have been Christmas of 2008. Geez, it's been seven and a half years. He backed away after he found out I was doing porn. But anyway, he wants to get together now. Maybe enough time has passed."

Aaron didn't say anything, but thoughts were swirling around in his head.

Ryan said, "You look like something's bothering you."

"Yeah. I'm not sure how I feel about this. I mean, you don't suppose he wants to get back together, do you?"

"I sure hope that's not what he has in mind. He and Seth have been together for almost nine years now. Besides, I'm not interested in that. I have you now. Even if I didn't, I wouldn't do anything to break up another couple."

"Yeah, but you don't know how their relationship is going. They could be having problems. Maybe they're about to break up."

"You're right. I don't know. But I doubt Chris would talk to me about getting back together while he's out here on a trip with Seth. In any case, it doesn't matter. I have you."

They finished dinner and cleared the table. Ryan sensed that Aaron was still uneasy about Chris's upcoming visit. He walked up to Aaron and put his arms around him. "Hey, relax. Don't worry. I'm not going to dump you for Chris or anyone else. It's you and only you. But if you're that uncomfortable with it, I'll tell Chris no."

"No, that's okay. It's important for you guys to re-establish your friendship. I know it would mean a lot to you."

"Yes, it would." Ryan kissed Aaron. "Thanks for understanding. I really appreciate it."

Aaron smiled and kissed Ryan back. "Just so I'm clear, you said, 'It's you and only you.' Does that mean we're committed to each other now?"

"It does as far as I'm concerned. What about you? Are you sure you're ready to settle down and commit to one guy?"

"Absolutely."

"No more San Diego weekends?"

"Absolutely not. It's you and only you."

Ryan asked, "Well, alrighty then. So… are you still up for getting in the pool?"

Aaron grinned. "With 'up' being the operative word."

"Okay! Well, if you'll excuse me for a moment…" Ryan turned and headed toward his bedroom.

"Of course!" Aaron smiled. He decided to visit the hall bathroom for a few minutes, just to be sure.

While he was sitting down, he pulled his phone out of his pocket and opened Facebook. He edited his profile and changed his status to 'In a relationship.'

Afterword

Thank you for purchasing and reading this book. I hope you enjoyed it.

This is the fourth in a series of six books that follow Ryan as he finishes high school, goes to college, launches his career, forms relationships, and comes to terms with his past.

I invite you to subscribe to my newsletter. I'll keep you informed about my upcoming books and offer them to you at a discount. I'll share background information about the stories and the writing process. From time to time, I may solicit your input which will help make the books even better! To join, visit my website: AuthorDaveHughes.com.

To thank you for joining, I will send my short story, *Cruise Virgins*. In it, Ryan (as a young adult) and Ted experience their first gay cruise – and confront their feelings for one another.

Now, I have a small favor to ask.

As a new, self-published author, it's incredibly difficult to get my books noticed in a world in which hundreds, if not thousands, of new books are released every day. It's challenging to build an audience for my work. If you enjoyed this book, please consider posting something about it on your social media platform of choice. All it takes is something simple, like 'I thoroughly enjoyed reading *If I Seem Quiet...*, by Dave Hughes. Check it out.' Also, please consider leaving an honest review on the website where you purchased this book.

Thanks! I truly appreciate it.

I would like to thank my launch team: Gary Brenkman, Aaron Chavez, Jeff McKeehan, Mark McNease, Trevor Schulta, Michelle Taquino, and Mike Triggs. And thanks to Amy's Bookshelf Reviews for the great reviews and all she does to support authors.

Thanks to my author friends for their invaluable support and advice (in no particular order): Mark McNease, David S. Pederson, Andrew Michael Flynn, Martin Wilsey, Debra Gaskill, Mike Triggs, Sandor M. Lubisch, Russ

Smith, and Kevin Allen McKeehan. (Sorry if I missed anyone!)

Thanks to my email subscribers for their loyalty and support. I've made numerous decisions based on their feedback. And thanks to the Chandler Public Library Downtown Writers Group, led by Andrew Flynn, for their support and useful, constructive feedback.

Special thanks to Gregg Edelman of Exposed Studio & Gallery. His charming art gallery is the perfect location for my book signing events. Thanks for all you do for the community!

Very special thanks to Mark McNease, prolific author of LGBT-themed mysteries and short stories (see MarkMcNease.com), for his priceless support and friendship. Mark hosts podcasts and runs a website and Facebook group called LGBTSt.com, and promotes my work through all those avenues.

Most important, I would like to thank my husband, Jeff McKeehan, who has supported and encouraged me every step of the way, provided great ideas and valuable feedback, and tolerated all those times when my mind was immersed in the world of my characters. Every spouse of an author knows exactly what I'm talking about.

Other Books by Dave Hughes

Fiction

Maybe Next Year
Instant Adult
Open Books, Closed Sets

Retirement Lifestyle

Design Your Dream Retirement
Smooth Sailing into Retirement
The Quest for Retirement Utopia

About the Author

This is author Dave Hughes' fourth novel. He has two more books in various stages of development.

Before writing fiction, Dave wrote three retirement lifestyle planning books, *Design Your Dream Retirement, Smooth Sailing Into Retirement,* and *The Quest for Retirement Utopia.* Dave created the website RetireFabulously.com, which enables readers to envision, plan for, and enjoy the best retirement possible. In addition to writing hundreds of articles for RetireFabulously.com, Dave's writing has appeared on US News & World Report, lgbtSr.com, Medium, Yahoo! Finance, CNN/Money, Next Avenue, Tiny Buddha, and others.

Aside from his writing, Dave is also a jazz musician. He plays trombone and steelpan in various bands in the Phoenix area. He owns an embarrassingly large collection of jazz, Brazilian, exotica, steel band, jazz/rock, and vocal ensemble CDs and videos.

Before retiring early at age 56, Dave was a software engineer for 34 years, working for companies such as Intel Corporation, Computer Sciences Corporation, McDonnell Douglas Space Systems, and NCR Corporation. Throughout his career, his assignments included software development, customer support, training, course development, and management.

Dave resides in Chandler, Arizona with his husband Jeff and their dog Maynard.

Dave is available for interviews, book readings/signings, speaking engagements, and panel discussions. You may contact Dave at dave@AuthorDaveHughes.com.

Visit AuthorDaveHughes.com to learn more and subscribe to his newsletter.

www.ingramcontent.com/pod-product-compliance
Lightning Source LLC
Chambersburg PA
CBHW020644120726
47906CB00001B/115